STATIC OVER SPACE

BOOK ONE
GRAVITY & LIES

C.G. Volars

Published by Outland Entertainment LLC
3119 Gillham Road
Kansas City, MO 64109

Founder/Creative Director: Jeremy D. Mohler
Editor-in-Chief: Alana Joli Abbott

ISBN: 978-1-954255-22-7
EBOOK ISBN: 978-1-954255-23-4
Worldwide Rights
Created in the United States of America

Editor: Alana Joli Abbott
Copy editor: Scott Colby
Proofreader: Lorraine Savage
Cover Illustration: Jeremy D. Mohler
Cover Design: Jeremy D. Mohler
Interior Layout: Mikael Brodu

Visit **outlandentertainment.com** to see more, or follow us on our Facebook Page **facebook.com/outlandentertainment/**

— CHAPTER ONE —

Izo

One more month—that's how long until the most popular celebrity golf tournament in television was coming straight to Izo's backyard. As long as Izo Lopez could keep his nineteen-year old, homeless, Latino ass from getting fired or arrested until then, he would be set. The second those cameras arrived and went live at the golf course, everything in Izo's life was going to change.

Izo smiled the way only excited hope could afford. Shielding his eyes from the sun, he sat up and climbed out of his ancient Volkswagen Golf. All five fingers glowed caramel brown in the early morning rays. Beyond his remote camping ground, a rolling sprawl of blue-green mountains careened in every direction. Dotted along the staggering landscape were mountain cliffs sheered in ascending diagonal stripes, like craggy waves. Boulders as big as vans sat in the foreground, precariously balanced in impossible stacks. Two healthy waterfalls sparkled in the far distance. Fifty feet below, Lake Tahoe shimmered up at him in all its massive, alpine glory.

Izo sucked a long, grateful breath and stretched. Then he cringed.

Shit!

A twinge of pain lit up the right side of his neck; it felt like an electric pterodactyl had caught him by one talon. Izo hissed and grabbed the tender spot above his shoulder. He was way too young for this kind of crap; this was what forty-year-olds felt like in the morning, not newly minted adults.

Izo turned to glare at the backseat of his car. Littered with peanuts shells, dollar menu wrappers, and his trusty Oaskys sleeping bag, the backseat stared back with perfect innocence. It was pretending it hadn't tricked him with its inviting cushions only to besiege him with its diabolically small space that never failed to make him regret trusting it. Of course, he'd fallen for it again. *Fucker,* he grumbled to himself. He flipped off the seat before kicking the back door shut.

Oh well. He wasn't going to let it ruin his mood. Going into the front, he snatched his pocketknife and glanced at the time on his middle console. It was 7:30—two hours before he needed to be at work; an hour before he needed to be at his bus stop. Plenty of time for a shower.

Even better, when he checked the garbage bag of water on his hood, it was warm! Lugging the hefty bag to a nearby tree, he tossed the rope tied around its top over a tall branch before hoisting the bag above his head and securing the end on a strong root jutting out of the ground.

The shower bag gently twisted in the air as Izo hurried to pull off his t-shirt and shorts. He left his underwear on, though. Hikers and other campers did occasionally venture this far into the park. No reason to go cheeks-to-wind and risk someone siccing la juda on him.

One quick poke of his pocketknife and he was in business. Warm, sparkling river water poured out of the bag to dribble down his bronze, sun-kissed torso—though sun-striped might have been a more accurate term. Even as an olive-skinned Latino, his summer job as a caddie made it a constant struggle to keep his tan even.

The water continued pouring, and Izo dialed back his thoughts to enjoy the present for a moment. Ambient forest noises filled the quiet of his mind...the rising rustle of wind-swept leaves...the playful bubbling of water tumbling over rocks...a melody of bright birdsong, varied and irregular, a veritable jazzy-nature festival of free-wheeling chirps and clicks, including the otherworldly undulation of the Warbling Vireo, a sound he'd recently been taught to recognize at UC Davis's free Tahoe Science Center (donations welcome!).

Izo sighed, filled with easy gratitude. Plucking his pine tar soap out of a nearby plastic bag, he started to scrub down. The pine bar made quick work, washing away any sticky residue-sweat from sleeping in his car while moisturizing his skin and leaving him fresh and clean with an alluring woodsy scent. Not bad for four bucks at the local co-op. It was normally more than Izo would spend on a toiletry, but this was worth it. If there was anything he'd learned in life, it was this: just because you lived in your car didn't mean you were allowed to smell like it. Especially at his job.

Speaking of...he was pretty much done. Izo glanced around to double check he was alone. Then—snapping to his car—he grabbed the duct tape out of his passenger's seat and—snapping back—he sealed the bag with three quick strips of tape. The water stopped. He poked the shower bag curiously. It still had about half its water. Nice—he wouldn't have to hit the river after work. Grinning, he secured the whole thing flatly around the tree trunk with a long strip of tape across its middle.

Izo walked back to his car to check the time on his console. 7:50. He needed to get a move on. Izo dropped the tape back into his car and hurried to get dressed in a pair of blue, water-slicking shorts and his official monogrammed white polo. Both name-brand, they were some of the most expensive clothes he'd ever bought. But it was worth it: at two bags a loop and two loops a day, most days he came home with $300 in tax-free cash. Not bad for a summer job. Sure, there'd been a little hazing from the other caddies at the beginning. But the hours were good, the views at the gold course were amazing and, best of all, it was going to launch him as the world's first Mexican-American superhero.

Izo grabbed his skateboard, sunglasses, hat, keys, and wallet before locking his car. He paused before leaving, though. He was forgetting something. He patted himself down. What was it?

Phone!

Izo unlocked his car and hurried to grab and unplug his precious iPhone. It was the first phone he'd ever owned, and he still wasn't used to having it on him. This was a bad habit, too, since aside from the car and clothes, it was his single most valuable possession on Earth. Three models down from the current one and bought with every cent of the graduation money from his various foster parents, it was a bonafide iPhone that, assuming you had the right case—which he did—was completely indistinguishable from the newest hardware. He was pretty sure it was the main reason he'd tricked his current employer into hiring him. More importantly, it had his only photo of Hanako on it.

Izo tucked the phone carefully away into a hidden zipper pocket on his shorts. Then, locking his car, he hopped on his skateboard and flew down the street.

Izo stood on the board and sighed with easy boredom. Underneath him, the wheels bounced and twirled on the rough dirt road. He wasn't worried, though. He'd rewrapped the board with electrical tape only three days before—the top still had plenty of stick to stay adhered to the bottom of his Walmart shoes.

"Do a kickflip!" cried a pre-teen camping with his family near the front. Izo just smiled and lifted a hand in greeting before soaring uphill and onto the main highway.

Kickflip? he chuckled to himself. *I don't even know how to push off.*

Izo hissed and looked at the time on his phone. His bus was late again. Running the math in his head, he calculated that even if it arrived in the next five minutes, there was still a chance he'd miss his first tee time. This was golf in June at Lake Tahoe—one of the most lucrative businesses in town during the middle of its busiest season. Five minutes wasn't a risk he was willing to take.

He lowered the brim of his hat and stood to move away from the bus stop. The morning traffic was thick on the sidewalk as locals and visitors wound around each other. Izo zig-zagged through the crowd, looking for a quiet building with no visible security. He avoided the jewelry shops and sporting good sellers like the plague. Soon enough, he stumbled upon a small pizza joint next to a souvenir shop with a private alley. With no parking or cameras around the side and only low-morning-traffic in the front, it was perfecto.

Izo looked around before slipping into the alley. The walls were made of red brick and stood three stories tall, with a metal fire escape clinging to the second floor. He approached the ladder curiously. But there was no luck—it was held in the up position by a thick padlock, impossible to lower at all, much less from his position on the ground.

Izo glanced both directions down the alleyway. No one was watching. Reaching one hand up, he rose vertically and hopped over the metal rail. Loping up the metal stairs three and four at a time, he quickly made it to the roof. The teen silently played his eyes over the shuffling heads and cars below. After a moment he was reassured; no one was looking up at him. Truth was, no one ever looked up.

Izo grinned and turned his gaze to the skies above. It was a wonderfully overcast day, with pillowy clouds stacked like magnificent fluffy kingdoms in the sky. Edgewood Golf Resort was due south, almost a straight line past Sand Harbor and Glenbrook following Lake Tahoe's eastern shore. Once there, he'd be able to find a spot to land in the forested ruffage surrounding the resort. For now, he just needed to worry about picking the path with the most cover. After making a few quick calculations based on wind direction, he reached down for the ground.

Izo breathed out and flattened his chest. Deep inside himself, he could feel the concentrated hook at his center, the strongest point of attraction between himself and his target. He turned his eyes to his chosen cloud. The connection linked instantly; he could already feel himself leaning forward at the pull, as if a giant invisible rubber band had been lassoed around his rib cage. He pulled on his end harder, building the tension until it felt less like a single stretchy band and more like a thousand screaming bungee cords begging to snap him forward. Adjusting his footing on the loose roofing material, he squared his shoulders, lowered his chin, and finally released. WHOOSH! He sailed into the air like a baseball heading for a grand slam.

He was soon flying at a fever pitch, zooming and darting through the clouds with an ease he'd long since stopped questioning. Within thirty seconds he was halfway there and gaining speed. Izo shook his head and slowed. The velocity liked to do this with him, building and growing without reason, always snapping for that next gear, of which he'd discovered hundreds over the years, many of them midway over the Pacific. But much as he'd love to accidentally stumble onto Hawaii again (or had it been Japan?), he couldn't do that today. He had somewhere to be.

Still, he supposed he could take a second to enjoy his inexplicable powers. Slowing to hide fully inside an especially thick cumulus (another thing he'd learned from the UC Davis center), he paused to let it drift across him. Izo breathed out slowly and basked in the perfect tensile catch—neither so light he drifted away nor so heavy he sunk, a perfect hovering balance between floating and falling that all clouds were born knowing how to perform.

The air was cooler up here too, soft condensation prickling his skin as the light dispersed in a cottony glow. In a minute he'd poke his head out and figure out where to land. But for now, he was satisfied to close his eyes, stretch out his fingers, and let the cool air play between them.

The wind shifted and grew, blowing first his bangs and then his cap suddenly free from his scalp. Izo gasped and dove to catch it, but he was too slow. It was lost in the murky whiteness. Dropping out of the bottom of the cloud, he could hear the cap hit the lake below. *Mierda,* he cursed, kicking his legs in frustration. He'd have to buy a new one now. Not that he couldn't afford it, but at $40 a pop it would definitely set back his money-saving goal for the week.

Izo groaned and crossed his arms. There was a chance he could get down to the water and back without anyone seeing. But was it worth it? Probably not. Then again...he was in the middle of the lake. And it was morning. Neither the boaters that regularly sailed the lake nor the hang gliders that drifted above tended to be "early bird" types. And there was a chance the people on the beach might not be able to see him, assuming he moved fast enough. Maybe if he could just figure out where his hat was and whether there was anyone nearby? It was a white cap after all...it wouldn't be hard to spot floating on the water.

By the time Izo heard the low thrumming behind him, he'd already been shot.

Three Months Later

Izo turned to the sound of the padlock outside his door beeping. The door was thick, round, and made of browning metal, heavily rusted and pocked from years of casual misuse. Behind it, the sounds of its exterior keypad beeped. Someone was coming in to speak with him. Looking around, he realized gravity had kicked back in too. *Ah.* They must have arrived.

He stood up from his narrow bed and brushed himself off, grateful for the chance to stretch as much as he could in his ten-by-ten cell. It wasn't an exaggeration to call it a cell, either; besides a bed, a sink, and a highly unintuitive gravity toilet that'd nearly left him chasing down space poops like Pan after Tinkerbell, there was nothing in the room.

The lock disengaged with a heavy click. A second later, the door popped open, revealing Izo's least favorite alien abductor. Seven feet tall, green, and covered in scales, Glongkyle scratched at his neck with two pointed claws, each nail wider and longer than Izo's fingers.

"We're here," said the reptile.

Izo nodded. Deep down, the fact that he could understand the reptilian's hissing noises as speech still unnerved him, particularly since his ears still ached every time he slept on the side of his face. He supposed it was a small price to pay for the omnilingual implants now permanently drilled into both sides of his head. Not that he'd been given much choice.

"Great. So how does this work?" asked Izo. "Do we hoof it from here? Or is spaceship parking more of a valet situation? More importantly, are spaceport personnel up to date on their shots? I'm a little worried about innocent workers forced to handle this intergalactic bucket of bacteria." Izo glanced around in disgust. "Seriously, when's the last time you cleaned this thing, Glongkyle?"

"Two or three Avarians ago," the reptile replied cruelly. "Don't worry. Unlike you, everyone here's been inoculated against major disease—another reason for you to keep close and do as you're told."

Izo saluted with sarcastic enthusiasm. "Yes, sir, Mr. Lizard Captain, sir!"

Glongkyle blinked slowly. "This isn't a vacation," he continued after a moment. "We are here for one reason—the job. Until it's done, you will not wander off. You will not make new friends. You will stay at my or Yula's side every second we're in public, unless told to do otherwise. Whatever we say, you will agree with. Whatever we do, you will do likewise."

"Whatever you haphazardly make up on the spot, I will confirm with blind and unflinching sincerity. I get it. We had assholes on Earth, too." Izo moved forward to leave. "Are Yula and Tearn ready to go?"

But Glongkyle wasn't budging out of the doorway just yet. Izo stopped short. Their chests were now nearly touching. He looked up at the reptile. "Is there something else, Chief?"

Glongkyle didn't immediately reply. He was carefully considering the human creature standing at approximately three quarters his size. "You understand I'm choosing to give you this chance to prove your worth. I don't have to do this."

"Don't see how you have much choice." Izo waved around the room. "Can't make money from in here, can I?"

Glongkyle's creepy, double-lidded eyes stared with unnerving, unhurried focus, an expression Izo had recently realized sentient reptiles could pull off especially well. "I'm sure I could come up with a couple of ideas."

Izo dropped back a step and laughed, hiding how his throat filled with bile. The reality was he'd been trapped in the *Atrox Killboard*, Glongkyle's piece of shit spaceship, for three months. With nowhere to go, nothing to eat except space gruel, and no attractive men or women anywhere in sight, he'd spent most of his time wondering how much farther he was from Earth than the day before. It'd been maddening. He'd never wanted to leave a place so badly in his life.

Just be cool.

The Earthling slapped on a goofy grin and put both hands up, high enough that he knew the cultural sign of surrender would translate. "You win. I give up. I solemnly swear no matter what happens I, Izaac Lopez, will be good."

Glongkyle's lipless face stared. He continued to scrutinize Izo with an unending, unknowable gaze. Izo had little choice but to stand and wait.

"All right," Glongkyle said, finally stepping aside. "But don't forget what I said about Earth."

— CHAPTER TWO —

Izo lifted his eyes to the Wuljerian beast in his way. With dark brown fur and upright ears, Yula resembled a grizzly-dog hybrid. Both of them wore matching orange jumpsuits, apparently a popular color in space and prison alike. Yula's was dingy and stretched over her enormous alien form. Izo's was brand new, and he was swimming in it.

Yula raised a manhole-sized paw. "Izo promised."

Izo tilted his head. Overgrown dark brown hair fell over his face. "I promised to be good, my friend. I never said what I'd be good at."

Izo stole a glance at the alien food court behind him. With his back to a low barrier, the floor was two stories down below—an easy jump for him and an impossible fall for Yula. Thousands of hungry aliens from all across the tri-galaxies and beyond glutted the stalls and tables, gorging themselves on fast food—and creating plenty of places for someone to hide in the crowd.

Izo brought his eyes back to the Wuljerian's. Behind Yula was the rest of IA's massive blue and white spaceport. Hundreds of terminals connected to countless other galaxies and solar systems. One of them had to pass near Earth, right? Of course. Izo just needed to figure out which one.

He also needed to make sure Team Kidnap didn't catch him and drag him back to their spaceship in the meantime. Izo smiled at Yula. He reached back to swing a leg over the barrier.

"I'm going to get something to eat. You want anything?"

Yula's ghostly white eyes narrowed. She lumbered forward, her snarling expression the stuff of children's nightmares. "Izo, do not!"

Izo grinned and hopped over the barrier. Dropping carefully, the teen landed gently on a table below. The table's occupants, a family of purple mantises, startled at his sudden arrival. Izo held up a hand. "I apologize. I also hate being interrupted while eating. Please continue." Careful to avoid their bowls of steamed insects, he grabbed the back of one chair and used it to swing himself off the table, accidentally taking a toddler's four-armed jacket with him.

"Oops!" He handed it back to the little alien. "Nice jacket, dude." Then, peering at what he assumed were the parents, he narrowed his eyes. "Any chance you know how to get to Earth from here?"

"Earth?" the mantis-parent on the left repeated awkwardly. Their expressions, though devoid of eyebrows, seemed confused. "Is that a planet?"

Izo shook his head. Mierda. "Don't worry about it. Enjoy your lunch." He was about to leave when he stole a glance up. He stopped dead in his tracks. "You might want to move," he said to the family.

The parents followed his gaze and gasped. They quickly dispatched their children and food with every appendage available.

Izo continued staring up from the foot of the table. "Yula," he called. "What the holy stupid crap do you think you're doing?"

The giant alien, unquestionably one of the universe's deadliest natural killing machines, clung to the wrong side of the barrier like a scared koala. Yula glanced over her shoulder at the ground. She let out a whimpering howl. Then she tried viewing the distance over her other shoulder instead.

"Yula, go back." Izo folded his arms. He groaned as Yula dipped one foot down. "That's not going to make it any shorter."

A pink-skinned alien with antenna stopped to stare alongside him. "What's she doing?"

"She's perfecting the universe's fastest way to break both her ankles," Izo answered, loudly enough for Yula to hear.

At this comment Yula changed her mind and hauled herself back to the safe side of the barrier. She pointed at Izo while plowing through a crowd on her way to the stairs at the end of the hallway. "Izo stays there," she commanded.

Izo rolled his eyes at the pink-skinned man. Then he tilted his head. "You ever heard of Earth before, ese?"

"Is that your friend's name?" He pointed at Yula.

Izo sighed and spun on his heel. Maybe he could ask someone that worked here? But then again, he was strolling around an Imperial spaceport without a ticket, personal ID, or any money to speak of, so possibly it wasn't the best idea to draw attention from anyone official. Izo scanned every direction. The spaceport rose dozens of floors and stretched for miles. Thousands of posted signs hung in brightly arrayed colors. He squinted at them, looking for some hint, a picture, or symbol that might give him a clue where to go next. All he saw was an ocean of alien squiggles, the magic of his translating ear implants showcasing a clear and important downside.

Out of nowhere, he was tackled from the left. Glongkyle laughed while pinning him to the ground victoriously. Izo groaned. "What the hell, Glongkyle? Back home we call that unnecessary roughness."

"If you ever want to see home again, you'll quit making a scene," said the lizard on top of him. Gasping under the weight, Izo was reminded how much bigger the brute was.

Glongkyle seized the Earthling's wrists and wrenched them up. Izo hissed. Much as he loathed to admit it, the lizard was also stronger by worlds. The last time Glongkyle had him on the ground like this, he'd fought back and lost badly. It had taken ten days for his shoulder to stop hurting once he'd finally gotten it back in its socket.

The reptile glanced at the confused crowd that'd begun to look their way. "Nothing to see here," he said. "We're having a business discussion."

"You mean the business of ABDUCTING and EXTORTING me?" Izo called out loudly from the floor. "Why yes. We've been discussing that for months, haven't we?"

"You think you're cute?" Glongkyle hissed into his ear, his weight and tone communicating the extent of the pain he was willing to inflict.

"Cute enough to be worth kidnapping from my planet apparently."

"Enough," said Glongkyle. "I knew I shouldn't have listened to Tearn. This was a stupid idea. We're going back to the ship."

Izo sucked in a long breath. Three months. He wasn't going back.

Shutting his eyes, he took a few breaths, relaxed, and waited, placid as a lamb. When Glongkyle grabbed and helped him to his feet, Izo let him, gingerly rising with the lizard until his feet were underneath him. Then he twisted, pulled a hand free, and cracked an elbow into Glongkyle's nubby snout as hard as he could. With an ugly cry, the reptile grabbed his nose and fell onto his butt.

Izo took a few steps back. Then he stopped. He still had no idea where to go next.

Glongkyle noticed. "What's the plan here? There's only one way home." He laughed while cradling his nose. "You're going to do what I want eventually, fly-by."

Izo's nostrils flared. He swung his gaze into Glongkyle like a sword. "Don't EVER call me that."

Glongkyle smirked. "Why? You don't like it or something?"

Izo stared daggers into the reptile. Yula, the big lug, would be down shortly. Between the two of them, it would take no time to drag Izo back to the ship. He needed to hurt one of them, and he'd prefer if it were Glongkyle.

He squared his stance, bent his knees, and hitched his jumpsuit a little higher, hating that even if it had fit, he'd still be twenty pounds lighter and who knows how much weaker since leaving Earth in full health. He waved his enemy in like he'd seen in a kung fu movie once. It was gutsy to stay and fight, particularly given how soundly Glongkyle had finished their last skirmish. But he also didn't know any other way to be. "You planning on getting off the ground?"

Glongkyle's mouth broke into a cruel smile. He rose slowly and cracked his spiny neck. "Been waiting to go another round with you, fly-by."

"Let's go, El Capitán."

Glongkyle beetled his bony brow. Then he hurtled forward, scaled arms and clawed fingers outstretched. There was no telling what type of damage he, a sentient alligator-alien come to life with a vengeance, could do.

Izo watched, waited, then stepped aside and stuck out his foot. He huffed out a laugh as Glongkyle tripped over him and sailed into the air, arms reeling. It was a beautiful ten out of ten arc, a perfect rainbow of shocked green. When he made impact with the ground, Glongkyle's long lizard tail went rigid for a moment.

Izo thought back to all the times he'd woken on Glongkyle's ship, helpless, trapped, and all alone. He reached both arms up to swing his whole body into the hardest kick possible. It landed directly into the reptile's torso. Then Izo stepped over his least favorite alien abductor.

"Sorry." The Earthling leaned down to re-fold the bottom of one pant-leg that had come loose during the kick. "Didn't see you there."

Glongkyle groaned like a deflating balloon. He didn't try to get up.

Izo looked around. There had to be some way back to Earth. Picking a direction at random, he began following the herd of ambling aliens while watching for Yula's enormous form. Once out of the food court, he lost sight of the higher floors as he moved along a long, glass hallway stretched out toward the next major intersection. Searching the mass of extraterrestrial faces, he failed to notice a red beetle creature in a chic red hat that'd stopped short in front of him until he was already almost on top of her. Stumbling over her, he knocked the hat from her hairless crown. She shrieked. Izo cringed. He spun to snatch the hat midair and did his best to calm and quiet the screeching beetle-lady (he assumed).

"I'm so sorry about that, ma'am," Izo said, returning her hat to her. She continued to call him names. "I will be more careful. I swear." Waving another embarrassed apology, he jogged lightly ahead to get away from the bright-red meltdown, turned a corner, and slammed into a fur-covered wall.

Yula wrapped her fuzzy arms, each thicker than Izo's waist, around the Earthling. Izo squeezed his eyes and lowered his head. "Screw you, beetle-puta," he whispered bitterly.

Yula tightened her grip. "Izo is finished."

Izo grunted and fought, but the fluffy chest refused to move. Within moments he was huffing from strain and failing to keep fur out of his mouth. "Izo is not finished," he growled in defiance of nature and physics. "Izo is figuring things out as he goes." But like so many times before, it was no use. Struggle as he might, fighting off a Yula-hug was like trying to pry open a cuddlesome version of the jaws of life.

Glongkyle, the loathsome reptile, rounded the corner with perfect timing, like an onerous cosmic fart. "You caught him! Good job, Yula."

Izo squirmed to look over his shoulder and nod at his least favorite kidnapper. "Nice of you to join us. How's the nose?"

Glongkyle glared. "Better than my side."

Izo tipped his head back and laughed. He'd forgotten about the kick. But then he paused. A thought occurred to him: the one thing that could always make Yula let go. He didn't exactly enjoy it, but there weren't many other options at the moment. Dropping his gaze to Yula, he gave the giant a silly smile. "Oye Yula."

Yula looked at Izo with her soul-shriveling eyes. Reading Izo's coy expression, the giant alien seemed to read his thoughts. Her fluffy body bristled with fear. "No, Izo. No! Is not fair!"

Izo took a deep breath and tried not to picture Lenny squishing that woman to death at the end of *Of Mice and Men*. Then he dropped his head into the furry chest and began squirming as hard as he could. His entire body—arms, legs, face, and belly—moved back and forth like a parent tickling a toddler three times their size.

Yula roared with booming laughter and collapsed to the ground, Izo still in tow. Her already tight arms crushed Izo now, threatening to squeeze the teen like a tube of fully conscious toothpaste. But still Izo continued, attacking the big beast with relentless and unending ferocity. Yula curled, bending him backward in the curve of her massive, ticklish torso. It would be close, but Izo wasn't giving up. He made a resolution: from this point on, it was escape or death!

"Don't let him go, Yula!" shouted Glongkyle.

Yula tried; she really did. She squeezed. She squirmed. She giggled and shook her head hard. But finally, after barely two torturous minutes, she gave up and threw the Earthling clear, like a professional weightlifter flinging a rag doll. Izo soared across the hallway, spun, and landed on his feet.

Free again, Izo's eyes flashed over his options. They were in a four-way intersection, glass hallways stretching to connect buildings across a seventy-story drop. Along the perimeter was a line of gleaming blue benches. White trash compactors floated nearby. Izo squinted. He couldn't distinguish any difference between the four directions. He tsked in annoyance and wondered if it really mattered anyway. None of this seemed to be getting him anywhere.

"Grab him, Yula!" said Glongkyle.

But Yula shook her wooly head. "Izo tickles mean," she said with a child-like accusation.

"Yula," said Glongkyle. His reptile voice had gone low and menacing. "If you get fired, you won't get paid. If you don't get paid, what happens to your aunt?"

The giant Wuljerian's shoulders stooped. She turned to the Earthling. "Sorry, Izo."

"It's okay, Yula," said Izo. He'd been hoping to avoid this, but it seemed there was no other option.

Giving the big alien a sad smile, Izo jumped to one side, grabbed a floating bench, and swung it in a high deadly arc. Yula ducked, the big beast hunkering down on instinct. But there was no reason for the duck. The bench swung past her harmlessly, smashed into the glass wall beside them, and fell. Busted and sparking, it tumbled down the seventy-story drop before smashing into the ground with a resounding crash.

Izo took off for the hole in the wall. Glongkyle, who's face had just begun twisting into a horrified expression, turned and tried to hold out his hands to stop Izo. But he was too slow. Shooting the reptile a salute, Izo jumped and sailed through the hole in the wall—then snapped upward toward the alien sky beyond.

He still had no idea where he was going, but he could figure that out later. He was used to figuring things out later. Besides, it wasn't like the spaceport was going anywhere. For now, he just needed to stay clear of Glongkyle's fart-riddled ship. Soaring toward the infinite city, Izo opened his arms.

"You'll never see Earth again, fly-by!" Glongkyle screamed into the horizon. "And you can say goodbye to your little dirt girl-friend, too."

Izo's eye twitched. He dropped his arms and decelerated. Hooking himself invisibly between two buildings, he spun to glare from on high. "You need to watch your mouth, lizard."

Glongkyle crossed his scaly arms over his chest. He jerked his head for Yula to step nearer to the hole. Then he looked back at the Earthling, suspended close enough to exchange insults, but way too far to grab. "You want to flutter off? Fine. But you're going to get lost, we're going to leave, and then you'll REALLY never see Earth again."

Izo's insides burned. With every cell in his body, all he wanted to do was snap forward and yank the reptilian butthead off the side of the building. But he also had a sinking suspicion Glongkyle might not be lying; the jerk and his grimy spaceship might just be his only way home. Izo considered his options. Eventually his stubborn side won out.

He shook his head. "You know what? Screw it. I'll live here then. I'll go...bartend at a cantina! Yeah!! And I won't be no punk like Luke either." Izo smiled and nodded at this decision. Then, for good measure, he shot Glongkyle the bird with both hands before beginning to drift backward toward the city.

"Fine. Have fun being lost and alone forever," said Glongkyle.

"I will. Thanks."

Glongkyle's brow beetled. He seemed to be considering other threats to hurl when something suddenly occurred to him. He reached into his pocket and pulled out Izo's cell phone. "Forgetting something?"

Izo stopped short. "When—?" His mind raced back. How the HELL did Glongkyle get his cell phone? Izo hadn't left his only remaining connection to Earth on the ship. He remembered grabbing and checking the remaining battery life before leaving for the spaceport. Sure, it had been a busy morning, crossing through miles of the spaceport's inner terminals and passing several Imperial checkpoints while awaiting the perfect moment to escape, but he'd been careful to pat his pockets for it regularly.

"You must have dropped it during our scuffle. This is it, right? Your only thing from home?" Glongkyle dropped the delicate iPhone to the floor before resting one thickly clawed foot on top.

Izo's face tightened. The lizard's broke into a cruel smile.

"It has your only picture of her, doesn't it?"

Izo didn't answer.

"That's what I thought," Glongkyle said with smug victory. "So here's what's going to happen: you're going to do what I say and like it, or I'm going to crush this thing and leave—"

Izo snapped forward, grabbed the phone from under Glongkyle's foot, and snapped back.

"—you here to rot..." Glongkyle paused. He lifted his foot. The phone was no longer underneath it.

Izo looked the phone over carefully. He was pissed beyond words. "Glongkyle, I swear to God, if this has even one new scratch, you're slipping off that building—coordinates to Earth be damned."

Glongkyle gulped and backed away from the wall's opening.

After careful inspection, Izo determined the phone was fine. He was tempted to cut on the phone and check its battery life. Even with all the alien technology aboard Glongkyle's ship, he'd yet to find a way to charge it—not that Glongkyle would have helped him. He forced himself to resist. Checking the phone would only drain what little battery it still had and make him feel worse for looking afterward. Instead, he unzipped his jumper and carefully tucked the precious device into a pocket against his chest. Then he zipped his jumpsuit all the way to his neck.

His eyes found Glongkyle's. "Anyway, I'd say it's been nice, but..." He shrugged.

"If you leave, you'll regret it," said Glongkyle. "It'll be the worst mistake you'll ever make."

Izo was pretty sure the worst mistake he'd ever made was not waiting for that bus. Regardless, he was free to do what he wanted now. And what he wanted to do was to be as far away from Glongkyle as possible.

Turning midair, Izo began snagging and pulling himself away from the spaceport and toward the giant capital beyond. Behind him, a low, whining howl tore across the open horizon. Izo glanced over his shoulder with a frown. Yula's face was crushed. She looked about half ready to cry. She reached for Izo to come back, but the Earthling just shook his head. "Take care of your aunt," he called back.

"Are you really this stupid?" yelled Glongkyle.

Izo held in a snarky response and kept moving. It didn't matter what he said. Soon Glongkyle, Yula, and Tearn would be nothing more than a distant memory.

Along with your home planet, his subconscious reminded him. He grimaced but shook his head. It wasn't important. He could figure something else out later.

"What about the girl? The one on your cell phone?" hollered Glongkyle, his voice coming in weaker despite screaming between two clawed hands. "How long are you going to keep her waiting for you?"

Izo's nose twitched. He stopped. He hated it, but Glongkyle was right—the chances of Izo finding another way back to Earth were tiny. The chances of him doing so before it was too late to help Hanako? Zero.

He heaved out a heavy sigh. In front of him, an immeasurable alien capital, bright and dark, tall and wide, half-covered in clouds and half-flanked by impossible buildings, stretched out before him in infinite freedom and possibilities. It was a beautiful thing, a whole giant wonderland filled with no-more-Glongkyles. Izo's shoulders fell as he slowly turned his back on it. As Glongkyle's smug face came into view again, Izo's chest was struck with an almost physical pain.

Yula's ears and back straightened upright. The sight of her little Earth buddy returning seemed to excite her beyond words. The big idiot even began dancing from foot to foot.

Izo snapped back to float a few feet from the opening of the building, still out of reach of his captors. He crossed his arms. "Mira—if I do this, there's going to be some ground rules. Number one: I'm not getting back on that ship."

Glongkyle ground his teeth. "Fine. We can stay in the city."

Izo nodded. "Two: we're doing this my way."

"Fine. But you have to come inside right now. Security's going to get here any second and—"

"That's him!" shrieked the beetle lady from exactly out of nowhere. Appearing suddenly behind Yula, she gestured at Izo to someone that appeared to be the same species as Yula, wearing an official uniform.

Yula yelped and went to move away from the shrill sound. Turning toward the source, she simultaneously jerked back. Then she fell out of the hole in the wall in an almost comically surprised yip.

Izo and everyone else looked down in confusion. Then the Earthling sucked in a breath and dove.

Yula was plummeting toward the ground exactly as unstoppably as the tank nature had built her to be. Izo had no idea what he was supposed to do. Worse, he only had about seven hundred feet to figure it out. In his mind's eye, he tried to picture getting beneath Yula, but a vision of a human trying to deadlift a grizzly soon shattered this idea. He quickly flipped through a catalog of other possible positions: Piggyback? Superman? Bridal? In every situation, he saw Yula slipping off his skinny body like a horse trying to balance on a ladder.

Izo realized there was only one way to do this. He cursed everything. Luckily for him, Yula was already in position. Face an ugly mask of fear, the massive Wuljerian was doing her best to reach for Izo with both her fluffy paws. Izo mirrored her, reaching down to grab the Wuljerian's limbs. Then he braced himself, seriously regretting not taking the time to stretch his back that morning.

He began pulling up. The reality of the task was immediately worse than he imagined. First off, it was almost impossible to get a solid grip on Yula's hands. He wasn't sure if it was the powerful wind buffeting their limbs or the fact that Yula's arms were as big as Izo, but every time they managed to connect hands all Izo came away with was handfuls of fur.

The cold, unforgiving ground loomed closer, about halfway from swallowing them whole like a massive, grinning god. Finally, in a tiny, split-second miracle, Yula managed to lock both her paws around Izo's forearms.

A shared look of relief flashed between them. Everything was going to be okay. Izo began pulling up.

Holy crap!

It was like trying to stop a train. No. That would have made more sense. It was like consciously letting a train rip your arms off at the shoulder. There was no point to this. Grappling with the cold futility of physics, Izo flipped his feet down and tried to lift with his legs, whatever that meant in this context. But try as he might, it was no use. It didn't matter what he did; they continued plummeting toward the ground like an overstuffed bag of cinder blocks.

Oh well. He'd tried. Today just wasn't his fluffy friend's day.

Izo let go and tried to pull away, but something stopped him. Yula hadn't released he grip on his forearms. He was still falling. Crap! She was going to drag him to the ground with her! He tried to shake her off, but it was the battle in the spaceport all over again. Shit! Yula wasn't letting go!

Izo opened his mouth to beg, but something told him he didn't have enough time between there and the ground to explain the noble nuance of self-sacrifice to the big alien. No, it seemed Izo was committed: he was either going to figure out how to save her or die covered in her fur.

Izo looked next to them at the building growing taller every second. Instead of trying to fly in his normal "rubber-band snapping" way, he started hurling every invisible line he could conjure at the building's roof. Soon, like Spider-Man slowing a runaway helicopter, there were enough invisible "cables" that their descent began to slow.

Izo grunted. His thoroughly un-invincible body was now the only linchpin between a network of invisible forces and the heaviest sentient creature he'd ever seen. *Oof.* This day was turning out rougher than he'd hoped.

Stretching the cables gingerly, he lowered Yula to the ground before dropping down beside her. Both instinctually slumped into low, wide-seated positions. They didn't want to lie down, but they also didn't want to stand. Their breaths were hard and ragged. Yula's were punctuated with vague whimpering sounds. Izo stared ahead, a sense of death still floating nearby like a faint but familiar smell. He rubbed a new sore spot between his neck and shoulder. "Don't know how Spidey does it," he said without realizing he'd said anything.

"Hey," said Tearn, Izo's third and smallest abductor. He'd appeared from a nearby exit, pushing a floating cart loaded with grimy boxes and crates. He waved at them genially. "I got our luggage pulled from the ship. Good news: they didn't charge us!" Tearn paused, confusion forming over his face. "Wait. What are you doing down here?"

Izo peered at Tearn blankly. Short, grey, and shaped exactly like a classic sci-fi Martian, the bald, bulbous-headed Ginarsian was the only one whose orange jumpsuit fit worse than Izo's. Folded over and pinned down to a ridiculously oversized accommodation, Tearn looked like a toddler wearing his father's suit.

Tiny Tearn took in the scene: the broken glass on the ground, the mangled bench nearby, and the massive hole in the spaceport above. His mouth fell open. Black reflective eyes dropped to settle on Izo and Yula. The Ginarsian crossed his tiny arms over his tiny chest. "What'd you idiots do now?"

"Don't look at me." Izo pointed at Yula. "She's the one that tripped out of a building."

"Izo break building," Yula tattled, pointing back.

"Because I can fly, you big, stupid dog!" But when Izo saw Yula's surprised and hurt expression, he felt about as heroic as a bug. "I'm sorry, Yula. I didn't mean that. You're not dumb. I have un humor de perros. I was recently abducted by a couple of alien jerks." He shot a meaningful look at Tearn.

Tearn shrugged with a nervous motion. "Well, life's not always fair."

Izo rolled his eyes.

"We need to clear out before security gets here." Tearn hurriedly waved them up. "It's almost lunch. Let's get out of here and get something to eat."

Izo wanted to get back to Earth more than anything—back to Hanako, back to normal, good-looking Earth humans, back to twenty-four-hour days and recognizable food. But sitting atop a floating white chair in an open air café a few blocks from the spaceport, he debated if returning to Earth was worth dealing with Glongkyle's crap for even one more second. He looked up at the nearly cloudless sky. He could go. He could fly away right now and never think about Earth or any of this ever again.

No, he urged himself again. *You made a promise to Hanako.* Come hell or...alien abduction...he was going to keep his promise and return home.

"I still don't understand your problem," Glongkyle interrupted from across their floating table. This was true. Glongkyle didn't understand Izo's problem. Why? Because it wasn't Glongkyle's problem.

Izo wiped a hand over his face. Yula needed to hurry back with their food. Izo didn't have enough patience for this without food. "Okay, Glongkyle," he said. "Then you wear a dress."

"Why would I wear a dress?" said Glongkyle. "You're the Avarian; not me."

"But I'm not an Avarian on Earth," said Izo.

"Does it look like you're on Earth?"

"No!" Izo stood to slam both his palms into the table. "I wonder what could have happened?"

Tearn reached out to place a hand on Izo's arm. They were beginning to draw the attention of passersby. "I realize you're upset. You have every right to be. But that's in the past. From now on we're on the same team. As long as we work together, we'll get through this quickly. What we can't do is panic."

"Hey, Douglas Adams—shut up." Izo knocked Tearn's hand away and sat. "I didn't have time to grab a towel, remember?"

Glongkyle glanced at Tearn in confusion. The Strungian was clearly expecting the team's resident linguist and cultural attaché to understand and explain Izo's reference. Instead, Tearn grabbed Izo's arm to give the pissed off teenager a reassuring rub. "Izo, calm down. Everything's going to be all right."

Izo felt weirdly better after that encouragement. Tearn's encouragement always made him feel weirdly better, even if it was occasionally accompanied by an overly familiar affection. He wasn't sure if it was because Tearn's hands were smaller and warmer than most, but in any case, a peaceful wave soon washed over the Earthling.

Izo blinked slowly. He tried to remember what they were arguing about.

"This is going to be easy," said Tearn. "We finally landed on IA. Half of the plan is done."

"How is this a plan?" said Izo, remembering. "Your whole strategy seems to be plunking me in the middle of a planet and waiting for money to appear."

"Which it will," said Glongkyle. "As long as you wear the dress."

"Which sounds smart," said Izo. "As long as you don't have a brain."

"Izo, you're right," said Tearn. "It's a simple plan. That's because we've done it before. The hardest part was getting you here. Now, all we need to do is find the right sucker, get a check, and you head home with the best alien tech Earth has ever seen. Everything's going to be fine," Tearn repeated for the millionth time. He gave the Earthling's arm another encouraging rub. Izo cringed when the little Ginarsian's fingers slowed to run over the lines of his bicep. Izo was bisexual, but he was keenly aware that there were plenty of aliens that were definitely not his type. "Heck, everything's going to be awesome!"

Izo dropped his chin to his chest. He glared at the tabletop. He didn't feel like arguing anymore. But he was pretty sure he didn't believe Tearn either. It would have been easy to. After all, the Ginarsian might have been telling him the truth. But he also knew just because he wanted something to be true, didn't mean it was. In fact, it was normally the opposite.

That said, his chance of getting home without them didn't look ideal either. "Okay. I get it. One big score, then back to Earth. Fine." Izo tapped a finger into the table. He shook his head at Glongkyle. "But I'm not wearing a dress to do it."

"Avarians wear dresses, dummy," said Glongkyle.

Not all of them, he wanted to say. But it'd be meaningless to point out—they knew way more Avarians than him. In a larger way, it probably was a meaningless argument. They'd gone to all this trouble of kidnapping, trafficking, and extorting him. Why was he so worked up about wearing a dress? It was stupid and stubborn to be this concerned over stereotypical dress codes. Particularly as a liberal, bisexual from California. But maybe that was the point. They could do a lot of things to him—shoot him out of the sky, lock him in a ship, drag him across the universe, and refuse to take him home until he made money—but they couldn't make him stop being stupid and stubborn.

"I told you not to call me an Avarian," said Izo.

"Izo," Tearn said pulling the teenager's attention back. "Can I ask you something? Why don't you like being called Avarian?"

Because Glongkyle uses it like an insult, Izo wanted to say. But that would be giving Glongkyle, the scaly, gleeful butthole, too much power. "The term is nonsense," Izo explained around his real reason. "There's no such thing as Avarians on Earth. You might as well call me a Heffalump."

"So it's culturally meaningless?" said Tearn.

"Sure," said Izo.

"Okay. I understand. But let me ask you this—why do you care?" said Tearn. "By definition, all it means is you're a rare variation of your species that can fly. Avarians appear on every planet. It's a good thing, Izo. You're a remarkable specimen of Earth's natural selection."

"Yeah, stupid," said Glongkyle. "You're lucky to be called an Avarian."

"Feel real lucky, thanks." Izo glared. But then he backtracked. "Don't get me wrong. The flying part is cool. I have superpowers. That's the jackpot. But there's also this creepy history and wearing dresses." Izo held his arms wide. "Doesn't sound like my kind of club."

"One: you have no choice. You are an Avarian. Get used to it. Two: creepy history?" Glongkyle swung a sharp look at the Ginarsian. "Tearn, you massive-headed moron. What the hell were you teaching him in the back of my ship?"

"Not how to read in alien, that's for sure," said Izo, remembering how he'd been unable to decipher any of the signs in the spaceport.

Tearn glowered at Glongkyle before focusing on Izo. "I told you—I can catalogue and add your language to the Imperial codex. But I can't magically make you recognize the syntax and written symbols of nearly a dozen vital languages. Literacy is a whole separate skill."

"Could have taught me the word for 'exit,'" Izo mumbled.

Tearn's eyes widened. He seemed to realize what many of their conversations aboard the ship, the *Atrox Killboard*, had actually been about. "W-w-well sorry I wasn't more useful in your grand escape!"

Izo shrugged. "You never are."

"Unlike what short-stack's been telling you," interrupted Glongkyle, getting a nostril flare from Tearn, "there's nothing creepy about Avarian history. Avarians are valued above anyone. You're treated like sacred treasure."

"I thought our history was one long string of imperial abductions, rape, and murder when it made your gods happy?"

"That's a little reductive," said Glongkyle. "Do bad things happen? Sure. But by far and large, Avarians are revered and respected universally."

Izo stared. "I'm being trafficked and extorted for money. Like... right now."

Glongkyle waved him off. "Anecdotal."

Izo threw his hands in the air.

"I think it's also worth mentioning, not for nothing," stammered Tearn, "w-we're technically smugglers. Not traffickers."

"Guess what, Mr. Linguist? When it's people, it's trafficking." Izo shook his head in disgust before looking away at the rest of the populace strolling the capital. He was once again struck by how many different types of aliens were basically humanoid with variant sizes, coloring, and features. Twenty-five percent could have easily posed as Earthling with a few minor adjustments.

His hair stood up on the back of his head. He scratched his arm. "Shouldn't Yula be back with the food by now?"

Pausing their conversation, the three of them spun their heads to see if they could spot the big Wuljerian. She'd left nearly thirty minutes ago to hunt and gather food. Izo was worried the giant was lost.

Izo spotted her first. "There she is." Sure enough, Yula was standing at the edge of the plaza outside the first row of floating tables, tray in hand, eyes blankly scanning the sea of tables with a confused expression. Izo floated high out of his seat and waved.

Seeing Izo, Yula lumbered to their table and plunked down a tray of stacked boxes. She handed a box to Tearn. "Table got lost."

"That's okay, Yula," Tearn said, taking the offered meal. "You did a good job."

Izo nodded and waited for Yula to hand him his food. But after passing a box to Glongkyle, and opening her own, Yula began eating. The fourth box of food remained on the tray.

Izo waved at the Yula. "Hello? ¿Me olvidaste? Forget anybody?"

Yula brought her meal, a large loaf of meat covered in sauce, toward her face with both hands. She acknowledged neither Izo nor Izo's lunch. "Sorry. Must be dumb dog," she said before taking her first bite.

Izo's shoulders sank. "Yula..."

"You know what's funny?" Glongkyle said, giving Izo a shit-eating grin. "You're always calling me an asshole, but you managed to piss off a Wuljerian, one of the nicest species in the universe. So who's the real asshole, fly-by?"

Izo's jaw clenched.

"Don't try to pin this on him, Glongkyle. You've been an asshole longer than he's been alive," Tearn said hitching up an eyebrow.

Izo couldn't help but grin. If anyone knew the truth about Glongkyle, it was Tearn. From what the Earthling had gathered during their long journey, the two had known each other since they were kids.

"Whatever. Yula, give him his food. Whether he likes it or not, he is an Avarian and Avarians are precious cargo." The reptile smiled cruelly at the Earthling. "Precious cargo needs to eat."

But the fourth box of food remained on Yula's tray like a guarded kill. When Glongkyle reached to grab for Izo's meal, the Wuljerian growled and the group's captain yanked his hand back.

"Oye Yula." Izo reached across the table to touch Yula's wrist. "I am sorry. I didn't mean to insult you." But Yula pulled her fluffy arm away. Izo sat back. "Great. Now my Wookie's mad at me."

"Yula not Wookie," said Yula. "Yula not dog."

Izo sighed. This was one of the weirder parts about what was already a really weird situation. As infuriating as all of this was, Yula was mostly innocent, and a soft-hearted person to boot. She didn't deserve to be caught in the crosshairs; she was being leveraged for her species, same as Izo.

Izo reached out, grabbed the giant's hand, and locked eyes with her. "You're right. You're not a dog," said Izo. "And you're not dumb. I'm dumb."

Yula frowned. She pushed her chin to her chest and seemed to consider it. Then, with the hint of a smile, she glanced at the Earthling. "Izo Wookie?"

Izo smiled. Throwing his head back, he did his biggest, loudest, best Wookie impression. It was a booming, lilting noise. Aided by the tall buildings that surrounded the plaza, it bounced and ricocheted everywhere through the Imperial streets. Aliens from across the universe stopped and surveyed in confusion. It was a beautiful scene, enough to make George Lucas proud, and, more importantly, draw the delighted applause of one overjoyed Wuljerian.

"Is better!" said Yula.

Izo shrugged with humility as Yula finally handed him his lunch. "It was all our practice on the ship," he said. But then, looking down into his meal, his eyes nearly bugged out of his head. "What's this?"

Yula's ears flattened. "Is sandwich?"

Izo gawked. Tall and drenched in a white sauce, it involved a thick brick of red meat bounded by two shiny green buns. "The bread here is green?"

Tearn blinked owlishly. "What color is it supposed to be?"

"Brown."

"Ew," said Glongkyle. "Like poop?"

"No. Like grain!" said Izo.

Tearn, Glongkyle, and even Yula all shared a look. "I hate to tell you this, but the grain on most planets around here is green," said Tearn.

"See? This is what I'm talking about," said Glongkyle. "I'm not going to let someone who doesn't know the color of bread decide what to wear during our big scam."

"Not the time, Glongkyle." Tearn was watching the Earthling with concern.

Izo was staring at the green and red concoction. It gave off a tart scent, like a bitter fruit jam. The dough was so dense, it looked more like baked paste than bread. His shoulders slumped. It was the universe's dumbest thing to be upset over. It was a sandwich. A stupid sandwich. But being stuck on their ship eating nothing but space gruel for three months, Tearn had assured him, yes, he could get anything he wanted once they reached IA. Call him crazy, but at some point during the journey, Izo had started to look forward to it a little.

"Tearn, you asshole—you promised there would be sand-wiches." Izo's soul contracted, and the abyss within him widened by double. "This is the worst thing that's ever happened to me."

"I'm sorry! I thought that's what you meant. You never know, though," suggested Tearn weakly. "Maybe you'll like it?"

Izo blew out two cheeks of air and looked down at the "sandwich." Maybe it wouldn't be terrible? He lifted it, braced himself, took one giant bite, and chewed. He got three chews in before retching. It was the exact flavor of creamy, sweet dish soap.

Izo opened his mouth and let the ball of food fall off his tongue and onto the table. Then he shivered.

Yula looked distressed. She held out her meatloaf for Izo to have. It was riddled with loose pieces of fur and presented in Yula's hand like a kindergartner's art project. Izo had to turn it down. "Thanks, though." Closing his box, Izo pushed it away.

Glongkyle tilted his head. "You're not going to eat?"

"I don't think I can."

Glongkyle gave Izo a derisive look. Then, without another word, he switched their boxes. "Try mine."

Izo eyed the meal curiously. Yellow-orangish and with a fluffy, crumbly texture, it gave off a pleasant, savory smell. "Are these... eggs?"

The reptile frowned. "More or less."

Before Izo could let himself ruminate on this answer, he hurried to pinch and try a bite of the delicious smelling food. "Hey!" He gave an appreciative nod. "That's not bad." Wiping his hands on his jumpsuit, he began eating. But then, after a moment, he slowed. He narrowed his eyes at their captain and commander. "Why are you being nice to me?"

Glongkyle opened Izo's box and picked up the so-called sandwich. "Like I said—precious cargo's got to eat." He nodded at Izo's lunch. "Hurry up. It's not as good cold."

Satisfied, Izo shrugged it off and continued eating as Glongkyle took a bite of the not-sandwich instead. The group fell into an easy silence. All around them an endless ocean of alien strangers flowed past.

When Glongkyle saw Izo was nearly finished, he took a slow, purposeful sip of his drink. He eyed the teen slyly. "To be clear... you're definitely wearing that dress now though."

Izo continued shoveling food into his mouth with one hand. With his other hand, he flipped Glongkyle the bird.

Glongkyle set his cup down loudly. He gestured at Tearn. "What is that? Why does he keep doing that? Tearn, you're the freaking linguist. You're supposed to know this stuff."

Tearn shrugged and continued eating. "If it's culturally meaningless, why do you care?"

— CHAPTER THREE —

Izo

We'll split up and look for dresses—"
"I'm not wearing a pinche dress," said Izo.
"—and meet near the fitting stations in fifteen
minutes." Glongkyle continued passing scanner guns to everyone
while ignoring Izo's interruptions. They'd left the café and
swapped locations for a fancy store that specialized in Avarian
clothing. Not that this made any sense to Izo. According to Tearn,
at least, Avarians could pop up in any species.

Also, as far as the dress discussion, nothing had been resolved.

"You could kill me and bury me in *Pet Sematary*," Izo continued.
He hopped onto a spinning shelf of folded shirts. "Zombie-
demon-me still wouldn't wear a dress."

Glongkyle glowered and brandished a glittery scanner for Izo to
take. The teenager stared with a flat expression. The spinning shelf
slowly carried him farther and farther away.

Glongkyle rolled his eyes and gave the scanner to Yula. He
handed the last glittery scanner gun to Tearn. "And don't pick
anything fancy." He gave Tearn a pointed look.

Tearn gestured with his scanner in confusion. "What did I do?"

"I don't want another Tmipian pie fiasco, Tearn."

Tearn's face turned red. He waved the scanner gun at Glongkyle. "Those were delicacies!"

"Repeat after me," said Glongkyle. "Nothing. Fancy. Especially if it's on sale."

Tearn folded his arms.

Yula pointed her scanner at her eye, shot it, and laughed. "Store tickles too!"

A purple-skinned store clerk holding a tall stack of clothes stopped and zeroed in on them. "Can I help you?"

Izo hopped off the shelf and joined the others in awkwardly brushing off their jumpsuits. They tried to look presentable in the high-end establishment. The store clerk—a cute, almost-human looking alien with an absolutely heart-breaking set of curves— glared, then flew away.

Izo's eyes grew huge. His heart started pounding in his chest. *That hot alien can fly like me!* His entire time on Earth he'd never met another flying person. But Tearn had promised him there were millions, sprinkled all across the universe like cosmic predetermined anomalies.

Izo snapped forward and grabbed the purple alien by the arm. "You can fly?"

The store clerk zapped him with electricity.

Izo yelped and let go. The others roared with laughter behind him. He slowly floated back, disheveled and morose as he tried to shake the stinging out of his hand. He glared at the store clerk who was continuing to put things away. "What the heck was her problem?"

"Lesson number one, that's a male—" said Glongkyle.

"That's a male!?" Izo whipped his head around to re-examine the purple clerk with the tiny torso and massive hips. Still hot as the California sun. He leaned his head. "Where's he from?"

"Anolita." said Glongkyle. "Lesson number two—don't mess with Anolituns."

Izo's hand remained raw and singed. He shook it out a few times while mentally making a note: *purple aliens—hot, but mean.* He knocked over a stack of shirts. Then he turned to Glongkyle and pointed at the store's exit. "Idiota, I don't have to be here."

"You do if you ever want to eat another Earth sandwich, fly-by."

Izo considered laughing him off. But Glongkyle pointed the sparkly pink scanner directly between his eyes. Izo gulped and tried to remember the lizard couldn't actually hurt him at the moment.

"Allow me to explain this one more time: if Earth hasn't heard of the tri-galaxies, the tri-galaxies haven't heard of Earth. In fact, I know exactly how far into uncharted territory we were when we picked you up—"

"Picked me up?" The California teenager's eyes drilled holes into the reptile's. "That's what you're calling it?"

"And you couldn't accidentally retrace that path with an army of prophets and a thousand years to kill. You want to leave? There's the door. I can find another Avarian." Glongkyle's lipless mouth broke into a smile of absolute victory. "How many home worlds you got?"

Izo clenched his fists. He wanted to punch Glongkyle. But if he did, it would just cause another in a long line of pointless scuffles with Yula when the big Wuljerian intervened. So instead he coasted forward, slammed his shoulder into Glongkyle's, and floated deeper into the store to do the one thing that calmed him down when he couldn't stand to be around the others.

Izo looked around the brightly colored extravaganza. Three stories tall and littered in an explosion of clothes, it was filled with free-floating platforms and dozens of towering columns of apparel that only Avarians could access. Soaring up to the highest un-in-habited place he could find, Izo huddled into a corner, unzipped his jumpsuit, and took out his cell phone.

With the click of a button, Hanako's smiling face greeted him, just as bright and warm as the day he'd taken the photo. He remembered that day. They'd spent it wandering around Old Sacramento, clacking down the wooden boardwalks while perusing the stores. It was sunny and cool, as it often was during spring in Northern

Cali. The crowds were as happy, colorful, and diverse as a hippy's favorite t-shirt.

They'd known each other since they were kids, shortly after Hanako's mother died. They met in foster care, Izo awaking in the middle of the night to the sounds of high-pitched crying as another child was brought in carrying nothing more than a trash bag filled with clothes and whatever they were wearing on the worst night of their life.

Hanako was trying to squirm out of Ada's arms as Marcus signed documents with the social worker. Ada, a sweet, heavyset Hispanic woman who loved children more than anything, did her best to soothe the screaming child. But Hanako was inconsolable, like a shrieking bomb ready to tear off the roof. Izo could see the reservation growing in Marcus's demeanor, the way his signature grew slower with every passing moment.

That's when Izo, exhausted ten-year-old he was, noticed what Hanako was reaching for—not for the ground to get down, but for the trash bag sitting on the ground. Padding over, he tore open its top to begin searching through it.

"Izaac," Ada admonished. "This is not yours!"

But Izo ignored her and continued looking, flipping through a mush of dirty clothes until he found what he was pretty sure he was searching for: a fuzzy, limp doggy in deep chocolate brown.

Holding it up, he was answered with a jealous scream from the tiny terror—all the proof he needed. He handed it to her. Hanako snatched it, her expression a hideous mask of distrustful fury. But it worked; she stopped crying, and Izo went back to bed. Years later, he made her a promise, and he'd be damned if anything was going to stop him from keeping it.

From his perch high in the Avarian store, Izo could hear the others calling his name below, Glongkyle with a whole bevy of more creative nicknames.

"Back to the Space Jam," he whispered to himself. Izo clapped himself on each cheek twice. He needed to shake his melancholy off. He could do this. He could finish this scam and get home. Sick alien tech. More money than he'd ever know what to do with. He was close. He could do this. Just a little while longer; then he was home free.

Swallowing hard, he looked down at Hanako's beaming face. "I'm getting back to you," he swore to her, "and we're going to be a family." In the top right-hand corner of his screen, the phone's battery life changed from eighteen to seventeen percent. Izo sighed, clicked off the phone, and put it away. He suppressed a staccato shake in his chest. But then, reminding himself he was a badass, he hopped over the edge of the floating platform for the fitting station down below.

From Izo's vantage point overhead, the fitting station mimicked a white and gold flower. Its center consisted of eight rooms cut in triangular wedges that formed an octagon. Its outside edges were rounded by semicircular sectionals that made up its petals. Spotting him from one of these, the team waved to get his attention.

Izo drifted down just as a petite Avarian in green and black approached their group from the air. He (or she?) was pretty cute, with shimmering gold skin, anime-like huge eyes, and a giant head covered in bombshell blonde hair. They kind of reminded Izo of a smaller, more bobble-headed version of Peter Pan.

"Hello!" the other Avarian said. "My name's Seemi, and I'll be helping you today!"

— CHAPTER FOUR —

Seemi

You're Avarian, right?" asked the tall, reptilian customer. Short yellow horns and a blunted snout identified him as Strungian, and likely on some exploitative scheme no doubt.

"I am," said Seemi.

"You're also..." The reptile glanced at Seemi's crotch. "Aurelian?" His gaze returned to Seemi's with a simpering smirk of innuendo.

Seemi's face clenched. Yes, he was Aurelian, a member of an intersexual species born with both internal and external genitalia. And yes, their history had been fairly straight-forward. With everyone equally concerned about carrying offspring, they'd perfected contraceptives long before agricultural farming. A notoriously liberated species, they were often treated like free entertainment for the dumb and huddled masses around the universe. And Seemi faced that stereotype. Every. Damn. Day.

The ironic thing? Seemi had been excited to get this job. He'd moved to IA out of the blue, a fight with his parents blown into an adventure for the ages. He had a friend in town and enough money for a ticket; the rest he'd figure out later. Once here, he knew he needed a job if he wanted to stay, and he'd applied at Loft, a chain of high-end clothing boutiques. It had been completely on a whim, a haphazard application at the store closest to IA's most popular intergalactic spaceport. Seven years later, it was with no small amount of bitterness he returned day after day to a store barely five blocks into the city that was supposed to represent his life's greatest adventure.

He honestly hadn't thought he was going to get the job. He'd applied for everything—bartending, waiting, teaching art, and even the Imperial army. When the renowned business had contacted him a few days later, he could barely control his voice enough to confirm his name and foreigner's ID. He couldn't believe it! He'd barely been on IA three days! Everything he'd heard about the big, bad capital that ate Avarians alive was wrong. He could do this. He was going to make it! Fate was on his side.

Seven years later, Seemi could officially confirm it wasn't fate that made his application stand out that day. Seemi was Aurelian, and this Loft location was on the tourist end of the capital. As time went on, Seemi noticed that this store had a funny habit of hiring different types of rare Avarians. Almost one of each, in fact. It had seemed kind of fun at first—cutting edge and super diverse, a multi-cultural microcosm in one location. A place where every Avarian could be seen and heard. It was certainly on-brand. But as employee concerns were continuously glossed over and turnover of "poor team-members" picked up, it became clearer and clearer that Loft was less a place for Avarians to be heard than a place for them to be seen.

To be clear, Seemi needed this job. It was a good job: good hours, good benefits, and decent pay. His complaints were environmental and spiritual, the type of complaints homeless and starving people wished they could make. So Seemi did what any smart Aurelian would do: he kept his head down, worked hard, and applied for a transfer after three years.

They offered him a raise and a promotion instead. Four years and two promotions after that, Seemi was as bolted into this store as the walls that held the ceiling up.

For one wonderful moment, Seemi imagined trading every pay raise and bonus for one heavy swing at the reptile's simpering expression, preferably with a blunt object. Of course, that wouldn't stop the stupid insinuations from the next person, or the one after that...

Seemi blinked and remembered his training. Non-reaction. That was the official Loft policy for inappropriate customer comments. Stay cool. Remain calm. Ignore inconsequential behavior. He turned to another customer in the group, a tiny Ginarsian. "Is there something you need help with today?"

"Yes," the tiny Ginarsian said. Short and with a round, hairless head, his species was known for their social acumen and powers of empathy. Why he was teamed up with a Strungian, the store clerk couldn't possibly imagine. "We need a couple of outfits for our Avarian friend. He may be a unique fit. Izo!" the Ginarsian shouted over his shoulder. "Come here!"

Seemi turned to Izo and was instantly confused. Although his gloomy self-propelled flight quickly revealed his Avarian nature, Seemi had no idea what species or galaxy the youth hailed from. Which was definitely weird. After years of working near the capital's central spaceport, he'd grown used to identifying virtually every type of customer that came through the doors. But this youth, from his matte golden skin to his small face and bright green eyes, had Seemi at a loss.

"Hello. How are you?" said Seemi.

Izo shrugged. He didn't look Seemi's direction. He instead resigned himself to peering about the room in dispassionate annoyance. "Fine. You?"

"I'm well. Thanks for asking. Did you have something particular in mind?"

"Nothing too 'Avarian' I guess." The youth waved his arms around the store in vague distaste. "No offense."

Seemi's eyes widened. In all his seven years of working there, he'd never heard anyone say something like that. How could something be "too Avarian"? Avarians came from every planet in the universe. Their style was as varied as the stars.

"Give it a rest, fly-by," the reptilian said. "You're an Avarian. Avarians are supposed to wear Avarian clothing. Stop being weird. You're making other people uncomfortable."

Now you care about making people uncomfortable? Seemi thought to himself. He cleared his throat and smiled at the youth. "Don't worry. Here at Loft we always take care of our customers. No matter what your style, shape, or species, Loft can find something uniquely designed and tailor-fit for you. Why? Because you're Avarian." Seemi broke into his picture-perfect smile before delivering the company's trademark tagline. "And you're worth it."

"You hear that? He always takes care of his customers, Tearn," the reptile said to his Ginarsian friend. "As an Aurelian, I wonder if that means he—"

"I'm sorry?" Seemi interrupted. He moved forward and tipped his head to one side. On the wide-angle cameras overhead it would look harmless. Probably adorable. But up close and personal, it was as fierce as an "accidental" shove. Seemi stared at the reptile with a perfect, unflinching smile. "Did you say something?"

The Strungian shook his head and looked down. "No."

"Are you sure?" Seemi waited another second. When it was clear the man wasn't going to double down, Seemi obliged. He clapped his hands and turned to the others, committing himself to change gears. "Wonderful! I am so excited to have you all here, because we have some amazing new stuff at Loft."

Seemi gestured for them to take their seats on the circular sectional behind them. Then he moved in front of their towering digital sales screen to begin his pitch. "The MyBody takes measurements with its state-of-the-art laser technology to render your digital mock-up here."

Seemi floated near the edge of the screen and tapped it twice. A ten-foot-tall avatar of the store clerk appeared, smiling and donning the latest fashion. "Any style in the store can be virtually adapted to your body type, regardless of species or size."

Floating higher, Seemi tapped on an outfit from the top of the screen. The digital Seemi blinked away and then reappeared, proudly donning its new outfit.

"That's when the real fun begins! Color, trim, print—anything can be customized to create your ultimate look." Finished, Seemi floated out toward them. He was proud. He had done it. He had held it together and delivered a killer product demonstration. "Any questions?"

The Avarian, Izo, raised his hand.

"Yes?"

"What kind of Avarian are you?"

The store clerk dropped to the ground. He could feel a surge of rage surging inside him like a magnetic volcano ready to explode. "Is this some kind of joke?" he said. "Because if you're not going to buy anything, you can all go and—"

"I am so sorry," the Ginarsian, Tearn, said sitting forward. "He's not from around here. I swear he didn't mean any offense. Did you, Izo?"

Seemi crossed his arms. Beside Tearn the reptile was laughing so hard he had nearly fallen over. The big Wuljerian, the last member of their group, looked like she had no idea what was happening. But none of them mattered.

Seemi glared daggers at the other Avarian.

The youth's face swiveled back and forth between Seemi and Tearn. "I'm sorry," he said, slowly gathering that he'd done something wrong. "Uh... my bad, ese?"

Seemi was on the verge of kicking them all out. Instead, he pinched the bridge of his nose. "It's fine. Do you have any questions about the clothes process?"

Izo shook his head. He pointed toward the fitting room next to the screen. "You're going to make a dress-up doll of me. Right?"

"Correct." Seemi gestured over his shoulder and the fitting room door popped open.

"Great." Izo pointed awkwardly. "Can I go ahead and...?"

Seemi nodded.

The other Avarian snapped into the room, again surprising and confusing Seemi with the unexpected movement. *Maybe he's some sort of sprite?* Seemi wondered to himself.

Seemi shut the door and prepared the program. A grid of lasers would appear and scan the Avarian's body before saving and transferring the information to corporate's central database. Though not a long process, it could sometimes take a couple of attempts to get it right if the customer was squirmy. Something told him this customer would be. "Let me know when you're ready."

A short while later Seemi heard the strange youth pat twice on the door from the inside. "Ready!"

Seemi started the program. Inside the lights would turn off as a grid of red strips would appear, starting first at the feet and then working their way up. The entire procedure might take a minute, though Seemi had never actually timed it—

The program stopped short. Cutting off, it turned the dressing room lights on and announced an error with a disapproving chirp.

Seemi read the error and frowned. "Are you still wearing your shoes, sir?"

"Yes?" came the other Avarian's muffled voice.

Seemi pursed his lips. "Kindly remove your shoes." After a moment's reflection, he frowned and added. "And your clothes if you still have them on."

"Ohhhh." A moment later the other Avarian's head popped out from behind the dressing room door. "How naked we talking, vato?"

"The point is to get accurate measurements," Seemi explained patiently. "If you buy clothes that fit when you already had clothes on, those new clothes won't fit. Do you understand?"

The other Avarian nodded. "Does this thing save the picture?"

Seemi was taken aback for a moment. He'd never thought to ask. "I think so. Yes. It's uploaded to the central databanks." He could see this wasn't the answer his customer wanted to hear, though.

"By the gods," said the reptile behind them. "How are you being difficult now?"

"I'm not uploading a nudey pic to some random alien databank!" The Avarian turned to Seemi. "No offense." He turned back to the Strungian. "I've seen how that shit works on Earth. Next thing I know, people are trading my picture behind my back, making who knows what plans. No, thank you. I didn't do it there, and I'm not doing it here."

"Izo!" yelled the reptile. "Get in there and take your damn clothes off."

"Screw you, lizard!"

"If you're uncomfortable with a nude rendering," Seemi said quickly. "I can help prep an ionic leotard. It takes a little longer, but the result is equally accurate and absolutely private."

Izo pointed at Seemi. "See? They have contingencies for this type of thing."

"Leave him alone, Glongkyle," said the Ginarsian, Tearn. "You know he's shy. He was shy the entire trip here."

Izo pointed at the Ginarsian. "Thank you, Tearn."

Glongkyle crossed his arms and stared at the dark-haired Avarian. There was something unspeakably antagonizing about his aura. "He better get over it. His return trip hasn't been confirmed yet."

A stilted silence followed. Seemi didn't know what the man meant. Intergalactic flights were usually scheduled months in advance, but could be shifted a few days forward or back closer to the date. It wasn't usually something people got upset over.

He looked back and forth between the group. A prickling sense of danger, like the vague shape of an unexpected shadow, passed over him. He wasn't sure what was going on. He considered calling the local guards. Though what would he say to them? *This jerk is acting suspicious. Could you check if he's a criminal?*

Seemi turned to Izo. "Did you want to try the leotard?"

"Yes," the Avarian said, sticking his tongue at the reptile. "That would be awesome."

Seemi nodded and the two quickly disappeared inside the fitting room.

Ten minutes later, Seemi had helped the new customer into a magnetic leotard and was shooting him with the ionic emitter. The emitter blacked out the store's all-seeing reader from recording any visuals while taking accurate measurements underneath. He was also trying to remain professional as his customer did his best impression of a one-man question machine.

"Why do they call the people from here Malforian?" Izo asked. "I thought the planet's name was IA?"

"Malforia was the old name, the ancient one," said Seemi. "IA is an acronym for the new name. It's short for 'Imperial Alliance.'"

Izo nodded, taking this in. Seemi continued to work. He prayed beyond reason that the curious foreigner was done. He was not.

"So what type of Avarian are you? And how many different types of Avarians are there? What planet are you from? Is it nearby? Have you ever heard of Earth before?"

Seemi blew out a long breath. Not exactly a sigh. He didn't have the energy to work up a sigh. "I'm Aurelian. My planet is Aurelia. It's in the Relegian system. It's relatively close—the next galaxy over. I have no idea how many types of Avarians there are." He tried to think back, but his brain felt like jelly. It had already been a long day and was getting longer by the minute. "Forgive me. What was your last question?"

"Have you ever heard of Earth before?"

"No. And not to be rude, but do you have any questions about fashion?"

Izo thought about it. "What are the most expensive clothes in the universe?"

Seemi responded without thinking. "Bgulvrian. Hands down."

Izo nodded. "Chido."

Seemi shook his head and continued to work. It occurred to him that he needed to get ahead of this conversation if he was going to survive it. "So... first time to the capital?"

"First time anywhere," said Izo, obeying as Seemi signaled for him to turn around. "This is the second planet I've ever been to."

Seemi raised his eyebrows in faux surprise. *You don't say.* "It's a great place to visit. Bunch of stuff to do and places to see." Seemi paused. He realized in horror he was coming up blank. The other Avarian had talked him into a stupor. "If you get a chance, you should check out the Fountain."

He winced. It was the single most obvious suggestion he could have made. Three blocks up, it was the definitive landmark of the entire district, the overblown icon that distinguished this area on tourist maps. He might as well have suggested visiting the Emperor's Palace while already on the Summit. *Really?* He imagined people asking with mocking sneers. *Do you think we ought to swing by?*

"People are always surprised by how big it is in person," he finished lamely. He needed to get out more.

The youth nodded again. It was obvious he wasn't impressed. "So, there's something I wanted to ask you," Izo said after a moment. He glanced at the door.

Seemi tensed. He recognized the tell-tale signs of someone working up the nerve to do something they weren't supposed to. "What did you want to ask?"

"It's kind of weird."

Seemi shifted uncomfortably. He wanted to say "no." He should have been able to say "no." Technically, he could say "no." But he was at work, paid to be polite to others even as they treated him like a free amusement. He gritted his teeth. "Weird how?"

"I'm curious..." The other Avarian turned back to face him. Bit his lip. Then looked down between them. "How does it work?"

Seemi closed his eyes in humiliation. He wanted to leave. He wanted to quit. He wanted to go back to Aurelia and never think about the capital again. But of course, as Seemi well knew, that wouldn't solve anything.

Yes, Aurelian society was notorious for its sexual liberation. As an intersexual species, pleasure was their biological gift and genetic right. They weren't going to squander it. The desire to seek the outer limits of their amazing bodies was one thing that many mature Aurelians shared. There was a saying—the day Aurelians stopped discovering new things about sex was the day the universe would go dark.

It was a label most people were happy to assign to Seemi. But what most people didn't know, because they'd never been to Aurelia, was the one exception to Aurelia's free-love standards regarded their Avarians.

Avarians were different. Avarians were mystical. Avarians might pop up once in a generation. Seemi, for example, was the only Avarian among twelve siblings and cousins. Avarians were rare and valuable and had to be protected. Kept safe. Being an Avarian meant everyone wanted something from you. You were unique and special, all the way down to your genes, which sex gave people access to. You couldn't open yourself up to them. You'd be ripped to pieces before you could give them one percent of what they wanted.

That's why it was so important to protect Avarians. That's why adults (parents and grandparents alike) sometimes lost their tempers at obstinate Avarian children. It was for their own good. These children needed to learn how the universe treated Avarians.

The irony of it all? Seemi had left Aurelia for IA to stop being singled out as Avarian. But having reached IA, he was instead singled out as Aurelian.

There was no winning. Seemi was an oddity everywhere.

Seemi clenched his jaw. He wondered if maybe he shouldn't try bartending after all. It wouldn't stop the stupid questions and innuendos, but he might be able to drink for free. "How does what work?"

"It. You." The other Avarian pointed down between them. "Your flying."

Seemi glared, paused, shook his head, and then blinked. It took him a moment to register what had been asked. He lowered the ionic emitter. The other Avarian wasn't pointing at his crotch. He was pointing at his feet.

Seemi looked down. Feet tucked under, he hadn't noticed he was floating off the floor. "I'm sorry, are you asking how I fly?"

"Yeah," said Izo. "How do you do it? Mine is like a snapping bounce. It feels like... rubber bands are pulling me. But yours looks smooth and kind of wavy. Like an up and down motion." He angled his head as if thinking how to explain it. "It looks like a boat bouncing over water." He searched Seemi's face with fascination. "What does it feel like? And when did you figure out you could do it?"

"Uhhhh." Seemi shook his head. In all his years as an Avarian, he'd never been asked either of these questions. "I guess it feels like I'm floating on a bubble?" He thought back. "I think I was three when I first did it?"

"Is it hard to do? Do you have to think about it?"

"Not really." Seemi performed a couple of lifts. "It comes easy."

"Wow. It looks cool."

Seemi chuckled in bewilderment as the other Avarian, unsatisfied to just watch him, put a hand on his shoulder and began following his motions with his own jerking bounces. Then, when Seemi laughed harder, the other Avarian began laughing too.

For a moment, Seemi was lost in an almost child-like revelry. The two of them were bobbing up and down like happy morons, higher and higher. Their laughter was rising, too; the fitting room turned into an idiotic echo chamber of ridiculously bouncing joy. And for a second, he let go and leaned into the feeling. It was dumb; just about the dumbest thing he'd ever done. But it was fun! They were breaking the rules. And yes, he'd probably feel a little embarrassed from cracking his professional armor. But screw it. He came to IA to meet other Avarians—hadn't he?

Suddenly the brunette jerked away. He was still laughing but something overwhelming was pulling his gaze inwards.

"Hey." Seemi grabbed the other's shoulder. It was a sympathetic reaction, foolish and unquestionably against company policy. But he couldn't help himself. The youth looked so upset. "Are you all right?"

"They're right. I am an Avarian." He peered at Seemi with horror. "I am what they've been calling me."

Seemi frowned, and even though he didn't understand the details, he was pretty sure he got the gist of why Izo was upset—being an Avarian in a place like IA could be a lot. He hugged the other Avarian. There was a part of him that wanted to lash out and scream, rail against the odious powers that be. *Don't you ever feel ashamed,* he wanted to say. *The fact that we don't burn this whole planet to the ground—we should all get medals!* But that's not what the youth needed right now. "It just means you can fly." Seemi patted him on the back. "That's all it means."

The other male sniffed hard, nodded, and stepped back. He was obviously a little embarrassed. "You're right. It's superpowers."

"Exactly," said Seemi. He pretended to adjust his hair as Izo got something out of his eye. "And hey—I remember when I first came to the capital. It's a lot to take in for anyone. But it gets easier, I promise."

The youth smiled. "Thanks."

"You're welcome. You know the best way to start?" Seemi held up the ionic ray gun. "An epic outfit."

Izo's shoulders dropped. "Can I ask you a favor? Avarian to Avarian?"

"Of course."

Izo flicked his head toward the door. "Don't let these cabrones put me in a dress."

Seemi's brow dropped in confusion. There was just no accounting for taste.

A few minutes later, Seemi finally pulled up a ten-foot-tall digital replica of his new customer. Chin up and arms crossed over his chest, the digital Izo gazed out at them with a tough sneer. Below this, he was outfitted in a small, light blue dress—Loft's default setting.

The real Izo took one look at his digital avatar and hissed. "Yo, can we change that?"

"Of course," said Seemi. He wasn't sure what was wrong with it but did his best. Bobbing up to the top of the screen, he opened a drop-down menu and selected a set of winter nightwear, instantly changing the digital Izo into a pair of fuzzy pajamas. He turned to his customer. "Better?"

"The shorts could be longer, but yeah," said Izo.

Seemi took note of this. "Okay. Who wants to start?"

"I had a couple of ideas," said the Ginarsian, Tearn. Lifting his scanner gun, Tearn quickly loaded his choices onto the screen. "First, I found this." He popped the digital Izo into a long emerald evening gown. With a high neckline, shimmering train, and dramatically plunging back, it looked like something straight out of high society.

Seemi eyed the impressive outfit then the group wearing dirty, matching jumpsuits. He had a sinking suspicion there was a disconnect here. "Umm, it's lovely," Seemi started, the picture of professionalism. "Where were you planning to wear this?"

Izo dropped his face into his hands. "To a job interview."

The Strungian bounced a small piece of trash off the top of Tearn's head. "What part of 'nothing fancy' did you not understand, short-stack?"

Tearn scrambled to pick up the wadded missile and throw it back. It missed. "The color matches his eyes. Don't be an asshole, Glongkyle!"

Seemi bit the inside of his cheek. Ginarsians, emotional wizards they were, seldom knew how to regulate their own emotions when riled. He was going to have to watch this group carefully. "While it certainly is beautiful," said Seemi, "could it be a touch too formal for the occasion?"

Tearn sank into a distraught ball of white hot rejection. "You like it, don't you?" he asked the other Avarian.

"I-I-" Izo stammered. He was at a loss for how to let his friend down. "I don't know where I'd wear it."

"You hate it too," Tearn moaned.

Seemi hissed.

"Stop moping," said Glongkyle, the Strungian. "You wanted to see him fancied up. Congratulations. Take a picture and jerk off later."

Seemi was about to defend the tiny Ginarsian when he was cut off by a burst of ugly emotion streaming into his brain. Seemi grunted. He'd forgotten how sharply a well-trained Ginarsian could throw out their tele-empathic projections. Waves of embarrassment flooded over him, radiating out from the Ginarsian like a radio. Seemi thanked his lucky stars there were no other customers around. They might have been seriously confused.

"That's disgusting. You know I don't think of him that way." The tiny Ginarsian's fists were balled up with shame. "Izo and I are just friends."

Everyone, including the big Wuljerian, squirmed in his painful mortification. Seemi tried to think of a way to calm the Ginarsian and ease his indignity. Luckily, the other Avarian beat him to it.

Reaching out from his spot on the couch, Izo grabbed Tearn's hand. "Glongkyle's being a jerk. He's always being a jerk." He smiled wryly. "Tearn, I know we're just friends. Good friends."

Tearn eyed the dark-haired Avarian. "You mean it?"

"Of course." The Avarian patted the Ginarsian's hand. "I always feel better when you're around. Plus, you were the first alien I ever met. Remember?"

"That's right. I was." A smile broke out on his face and, like clouds shifting from the sun, the mood instantly brightened. Everyone but Glongkyle breathed a sigh of relief. The Strungian, with his low reptilian emotional sensitivities, probably registered the whole ordeal as nothing more than an off-kilter conversation.

Izo smiled at Tearn and tried to get his hand back. But now that he had him, Tearn wasn't letting Izo go. Seemi looked away and almost shivered. He did not envy the dark-haired Avarian. "Were there any other selections?" the store clerk asked, hoping to move on.

"How about this one?" Tearn said. He popped the digital Avarian into a different outfit.

Seemi nodded with approval. It was a short green romper in a bold, geometric cut. Flattering Izo's slender build, it sliced open a few inches in the front and the back, revealing two peaks of the wearer's bare skin. A signature piece from a trending designer, it was a perfect choice—playful and current, yet professional and high-end.

Impressed, Seemi turned to the group expecting good things. But, seeing the other Avarian's expression, Seemi realized it was a non-starter again. He eyed the Ginarsian. "So…what does everyone think?"

The dark-haired Avarian opened his mouth but didn't immediately speak. He seemed to be considering his words. "It's very chic."

Seemi nodded. "It is."

"You don't like this one either," Tearn said. His tone was as low and mournful as a re-injured animal.

"No, I do!" Izo said. "But…the material's a little thin. Right?"

Tearn sank even lower. "IA's in its warm season."

"But—" Izo shifted uncomfortably. His gaze flew to Seemi for help.

Seemi was half ready to fly out of the store. "The capital is in the mountains," he said, trying to help. "It gets cold at night. If you'll be wearing it in the evening, you might consider something warmer." Then he cringed back in anticipation of another burst of emotion.

Tearn pointed up at the menu options. His finger was short and incredibly steady. "It comes with a matching jacket."

Seemi searched where he was pointing. He was right. It did come with a matching jacket. Seemi started to open his mouth and come up with a different excuse when he was cut off by the reptile.

"It's perfect. We'll take it," said Glongkyle. He gestured approvingly at the Ginarsian. "Good job, Tearn."

Seemi gave Izo an apologetic look. It was the Strungian's employment credentials and ID they'd use to open the line of credit. He had final say. But when Izo refused to meet his gaze, Seemi felt about as useful as a booger. Seemi started the order. "Excellent choice, sir."

The dark-haired Avarian sat back and crossed his arms. He was upset. Adorably, the big Wuljerian sitting next to him took notice. Her fluffy ears drooped with concern. She pressed the smaller, hairless creature with her paw, jostling the Avarian to one side. "Clothes is pretty," she reassured.

Izo clenched his slender forearms. "That's the problem, Yula."

The Wuljerian tilted her head, a mass of fluffy hair falling in a confusion. "Pretty is not problem."

"Maybe not a problem for you," said Izo.

The Wuljerian's eyes went wide. She looked like she would burst into tears. Without another word she jumped up and lumbered away, brown shaggy hair bouncing in sad waves behind her.

"That's not what I meant. Yula—you're pretty. You're pretty!" Izo called out. But the giant was gone. The youth sat forward and covered his face with his hands. "God damn it."

"You need to get over this," said Glongkyle. "There are millions of Avarians floating around this capital, and you need to look twice as hot as all of them to make this work."

Seemi considered this. "You don't need to look pretty to look hot though."

"Yes, you do," said the Strungian.

Seemi dragged a hawkish gaze at him. "Excuse me—I work in fashion. You don't." He pulled up one of his favorite hot new designers. "This is the absolute latest from JepaGult, an up-and-coming designer from Anolita. There's nothing pretty here, sir."

It was unquestionably true. Her newest street warrior collection was a compilation of cropped hoodies, square shoulder vests, and edgy tunics arranged in a variety of smoking and darkly jeweled colors. It was fierce, aggressive, and in-your-face. There was nothing dainty or demure in the entire line-up. It was also unquestionably hot. So what the hell did that Strungian think he was talking about?

The dark-haired youth happened to glance up. Then he leaned forward. His mouth popped open as he inspected the outfits one by one. "Whoa," he said after a second. He looked at Seemi like he'd been visited by a god. "What else you got?"

Seemi, remembering the comment about the pajamas, considered and went in search of a full-length pant. He soon stumbled on a classic street trouser. Following sheer instinct now, Seemi switched the fit, darkened the color, and added a little length in the cuff for good measure. What was left was something casual, but nimble in a dark silvery grey.

Seemi floated back. "What do you think?"

Izo nodded. "Looks cool, man."

Seemi beamed.

"That's not an outfit though," said Glongkyle. "It's just pants. Is he going topless?" He laughed.

Seemi bit his tongue. He scanned the collection. It would need to be eye-catching, but subtle. Drool-worthy, yet tough. Spotting something, he clicked it and turned to gauge the group's reactions.

Their faces told him everything. He'd found it. He turned to Glongkyle, also impressed, and started his sales pitch. "This handmade piece marries street-tough flavor with figure-flattering design. Available only for a limited time, this designer piece is sexy. It's fierce." Seemi grinned. "It's everything."

Spinning back around, he took in his choice for the first time. He was a little stunned at the vision he'd created. The black mesh top draped over the digital Izo fit neither too loose nor too baggy. It highlighted his youthful figure, slender strength, and natural symmetry. But its most defining feature was the wide, two-toned hoodie. Half black, half red, it fell over his customer's shoulders like a sacramental cape.

The Ginarsian began applauding. "Can we get it in green?"

"You can change the color with any handheld device," Seemi said slowly. He was experiencing a strange moment of having tapped into something within himself he hadn't known was there.

"Color-changing fabric on a designer piece?" Glongkyle laughed again. "Nice try. We're not buying any upgrades."

"Color-morph is standard in most limited-edition pieces. It used to be as big a deal as size-morphing is now." He let the tiniest bit of snark into his voice. He'd earned it. "Not anymore."

"Color morph? ¡No chingues!" Izo looked at Seemi in amazement. "This thing can change colors?"

"You bet your Avarian ass," said Seemi. "Color, pattern, and saturation—all customizable at the touch of a button."

"How cool is that?" said Izo.

"We'll take it. All of it," said Tearn.

"Great." Seemi clapped his hands proudly. It had turned out to be a good day. "I'll ring it up and get your design queued for creation."

"Whoa! Tearn, you want to buy him this overpriced piece of junk?" said Glongkyle.

Tearn looked confused. "Why not? It looks great on him. It's name-brand. And, best of all, he might wear it."

"That's why he hates it," said Izo. The Avarian shot a chilly look at the reptile. "He won't spend a dime unless it makes me miserable."

Glongkyle peered at the custom-created outfit without answering. His jaw slowly worked circles under his dead set gaze. He seemed to be considering something. "You know what? Fine. We'll get both. But it'll be up to you to show us which one works better."

"Meaning what?" said Izo.

Glongkyle pointed at Seemi. "Prove it's as alluring as he says."

Seemi beetled his brow. He wondered if he shouldn't call the authorities after all.

"Well?" said Glongkyle to Izo. "You want to get it? Or am I right that the other one's the better buy?"

Seemi's eyes went to search the other Avarian's. Izo was busy staring at the outfit though. He seemed neither happy nor confident about this new arrangement, but he reached out to grab the reptile's hand anyway. "I want to get it."

— CHAPTER FIVE —

Tearn

Tearn laughed and pointed at another stranger as Izo strutted alongside. The stranger, approaching them from the opposite direction of the crowded walkway, was a tall, green Nertian with roving antennae who'd glanced Izo's way.

Izo quirked up an over-the-top smile. "Hola, handsome." The Earthling gave a finger-wagging wave. "Come to this planet often?"

Tearn burst out with embarrassed laughter as the stranger paused to eye Izo with curiosity. Izo blew the stranger a kiss and continued, drawing more than a few confused looks from the other pedestrians surrounding them. The man turned, and Tearn gasped when one of the man's stalked eyes bent backward to continue following the Earthling.

"By the gods!" Tearn whispered ducking down. "He's still looking!"

"Of course he is. He can't help himself." Smoothing down his hoodie, the Earthling grinned back at Glongkyle, who was following closely behind. After leaving the high-end Avarian store in his favorite new outfit, the teenager had proudly begun cat-walking all over Glongkyle's theory about the romper being more alluring. Tearn, excited to see Glongkyle put in his place for once, had reveled in the silly battle of the species.

The truth was, after decades of dragging Tearn on a never-ending saga of intergalactic extortion schemes, their intrepid captain had finally met his match. The fact that it was a teenage Earthling barely taller than Tearn? Amazing.

"Knock it off," said Glongkyle, voice betraying his testy mood. "Classy Avarians don't proposition strangers."

"I thought that was the plan, jefe?" Izo said over one shoulder. "And don't be sore. I can't help that my spot-on fashion sense is working better than I thought."

"One: the plan wasn't to get attention on the street. And two: they're not interested in your fashion sense. Trust me," said Glongkyle.

"Hush, peasant." Izo gave a dismissive wave over one shoulder. "You think you're being cute?"

"No, but she does." Nodding ahead of them, Izo flashed a naughty smile at a female Fudomadern with four arms. Looking him up and down, she placed her bottom hands on her hips. "That's right." Izo gave her a nod. "Lady Goro likes what she sees."

Who could blame her? Tearn thought. Watching Izo saunter through the pomp and glamour of the capital, Tearn was again left to wonder how perfectly their unique Avarian seemed to fit in. Side by side, both equally elegant and mysterious, it was as if Izo and IA had been hand-painted to match.

Tearn gazed at Izo in adoration. Young and brown and tall and lovely, Izo was more perfect than Tearn ever could've imagined. There were days during their long journey aboard the *Atrox Killboard*—Glongkyle's ridiculous name for his ship—that Tearn could barely believe Izo was real. It was like something out of a fantasy: the beautiful Avarian imprisoned by evil forces and befriended by a pure-hearted Ginarsian. Two worlds collide. The Avarian grows to rely on the Ginarsian until, despite all odds, something magical happens, and the two become lovers.

Not that Tearn was expecting anything like that to happen. That was silly. Izo had been clear on the *Atrox*—they were just friends. But then again, Tearn thought to himself, friends accidentally became lovers all the time. Especially here in the capital.

IA—the capital of Malforia—the military and state headquarters of the Tri-Galactic Empire and, by extension, the universe. It was also the place where fame and fortune came to play with politics and power. When Tearn first described it to Izo, the teen had said it sounded like "half L.A., half D.C." Tearn didn't know what that meant, but Izo seemed impressed. And why wouldn't he be? IA was the single most recognizable city in existence. Every other corner held some famous piece of history. There was the Vitruvian Stairwell where Princess Snowen had tripped into the arms of her rescuer; the Aurelian boutiques where Audrilu had hidden from his regal stalker; Madytun Avenue where the most renowned brands and famed celebrities flocked day after day. All of it was real and here, brightly arrayed and waiting.

Tearn glanced up at his captivating Avarian. "So, are you excited by it?"

The mythical creature looked at him quizzically. "By what?"

"By here—being in the capital!" Tearn raised his hands awkwardly. "Only the most beautiful and talented Avarians ever make it all the way here. People from all over the universe spend years saving to finally visit. I know I've been looking forward to it for years."

"Ah, so it's your first time in Disneyland too." The teenager's perfect eyebrow lifted in faux amazement as he took in his surroundings with a sarcastic expression. "How lucky of me to win a free trip on this momentous occasion."

Tearn laughed nervously. Izo was always joking about their bringing him without asking. And sure, kidnapping was wrong and not the way you were supposed to treat others. But a free trip to IA had to buy a little something back, right? Most people waited their whole lives for one opportunity to visit. Izo was going to be working here! True, he might not have asked for it, but surely most would agree the situation was a dream come true. "You don't think it's at least a little bit enchanting?"

The Avarian surveyed the area with apathy. "It's así así."

Though he hadn't understood the last half of Izo's sentence—because the stubborn Avarian had refused to let him translate his second language—Tearn smirked, picking up on the general idea nonetheless. "You're joking! This is a wonderland of Imperial tech and intergalactic culture! It's like being in an Avarian fairytale!"

"Don't know a ton of Avarian fairytales," said Izo, "but I doubt many begin with the protagonist getting abducted."

Tearn thought about this. "Now that you mention it, many of them do start with—HEY!" Tearn said. He'd run into the back of Glongkyle when the group stopped short going around a crowded corner.

Tearn was about to complain more when, seeing why they stopped, he hiccupped instead.

There it was. The most beautiful and famous landmark in the universe. Carved from a single block of white Vitruvian stone, it gleamed like glass. With a seamlessly untouched and nubile quality, it was as white and pure as fresh snow. Massive, it stood over three stories tall and took up half of its namesake plaza.

"I never thought I'd see it in person," mumbled Tearn.

"See what?" asked Izo.

Tearn pointed ahead. "Ara's Eternal Fountain of Avarian Purity."

All the details came pouring back to Tearn's steel-trap mind. A multi-tiered fountain of bubbling waters and intricately latticed spumes, it was the definitive installation of the Malforian capital. Situated almost directly outside IA's intergalactic spaceport (*or, more accurately,* Tearn corrected himself, *the spaceport had been built next to the Fountain),* the Fountain's millennia-old origin and history were semi-mythological. IA, after all, was an ancient land of many myths and legends, a place where truth and mystery danced in tangles and nothing was exactly as it seemed. Naturally, IA's nominative fount was no exception.

"Is it covered in floating statues?" asked Izo, bringing Tearn back to the present.

"Yes! They represent the eighteen most celebrated Avarian virgins of all time. Some are fictional, some are real," Tearn explained. "All forever orbit the Fountain in rapturous suspense. With uplifted faces and half-naked bodies, these wondrous creatures draw the viewer's eye up in an ever-rising crescendo of mystical and sparkling delight. Although idolized for its statuary, however, it's the water trapped within the Fountain that's the source of the legend."

Izo zipped higher to peer into the Fountain's sparkling blue contents. "It's got legendary water?"

Tearn nodded. "Long before discovering space travel or magnetic energy, ancient Malforian tradition held that Zaeus, Ruler of the Gods, had looked down from his palace in the heavens to see Ara, a beautiful Avarian, bathing in a nearby stream. Falling in love instantly, Zaeus traveled down to the mortal realm to seduce and return with the object of his desire. But Ara, desperate to escape the lusty god, pled to Vestigia, God of Virgins, to save her. Taking pity on the hapless Avarian, Vestigia transformed Ara into a natural spring. Those pure running waters have nourished and sustained the city ever since.

"And so, Ara's name, purity forever intact, was passed down to the Fountain, which drew water from the Spring. The statues are all celebrated symbols of virginal Avarian beauty, commissioned and placed here to continue the legacy."

Izo considered this. "So you're telling me some dude tried to mack on an Avarian, and the God of Virgins saved them by 'turning them into water.' Sounds like a shitty way to bless a believer." Izo seemed to consider this. He laughed. "Actually, it sounds more like someone went missing in the river, and they've been floating half-naked statues over it ever since!"

Tearn blinked. "N-no. It's a very sweet and mythic story. It's been passed down for hundreds of years—"

A high-pitched, excited bark from Yula snapped Tearn out of his confusion. "It is! It is her!" whimpered Yula while squirming. Unable to control herself any longer, the giant Wuljerian broke forward, plowing through first their group and then the larger crowd to move closer to the Fountain.

"Yula!" cried Tearn, trying to follow. "Slow down! You're going to hurt someone!"

"It's Ari!" howled Yula.

Tearn froze. He sucked in a breath so large it hurt his Ginarsian lungs. Whipping left and right, he strained to look through the crowd for any hint of the famous, blonde singer. "Where? Where!?" Tearn begged.

"Hey!" said Glongkyle from behind them. "Wait up."

"Just hang on," Tearn shouted back at Glongkyle. Then, pushing through another two dozen people, he hurried to catch their team's Wuljerian. "Yula, where's Ari?"

"There!" Yula pointed at the Fountain.

Tearn's shoulders fell as he realized what Yula meant. She'd seen Ari's statue, not the intergalactic superstar herself.

"By the gods, you guys aren't that nerdy, are you?" Glongkyle groaned loudly as he finally caught up. "Ari fans? Still?"

Their Avarian floated down behind them into the dense crowd from above. "Who's Ari?"

"She is sun!" said Yula.

"No! She's better than the sun!" said Tearn.

"She's a cheesy pop star that was big a million years ago," said Glongkyle.

"Excuse me? Her last intergalactic tour sold out in seconds. I know. I tried to get tickets." Tearn shook his head. He turned to focus on her statue. Nubile and slight, it depicted her at the start of her meteoric career, back when she was a virginal Aurelian Princess plucked for greatness at the tender age of sixteen. He sighed with adoration. Even in stone, she was still the most elegant thing he'd ever seen.

"It's a stupid statue," said Glongkyle.

"Glongkyle will hush," Yula growled. Her mouth curled back in a snarl.

The reptile stepped back into two strangers. He didn't say anything else about Ari.

Yula turned to Tearn. "Ari comes." The Wuljerian gestured at the Fountain, now only a few feet away. Sure enough, the famous singer's statue was slowly making a circuitous descent to its lowest point.

Tearn pulled out his digital device. "Recording?"

Yula raised her giant fluffy arms over her head like an exuberant toddler. Then she scampered up the last few feet to the base of the Fountain and spun around, knocking a half a dozen people over. Tearn, holding in a laugh, prayed they wouldn't need to fish her out of the Fountain in a moment.

"Yula, give us a smile!" Tearn yelled as the statue slowly neared.

"Tearn picture too," Yula said, waving Tearn over.

Tearn started to refuse, but then thinking, *What the hell? We're already here,* he shoved his device at Glongkyle and rushed to Yula's side. Yula grabbed Tearn and lifted him onto her shoulder.

"Smile," Glongkyle grumbled, holding up the device. And Tearn did, wider and bigger than he ever had before. Taking what Tearn hoped were a couple of good recordings, Glongkyle lowered the device with an eye roll.

Satisfied, Tearn glanced over to shoot Izo a silly grin while still atop Yula's shoulder. But as he spotted the Avarian, Tearn's expression dropped.

The nineteen-year-old was rigid as a statue. A hunched figure stood behind him. A large claw was wrapped around his neck. Razor-sharp nails were indenting the delicate skin of Izo's throat. The attacker's body was obscured. Pressed against Izo's back, he held the Avarian still while hiding behind him. Over Izo's shoulder, the end of a thinly furred muzzle could be seen. Two long, sharp fangs hung off it like curved daggers.

"Izo," Tearn whispered.

Seeing Tearn's face, Glongkyle spun and sucked in sharply. He unholstered his weapon, an unregistered laser emitter he'd bought on Flarion, and began gingerly moving toward the Earthling. Yula, noticing too, headed in the same direction, Tearn still perched high on her shoulder. But Izo's assailant must have noticed them, because a moment later the person disappeared, vanishing into the crowd like a shadow on a cloudy day.

Glongkyle reached Izo first. He grabbed his shoulder as the Avarian hunched over.

"Izo, are you okay?" asked Tearn as Yula set him down.

"Yeah." Hands on his knees, the Avarian gasped for air. "I'm fine."

"What happened?" Glongkyle stretched his neck at its full height, gazing around protectively.

Izo shook his head. "I don't know. He was standing behind me and he said something about the Fountain. I sort of nodded but wasn't listening, and then—" The Earthling rubbed his throat. "He grabbed me. I thought he was joking but then he said I was pure and he—"

Izo squeezed his eyes. His face tightened. "I don't know. I don't know what happened." He shook his head. "He just kept saying I was pure." He turned to the Fountain in confusion. "That I was pure like Ara."

"And?" Glongkyle waved impatiently. "What did he DO to you?"

Izo swung his green eyes into Glongkyle like a pickaxe. Then he flicked them to Tearn. "I'm not talking about this with him here."

"What? Why not?" Glongkyle held out his scaly hands in confusion.

Tearn held in an eye roll and instead wrapped Izo into a tight embrace. Tapping deep into his Ginarsian powers, he quickly set to performing his real job on the team.

Tearn was a Ginarsian tele-empath. Or, more accurately, he was a tele-empathic master. All the years of Tearn's training made their whole operation possible. Sure, Yula could hold someone down without hurting them and Glongkyle owned a space hardy cargo ship that could travel hundreds of galaxies within a few months, but if it weren't for Tearn's powers, all they'd arrive with would be dead or half-suicidal Avarians. Proud of it or not, it was Tearn's ability to soothe and convince their victims to go along with their schemes that allowed the operation to continue making buckets of money every year. It simply didn't work otherwise.

Tearn sent wave after wave of projected ease directly into the traumatized teenager's neural system. Izo's carbon-based brain didn't know the difference and, soon enough, it was working. Izo's heart rate slowed. He relaxed into the Ginarsian's embrace.

"Did he hurt you?" asked Tearn.

The Avarian youth let out a slow and shuddering breath. He pushed Tearn away. "No."

"He is gone," said Yula. She examined Izo with genuine concern and gave Izo her own encouraging hug. Tearn tilted his head. He was again left wondering how much of the underpinnings to their business Yula understood.

"Thank goodness you're okay. But that was way too close. Izo, you have to be more careful!" scolded Glongkyle. And then, for about the millionth time since they'd left Earth with the hot-headed Avarian, Glongkyle jumped in to completely undo all Tearn's best efforts to calm their captive. "This is why you can't go around flaunting and flirting with strangers in public. You see what kind of attention it brings."

Tearn's eyes went big as saucers. He wanted to scream, *are you kidding me!?* He could physically feel the tension and rage rising off the teenager like a storm cloud.

Izo squinted at Glongkyle. "Hey, puta—you trying to say this was my fault? That some weirdo grabbed me in a crowd?"

"No, but—" Glongkyle gestured around them. "There are bad people out there. As an Avarian, you have to be smart. You can't make yourself a target. I hate to say it but—" Glongkyle shrugged. "I tried to warn you. You were too busy making jokes."

Izo lunged at Glongkyle, but Yula moved between them before the Earthling could reach. She faced their captain. "This is wrong."

"Yula, it's okay," said Glongkyle. He patted the Wuljerian on the shoulder. "I know you want to protect him, but Izo has to learn he's not on Earth anymore." He gazed mildly at the youth. "The rules are different here for Avarians."

"Hey, puta madre—screw you!" Izo bobbed up. His energy was itching for a fight.

But Yula shook her head and held her hands up to stop them both. "Man was Wuljerian." Yula pointed at her snout. "Man smells pure. Man attacks pure."

Tearn squinted at their massive colleague. "Yula, what are you talking about?"

Yula pointed at the Fountain. "Ara is pure." Then she pointed at Izo. "Man attacks pure."

Tearn, both as a trained linguist and long-time Yula translator, widened his eyes as he suddenly understood. It took the Earthling a little longer. The second he did though, he pulled his arms in tight. His mouth fell open and he cringed like a Ginarsian child who'd just seen a Hutrling beetle disappear into his lunchbox. "What!? I'm not pure like Ara! I've had sex before."

"Izo, he was using a sense of smell," Tearn explained, understanding but wishing he didn't. "We've been traveling for months. Any pheromones from a sexual partner would've washed off you ages ago. The scent difference between you and an actual virgin would be indistinguishable."

Yula nodded. "Pure smells same."

Tearn looked at Izo sadly. The teenager now looked like he'd discovered he'd eaten a Hurtling bug. Tearn patted Izo's arm in sympathy.

"My point still remains," cut in Glongkyle suddenly. "If you're going to go around smelling like a virgin, the least you can do is not draw attention to yourself. That's all I'm saying."

Izo's blazing green eyes snapped toward Glongkyle. He flew around Yula at the reptile again.

"Yula!" Tearn yelled.

Yula grabbed the teenager from behind and pulled him away, wrapping their Avarian in a giant bear hug. At the same time, Tearn held Izo's hand to gently ring out tele-empathic calm like a jingling bell. And, like so many other times with so many other Avarians, their tag team method of hold-and-soothe worked. Izo calmed and resigned himself to his fate.

The Avarian quietly spit a few choice words from his second language, the one Tearn had ultimately left untranslated, partially from sheer exhaustion, partially in admiration for Izo's unflinching defiance. Besides, Tearn had a sneaking suspicion that Izo liked to curse in the second language, and he didn't necessarily need to translate the exact words to catch Izo's meaning. He couldn't help but give the Avarian a proud smile. It took a lot of steam to kick through a master Ginarsian's projected emotions. Their Avarian was quite the force to be reckoned with.

Still, impressive as his fiery personality was, they needed him to move on now. Tearn dug deep and hit the youth with an especially heavy wave of cool. Izo's eyelids drooped shut and Tearn could feel his last traces of fear, anger, and frustration melt away. He waited a moment then tapped for Yula to let the youth go.

"We're just glad no one got hurt," said Tearn. "Right?"

Izo nodded. His eyes opened slowly. He looked peaceful and calm. Relieved even. "Right." He rose slowly to his feet and gazed around. "No one got hurt. That's all that matters."

Tearn had to hide a smile behind his hand. As a master of emotional manipulation, it was sometimes laughable how fast people would accept a logical explanation (almost any logical explanation!) rather than admit an underlying emotional one. Not that he was complaining. People's reluctance to face their own emotions made his job easier. Izo, the tough and peppery youth, had been a cakewalk.

Izo ran his hands over himself, some mentally abandoned sense of danger still confusing him. His eyes shot up. "Wait. Where'd my phone go?"

Oh no.

"Your what?" asked Glongkyle.

"He means his device," said Tearn. He quickly stepped closer. He knew exactly how important that phone was. It was talismanic. Losing it was like losing any chance of returning home. It was the embodiment of Izo's hope and, more literally, the only thing besides himself from planet Earth.

Tearn hissed. He had seen what happened to Avarians who slammed into shock after having their normal emotions halted. It wasn't pretty. Had he known the stupid phone was missing he would have waited until after Izo discovered it to hit him with calm. "Could it be back at the store?" he suggested.

Izo shook his head slowly. "I checked. I had it before we left." He looked around the crowd still flowing past them to get closer to the statue. He seemed lost. "I think that guy took it." Floating up, he sailed slowly overhead like a dazed ghost trying to remember who killed him.

Izo eventually drifted back down. "I don't understand." His expression held zero emotion. "Why would he take my phone?"

Tearn shot a warning look at Glongkyle. He recognized the signs of someone nearing an emotional break. The clash of adrenaline and tele-empathic downers were over-working Izo's system. He might not be able to handle another fray with the lizard.

"Devices hold personal information," said Glongkyle. "He probably thought he could figure out where you were staying and come visit you later."

Izo shoulders fell. He looked completely hollowed out. "He stole the only thing I own so he could stalk me?"

"Look on the bright side," said Tearn. "It doesn't have your address. He was a moron. He can't find you. You're safe. Okay?"

Izo gazed down at Tearn. "I'm safe?" There was something pathetically distraught about the question, like a child asking if everything would be all right as the roof collapsed.

"Y-yes," said Tearn.

Izo took in a shaky breath. He moved his gaze to peer out into the crowd. Tearn waited, unsure what would come next. Nothing did. The Avarian simply continued to stand, shoulders back, chin high in a strong and watchful gaze. That's when it hit him—Izo was trying to be brave. The Ginarsian's heart almost broke. Of course. It was a point of pride with their funny little Earthling. It was when Izo was most upset that he most refused to show it.

"Exactly. You're safe," said Glongkyle. "What did you need a stupid device for anyway? It's not like it was going to work here."

Izo gazed blankly at Glongkyle. "It would have worked when I got back to Earth."

Glongkyle glanced at Tearn. "So? Can't you get another one when you get back to Earth?"

"Glongkyle, do everyone a favor and shut up," said Tearn. He rubbed a hand over his eye before taking the Avarian's arm one last time. He could already tell they'd both be sleeping like rocks tonight. "Everything's going to be all right." Squeezing Izo's hand, Tearn released one last wave of peace and encouragement. "I promise."

Izo's chin dropped to his chest like a stone tipping down a ravine. He breathed in through his nose and out through his mouth—a long healing breath. "You're right. It's just a phone."

Tearn nodded while gesturing for Yula to help move Izo away from the plaza. Together the two of them guided the placid Avarian out of the horde and into the nearest café.

"Hey, gorgeous," Tearn watched Izo say to the beautiful purple Anolitun waiting on them. Curvy and flirtatious, the service industry Avarian was a picture of loveliness in gold and black.

Izo held up his drink. "Can I get another one of these?"

Tearn tried to shake his head "no" at the Anolitun, but the Anolitun was too captivated by the Earthling's smile to notice. Taking Izo's offered cup, she gave the Earthling a flirtatious wink. "Be right back, cutie," she said before flying away.

Izo whipped his quick green eyes, swimming with alcohol and neuro-chemicals, to follow the Anolitun. In doing so he nearly fell out of his chair. "First thing: what gender is that alien? Second thing: forget the first thing. How do I get them to make out with me?"

Glongkyle glanced over his shoulder to where Izo was looking. He let out a low whistle. "I don't know, but I'd be willing to help if I can watch."

Izo shuddered and finished his drink. "No offense, I'd rather never kiss anyone again."

Tearn touched Izo's hand. No juice. Just an encouraging pat. A well-trained master knew when to throw in placebos. "It doesn't matter. You're not going to be here long enough for it to matter."

Izo snatched Tearn's cup. "Cheers to that! No offense." Izo swung his new drink at the other patrons. "It's a nice bar. Great drinks. Shit planet though."

Izo was right: it was a nice bar. Colored in deep reds and brassy golds, it smelled of expensive perfumes and regularly cleaned carpets. It was the fourth closest bar to Ara's Fountain and looked every bit the lush and central venue that rent prices near the landmark must have demanded.

Their staff, it appeared, was also selected sparing no expense—a fact that, somewhat ironically, Izo had zeroed in on with approval.

"Tell me la neta, do you think they were flirting with me?" Izo whispered to Tearn. "Do you think it's they knew I'm Avarian too? Like, can they tell?" Izo jerked his hand in a circle while lowering his voice even more. "Or do you think I should do a lap, like as a signal?"

"I think your supposed crush is at work," Tearn whispered back.

"So?" Izo sat up to finish Tearn's drink. "You can't run into someone cute at work?"

"Excuse me, I'm sorry to interrupt," a stranger said from behind them. "But I couldn't help overhear—did you say you're Avarian?"

Tearn gaped. Nothing could have prepared him for the stranger's scent. It was like being hit in the face with an abandoned fish market. His visage was almost as startling too. He was a giant floating octopod, face filled with four orange eyes and a small vertical mouth, and he was covered in a glittering, iridescent skin that looked slimy to the touch. Rather than standing on any discernible trunk, his huge head was held up on tentacles—quick, powerful tentacles that continued twirling underfoot at every moment, as nimble as fingertips near the ground and thick as branches near the top.

Tearn covered his nose and tried not to wretch up their expensive drinks.

"Uh, yeah," said Izo. He was also covering his nose with his hand.

"That's great," said the stranger. "So listen, I was wondering if I could take a minute of your time to talk about an amazing opportunity?"

"Opportunity?" Glongkyle repeated. He tipped closer. "Like a financial opportunity?"

"Yeah. A good one too. I'm a talent scout for a big name agent in the area," the stranger said. "My job is to comb the city for unique Avarians. And, if I may be so bold—" They held three tentacles out toward Izo. "I think I just hit the jackpot."

Tearn frowned. He hadn't expected an opportunity to present itself this fast. After all, Izo had lost a lot of weight during their long, cramped trip from his planet. Despite Tearn's efforts—tele-empathic or otherwise—the youth had been uninterested in their alien food. If anything, having seen Izo's strong and youthful physique at the beginning of their journey, Tearn had thought that Izo, perfect as he was now, would need months to regain his fully glory.

Izo seemed reluctant to accept. "I don't think so, vato. But thanks for the offer."

"He's kidding!" said Glongkyle. He scrambled off his seat. "We'd love to meet with an agent."

The stranger laughed. "That's what I thought. A face like that with a body like his?" The scout waved his tentacles in worshipful circles at Izo, as if conjuring him on the spot. "Someone should be paying you for that. So here it is: if you aren't doing anything, I know my employer would be real interested to meet you guys."

Tearn peered at Izo. The Earthling looked about as interested as a person offered a chance to sell their feet in exchange for shoes.

"Thanks, but no thanks," said Izo again. "It doesn't sound like my sort of—"

"You should give it a shot," interrupted Glongkyle. He was staring the Avarian down like Izo owed him money. "You never know. Might be lucrative." He tipped his boney head. "Weren't you trying to save for your big trip home?"

Izo blew out a hard breath. His eyes flicked back to the scout. He gave him a pinched smile. "You know what? Let's do it."

The scout giggled deliriously and held up his shiny tentacles. "Don't know about that. Let's do the interview first!"

— CHAPTER SIX —

Glongkyle

Glongkyle was worried. The squid-shaped scout that grabbed their attention in the bar was guiding them deeper and deeper into the backend of downtown IA.

The storefront district of downtown was quaint and curious, a haven of fresh paint and welcoming verandas. The backend was a hidden universe of dark passageways and dingy businesses, a labyrinth of well-trafficked gutters crowded with glaring people that froze and swiveled their heads at you. There was no telling how deep you'd waded in and almost zero hope of returning on your own. It was as if an entire shadow city lay in hiding behind that first back-alley door.

By the time they stopped in front of a nondescript office covered in dusty yellow cracks, Glongkyle couldn't have said whether they were closer to the spaceport or their hotel in central downtown. He didn't like that.

"Found you another one," their underworld guide said, pausing outside the door on his spinning appendages. "And you don't have to ask—he passes Rules 1 and 2."

Glongkyle's nostrils flared. He recognized the reference. He'd heard it many times over the years as a vendor of exotic Avarians.

Though the punchline sometimes varied from planet to planet, the basic gist was the same everywhere.

How can you spot an Avarian from a distance?

Rule #1—Can it fly?

Rule #2—Did you want to sleep with it?

Glongkyle stretched his neck higher and looked down the long alleyway in both directions for exits. He was starting to wonder if it had been the best idea to come here.

"Great. Bring them in," said the voice from inside.

The scout moved away from the door and motioned them all in. Pushing Tearn back, Glongkyle stepped to the front of the group while gesturing for Izo to follow closely. When he saw what was waiting for them, he was glad he did.

Cool grey skin, long silver hair, rows of jagged teeth and a mammoth head—a native Malforian. Coolest and cruelest of all the universe's sentient species, they'd been conquering and pillaging planets as they pleased for the good of their massive empire for almost as long as interplanetary contact had existed.

They'd originally been fish, if you could believe it.

They were one of the oldest species in the known universe. Their descendants had risen straight out of the Malforian waters onto their newly formed back legs, enabling them to learn how to work with tools while remaining the unquestionable apex predator of their natural habitat. How they'd bypassed all the nuanced evolutionary tracks that led most organisms toward reptilian, mammalian, or amphibious breeds was still a mystery for the ages.

They didn't mate the way other species did, either. Not that there was one normal way for species to procreate. Glongkyle's people were born in external eggs. Tearn's were hatched live from their mothers' wombs. Yula had come out a mere hundredth of her current size in a litter of twelve. Mating rituals and fertilization processes were as varied and diverse as the plants on the ground. It was life, and life was beautiful.

But no one mated like these guys.

Back in the warm, conducive waters of ancient IA, the female (which was all of them) would scatter eggs in a safe, secluded area. The half that were also male would spread sperm over the eggs and a new generation would come swimming out a few weeks later. The key to this method was the environment—water allowed the sperm to swim toward the eggs. But as the primeval Malforians began emerging on land, they tired of returning to their ritual waters to procreate.

According to legend, this is when a few of their wisest ancestors noticed the beasts of the land. These animals didn't create young in the water. These animals created young in another. And though it undoubtedly produced fewer offspring, the children were larger, stayed closer, and were seldom carried off by strong rains. So the Malforian females (which was all of them) evolved specialized body protrusions, oviducts, that carried eggs further outside their bodies. The males, to ensure fertilization, evolved sperm that could remain dormant and ready for several egg-laying cycles.

Then both went out into the world, implanting and fertilizing or fertilizing and implanting their young all over their planet in whatever they could catch and hold down. Their species thrived. Thousands of years later, when they discovered space travel, they continued their proud tradition on the rest of the universe too, much to the surprise of several stubborn conquered heads of state.

They were the universe's hardiest species, a people obsessed with hyper-domination and aggression. Six fingered, highly intelligent, and built to breed, Malforians were arguably the meanest and toughest species out there. They were also the absolute last people Glongkyle would want to go into business with.

The Malforian gazed at their half-delirious Avarian with vague curiosity from behind a large and dusty desk. His chin rested on his hand. He smiled at Izo, then flicked his eyes at Glongkyle.

Glongkyle gulped and refused to give the man the satisfaction of seeming intimidated. Instead, he yanked back the nearest chair and loudly took his seat, spreading his arms and legs wide in a way that made himself feel bigger but also hurt his tail.

"Wait..." Izo stopped short as he also bent to sit. He tilted his head curiously at the Malforian. Then he turned toward Tearn. "Is he like a shark-dude?"

Glongkyle wanted to rake his nails down his face. Of course, during all their weeks aboard the *Atrox*, Tearn forgot to teach Izo about the native species of the one planet they were going to.

"He's Malforian," Tearn corrected quietly. He'd chosen a spot against the back wall next to Yula. Cracked and tan, the wall was covered in large digital frames depicting Avarians that Glongkyle vaguely recognized, possibly from ads.

"Malforian," repeated Izo slowly. "So he's from this planet?" he asked.

"So he's way scarier than a shark," Glongkyle answered for Tearn. Not that he had any idea what a shark was.

"Who? Me?" the man behind the desk said. He broke out in a playful grin. "Don't be silly."

Glongkyle could feel his reptilian muscles freeze. The man's wide, jagged teeth were shining across his face and seemed fixated on him. Glongkyle imagined them tearing easily at his throat, his armored scales no match for their endless serrated points. And sure, Glongkyle had teeth, claws, and muscles too, but looking at the Malforian's skin up close, he remembered the textbooks that had taught him how thick, floating, and deadened Malforian nerve endings were, how easily they could take even savage attacks with barely any damage and return it one-hundred-fold. It unnerved him beyond words.

"Name's Deneus," the Malforian said. He motioned a greeting at Izo. "What can I do for you?"

"Hi, I'm Izo," the Avarian said, raising a hand in return. "I would like some money for being Avarian, por favor."

Glongkyle watched the Malforian's eyes dance over Izo's face. He seemed pleased. Then, gaze flowing over the rest of them, it paused for a moment on Yula. If he hadn't known better, Glongkyle would have thought it stayed there for a second longer than it needed to. He suddenly remembered—Yula was Wuljerian! One of the few species comparable to Malforians in size and strength, a Wuljerian's thick fur left the big grey bastards at a dead tie when it came to defense.

Glongkyle, relaxed back against his chair. They were going to be fine.

The agent glanced at the scout with a nod. "You can go. He looks good."

"Yes!" The scout said, pumping a tentacle. "What did I tell you? That fountain is pure gold. That's three Avarians I found for you today."

The Malforian shot the scout a confused look. "Three?"

"Sorry, my bad." The scout said. "The other one went to Tasdid."

Deneus leaned back with disgust. "Why are you still taking anyone to him? I told you: I'll pay you and your boys twice his fee."

"I know, I know, but I've got to send him something. Besides—" the scout insisted, holding three tentacles toward Izo. "I bring you the best ones, right?"

"I'll decide which ones are best," Deneus deadpanned. "You want to keep making double? Bring ALL of them to me FIRST."

"Damn. Greedy much?" said the scout. "It won't matter anyway. This one's going to be your big come back," he said, pointing at Izo. "He's fancy. I can tell."

"I bask in relief at your assurance. Don't forget what I said, okay? Come to me first," ordered Deneus.

"Love you too." Blowing the agent a kiss, the scout left.

"Ignore him," said Deneus before taking out a wide handheld device. Behind him, a large screen built into the wall lit up, revealing a "new client" file, blank and ready to go. Skipping the contact information at the top, Deneus scrolled straight to the personal info.

"So, tell me about yourself," said Deneus. "What's your name? Where you from?"

"Izo. And he's from uncharted territory," Glongkyle answered before the fly-by could say anything to give them away.

"Really?" Deneus swung his eyes at Izo with interest. "Exotic beauty hailing from deep within unexplored lands...not a bad start."

Glongkyle grinned. "Thanks."

Izo made a face and looked away.

"You're welcome. So, tell me more," Deneus encouraged, sitting up as he took notes. "What made you come to big, bad IA?"

"Me chingaron," said Izo, jerking a thumb at Glongkyle then Tearn.

"I'm sorry?" said the agent.

"He said career change," Tearn said from the back of the room.

"Ahh. Get a lot of those," said the man. Then, peering up at each of them, he cocked his mouth to the side. "Sooo...you got any official documents?"

There was a long, awkward pause. Time ceased to move. For one terrifying moment, Glongkyle wondered if the kid was going to spill everything right there and then.

"We're a touch light on those at the moment," Tearn finally said, "but they're in the works."

"We filed everything, but there were issues with his homeworld," added Glongkyle, catching the Ginarsian's drift. Intergalactic bureaucracy was a universal annoyance of nearly every corner of existence. "Their office is always losing stuff. Misplacing files."

"Don't you just hate it when things go missing on Earth?" said Izo with a glare at Glongkyle.

Tearn coughed nervously from behind them. Glongkyle sat up in his chair. He didn't appreciate when any of his fly-bys hinted at their kidnappings in public. Izo's tendency to bring it up made him especially nervous.

"Absolutely," Deneus agreed once it was clear no one else was going to speak. "Either way, I won't ask again." Then, skipping past the next three pages on the form, he stopped above the section labeled "Job Placement." Opening a search bar, he turned and smiled widely at Izo. "Now for the fun part—what do you want to be?"

Izo looked around the room in confusion. "¿Qué?"

"Model, actor, dancer, extra—everyone's looking for fresh-faced Avarians. Type 'Young, Outgoing Avarian' in any search bar, ten thousand jobs pop up." And, demonstrating this, he soon had dozens of page results ready to cue. Sorting them by highest pay, he soon had even Glongkyle's eyes popping out of his head. "The world is yours. Only question is, how do you want to get paid?"

Izo beetled his brow at the screen. Glongkyle remembered the kid couldn't read.

"Got anything for a Chicanx comic?" asked Izo.

"What?" Deneus looked at Glongkyle in confusion, who shrugged as if to say, *I never know what this kid's talking about, either.* "No. We're talking nice, normal Avarian jobs." Turning, Deneus gestured at the first thirty listings. "Like...this one! Amazing company; better pay. All you do is sit in a club and drink for free."

Glongkyle's eyes went wide. His hand shot out over Izo before he'd realized he'd done it. "Absolutely not."

"Hang on," said Izo. "Free chelas? I want to hear this."

"No, you don't," Glongkyle hissed at their Avarian. He whipped his face at the agent, the anger at the idea overtaking his fear for the moment. "He's not interested in anything like that. Move on."

"Could we maybe let him decide for himself?" asked the agent.

"Yeah, man. What the heck?" said Izo, pushing Glongkyle's hand away. "You're not my mom."

"I'm sorry. You're right," said Glongkyle. "Please, let's stop and hear all the pros and cons of unregistered Avarian prostitution."

"Wha—?" The youth turned to the agent. "¿Estás loca? I'm not doing that."

"Now hang on," said Deneus, speaking quickly. "This is a cool opportunity. All you have to do is hang out in a club while wearing a special device. If you find someone you like, maybe the two of you come to an understanding. They pay you with their special device. Nobody keeps any records. The house gets a small cut. Nobody gets in trouble and nobody tells you what to do.

Payments, clients, hours—all the control lies with you. You don't like anybody? Fine. Just sit and drink for free."

"Assuming he hits his drink quota and doesn't owe the house money at the end of the night," snarled Glongkyle. He wasn't entirely sure where this was coming from, except some small screaming rage that knew for a fact Izo was worth more than this and that Glongkyle hadn't traveled all this way to the Avarian entertainment capital to let the kid slog away at earning tips for compliments and sexual favors every night.

Turning to the Earthling, he did his best to explain. "Izo, listen to me—I know these places. Shit, I love these places. They're date-rape central. They get freelance Avarians to peddle over-priced drinks by flirting with losers who know you're nailed to the floor until your shift is over. We're talking entire businesses built around their customers' hopes of getting an Avarian drunk or desperate enough to sleep with whatever random person slithers in. They'll say you don't have to sleep with anyone—but in real life, people get pissed at rejection. They'll say you're perfectly safe, but if something did happen to you, you were never legally their employee."

"That's a little overstated," said Deneus.

"Want to bet? Izo, if you got hurt, killed, or disappeared, this place would have zero liability for you."

"Hey! I take care of my clients," the agent said, rising.

Glongkyle paused, the full combat-ready height of the Malforian throwing him off for a moment.

"You don't approve of prostitution—fine," said Deneus. "Go complain to a church. But don't ever say I put my clients in danger. I have gladly busted-in heads to keep my employees safe. I only work with above-board places—bouncers, cameras, and state-of-the-art locators on and recording at all times."

Glongkyle tipped his head back and laughed, probably too hard but feeling justified anyway. "On and recording, until you get into the back rooms."

Deneus crossed his arms. He lifted a hairless brow. "Don't be so sure."

Glongkyle's face dropped. *Oh shit.*

Luckily, Izo had stood and held his arms between them. "¡Ya basta! I'm not interested."

The agent leaned over and planted his six-fingered palms on his desk. He let out a long sigh. "Are you sure?" He gestured with his head at the high salaries listed on the wall. "A lot of these places pay well for exotic looks."

"Ni lo sueñes. That's cool, but no thanks."

Deneus held out a hand. "Compromise: why don't we try it for a couple of weeks? No schedule, no contract. Just a heads up if they need people on busier nights."

Yula let out a low, rumbling growl from the back of the room. The noise, while soft, had been as menacing and purposeful as the unsheathing of a weapon. The Malforian dropped back a step. He eyed the Wuljerian.

"Izo say no," said Yula simply.

The agent, still standing straighter and at the ready, shifted his eyes gradually to Glongkyle, who smirked, then to Izo. "Didn't realize you'd come to this interview with two bodyguards," he said.

"Like your scout said earlier, I'm a fancy Avarian," Izo replied. He jerked both his thumbs to himself.

"Clearly," Deneus responded before taking his seat. He tapped a few buttons on his device. A moment later the listing updated; over sixty-five percent of the positions had vanished. "On to the next life-changing opportunity," said Deneus flatly. "Can you act?"

Izo shook his head. "No."

Deneus updated the list. Another half of the jobs were gone. "Can you dance?"

Izo considered. "I can do a decent moonwalk."

"What's that?" asked the agent.

But then Izo shook his head again. "I'm not going to front, ese. I like dancing, but I don't want to do it for a living."

Another click from the agent. Another chunk of jobs gone. Glongkyle rubbed a hand over his face. They were down to maybe ten percent of the original number, some nine hundred jobs, a handful of which were now highly specialized. He could feel the nervousness batting at him. Maybe the club gigs wouldn't be so bad?

"Last chance for the big bucks," said the agent. "Have you ever modeled before?"

Izo shrugged up both his shoulders. "Sorry."

Deneus turned off the device. He moved around to the front of his desk. He leaned against it. "Okay, let's back up." He held out his hands. "What can you do besides fly?"

Izo frowned. Glongkyle frowned. No one said anything for a long time.

"I know this isn't the answer you were looking for," Tearn said from the back of the room. "But he's fast."

"How fast?" said Deneus.

"En chinga," said Izo proudly.

The agent looked to the others. "How fast is that?"

"It's really fast," said Tearn. The Ginarsian snapped his fingers at Izo. "And knock it off. I know what that word means."

"I don't give a chingada," said Izo.

"It's true. He's stupid quick," Glongkyle jumped in, hurrying to move on. "Faster than a cargo ship." Glongkyle said, giving Izo a meaningful look. "Assuming you don't catch him by surprise."

Izo shot Glongkyle his favorite finger. "Vete a la chingada."

The agent gave Izo a funny smile. He'd propped his chin on his fist. He seemed to be considering something. "You're not from around here, huh?"

"You can say that again," said Izo.

"Interesting, but not the point," Deneus finished. His expression disappeared as he sat back. "Being fast is cool, but it's not a job."

"It's a job for Imperial Racers," said Tearn.

Glongkyle made a confused face. *Imperial Racer?* Why would Tearn bring them up? A team of professional Avarian athletes, all they did was train year-round to prepare for their bi-annual races. Sure, the fly-by would probably get a kick out of it, but where was their money?

He gasped. Tearn was a genius! Professional athletes needed a ton of start-up cash! Investors and bigwigs were always looking for fresh-faced athletes to sponsor. Plus there were grants, endorsements, scholarships, and maybe even a sign-on bonus. It was a payout bonanza!

Glongkyle looked back at his short best friend and wanted to kiss him.

"You can be a flying racer on this planet?" Izo twisted around in his seat to point at Tearn. "That one. Let's do that one."

The agent tipped his head back and broke into laughter. "You can't be an Imperial Racer, kid."

"Why not?" said Izo.

"There are only twenty-five of them on the planet," said Deneus "Those teams are notoriously small and elite. You may think you're fast, but these guys are impossibly fast. Like blink-and-they-left-the-city fast. The kind of fast that only computers can see."

"That's what I'm telling you," Glongkyle insisted. "When he moves at full speed, you can't see it."

Deneus narrowed his eyes. "Bullshit."

Tearn nodded at the door. "Izo, go show him."

And for a split second, the agent seemed like he wanted to see it, but he shook it off. "Doesn't matter—this is IA," said Deneus. "People go bankrupt trying to hit it big. Launching a pro athlete? It's a money pit."

"So we'd need an investor," said Tearn. "Big deal."

"Uh-huh. And where do you suggest finding this investor?" said Deneus. "Can't exactly pick one up at the investor store."

Tearn and Glongkyle shared a look. "Well..." Glongkyle began slowly. "I'd assume that'd fall under local management."

Deneus crossed his arms. He looked pissed. But, after taking a deep breath, he instead turned to the Avarian and broke into a sweet smile. "Here's the thing, cutie pie," he said in a voice dripping with gentleness. "I love your team's passion. I do. But it's time to grow up. We're over-thinking this. You've got a face. You've got a body. Let's make some money."

He turned and went back to the other side of his desk to switch his device on. He pulled up one listing in particular. "I've been holding this job for someone special. It's a three-day gig looking for extras. All you have to do is curl up naked in a clear glass ball for a couple of hours. The last person who did it slept through the entire job. Literally got paid thousands of dollars to take a nap!" He held out his arms like this was the simplest, most hilarious thing in the world. "Name one way to make money easier than that. So come on, gorgeous. What do you say? Can you lay in a ball for me?"

Izo peered at the man flatly. Then he turned to Glongkyle. "Can we go yet?"

"I was waiting on you," Glongkyle said, standing and heading to the door.

"Wait, where are you going?" asked Deneus. "Sweetheart, I can find you work."

"Es claro," mumbled Izo.

"We appreciate your time," Tearn cut in politely.

The agent looked floored. "You're leaving?" Jumping around his desk, he hurried to stop them. "Sweetheart—please come back. I'm sorry if I offended you."

"You didn't offend anyone. But you can't do what we need either," said Glongkyle before leading the other outside.

"The racing thing? Are you kidding? Do you have any idea how impossible it would be? There's one team on the entire planet. ONE. And they're mid-season! The odds of anyone walking-on right now are astronomical."

"Maybe for some agents," answered Tearn coming outside the office last.

"Beautiful, please," Deneus said, going around the others to stand in front of Izo. "Have some sense. We're talking about a seven-figure investment just to get started. Where's that money supposed to come from?"

"Izo, ignore this silly man," said Glongkyle.

But Tearn stopped. "What if he was fast enough?"

"For what?" asked Deneus.

"To join their team. You clearly have a lot of connections. Could you find someone?"

"To invest in him?" The agent made a weird face. "Maybe?"

"Great. Let's start there." Tearn turned to Izo and took off his shoe. He held it flat in his hand. "Izo, I want you to close that door over there and then hand me my shoe."

Izo looked behind himself to find the opened door. It was at the far end of the alleyway, three blocks from them. "Okay?"

Tearn leveled the Avarian with a meaningful look. "Don't let my shoe touch the ground."

"Ohhh," Izo said, catching on. He spun and dropped into a starting position. He nodded. "Ready."

Tipping the shoe out of his hand, Tearn yelled: "Go."

The shoe fell toward the ground.

Izo disappeared.

The door slammed.

Izo reappeared holding the shoe. It had barely dropped.

The agent had frozen. For a second, his gaze was wary and his stance reserved, as if he'd discovered he'd been speaking with a small monster for the last several minutes. After a moment he seemed to slowly warm up to the idea. He gave Glongkyle a skeptical look. "He can do that again?"

"Oye, I can do that all day."

The agent chewed his lip. He looked at the door at the end of the alley. Glongkyle could almost see his Malforian gears turning. "I can't believe I'm about to say this," the agent finally responded, "but I'll give you one week. After that, you're paying me to consult and working in one of these clubs in the meantime. Got it?"

Glongkyle and Tearn threw their arms up in the air. "Yes! Thank you," they said together.

"He won't let you down," Tearn assured the Malforian.

The agent rolled his eyes. "We'll see about that. DON'T get excited. This isn't going to be easy or glamorous."

"Great! Neither are we," said Izo.

"So what do we do? How do we get started?" asked Tearn.

Deneus rubbed his six-fingered hand over his wide jaw. "There's only one way to get an unknown talent started in this town."

"What's that?" asked Glongkyle.

Deneus eyed Izo up and down. "You network. Quickly."

— CHAPTER SEVEN —

Deneus

Later that same day, Deneus's new client was complaining hotly and waving his hands around in disgust. Deneus was regretting buying him a perk-up beforehand instead of simply holding off another day or two to let him rest and get settled into the town. But what choice did they have? Avarian night only happened once a week in Malacorp Tower, the famous Member's only club.

"How exactly is this supposed to be networking?" Izo asked.

"Sweetheart, I love you, but don't knock what you don't know." The agent grinned and pointed proudly at the enormous, seven-story tall nightclub located in the most expensive block of downtown IA. "This is going to be huge. You want to be a racer? You need an investor. This place has hundreds."

"I get that, but why are we in the alley?"

Deneus held Izo's gaze to distract the youth from their surroundings—a slim walkway wide enough for a string of dumpsters to float over a stream of putrid liquid that smelled of rot, alcohol, and urine. The truth was Deneus wasn't allowed in. It was an invite-only club, one of the most exclusive in the city (and by extension, probably the universe). A joint venture between some of the scariest Sword members on the Mountain, their membership backlog stretched for decades. And sure, Izo could have gotten in with a float and a smile. But the rest of them? Yeah, right.

None of which his client needed to know.

"Here's the thing, Izo," said Deneus. "Quality Avarians—they never pay for anything."

"¿Nada?"

"Not even once. Drinks, rides, clothes, clubs: anything a quality Avarian wants, they get for free. So the only question is—are you a quality Avarian?"

"Would a quality agent need to ask?"

Deneus smirked. *He's got spunk. They're going to love him.*

"We found a side door!" the dumb reptilian, Glongkyle, interrupted from farther along the alleyway.

They followed Glongkyle around the side of the building, careful to dodge wet miscellanea strewn on the ground. As they turned the corner Deneus winced at the sound of Yula slamming into the freshly discovered door with an echoing boom. Backing up, Yula was positioning her shoulder to try again.

"What the hell are you doing?" Izo zipped over to push Yula out of the way. "That isn't going to work!"

To Deneus's surprise, the massive Wuljerian backed away with an annoyed look. Deneus shook his head in amazement. He doubted if he'd ever seen a fierier Avarian in his life. *They're really going to love him.* He hurried to his client's side.

"Of course it's going to work, fly-by," said Glongkyle. "Yula locks her keys in her room all the time. She gets it to open eventually."

"And how many people are going to get wiped out in the process?" countered Deneus. He pointed at the building. "That's the most exclusive privately owned Sword club in the capital. If that door hits anyone you're going to have twenty Sword attorneys up your ass by morning." He waved Yula away. "Move please."

Shooing them off, Deneus approached the security reader next to the door. It was made of tnilium, one of the strongest military-grade metals in the tri-galaxies. Feeling along its edges,

Deneus chose one side to gently pry apart with his thumbs. Sliding a finger inside, he blindly felt around until he located the main power cord connected to the building's energy supply. He wrapped his finger around it and pulled until a tangle of embedded wires popped out of the box in a cloud of dust.

"There. That should do it," Deneus said.

"I forgot how strong Malforians are," Tearn whispered to Glongkyle.

Deneus smiled and pretended not to hear. He pushed the door open with one finger.

Inside was a back room, filled with clunky sound equipment and dusty piles of half broken furniture. Picking through it, they quickly made their way to the innermost doorway. Outside, the club was a decadent, chaotic mess of gleaming reds and whites bursting with people from all species. They were bouncing to music and bouncing into each other, flailing in a churning kaleidoscope of laser lights and smoke shadows, a drunken mass of lewd and drunken flesh. Hanging cages and floating platforms displayed Avarians wearing little more than sparkling necklaces and inviting smiles. Dozens of bars spread out in the middle of the enormous space surrounded by rows of patrons shouting for drinks four and five people thick.

Deneus waved the others in.

Glongkyle entered first, snout curling as he surveyed the buffet of Avarian flesh, seeming neither terribly embarrassed nor surprised. He turned to the others behind him. "Yula, stay close to Izo."

Yula nodded and moved out in front of their Avarian. Glongkyle was right to be on alert. Petite, sharp-tongued, and with a gorgeous, symmetrical face that you couldn't quite place, Izo was exactly the type these clubs craved.

Their Avarian entered and looked around. "It's packed!" he told Deneus loudly over the music.

"You want to see if there's a table?" Deneus yelled back. He made an upward motion with his hand.

Izo nodded and zipped up. Conversations slowed mid-sentence as every patron nearby eyed his performance with interest. To Deneus's delight, many of them were in incredibly expensive suits.

Izo searched the rows of semi-circular booths lining the walls. Spotting a free table, the short Avarian snapped forward and disappeared. He reappeared above the empty table just in time to slam into another Avarian who'd also been racing overhead to reach it.

Rebounding in the air painfully, they backed up and glared at each other. She was a beautiful Anolitun with deep purple skin and long, curly blue hair. More telling than that, she possessed the tiny torso and wide base that was the tell-tale sign of long, intensive training to the core muscles and organs that gave Anolituns their powers. Worse still, a male with a similar build appeared beside her, along with a green, slim-hipped Nertian.

Deneus hissed. These weren't just any Avarians. These were professional athletes. There was no telling what electric damage the Anolituns could do, and the Nertian could probably knock over the whole club if he felt like it. Shouting "Yula!" over his shoulder, Deneus hurried to reach his client before he could say something stupid. But it was no use. Deneus watched in helpless horror as the four immediately began to bicker.

"We were here first," said the purple female.

Izo laughed. "Does 'first' means something different on your planet? I beat you fair and square, loca."

"Fair and square?" The female folded her arms. "You ran into me."

"Sí," said Izo, lifting up both hands to explain. "Knocking you squarely out of my way."

"We already had this table," explained the green Nertian mildly. "We left to go get drinks."

Izo eyed the Nertian. He seemed intrigued for a moment, but then he shook it off and gestured at the table. "Mira, did you leave anything to claim it? A jacket or a purse?"

"Why would I leave my purse when there are people out here shamelessly stealing tables?" said the female.

"Oye, Jessica Rabbit," said Izo. "It's not my fault your big butt was too slow to get here before me and that you were too rude to ask for it graciously. Had you been a lady, I might have been a gentleman. But you weren't. Oh well." He waved her off. "I'd suggest you start looking elsewhere. Something tells me it's going to take you a while."

Tiny arcs of electricity flickered off the female's back where Izo couldn't see them. Deneus dove to get there in time.

"Any last words?" said the female.

"Yeah. An apology would be nice." Izo looked at her and then examined the Nertain up and down. "But I'd settle for either of your numbers."

"Ohhhh, I'm going to enjoy this," said the female while rubbing her hands together to gather more voltage.

"Tobith, forget it," said the Nertain. "Coach is going to kill you if you get in another fight over the weekend."

"Come on, cuz. Forget this clown. He's not worth your time," said the other purple male. Grabbing her by the shoulder, the male Anolitun tilted his head in the opposite direction. "We'll find another table."

The purple female, Tobith apparently, glared balefully at Izo. She jabbed a finger at his face. "You're lucky my cousin's in town and I'm supposed to be on best behavior. If I see you again, I'll light you up like an electron star." Then she turned and pushed past the crowd, her cousin and the Nertian following close behind.

Izo waved at their backs. "Have a good night!"

Careful to stay clear of touching her, Deneus whipped on his client. "What the hell were you thinking?"

"What? I got here first." Then the Avarian bobbed and signaled for the others.

Deneus shook his head and sat. He needed a drink. And a different, less ridiculous client. But then again, considering the ridiculousness of their venture, he supposed maybe it was for the best. In fact, he thought as he gazed into the club's massive belly, it might be exactly what they needed.

It was an impossibly exclusive club, each of its seven floors representing another checkpoint of increasingly exclusive VIP access. The system of excluding people was simple—money. The more money you had, the higher you could go. Which made perfect sense. Ten bottles of liquor on the bottom floor wouldn't buy one cup of the premium stuff on the top.

There were plenty who might find a system like this crass. It reeked of finance-based classism. But what did you expect from a place owned and operated by the Sword party? Subtlety? IA's premier political party was made up of hawkish billionaires and aggressive CEOs. Their policies and lifestyles were gleefully bold. As a lifelong supporter of the Sword party himself, Deneus found the simplicity refreshing. Why wouldn't the wealthy expect more for their money? They'd worked hard for it, just like him.

Deneus ducked his head as a guard went by. Not that political allegiance was going to mean shit if he got caught in here. One scan of his face (and by extension, his financials), and they'd all be booted faster than he could say "Vote Mortaco for Emperor." Resting his chin on his fist, he tried to think of a plan.

"It's a nice place, Deneus," said Glongkyle, finally arriving with the others. He examined the area and gave an impressed nod. "I'll be honest—this might do it."

"¡Órale!" Izo rubbed his hands together while examining the room. "We're definitely going to get some action here tonight."

Tearn giggled, climbing into the seat next to the Avarian. "You promise?"

Izo's lip curled as he glanced down at Tearn. "No, I meant... nevermind."

"Not to interrupt whatever this is," said Deneus, pointing between the two, "but we need to get moving here." He turned to the Avarian. "Izo, if you want to find a wealthy investor, we need to get you into the higher floors."

"Cool," said the Avarian. Looking around, he pointed left. "I think I see an elevator over there."

"Yeah, but you can't get on it. VIP starts on the second level." Deneus pointed around at some of the other people on the dance floor. "We need to find someone with access to take you up."

Izo considered this. "They wouldn't already be up there?"

"Not yet," said Deneus.

"Wait, I don't understand either," said Glongkyle. "Why would anyone be here if they had better access?"

Deneus pointed at Izo. "To find an Avarian to take with them."

Everyone turned to the youth. His eyebrows lifted sharply. "Oh shit." His gaze turned inwards. "I'm the action."

"See? I told you," said Glongkyle. He broke into a shit-eating grin. "Should have worn the romper."

Izo snapped back to himself to level Glongkyle with a blistering glare. "Would you drop it? It was an accident. Sometimes things get lost."

"Yeah right. Do they also get stepped on, ripped, and stained in one night, too?"

"They do if they're a romper," said the Avarian.

Deneus looked back and forth between them, confused. "He looks fine. You all do." Glancing around the table, it occurred to him with surprise that everyone was wearing luxury, name-brand stuff. He squinted at the Ginarsian's in particular. Notoriously a difficult species to find clothes for in high-end shops, his suit fit perfectly...and was of a very distinctive print. Deneus' eyes bugged out when he recognized it. "Is that Bgulvrian?"

Tearn beamed. "It's a good knock-off, right?" He looked down at it proudly, smoothing his hand over the front of the pristine piece. "It was a little pricier since they had to hand-tailor it. But when in IA, right?"

"We're all very impressed with your fancy knock-off, Tearn, but if we could get back to the point." Izo held out a hand to Deneus. "How do I convince someone to take me upstairs?"

"How do you think?" said Glongkyle. "You flirt with them, fly-by."

But when Izo's face soured at this, Deneus immediately jumped in to smooth things over. "We're not saying you should do something you're uncomfortable with." But when Izo only responded with baleful suspicion, Deneus rushed to find more words. "This is a professional networking opportunity. It's a chance to interact face to face and increase your exposure with the right class of people."

"Uh-huh," Izo deadpanned.

"Look," Deneus said, sitting forward and praying he'd come up with something good for the end of this speech. "Avarians are special, right? Everybody knows that. You've got these great powers. You're nice to look at most times. It's the whole package. And you, Izo," he continued, "you're even more special. You have a unique look. Plus, you're really fast. You're a fascinating person. Right?" he said, looking around for help.

Everyone nodded.

"So people are going to want to meet you. They're going to want to talk to you. Most importantly," Deneus said, figuring out where he was going with this, "they're going to want to impress you—because you're impressive. That's all you have to do, sweetheart. Stand back and let them impress you."

Izo blinked. "Yeah…I don't think I'm comfortable with that."

"Of course you are. Don't overthink it. It's easy." Sitting up, Deneus pointed at a cluster of expensive suits. "All you do is strike up a conversation. Then after a little bit, once the conversation gets going, you act a little bored. Like, hmm, maybe you're going to blow them off. But before you do, you say 'You know where I've never been? Upstairs! Is it nice up there?' Now whether they've even been up there or not, they're all turning into personal tour guides on the spot."

"I don't know," said Izo. He bit the inside of his cheek. "Deneus, can I ask you something?"

"Of course," Deneus said while turning away. He was looking for a waiter. The perk up from earlier was clearly a mistake. He needed to get a drink into his client.

"I know you call yourself an agent, but between those jobs at the office and everything going on here, I can't help but wonder…" The youth hesitated, seeming to consider how to word his question. "Are you really just a pimp, dude?"

Deneus narrowed his eyes. Something weird was going on. "I don't understand."

"Are you a pimp," the Avarian said, repeating his strange word, "or an agent?"

Deneus looked around the table. "Someone want to help me?"

"I'm going to jump in as official linguist here," Tearn said, sitting forward. "Izo, in Malforian 'pimp' and 'agent' are the same word."

"¿Qué?" asked the Avarian.

Tearn made a face like he was struggling to explain. "Remember when we translated all the words from English and figured out you guys have like fifteen words for 'blue'?'"

Izo nodded. "Because there's a lot of shades of blue."

"Okay, so to him—" Tearn said pointing at Deneus. "There's no shade between 'agent' and 'pimp.' It's the same word. Loosely translated, it means 'one who sells the skills of others.' To him, you basically asked if he's 'planning to sell your skills' or if he's 'planning to sell your skills.'"

The Avarian blinked owlishly. "If they aren't different words, how do you tell them apart?"

"That's what he's trying to tell you, fly-by. You don't tell them apart." Glongkyle sneered.

"But...what does that mean?" Izo pointed at Deneus in confusion. "Which one is he?"

"He's both!" said Tearn and Glongkyle simultaneously.

"...then there's the son of a Hriesn board member over there," said Deneus, indicating someone in a group standing near the other end of the dance floor. "He's acting like he's slumming it, but the truth is his dad's I.C.O. may drop twenty percent next week, depending on a bill coming up. He'd be a great one to talk to."

"How do you know all this?" asked Tearn in amazement.

Deneus shrugged. "It's my job to know all the corporate sweethearts and trust fund babies. Speaking of, bottom's up." He reached over and tipped up Izo's drink as the Avarian went to take a sip. The concoction cost a small fortune, but it would've made a Risheldian Bullwhale friendly enough to ride. "Time to find you an investor."

"I don't want to," the Avarian complained. "It's weird now!"

"Kid, this was your idea. You want someone to bankroll your big dream?" He gestured around the room. "Fetch."

The Avarian grumbled and finished his drink.

Deneus helped Izo up, a gesture the Avarian didn't appreciate. Rearing back, he nearly had Yula on her feet and in Deneus' face. But the agent was quick to respond, moving away and apologizing profusely. Annoyed and a little drunk now, the kid eventually allowed himself to be led to Deneus' first pick of the night—Sheost Psegre.

The nephew of a notorious oligarch and junior aid at Malacorp, Sheost and his friends had been easy to spot the second they'd walked in. Positive they'd be heading upstairs with their lower-level candy soon, Deneus hurried to think of a way to get their attention.

Coming up to the group, Deneus turned his back and pretended to dance with his Avarian. "The one we want is Sheost. He's wearing the custom Rurjin," he whispered.

Izo scanned the group behind Deneus. "What's a Rurjin?"

"It's a wearable device."

Izo nodded. "What's a wearable device?"

Deneus stopped dancing. He dug a thumb into his temple. *How could anything so attractive be so dumb?* "Never mind. He's the one wearing blue."

"The short one that's kind of cute for a shark?"

"Sure?"

Izo nodded. "Got it."

"Great. Good luck." Then moving behind Izo, he shoved the Avarian into the center of the group.

Across the room, Yula jumped up from the table.

"Whoa!" said the group of Malforians. They all moved forward to catch the smaller creature. But this wasn't Deneus' first time. Like a perfectly planned throw, when everyone straightened and moved away, it was Sheost helping the drunken Avarian to his feet.

"Hey now," Sheost said gently. "You okay?"

"I'm fine." Izo glared at Deneus, but the agent was already pretending to talk to a red-headed Avarian. "Some asshole knocked into me for no reason."

"I'm sorry," said Sheost. "If you want, I can call my attorney. He could probably get you a couple grand."

"Think you could get more than that," said one of Sheost's friends. Tallest in the group and with long shaggy hair, he wore a device that was last year's model. He looked Izo over with aggressive interest. "He looks expensive."

Izo's face cringed with disgust. "Thanks."

But Sheost ignored his friend. Deneus could almost see the rich, young Malforian struggling to place Izo's features, eyes anchored to the kid's face. "Where are you from?" asked Sheost.

"Earth. Wait. No." The youth stared down, holding out a hand. "¿Qué chingados do you call it?" Remembering, he snapped his fingers. "Uncharted territory."

"Is that so?" said Sheost. The agent could see all the same thoughts in Sheost's eyes that had occurred to Deneus early that day—mysterious stranger, unknown lands, something fresh, something different, something new.

The spell was instantaneous. The young Malforian's gaze changed from curiosity to focused intent, like a hunter stumbling onto its next meal. "Guess you're a long way from home," said Sheost. "How long have you been in town?"

"A couple of days." Izo frowned. "One day. I've been in town one day so far." His gaze turned inward. "Jesus-dang-Christ, is that right?"

Sheost nodded in humor at this response. Then, easy as that, the heir-apparent pointed up. "You seen the upstairs yet?"

Behind them, Deneus waved Yula down as fast as he could. The Wuljerian, her features alert and angry, was still standing next to their table. Snorting, she sat.

"So, Izo," the shaggy-haired one said, pounding back another drink. "They got any more like you on your planet?" Gaze hostile and drunk, Sheost's angry friend was sitting across from the rich Malforian and his new Avarian jewel.

Izo shook his head. "Nada."

Sheost's friends tipped back with jealousy and laughter. Behind them, Deneus silently pumped his fist. He couldn't have asked for a better response. The kid, go figure, was a natural at the "innocent foreigner" schtick.

They'd arrived on the fifth floor a half-hour ago, the group's Avarian dates sauntering in like they'd owned the place. Deneus had snuck upstairs among Sheost's drunken group of Malforian friends with the red-headed Avarian he'd been talking to. Together, the two of them silent as clouds, they'd slipped into the back of the group as Sheost confirmed his access at the elevator.

The guard, seeing the heir's ridiculous credit line, had confirmed the giant entourage's fifth-floor access.

For the first time in his life, Deneus had stepped into a VIP lift. A stock feature in clubs like this, the apparatus's appearance conveyed everything of the literal mobility it granted. Perfectly spherical, one sheer globe of glass with a gold floor, it seamlessly displayed every inch of the life you were leaving as you rose in gilded ornament.

By the gods, if the fifth floor wasn't magical. Cleaner, richer, sparser—no crowds squishing past each other up here. Instead, it was a relaxed atmosphere filled with tufted Dresrdian leather, complimentary drinks, and a stylish Avarian for every guest. This, Deneus realized with a dreamy sigh, was what real money felt like.

Deneus nodded blankly at something his date said. From the corner of his eye, he continued watching Sheost and Izo.

"So you're the only one, huh?" Touching Izo's nose, Sheost smiled. "Guess that makes me sort of lucky."

Izo, clearly affronted at the nose boop, gave the young Malforian a strange smile. His voice dropped sharply. "Don't do that again, vato."

And like magic, a new fire lit up in the heir's eyes. Sitting up, he bore down at the assertive Avarian like a playful predator. "Why? What are you going to do to me if I do?"

"Bullshit he's the only one," Shaggy said, interrupting loudly. He stood fast, nearly tipping into his Aurelian date. "You're telling me no one else on your planet can fly?"

Izo glared at the drunken Malforian. "I haven't interviewed everyone, but yeah—as far as I know, I'm the only one."

Shaggy looked at Izo like he was stupid. "What about your parents?"

The youth sucked in an angry breath. "Oye—don't talk about my parents, cabrón. It's none of your chingado business—"

"Izo!" Deneus said, moving toward him quickly. "There you are, you little scamp! You got away from me. Hello, nice to meet you. I'm Deneus." He pulled out a stack of digital business cards and began passing them out, redirecting everyone's attention.

"Thanks," said Sheost, taking his offered card with a slow, unsure motion. Deneus could see him assessing his clothes and tech with confusion. Sheost turned to Izo. "You know each other?"

"He's my—"

"Step-uncle," said Deneus, cutting off the Avarian. "Soon to be crippled step-uncle if I lose him again." He shook a finger at Izo. "Izo, you're in a lot of trouble, young man. You know your mother just moved here and is terrified of the city. If she knew you were out here wandering by yourself, she'd be worried sick. Now we both know she appointed me your guardian. I swore as a Malforian to keep you safe! Yes, I know I promised we'd have a good time, but think of your poor mother! This is unacceptable. Get up. You're coming with me and calling her right now."

Izo squinted at him in confusion. "Qué?"

Deneus tutted in disappointment. "Don't play innocent with me. I told you to stay close to me. This one!" he said, turning to the group with a laugh. "I have to watch him all day! Of course, his mother's always on my case, but it makes sense. Look at him. Absolute heartbreaker. Mother was too, but my brother beat me to it," he said, suddenly turning his gaze to Sheost. "Isn't that always the way?" He shot a begrudging smile at the shaggy-haired kid. "Oh well. That's family for you." He turned back to his client. "Izo!" he said, snapping his fingers. "You better start marching, young man."

"You can use my device to call her," said Sheost. Taking off his Rurjin, he held it up for Deneus to take. For a split second Deneus was tempted. He could sell it for a house...and Deneus needed a house at the moment. But he shook his head. "Thanks, but no. There might be tears." Then turning away, he signaled for Izo to go.

Rising, Izo left with Deneus shepherding him from behind.

"I'll be right here!" Sheost called after them.

"Head to the back," Deneus whispered, pointing at the far corner. Going into the lush hallway, they quickly made their way past the bathrooms and into one of the private rooms.

Decked in warm wood paneling buffed to a shiny, reflective glow, the room was filled with low lighting and a large window revealing the skyline and mountains beyond. It was a delightfully romantic space. With little more than a bed and chair for furniture, it cut straight to the point.

Dropping onto the bed, Deneus grinned at his client. "How easy was that?" He stared at the Avarian in amazement. "You were out there two minutes and you already got a billionaire heir on the line with nothing but eyes for you."

The youth held out his hands. "I still don't get it. How does this turn into dinero?"

"He's rich. He likes you." Deneus shrugged. "Do I need to draw you a picture?"

"Of me asking for money? Because that sounds like an awkward picture."

"You don't—ugh." Deneus dropped his head. *How could anyone be so bad at something they were naturally so good at?* "You don't ask rich people for money, Izo. You offer them a chance to get in on the ground floor of something big: you."

"Ohhhh," said Izo. "He has the chance to invest in a racer."

Deneus pointed at the lad. "Now you're getting it. And don't let the rude friend rile you either. He may be a good place to grab some money too."

Izo nodded. "Okay, I'm ready."

"Good. But first—" Rolling onto his side, Deneus leaned onto one elbow. "I've never been in the back room of a club this fancy before." He wagged his eyebrows. "You want to fool around?"

Izo's face pinched. "Lo siento. No offense, but I'm starting to think Malforians aren't my type."

It took Deneus' translator a second to catch the Avarian's meaning. When it finally did, Deneus narrowed his eyes. "What? Who doesn't like Malforians?" He looked around the room in confusion. "We're on my planet!"

Izo waved this off. "It's nothing personal. You just remind me of…something from Earth."

Deneus stuck his tongue in his cheek. The idea seemed ridiculous to him. What kind of Avarian, especially one so foreign, would come all the way to IA just to decide he wasn't into Malforians?

But then, after a moment, Deneus realized what the Avarian was saying. *Of course.* He didn't mean he wasn't attracted to Malforians. He meant he was waiting for the right one. The translator couldn't catch the nuance, he supposed. Deneus nodded approvingly. "You know what? That's really admirable. I can tell you really respect yourself." He gave the Avarian a thumbs up. "Good on you."

"Great," said Izo with a weird expression. Reaching back, he opened the door and started through it. "Can we go now?"

Deneus rose and followed. "It's probably a good thing," he said with a laugh. "Your mother would've killed me."

— CHAPTER EIGHT —

Izo

Izo didn't like IA. Point of fact, he hated it. The whole place could go up in flames for all he cared. "If you ever need a test planet," he'd have told them on the Death Star, "let me know." But what could he do? Starting over would only mean more time stuck there. Plus, the idea of being a flying space racer...maybe not the worse forced labor out there. And as Glongkyle and Tearn had painstakingly explained back at their tiny hotel room while getting ready for the night, the signing bonus for something like that could easily split five ways. Basically, if he could get this done, he was home free.

Izo spotted Sheost searching for him. He forced himself to smile and wave. Sheost was a nice enough bro. True, the whole "capital investor with the hots for you" situation was a little weird, but that's what a hero's adventure was—navigating hairy situations. Right? Yeah. This was a hero's journey. A weird one, yes, but one he was going to figure out nonetheless. He'd do great. He could do anything! He'd slay this dragon and be back on Earth in no time.

Izo made a face. He'd also figure out a better metaphor.

"Hey, how's your mom?" asked Sheost, meeting him and Deneus near the back hallway's entrance.

Still dead since before I can remember. Thanks for asking. But he made himself slow down. The alien-güey meant well and, more importantly, Izo was here to make friends. He needed to change his approach. Tipping his head to one side, he smiled like he'd seen on a K-pop advertisement once. "She's fine! Thanks for asking. You're so sweet!"

Sheost nodded. Izo could see the clear look of interest in the alien's eyes. It was the same desirous look he'd caught Tearn giving him several times. Mulling it over, he realized he didn't like it much more on Sheost.

"Did she ground you?" the heir asked.

Izo rolled his eyes and pretended to spin his hair around one finger. "No, thank God." But then, like a flash of lightning, an idea hit him. "But she did remind me to get plenty of sleep and be ready for practice first thing in the morning!"

The young alien's shoulders slipped down. "Oh. Does that mean you're heading out?"

"I probably should," Izo said with a frown.

Sheost nodded sadly. It was clear his night had been ruined.

"But maybe we could schedule a meeting later to talk about racing?" said Izo.

Deneus laughed hard and loud to try and redirect everyone from this overly obvious ploy. "No, that would probably be weird. Why don't we stay a little longer?" He widened his eyes at Izo. "We did just get here."

"As long as we're not out too long. I'd hate to be sore and tired tomorrow for practice," said Izo.

"I'm sure you'd survive," said Deneus.

"You're not the one who has to go practice," muttered Izo.

"Hey," interrupted Sheost's angry, drunk friend before Izo and Deneus could argue further. Brandishing a long, thin cup, he shoved it under Izo's nose. "I bought you a drink. Here."

Izo grimaced at the scent. It smelled like it was equal parts vinegar and rubbing alcohol. He moved away and covered his nose. "Ni madres. No thanks, cabrón."

"Why are you being rude? I got it for you. You think you're too good for it? Ha!" Turning his watch toward Izo, he shot a projection into the air. "That's how much money I made last week alone."

Izo scanned the mess of alien symbols with a flat expression. Then he shrugged. "Ese, that literally means nothing to me."

The Malforian's face lit up with anger. "Bullshit. You're impressed." He shoved the drink toward the Earthling's face again. "Take it."

"For heaven's sake, Echi. Leave him alone," Sheost said.

"Why? Because you think he's sooo attracted to you? Grow up, Sheost. He likes your name, not you," said Echi.

Sheost shoved his taller friend's shoulder. "I am my name!"

"You realize he doesn't have any actual money, right?" Echi said, spinning on Izo again. "It's all locked up in trusts. This." Echi pointed at the fifth-floor room, the ceiling, and finally at Sheost's clothes, shoes, and wristwatch. "It's all debt."

Sheost burst out laughing. "Are you kidding me? How stupid are you? Two years from now all this gets paid off. This isn't debt." He held up his watch. "This is credit!" He laughed again before pointing at Echi's watch like someone gesturing at trash on the street. "You're going to be recycling last year's models for the rest of your life."

Something ugly flashed in Echi's eyes. It was as if he had a secret demon living in his head and, at that exact moment, had decided to hand it the reins.

He flashed his teeth. "Yeah, but I'm still liquid, which means I can cut through the bullshit." Snatching Izo's arm, he yanked the Avarian toward the back hall. "I'll give you fifty thousand dollars right now to magically start liking me."

"¡Aguas, aguas, aguas!" Izo hissed. He fought to pry the Malforian's fingers off his arm, but Echi had a grip like the Terminator. Leaning back, the Earthling tried to dig his feet into the ground, but they slid over the lush carpet like skis. Izo shot a worried look at Deneus. "Hey, Deneus—a little help?"

Luckily, Deneus was there as quick as lightning. He stepped in front of the angry Malforian, stopping and surprising him just long enough for Izo to twist his arm free.

Echi glared at the freed Avarian, but Deneus patted the angry Malforian on the shoulder, drawing his attention to himself. "Look, I don't know what's up between you and your friend, but it's got nothing to do with the Avarian. Why don't you and I go take a walk—"

"Back off!" shouted Sheost from behind all of them.

Turning toward the noise, they all watched as Echi moved his face directly into Sheost's swing. The punch landed in the center of his nose, crunching through bone and cartilage.

Echi screamed and retreated, arms swinging wildly. Eyes trained on Sheost, he cackled. "Ohhh! You're so dead. I'm going to sue you into the ground!"

"You? Don't make me laugh," said Sheost. "You couldn't clean a decent lawyer's toilet. You've got less money than a Shield!"

"Screw you!" said Echi.

"No, screw you!" said Sheost.

"Sounds like you guys have got this handled." Izo whipped toward Deneus. "Can we vamonos, por favor?"

"I don't know what that means, but we need to get out of here," said Deneus. But they turned for the elevator just as eight security personnel, all of them Wuljerian, surrounded the group.

"This asshole attacked me," Echi wheezed, pointing at Sheost. "I'm calling my attorney."

"No lawyer. Upstairs," said one of the security guards. Taller than everyone else in the room by at least a foot, the Wuljerian was covered in cool grey fur. She gave a menacing smile.

"Screw that!" said Echi. "If you don't move right now, I'm going sue to this whole place for medical negligence—"

"No lawyer. Upstairs," repeated the guard. Something about the second command was so final and compelling, Izo wasn't sure if he was more scared or more grateful for Yula at the moment.

Echi started to argue more, but Sheost waved him down. "Shut up. We're already in trouble." He surveyed the security guard. There was clear worry on the rich Malforian's face. "How far upstairs?"

"Seventh floor."

Upstairs the guards pushed the offenders out of a secret black and gold elevator. Leading them through two looming gold doors, they entered a tawdry circus. Izo gasped and spun his head. He didn't know where to look. There was so much to take in. It was like nothing he'd ever seen before—a full-on, no-holds-barred, sprawling alien spree.

Whoever designed the seventh floor had known exactly what they were doing. In its central space were twelve hovering platforms fitted with attached sectionals. These floated freely about the room, encircling twelve monstrous statues that held up the ceiling like massive, shining servants. These statues possessed no arms, legs, or faces. Existing only as tautly carved torsos, they were captured and installed for construction while projecting all the ego-less grace of art.

And sprinkled across the gilded, entombed torsos? Hundreds of Avarians, resting vertically in small groups, as they beckoned and waited to be summoned to a floating platform nearby.

Izo's eyes had never been wider. His senses were on maximum overload. The sounds and sights coming in from all directions were too much to understand, much less emotionally process. It was like a madhouse. He was a wild mix of opposite reactions. The side of him that had always been excited by the ideas of vampires and opium dens was immediately drawn in. But the other side of him that had secretly cringed when Belle fell in love with the Beast and hated Gothic scenes of helpless damsels was repulsed. Here was a place of utter abandon and guilt-free freedom...and yet the very idea of it seemed to hold an exacting pressure. When Deneus had mentioned the job for an Avarian to lay naked in a clear ball, Izo had assumed it was a one off. But standing here now, the blinders were starting to come off. Avarians weren't customers here; they were products.

The guards led the group deeper inside.

"Psst. Hey."

Izo peered over his shoulder, grateful to be brought back to himself by Deneus's summoning. "What?"

Deneus's head jerked toward the platforms. "Do you understand who those guys are?"

"No," said Izo. "Who are they?"

"They're Imperial Senators."

Izo shook his head, unfamiliar with the term. "Cool?"

Deneus's jaw clenched. Something in his eyes was screaming danger. "Not cool. We're not supposed to be here." He surveyed the guards in front of and behind them. They didn't seem to be paying any attention to Deneus's mini lecture. Still, he pressed a fist over his mouth. "Whatever you do—don't lie to them, don't get nervous, and don't get angry. Keep your answers short. Keep your face flat. And for the love of the gods..." He gave Izo a deadly serious look. "Don't piss anyone off."

Izo peered up at one of the platforms. He suddenly realized everyone on it seemed to be reaching or performing for only one participant. Izo's mixed feelings faded; he was definitely just uncomfortable. "Why? Deneus, who are these guys?"

Deneus peered up at the same platform. There was a lot going on atop it. The agent gulped. "They own IA."

Izo's brow furrowed. He turned to ask more, but before he could, their group came to a sudden stop in front of a wide, glittering pool.

A particularly large platform, the largest in the room, slowly floated down toward them. From their vantage, they could only see the bottom. Izo cringed at the idea of what it might be holding. At the last moment before it rested in front of them and came into view, Izo made a shivering grunt and covered his face.

In the darkness behind his hands, he could hear a soft hissing noise in front of him. It was soon followed by a lengthy silence and finally a confused chuckle.

"Is he covering his face?" asked someone from the platform. The voice, deep and easy-going, seemed vaguely amused.

There was another silence as the owner of the voice waited for a reply. Izo felt a nudge in his side—Deneus, pressing him to answer. But Izo just shook his head no.

"I-I think he's a little nervous, Senator," said Deneus.

"You can say that again," Izo murmured. He peeked out from between his fingers and let out a breath. The platform only held a cluster of maze-like seating that slowly gathered in height toward the center, like a miniature mountain made of cushions. It was still decidedly M-rated—a mess of attractive, scantily-clad Avarians in various shapes and genders, all giggling and playing with each other in a lurid heap. Compared to some of the other stuff happening in the room, it was almost mild.

At the top sat the man who had spoken, still peering at Izo curiously. Tall, with arms spread out over the back of his chair in an easy seven-foot wingspan, he was the biggest Malforian Izo had ever seen—and he'd seen plenty so far in the club. He had long, silvery hair that fell in a mane about his shoulders and a large, powerful body colored in the typical thick grey of his species. With a strong brow, wide nose, and a chiseled jaw, he was conspicuously masculine. There was something utterly self-assured in his attitude. It was more than confidence. It was predatory. It was a fifth-grade bully gazing down at the second-graders, the type of person who was used to humiliating and pulverizing others on a whim and who always got away with it.

It was one of the fastest complete boner bummers Izo had ever experienced. He might as well have been watching that lady from the internet step on a puppy again.

The Malforian on high gazed down at the Earthling with curiosity. "So you're the one causing trouble?"

"No," said Izo. He pointed at Echi. "That's the guy you're looking for."

"Oh?" The Senator's gaze danced over Izo. As his face turned to Sheost and Echi, all mirth disappeared. He glowered. "So? What did you do?"

"I didn't do anything," said Echi. "He attacked me."

"Respectfully, sir, that's not how it happened. He grabbed my date and was dragging him toward the back rooms. I was protecting an Avarian. If that's wrong"—Sheost shrugged—"I take full responsibility."

"How terribly noble," said the Senator with a bored expression. Looking Sheost over, he suddenly titled his head. "Say, aren't you one of the Psegre's kids?" He snapped his fingers. "Don't I work with your brother in the capital?"

"Y-yes, sir," Sheost answered, his voice faltering suddenly. Looking down, his face flushed. "My older brother—"

"Is one of our more famous Senators. Which makes sense as he's part of one of the oldest families on the Mountain." The man narrowed his eyes in barely contained contempt. "I wonder what he'd think if he knew his kid brother was throwing punches over Avarians in front of anyone with fifth-floor access." Leaning back in his seat, he tutted. "More importantly, I wonder what the rest of your family would think."

Sheost shut his eyes painfully. His abject humiliation was hard for Izo to watch. "Please don't tell them," he said quietly.

The Senator shook his head while looking around the room in disappointment. "The Psegres are an important name on the Mountain; an important name with even more important holdings." The Senator steepled his fingers. "Tell me, Mr. Psegre— do you know why we don't like scandal in the capital?"

Sheost hesitated. Izo could tell the Malforian, eyes trained firmly on the ground, was fighting to come up with the exact answer the Senator wanted to hear. "Because it hurts our reputation," he started. "It creates doubt with the investors. It draws unnecessary attention and causes risk."

"One hundred percent wrong," snapped the man from on high. Sheost winced.

"Since you don't seem to understand, allow me to explain. It's really quite simple, you see. It's because your family's holdings might shrink. And if your holdings shrink, mine might shrink. If my holding's shrink, someone else's might shrink. Next thing you know, there's a chain reaction and the whole Mountain gets smaller." The Senator's eyes burned into the younger Malforian.

"Now if you were a Shield, I couldn't care less. Those candy-asses can all go belly-up," he continued. "But you're not a Shield. You're a Sword. Which means when you look bad, we all look bad." He held his arms out to the room.

Sheost had frozen completely. Eyes glued to the floor, he looked like he actually might piss himself.

The Senator's gun-metal gaze flashed at Echi. "You look young and hungry. I'll give you one sentence to prove you belong."

Echi puffed out his chest. "Avarians aren't worth fighting over."

The Senator broke into a hearty laugh followed by a loud clap. "See how smart that was? It took him one second to spit out the only thing I wanted to hear. Psegre's youngest is over here struggling with all these big principles and ideals. You can tell he went to a real fancy school. You're a Sword—we don't have ideals. We work for the good of ONE thing. What is it?"

Sheost sighed. He finally looked up. "The Mountain."

The man nodded in satisfaction. "Correct." He motioned for the guards to grab the two young Malforians. They quickly did. "The two of you are banned from accessing anything higher than the third floor for a month."

"No!" gasped Echi. The way his face contorted, Izo would have thought he'd been shot in the stomach.

"I am also giving you a gift, however." Snapping his fingers, he pointed for a pair of beautiful twin Avarians—one male, one female, if Izo guessed right—to float down next to the two. "These will be your companions during that time. I guarantee you won't be able to catch anything better than them. Let this be a lesson to never embarrass the Swords again."

"Thank you, sir," said Echi and Sheost.

"Don't thank me, morons. Today you've received a great and undeserved mercy." He paused to rake them with a glare. "Disappoint us again and you'll be fresh out."

"Yes, sir," said Echi and Sheost.

The Senator waved a hand. "Get out of my sight."

Nodding gratefully, Izo turned to go.

"Not you," said the Senator to the Earthling. "You stay. I've got a few more questions for you."

Izo spun to Sheost for help. But the young Malforian already had his hand over the back of his new companion. Avoiding Izo's gaze, he left without another word.

Izo gulped and glanced up at the Senator again. *What the hell does he want?* But as their eyes met and the man's lips split into a terrifying and toothy smile of pleasure, Izo had a sinking suspicion he knew exactly what the Malforian wanted.

— CHAPTER NINE —

Deneus

Deneus's brain was having difficulty processing his intense sexual arousal and unspeakable mortal fear. He wanted to curse. If only the stubborn Avarian had been a little less priggish about his line of work, none of this would've happened. But he was and it did and here they were. Which was just great. Now Deneus was going to die with a half-boner.

The seventh floor had turned out to be everything he could have imagined and more. It was a Malforian dream. He wanted to groan and never leave. He'd never seen so many perfect Avarians in one place before. It was as if someone had opened a mystical cavern deep within the mountain, and they'd all come pouring out in a shimmering waterfall at once.

There were purple-skinned Anolituns in plunging white teddies; light-grey skinned Cristovalians in tight black bustiers; tiny, pink-skinned Azarians donning little more than fire-resistant ropes; one deep-green Nertian wearing nothing but a shiny, curve-hugging amoeba that traveled up and down his body like an amorphous pet. All the universe's rarest and most exotic beauties gathered in one place and hell-bent on one task: to offer themselves up like crazed sacrifices to twelve wildly rich and bored Malforians.

And at the front and center of it all? IA's most famous and favored son, the man most likely to take over the Empire—Senator Malogue Di'Mortaco—the single most powerful living member of the Sword party.

"So why were they fighting over you?" Senator Mortaco asked Deneus's client.

"I don't know. Ask them," said Izo.

"I'm asking you," said Senator Mortaco.

"And I'm telling you I don't know." Izo shrugged. "Ask them."

The Senator knit his brow. "The Presgres are one of the oldest and richest families on the Mountain. Sheost wouldn't humiliate himself over nothing. There must have been a reason he was fighting over you."

"Te prometo, I don't know anything. I just—" He paused. An especially lovely Anolitun had interrupted to crawl closer to the Senator's feet. Covered in her kind's wonderfully smooth, electric skin, her body was shrouded in nothing more than a sheer dress of loosely woven gold. Izo's mouth fell slightly slack as he watched her.

The Senator noticed. Flicking his fingers, he signaled for the Anolitun to come closer. She obliged, floating up to lower herself onto his lap with apathetic sensuality. Her shoulder fell under his hand as he tenderly turned her until the entirety of her amazing body faced them. The Senator, far larger than the female, spread one arm over his chair's wide top. The other he sent down between her legs.

Eyelids dropping closed, she tipped her head back against his chest.

"You don't have to play coy here." The Senator told Izo. "Something you did must have got their attention. Don't be shy. Why don't you show me? Or, if you prefer," he said flicking his eyes down at the Anolitun in his lap. "You can show her."

The Anolitun was growing increasingly excited. Her hands were reaching over her head and down her torso to feel along the soft curves of her body and the hard edge of the Senator's jaw. Deneus gulped. It was the single most erotic thing he'd ever witnessed.

Deneus's client seemed to be seriously considering the Senator's offer. At the very least, he was obviously enrapt with the Anolitun female. After a moment he started to move forward toward them— but then he suddenly stopped. His fascination seemed to fade. "No. I don't think so."

Senator Mortaco narrowed his eyes with humor. "Why not?"

"I don't think I should." Izo bit his lip. Something seemed to be rolling around his head. After a moment he snapped out of his thoughtful revelry and was back to being ridiculous and brash again. "Basta, can we go? No offense, you seem like you have your hands full here."

The Senator laughed so hard his eyes crinkled.

Izo crossed his arms and waited until the Senator was finished. Then he repeated himself. "Is that a yes? Or are your guards going to grab us and take us to an even weirder alien party?"

The Senator broke into a faux, hurt expression. Brushing the now sleepy Anolitun away, he turned to Deneus. "Is he always this rude?"

Without thinking, Deneus took on a strangely formal and bored tone. "I apologize, Senator, but my client is far from home. I fear he may be a little flummoxed by tonight's events."

The Senator frowned and inspected Izo with curiosity. Deneus waited, expecting more, but nothing came. It took far too long for Deneus to realize what was happening. Eyes intent and still, the Senator had to be using an embedded device to analyze his client's features.

Embedded devices: instruments so uncommon to the masses that Deneus had forgotten they existed. Even Sheost Psegre, with his untold wealth and family name, had a wearable version—a ridiculously expensive and powerful one, to be sure, but a wearable device all the same. The embedded device being deployed by the Senator now only served to further show the worlds, powers, and privileges still separating sweet, rich Sheost and the mortal god sitting before them.

Tools of ineffable power, embedded devices were relegated only for a tiny collection of the ultra-wealthy and elite. Consisting of a digital implant and processor, they connected cutting edge applications and untold research databases—including classified ones—directly to their owners' frontal cortexes. With instant access to every piece of information ever written, the Senator and anyone else with embedded devices were equipped with what was essentially technologically induced omnipotence and access. It was like having superpowers.

Deneus clicked his tongue sadly. There was a part of him that liked the mystery of Izo's origins, the funny little narrative of the enigmatic beauty from unknown lands. But all good things had to end eventually. In a few moments, the Senator's search would return an answer, and they'd know, once and for all, exactly where the Avarian youth hailed from.

But after a while, the Senator only frowned deeper. He blinked a few times as if clearing his vision. Then he sat up. He seemed vaguely intrigued. "Where are you from?"

"Uncharted territory," said Izo.

"Yes, but where in uncharted territory?" said the Senator.

"Uhhh…" Izo glanced at Deneus for help. "Deep in uncharted territory?"

Deneus nodded with approval, but inside he was completely lost. Shouldn't the Senator's search have answered this? And, regardless of whether it had, why was Izo being so shifty?

And then, like a thunderclap, an idea occurred to Deneus. He straightened his back and gazed firmly at the man. "Senator," he said, his voice as loud and commanding as he dared, "I sincerely apologize, but my client is under no obligation to answer your line of questioning. He has repeatedly and clearly asked if he could leave. You have repeatedly and firmly ignored him. It would seem not only is your colorful establishment an obvious health code violation, but it's also one where Avarians are harassed and obliged to remain against their will."

The Senator's face flashed in genuine embarrassment. "No one is holding him against his—"

"So we're free to go?"

The Senator sputtered. "If you would let me finish, I was merely trying to—"

"Apology accepted." Deneus held up a hand. "Are we free to go?"

"Of course, but it's highly irregular for—"

"Thank you." Deneus grabbed Izo's hand, spun, and went for the elevators.

"When we get to the bottom floor, head straight for the front door," Deneus whispered as they reached the lift. "Don't say anything and don't look back. We need to get out of here before they figure out we didn't have access."

"Just a minute," said the Senator. Stealing a look over his shoulder, Deneus watched as the leader of the Swords struggled to pick his way down his giant platform. Exasperated, he stood up straight. "Shoo!" he said waving his arms at everyone. But it only caused a mass confusion of flying, colliding bodies.

Reaching the lift, Deneus waved for the call sensor and waited desperately for the door. The guards, having not been told to grab anyone, stood by while silently watching. If given the command, Deneus knew they'd waste no time. He looked to the elevator and prayed it would arrive quickly.

It did. Door sliding open, it revealed a tall, but slightly thinner, Malforian in a lush black robe. It took Deneus a moment to place him—Senator Jsien Lrasa. Nearly as famous as Senator Mortaco, Senator Lrasa was from a family closely allied with the Mortacos for centuries. Both with an equally ancient and prominent legacy, the two had been inseparable since childhood and competing for leadership in the Sword party—or at least they had been until two years prior, when a tax overhaul had decided things. His version gaining widespread support, Mortaco had come out victorious, his position as the champion of the Swords cemented.

Lrasa looked Izo up and down. He smiled approvingly. "Need a lift, cutie pie?"

"Hilarious," said Izo. Stepping into the elevator with Deneus, he gestured at the wall of nothing. "How does this thing work?"

"Need the right equipment," said Senator Lrasa. He pointed at his temple. "Lucky for you, I've got everything you need and more."

"Lrasa, don't you dare shut that door!" said Senator Mortaco. Having finally reached the floor, he was jogging over.

Lrasa peered at Deneus mildly. "See...now I have to shut the door."

Deneus nodded in complete understanding.

The door slowly began to close. Senator Mortaco, still half a room away, yelled in exasperation. Deneus cheered inwardly. It was going to work! They were going to make it out. But as the door went to fully close, a guard stuck his paw in just in time to stop it. The door reversed trajectories and began opening.

Izo glared at the guard. "Perro malo."

Senator Mortaco thanked the guard and stepped onto the elevator. The doors shut. Together, the four of them slowly started down the club.

"Why were you trying to escape?" Senator Lrasa asked Izo.

"He wasn't trying to escape. We're changing venues. Right?" Senator Mortaco said to Izo.

"Izo, do not feel it necessary to speak to either of these men," Deneus said loudly. Nodding, Izo stared at the front wall and didn't respond.

Senator Lrasa eyed Izo, then Senator Mortaco, curiously. He turned to the Avarian. "It was the seventh floor, wasn't it? It's creepy. I tried to tell him that, but he wouldn't listen. He never listens to me. He's always creeping out Avarians and making them leave."

"It's not creepy," said Senator Mortaco.

"It's a little creepy, ese," said Izo.

Senator Lrasa pointed at Izo. "Straight from an Avarian himself."

"He doesn't count. He's got something against sex," said Senator Mortaco.

"I don't have anything against sex," insisted Izo. "I like sex."

"Oh really?" Senator Lrasa and Mortaco responded simultaneously and with matching wolfish expressions.

Izo turned to Deneus. He gave a begrudging frown. "That's on me. I walked right into that one."

Beside them, both Senators bubbled with mischievous energy. Deneus stared in amazement. Gone was the terrifying colossus that only moments ago had been commanding the whole room with hardly a gesture. In his place was a giggling, puckish child. *Of course!* Deneus realized. Senator Lrasa and Mort had gone to school together. Individually, they were the next two heir-apparents for the entire Malforian Empire. Together and alone, they were nothing but goofy schoolboys.

Deneus had an idea. "Gentlemen," Deneus started slowly. "I believe we were clear before. I cannot allow you to continue harassing my client. Now, while I appreciate you personally escorting us down, I feel it only fair to warn you that my client's people are not in the habit of allowing the interference or mistreatment of any of their Avarian citizens. Furthermore," Deneus added, glaring at the two Senators with wide, disapproving eyes, "this is not a good example for the Empire."

Senator Lrasa quirked up a toothy grin. He leaned back on the nearest wall. "Is he lecturing us, Mort?"

"Ignore him," said Senator Mortaco to Deneus. "Please." Bowing his head and covering his mouth, he made the sign of a deep Malforian apology to Deneus. "I'm sorry. I never meant to offend or harass. Let me make it up to you. Allow me to buy you dinner."

Arriving at the bottom floor, the doors opened to reveal a long hallway and a fresh group of scantily clad Avarians waiting to go up. Seeing the Senators, they cheered and hurried on board. Izo and Deneus quickly wove their way out.

"Wait! Don't go!" Senator Malogue Di'Mortaco called out. But he was forced back by his excited fans. Senator Lrasa, equally confined by this new wave of people, seemed satisfied to forget the escapees.

Hurrying away, Deneus was beginning to recognize the loud, booming music from the main floor coming from the end of the hall. They were almost free.

"How about Tablaeu D'Ciel?" came the Senator's voice from behind them.

Deneus stopped. It was the most expensive restaurant in the tri-galaxies. Its waiting list spanned decades and was beyond exclusive—an impossible venue to secure. Because of this reputation, it was also a metaphor for a ridiculously tempting deal. *You sold your house? Yeah. They offered me dinner at Tablaeu D'Ciel.*

Deneus turned before Izo could answer. "Are you being glib? Or do you really intend to get a reservation?" He wasn't sure if the Senator was being literal or figurative at the moment. Deneus's brain fired faster than he could register. Somehow, he managed to keep his expression flat. "It's the middle of the night."

Waving bye to Senator Lrasa, Senator Mortaco jogged lightly toward them. "I own the place. They'll make room."

So he was being literal. Impressive. Deneus considered the offer carefully. Once free of the club, there would be little worry of being discovered. *Hmm,* thought Deneus. *It might not be a bad idea.* "Since you're inviting us," said Deneus, "I assume you're buying?"

"Of course," said the Senator.

In fairness, they had set out to accomplish something exactly like this. He decided to check in with Izo. "What do you think? Shall we let the Senator entertain us? He might have some career advice for you."

Face flashing interest at this line, the Senator also peered down at the Avarian. "Definitely. I love giving career advice to Avarians."

Izo crossed his arms. He glared at them both. "Mentirosos." After a moment, he rolled his eyes. "Fine. But they better have normal pinche sandwiches at this place."

— CHAPTER TEN —

Tearn

Tearn hadn't taken his eyes off the gold and glass lift since Izo had entered it and disappeared to the lofty heights above. He hated the idea of letting their prized Avarian out of their sight, but what could he do? Only Avarians were being taken to the upper floors. It'd been a surprise that Deneus had snuck in too. The club was working exactly as designed—the more the night waned, the more floating creatures were ushered upstairs. The main floor, so packed and promising at the beginning of the evening, had now been virtually emptied of all Avarians, like an over-fished lake.

Not that Tearn cared about anyone else. All he wanted was Izo to come back. But he never would. It had only taken one day and poof! He was theirs now—the Mountain's. Sure, Deneus would send them a check now and then, and Izo might eventually show up for his ride home. But until then Izo was, literally and figuratively, too far above him to touch. After all, what Avarian in their right mind would ever return to these lowly spaces after having tasted the towering, glamourous life up above?

Yula was off dancing with a group of people, fluffs of fur flying everywhere and having a great time. Even Glongkyle, Tearn pouted, had found a barely-flying Avarian to snipe with and argue the night away, though whether it was romantic or not, Tearn couldn't tell. He would have gladly taken either of their spots, but it seemed no one in the enormous, packed club would talk to him.

No, sadly, the only person he cared about was already gone.

Tearn groaned and picked up his drink. It was a bitter but powerful concoction, a rare spirit that few could appreciate, which was fitting since he'd never felt so lonely in his life. Thinking maybe he was fated to be alone forever, he failed to notice a small cluster of nearby strangers shiver unconsciously before stepping further away.

Tearn tipped his head down onto the table. He was in physical pain. Nothing had ever hurt like this. He'd never be able to find anyone like Izo again. Maybe he was better off just going home. He had enough saved to get a decent place on Ginarsia. Maybe he could finally go back to school to be a therapist?

And then, fresh and sudden as an unexpected rain, there was Izo.

Tearn stood. He moved around the table. "He's back. Yula, Glongkyle—he's back!" Pushing into the crowd, he hurried to meet their Avarian and his new agent.

But Glongkyle beat him there. "Where the hell did you go?" he hissed at Deneus. "We've been stuck down here for two hours, waiting."

Deneus signaled everyone to follow. "We're meeting Senator Malogue Di'Mortaco at the entrance of the club."

Glongkyle blinked. "I must have misheard that. You said we're meeting who at the where?"

Deneus waved them along. "Senator Malogue Di'Mortaco at the entrance of the club."

"We're meeting a Senator?" Tearn asked while following quickly.

Izo nodded. "Yeah. He's sort of an asshole."

"Back up." Glongkyle stopped short. "Why are we meeting a Senator at the entrance of the club?"

"Because he invited us to dinner. And before you ask—no, I don't know why. For some reason, he's very interested in Izo. I haven't figured it out. Either way, I think this could work in our favor as long as...and I really hate to ask this but..." He made a cringing expression at the group. "Are you guys comfortable lying to someone for a while?"

Tearn and Glongkyle froze.

Izo had covered his mouth and was making a strange, wide-eyed expression of amazement. "I think we could probably manage that," he answered for everyone.

"Good. Because I need everyone to basically act like Izo's royalty. Yula." Deneus drew the attention of the inebriated Wuljerian still bopping along to the music. "You're going to be Izo's bodyguard. If Izo's in danger or uncomfortable, you'll come to his rescue. Okay?"

The Wuljerian frowned. "Yula protects Izo."

"Exactly. You got it," said Deneus, impressed.

Shrugging, Yula turned to continue dancing.

"Tearn." Deneus looked at the tiny Ginarsian. "You're the snippy best friend. Everything Izo doesn't like, you don't like. Everything he sneers at, you sneer at. You always back him up. You laugh at all his jokes. As far as you're concerned, he's amazing and magical and no one's ever going to be good enough for him."

Tearn gazed up at Izo with adoration. "Doesn't sound that hard."

"YES! You're secretly in love with him! That's perfect. Use it," said Deneus.

Izo and Tearn looked away from each other awkwardly.

"Glongkyle." Deneus turned to the last member of the group. His face split in a pained expression. "Do you want to meet us back at the hotel?"

Glongkyle brandished both hands angrily. "No! I am pivotal to this team, gods dammit! If it wasn't for me and my ship, none of this—"

"You're the driver! That's great. Stay off to one side, don't talk much, and if anyone says anything to you, be as gruff and abrasive as possible."

"Think you can do that?" said Izo sarcastically.

Glongkyle huffed and didn't answer.

"Izo, you have the most important part." Deneus spun to the last member of their group. "You're the object of desire: the mysterious and aloof beauty. Everything you do adds to your mystique. You are an enigma of bewildering allure and utter unattainability."

Izo frowned. "But I'm also like really tough and street smart too, right? Like, I may be good-looking, but I can secretly handle myself."

"Sure." Deneus spun to everyone. "We got this? Do you understand how this works? We have a really big fish on the line and all we need is a little finesse to reel him in."

"Plus free meal," said Yula.

"Can I get an amen?" said Izo.

"Wait," said Glongkyle, waving his arms angrily. "Does this mean I have to go around kissing Izo's butt all night? Hell no! I'm never going to hear the end of it. This is a stupid idea. I'm out."

"We don't have time for this!" Deneus said. He whirled on Glongkyle angrily. "You realize we've already been defrauding an Imperial Senator for the last twenty minutes after breaking onto his property? Do you have any idea what kind of charges could be brought against us? Izo has no documents. We're not supposed to be here." Shoving a finger in Glongkyle's face, he looked ready to bite the reptile's head off. "If we are doing this, there's no backing out. Do you understand?"

The group hesitated. The agent was right. Tearn and Glongkyle had been kidnapping and extorting Avarians for years, but they'd never run a scam on a high-ranking official before. In a way, Tearn wasn't surprised though. Like everything in life, they were bound to get better at scheming eventually. It had always been dangerous and, sure, the stakes were higher. But wasn't that a good thing?

It was weird. Tearn was so used to ignoring that little voice that said this was wrong, he wasn't entirely sure how to objectively take stock of his choices anymore. In a strange way, the bigger and more terrible their actions, the less any individual choice seemed to matter. But the truth was these were big decisions—enormous decisions, actually, with massive consequences. He knew it because every time he stopped to imagine any of it actually being exposed, a cold spiral of panic filled his chest.

He looked at Glongkyle for reassurance, but their captain's normal brash confidence seemed equally halted.

"What do you think?" Tearn asked Glongkyle. "Dinner with a Senator?"

Glongkyle chewed on one of his claws. Finally, he let out a stilted shrug. "We already used the gas to get here."

Tearn stepped into the Senator's private shuttle and stopped. It was the most amazing vehicle he'd ever seen. With six tan captain chairs near the front and two creamy sectionals near the back, it featured black and gold Virtuvian stone and two touchscreen panels running its full length on either side. A vision of luxury, it looked more like a parlor in a penthouse than one of the fastest small-cabin spacecrafts in the universe.

Glongkyle whistled and moved around Tearn. "Snazzy." He and Yula plunked down into the two captain seats, pointing out and playing with all the dials and controls. "This isn't some bucket of bolts with crystals glued in. This thing is solid." Seeing one knob in particular, Glongkyle's mouth dropped. "This is an SVS?"

"Of course." The Senator dropped into the middle of the nearest sectional. "Why would you fly anything else?"

Because you couldn't afford it, thought Tearn. He glanced at the tall and handsome Senator with quiet disdain. Impossibly rich and famous since birth, he'd probably gotten the best out of life without ever giving it a second thought. He'd never stretched a meal two days between four people or had to figure out which one of three major ship problems could wait the longest to be fixed. He was the type of person whose needs and wants were so utterly guaranteed, he'd missed ever distinguishing them.

Patting the seat nearest himself, the Senator made a summoning noise at Izo.

But their Izo was no docile beauty. Instead, the Avarian ignored this and continued wandering around, taking in the ship's screens and consoles with interest. "Tearn, what's an SVS?"

Tearn smiled. He could already feel his mood brightening as some of his favorite memories from the *Atrox* floated back. Izo, the ever-curious beauty, had spent weeks aboard the ship asking and learning about alien civilization and life as they slowly cataloged Izo's native language.

"It stands for Super Versatile Spacecraft," Tearn explained, stepping closer to the Earthling. "Ships like this can take off or land almost anywhere."

"We could touch down on a lava planet in the middle of hurricane season. You'd never feel a thing." The Senator spread his wide arms out over the back of the chair. "Trust me, there's no place safer than in here."

Izo's sharp eyes shifted to the Senator. "It can go to other planets?"

"Anywhere you want." The Senator kicked off his shoes. "Though, you do have to sit down first."

Izo frowned but relented. Padding over, he chose a corner spot further down from the splayed Senator. Tearn, following, took the seat next to him while Deneus, ever the hovering agent, sat a short distance over from Tearn.

"Could it get to another galaxy?" asked Izo.

Tearn, realizing where Izo was going with this, shared a wary glance with Glongkyle.

The Senator touched his mouth and seemed to think it over. Then, sliding over suddenly, he wrapped Izo under his arm. "You know, I think it could."

Izo bristled and moved to rise, but the Senator held him tight.

"Sorry, gorgeous, but passengers have to stay seated during taking off." The Senator peered down at the Avarian with twinkling amusement. "Wouldn't want you to get hurt."

Izo glared, but, sure enough, a moment later they could feel the rumble of the powerful machine lifting them into the skies.

Glongkyle whistled as the seven-story nightclub dropped away like a drawing falling past the window. "How does it climb like that?" He looked around in amazement. "I didn't even feel it."

"It's the anti-drag absorption. Tiny turbines swirl the cabin to keep your liquid and solid masses balanced during takeoff." He grinned at Izo. "Latest and greatest of Malacorp. Pretty cool, huh?"

Izo pushed the Senator's arm off his shoulder and managed to scoot a few inches away. "How fast could it get to another galaxy?"

"Depends."

"On what?"

The Senator shrugged. "Bunch of stuff: the galaxy's quadrant, the gravity flux nearby..." He grinned and poked Izo in the cheek. "How good its passengers are in bed."

Izo cleared his throat loudly while shooting a savage glare at Deneus.

The Senator laughed. "Something wrong?"

"No," Izo said in a testy voice, but he pushed into Tearn as he continued to scoot further and further away, exciting Tearn beyond words. "I just don't usually talk to strangers about sex."

"Why not?" asked the Senator. "The best sex is with strangers."

Izo, satisfied with his new spot, sighed and put his hands in his lap. "I suppose that's one opinion."

"Opinion? It's a universal fact. What, you think it's better when both parties have known each other? Why? Because of some deep, metaphysical connection? Because you've discovered all each other's likes and dislikes?" Stretching an arm out, he wiggled his fingers over Izo's shoulder. "All each other's secret tingly places?"

Izo knocked the Senator away. "Hands off, burro."

Senator Mortaco gave Izo a sympathetic frown. "Don't be silly. Most species have roughly the same tingly places. It doesn't take years to figure out. Just a little honest bravery."

Izo started to respond, but the Senator held up a hand. "Don't get me wrong. It's adorable that you still think a relationship is important. Admirable even. But the truth is, going to town on someone you just met?" He breathed in as if reveling the idea. "Pretty much the most fun you can have in life."

Izo's lip curled. Tearn could feel that disgust pouring off the Earthling like rusted molasses. But he was in character. He didn't respond.

"You don't believe me? I'll prove it." The Senator laughed, sitting up. "It's dirty. It's exhilarating. Best of all, it costs nothing. All the time and effort we spend designing diversions and amusements—how many people wouldn't trade it all for the chance to be with a beautiful stranger?" He shrugged. "It's no one's fault. It's a carnal impulse, a natural function of biology. Your own brain was hardwired to reward you for doing it." He tilted his head at Izo. "No point in fighting nature, beautiful."

Tearn's jaw clenched. The dark, rich politician hovered over their pure Avarian like a dusk-to-evening shadow. The Ginarsian wanted nothing more than to hop off his seat and kick the man in the shin.

The Senator had leaned one cheek onto his fist. He was still waiting for Izo's response.

"That's a weirdly convincing monologue," said Tearn.

"You're too kind," said the Senator without taking his eyes of Izo.

"Do you use it often?" said Tearn.

Tearn was gratified to see Izo tip back with laughter. "It's neta! You're right. He probably says this stuff to Avarians all the time. Damn, ese. You almost had me going for a second!"

A look of confusion flashed over Malogue Di'Mortaco's face. "I'm sorry?"

Reaching over Izo, Tearn patted the larger man on the leg. "Good hustle."

Izo clapped his hands and laughed even harder. "I forgot about 'Good hustle!'"

"'Good hustle?'" the Senator repeated, confused. Tearn laughed. He already knew how his automatic translator was confusing him with the literal meaning of the sport's metaphor. How did he know? Because Tearn had got the meaning of the phrase wrong the first time through.

Tearn waved it off. "It's an inside joke."

The Senator shot an angry look at Tearn. "Maybe you could elaborate?"

Tearn broke into an impish smile at Izo. "How should I explain it?"

"It's a phrase for when someone's playing a game and loses," Izo said.

Tearn nodded, remembering back fondly. Bored for weeks on the *Atrox Killboard*, the two of them had spent countless hours inventing silly games and distractions in Izo's tiny, locked cabin, shooting dried vegetables into a bucket or spitting water at cups. They'd come up with all sorts of dumb competitions to play while stuck in zero gravity.

Tearn, naturally, had lost by droves. Afterward, Izo would always tell him the same thing: "Good hustle." When he originally translated it, he'd only put it down as "running quickly" because Izo hadn't understood he needed to explain its metaphorical meanings too. It was only later during their games that he'd figured out its normal context and use. He'd liked the meaning of the phrase so much he'd started using it whenever Izo tried to convince Tearn to help him escape: "No can do, kid. But good hustle."

Toward the end of the trip, when it was time to edit and compile Izo's language, Tearn had decided on a whim not to add the second meaning. Why? Because it was their inside joke.

"It basically means 'Nice try,'" finished Tearn.

"Try? You think this is me trying?" It was the Senator's turn to laugh now. "You poor, sweet thing. This is me taking my time."

Izo's laughter died away. "Do you mind doing it a little further over, vato? This pobretón can still smell how you were killing time upstairs."

"You want me to move over? Fine," said the Senator. "But I need a favor from you."

Izo crossed his arms. "What is it?"

The Senator smiled and twisted around to face a walled panel above and behind them. Magically, it popped open.

Inside was a cascading collection of some of the finest spirits in the universe waiting patiently in static chill. And then, with zero prompting, a Dfritian liqueur suddenly pulled away from the group and moved forward to the front with two glittering cups.

Grasping and filling the cups, the Senator handed one to Izo. "Don't make me drink alone?"

Izo took the cup and smiled. "Wouldn't dream of it." He handed it to Tearn.

"Oh. Thank you." Tearn brought the cup to his nose. It smelled of honeyed flowers. He couldn't help frowning with an impressed look. Dfritian liqueurs, after all, were powerful, bitter intoxicants that took several decades, sometimes centuries, to fully smooth out and mellow. This one had been carefully aged to a sweet and delectable perfection. He lifted a brow at Izo. "This is quality stuff."

"¿Verdad?" asked Izo. He turned and called out to Glongkyle and Yula at the other end of the shuttle. "You guys want some?"

"We getting drinks?" asked Glongkyle, hopping up.

"Drinks are good," agreed Yula, getting up as well.

Izo grinned and turned back to the Senator as the others gathered. "You heard them. Drinks for everyone."

The Senator laughed, his gun-metal eyes twinkling with delight. "You're a little troublemaker, huh?"

Izo held up his hand. "Five more, please."

And the Senator obliged. But it didn't make Tearn any less nervous.

— CHAPTER ELEVEN —

Mort

I hope this is okay," Mort said to Izo as he led their group inside the Tablaeu D'Ciel. "It's probably one of the nicest places on the Mountain," *and, hence, the universe.* "But we can go somewhere else if you want."

Stepping out into the lush, open restaurant, the group looked around in amazement. Between its cloud-grazing location, wall-to-wall windows, and understated interior elegance, there was something unspeakably magical about the monochrome space. Decked in white-columned walls, tables, and leather chairs—occupied by the usual crowd of guests—it sported as decoration only two large sculptures trimmed with blue jewels on either side of the restaurant, both situated on opposite balconies.

"Oh, I get it." Izo nodded as Mort led them to a private room reserved for VIPs near the back. "It's supposed to look like heaven, right?"

"I don't know about this heaven place, but I can assure you this is a completely original design." Mort shrugged. "But back to what I wanted to talk about: this weird issue you have with sex."

Izo sighed. "Mi problema isn't with sex. It's who sex is with."

Mort turned to walk backward in front of the youth, trying to catch his eye, but the Avarian was being obstinate and refusing to meet Mort's gaze. It was cute. "Hey," he said, snapping his fingers. "Short and angry—"

"Yes, tall and rapey?"

Mort smiled as he continued walking backward. "That was good. That was quick."

The Avarian looked away.

Mort stopped short. The Avarian, who hadn't been watching, ran into him. Mort grunted with delight. It seemed there was a tight little frame hiding under all those loose-fitting clothes. He grabbed Izo's wrist and held it high. "You know what I think? I think this is all an act."

Behind them, the Avarian's ward and watcher, Deneus, cleared his throat loudly.

Mort turned to face him. "Yes?"

The Malforian gave him a withering look of disapproval. "If you could kindly unhand my client, I would deeply appreciate it."

Mort licked his lips. Trapped in his grasp, the tiny creature with gorgeous green eyes yanked his arm to pull himself free. His attempts were marked distinctly by an Avarian's full strength, flying powers firing at their best. But it was no use. The youth could have lifted and spun them around the room half a dozen times. All he'd accomplish was breaking his own wrist and maybe some furniture. Mort still wouldn't let go.

The Avarian paused to glare up at him with more fire and fury than Mort had ever seen. "Knock it off."

Mort stepped in closer. He could smell the sweat coming off the Avarian, though whether it was from fear, effort, or both, he couldn't say. He broke into a mild grin. "What are you going to do about it?"

A sound like rolling thunder issued across the room. The Senator glimpsed back. Behind him, the Wuljerian made a growling noise with no attempt to conceal her hatred. Mort sized her up. She was an enormous being. Even among her species, she probably stood half a head taller than most. Her body was covered in an almost impenetrable layer of shaggy hair. A Malforian's razor-sharp teeth would have difficulty finding a way through. And attached to her massive paws and jaws were her own set of cutting utensils. Though far blunter and less sophisticated than a Malforian's, the damage they could inflict was nonetheless worth noting.

All around them, the other inhabitants of the private room seemed to be holding their breath. He couldn't help surveying each stunned expression in turn. He could almost taste the tension. Beneath his skin, his muscles trembled and begged for an excuse to attack. It had been ages since he'd felt anything like this. Here was a real, tangible scramble for power. Something he could sink his teeth into...maybe even literally.

It was almost too good to be true.

He turned to peer down at the Avarian. "Ask me nicely like a good Avarian, and I'll let you go."

The Avarian's eyes flashed. "Yula, if he doesn't let go in three seconds, rip his throat out."

Yula's growl kicked into a lower octave. Mort, still staring down, smiled. The Wuljerian took a step toward them. Then another one...

"Yula," hissed the reptile behind them.

Yula stopped and tore her gaze away from the Senator. She stared at Glongkyle, intensely pale eyes wide with confusion. "Yula protect Izo?"

Glongkyle advanced. "Izo can protect himself," he said with unhurried concern. As he passed the struggling couple, he flashed the Avarian a mean look. "Can't you?"

"Yeah," the Earthling replied quickly. At first, Mort was confused by the driver's nonchalant attitude. But when Izo glanced up at the Senator, his brow knit with concern, Mort decided he didn't care. There was a mystery far more pressing flashing behind those gorgeous green eyes. Everyone else in the group slowly followed the driver, first the bodyguard, and then best friend. Only the Avarian and the two Malforians remained.

"Are we going to stand here all night?" asked Deneus.

Mort held Izo's wrist a few more seconds. He was waiting for something, though he didn't know what. But as the moment stretched out, it suddenly happened—Izo's expression broke. Like a mirror losing anything to reflect, his face dropped, his volition fell away, and he blossomed into a perfect picture of resignation and stillness. It was a vision of abject beauty unlike anything the Senator had ever witnessed. He suddenly looked more like a piece of art than a person.

Mort let go.

Izo yanked his hand back. "Do that again and I'll break your nose."

The Senator nodded, understanding the reaction completely. "Of course."

Izo narrowed his eyes. He was still hanging onto his hurt wrist, but his gaze blazed with renewed fire. He jabbed a finger at the larger male. "Just watch yourself, cabrón."

Mort tilted his head. Was he serious? If so, Mort had never seen anything half so headstrong or endearing. The need to save face was strong with this one, a fact that Mort respected and, if he was honest, only made the youth that much more likable. He examined the Avarian through a cloud of fresh adoration. Finally, he waved an apology, and even bowed his head to show sincerity. "You're right. Forgive me."

Izo huffed and went to the other end of the table to take his seat. Deneus seemed to be holding in the urge to say something more. Instead, he resigned himself to silently following his client to the other end of the table, eyes never leaving the Senator.

Mort whipped out a chair and sat back, satisfied to simply watch the spirited Avarian gather his guardian and short best friend in a lopsided attempt at protection. He could see the three of them talking quietly. He could have analyzed their mouths to see what they were saying, but didn't. It was more fun to let them try to strategize.

He instead peered with disapproval at the Avarian's other two companions—the bodyguards. Ever-vigilant professionals, they were competing over who could lean further out over the private room's balcony. The Wuljerian, easily the longer and likely winner of the two, seemed strangely timid around the height. Mort smiled. They'd be easy enough to get rid of, if it came to that.

Mort shifted his gaze back to Izo to partake in his favorite new pastime—running a digital scan on the Avarian's mysterious features.

There was a gentle, automated rush as his augmented brain circuits broke the youth's lovely face down into triangles. This information he translated to an easy algorithm, adding genetic variations and natural anomalies, before passing it all to the major databases. In a moment, the search would return its results and he'd have his answer as easily as spelling out a word in his head.

A real-life mystery. Was there anything more intriguing? For a man like Senator Malogue Di'Mortaco, all untried things were delightfully rare. He'd been everywhere worth being, seen everything worth seeing, owned everything worth owning. His was a life of perpetual blessings and boredom. Nothing excited him; he hadn't felt his pulse quicken in years.

His internal device notified him it had his search results. He opened them.

Searching Error: Match Unknown.

Senator Malogue Di'Mortaco sighed with longing. Was there ever a more beautiful combination of words? And in an instant, he was caught up in a surge of love. Not for the Avarian—for the universe. After all, it was the cosmos themselves that continued dropping new discoveries at his feet like shiny, far-flung diamonds.

Mort rose and stretched his back. He wanted to play more with the new mystery in his life. He wanted to poke it until it gave him another perfect green-eyed glare. The Senator liked the way Izo glared.

He stood and strolled around the table. "Mind if I join?"

"Please," answered Deneus, gesturing at the empty seat on the other side of himself. "We were just discussing Izo's new career plans for the city. Maybe you could give him some ideas?"

Mort wanted to cover his mouth. It was so adorable. Watching them plot and scheme was just about the cutest thing he'd ever seen, most especially because they were terrible at it. Mort held in his reaction and gestured at the Ginarsian's seat. "Sure, let me sit down first."

"Tearn's already there," the youth answered stiffly.

"Tearn can move." And grabbing Tearn's chair, he jerked it back a few inches. To help.

The change in the trio's expressions was priceless, and none more so than the hot-headed beauty's. The offense, apparently, was beyond all words. Mort couldn't help letting out a cheeky grin. The whole scenario had him feeling like a colossus. Pushing little people around—better than therapy.

But then it occurred to him that the Ginarsian wasn't moving. Bald, big-headed, and small enough to toss overhand, Tearn was holding his ground like a fiercely loyal pet.

Mort frowned. He waved Tearn up. "Move."

"Tearn's fine where he is," said Izo.

"How can he be fine? He's in my seat." Looking down at Tearn, he let his smile drop. "And my city."

"You could play him for it," suggested Deneus out of nowhere.

Mort shot him an offended look. "Excuse me?"

But Deneus didn't seem worried. Leaning back and crossing his arms, he gave Mort an easy Malforian shrug. "It's a friendly disagreement. Settle it with a friendly competition."

Mort, now making his own disgusted noise, started to say how far below him and ridiculous the mere idea was—an Imperial Senator, one of the main levers of power within what was arguably the single most influential planet in the universe, reducing himself to compete with some no-name Ginarsian too stupid to know when he was in clear danger.

But before he could, the Avarian let out a slicing trickle of laughter. "I don't know, Deneus. The Senator seems a little scared to me."

Mort chuckled lightly. Internally, he was thundering.

"All right, does everyone have their slips in the bowl?" asked Deneus.

"Yes!" cheered Yula.

"Good. Now let me explain the rules one more time...Glongkyle!" snapped Deneus. "Pay attention."

"Sorry." Glongkyle sat back. Mort suspected the Strungian had been trying to figure out what metals the dessert trays were made of.

Deneus rolled his eyes and held the bowl higher. "Glongkyle, Yula, and I have written eight different words from eight different languages onto these pieces of paper. Now the two of you"—He pointed at Tearn and the Senator.—"will take turns choosing them at random to identify the language. Every language correctly identified earns one point. There are no passes or steals. The person with the most points at the end—"

"Gets to take Izo home and defile him," Mort crowed.

"Sí, but only after surviving a very long fall," added Izo with a pinched smile. Arms crossed, he was sulking low in his chair. He didn't seem to be enjoying himself.

The Senator grinned and shot the Avarian a slow and purposeful kiss. The youth exhaled hotly and looked elsewhere. It was adorable. "Enough stalling." Mort grabbed the bowl and shoved it toward Tearn. "Let's play."

Tearn awkwardly caught the bowl. Then, grabbing a slip of paper, the Ginarsian opened it. "Cristavolos," he said, holding it up for everyone to see.

"That is correct," confirmed Deneus.

Snatching his own piece of paper, Mort shook it open. Though the auditory translators everyone wore didn't translate print, his embedded device made the game a cake walk. Not that he needed his device for this particular language. He'd seen enough nasty messages from Ari carved into his shuttles and outside his office door to have it memorized forever. "Aurelian."

"Correct," said Deneus.

Tearn grabbed the next one. "Wuljerian," he said.

"This is also," Yula cried happily.

Mort rolled his eyes and snatched up the next one. The group was kind of cheating, taking advantage of the fact they were clearly familiar with each other's languages. But Mort could kind of cheat too. Running a quick search in his head, he pulled up the answer immediately. "Strungian."

"Correct," confirmed Deneus.

Tearn unfolded and held up the next one. "Anolitun."

"Also correct," said Deneus.

Damn, Mort thought to himself as he grabbed another. The little shit actually knew his languages. But then, looking down, he grinned. "Strungian. Again."

"What?" Tearn looked around in confusion. "That's not allowed."

"Not my fault," Mortaco said nodding at Deneus. "We told them to pay attention."

Deneus frowned and seemed to think it over. "We'll count it as half a point. Agreed?"

Mort shrugged. "Fine."

Tearn gulped. Reaching into the bowl, the Ginarsian vacillated between the last two slips of paper before ultimately grabbing the one on the right. But as he opened to read it, all the blood drained out of his face. "Um..." Tearn started weakly. "The handwriting is a little tough to read..."

"Tick-tock," said Mort.

Sighing, Tearn tossed the paper down. "I don't know."

Mortaco glanced over at it to run a quick search. "It's Utslectian."

"He's correct," Deneus said with a deeply disappointed look at Tearn.

"You'd think he'd remember the language of the Southern Chancellor's people," said Mort to Deneus.

Tearn grabbed his face and hunched over in his seat.

Mort opened the last slip of paper and rolled his eyes. "Ginarsian." Then, balling it up, he dropped it into Tearn's drink. Mort stood to make a show of stretching, pausing to flex his arms and shoulders a few times. "And now, I take my prize."

"You didn't win," said Izo.

Mort gave the youth a sympathetic frown. "Yes, I did. Your boyfriend lost fair and square, so now it's time to hush." He held a finger to his lips. "Trophies don't talk, beautiful."

"Deneus said the person with the most points wins. Not the most half points. You had three and a half. Tearn had three. You tied."

Mort squinted. "You round up."

"Deneus never said to round up," said Izo. "You can't make up rules whenever it suits you."

"Sweetheart, I'm a Senator." He held his hands out. "That's literally my job."

"It's not your job here," Deneus said. Rising, he turned to Tearn and the Senator. "We'll settle this with sudden death. One final round; one final language. We'll choose one word—something obscure—and the first one to identify it wins. Agreed?"

"Okay, but who picks the last language?" Tearn said. His voice was strained and nervous.

Mort shrugged. His embedded device could find anything. "Doesn't matter to me."

Deneus nodded. "Izo, would you like to choose?"

"Me? I don't—" But something seemed to occur to the youth. He uncrossed his arms and sat up. "Sure. What do I do?"

"Write down one word from any language on this piece of paper," Deneus said holding up a sheet. "Then, once they're ready, you'll show it to them at the same time. The first one to name it wins." Deneus turned to Mort and Tearn. "Make sense?"

Mort beetled his brow. Something weird was happening, though he wasn't sure what. Then it hit him. Of course! The Avarian was from an uncharted planet and Tearn was his personal linguist. They'd share some secret language that would be impossible to search. Mort chuckled, impressed. He surveyed the Avarian youth. He was proving to be quite the wily target.

Mort sat back in his seat mildly. He needed to think about how to play his next move. "All right," he finally agreed, with a nod. "But if I'm going to agree with this, I want something in return." He turned at Izo. "Win or lose, you have to get drinks with me."

"Sure," Izo said, holding up his cup. "We can order them right now."

"Not here. Somewhere else. And with no one else around." He jerked his head toward Yula. "In other words, you leave the entourage at home."

Izo's expression stiffened. "I don't think..."

"Deal," said Glongkyle. "But if we win, you have to use your connections to get Izo a professional contract with the Imperial racing team."

Mort blinked. He turned to the reptile. "I have to do what?" He spun back to the Avarian. "You want to join the Imperial racing team?"

Izo shrugged. "Sure."

Mort grabbed his chin. He was now positive there was something fishy going on. Even so, he had to admit it was an interesting wager. "And you'd swear to hold up your end?" he asked Izo. "Win or lose, you'll have drinks with me alone?"

The Avarian rolled his eyes. "Fine."

"I don't think it's a good idea." Tearn cut in. "It's just a game!" Laughing, his bulbous face was a mask of confusion and fear.

Mort narrowed his eyes. Whatever was going on, the Ginarsian wasn't in on it. That sealed it for him. Mort stood to face Deneus directly. "I get to choose the venue and meeting time for drinks," said Mort.

"And we get final approval of the racing contract," said Deneus.

Mort nodded and reached for a tooth. "Deal?"

Deneus nodded and reached for his own. "Deal." And then, following Malforian tradition, they each twisted out a tooth and handed it to the other.

The Avarian yelled and jumped out of his seat.

"What?" Mort searched the room in confusion. His device hadn't alerted him to any sudden movements or noises. In fact, there was nothing out of the ordinary anywhere around. He gazed back to the ashen-stricken Avarian. "What happened?"

But Izo was too busy staring at the razor-sharp barb in Mort's hand. "What the psycho-crap was that?"

"It's how they make verbal agreements," Tearn explained to Izo. "It's like making a pinky promise on Earth."

"By ripping out their teeth!?"

"What's wrong?" Mort flashed his bleeding gum at the Avarian. "You don't find that attractive?"

The youth covered his mouth. For a moment, it looked like he might actually vomit in front of everyone. But he eventually managed to swallow it back down. "Ugh. Holy shit, we better win this thing."

"Izo, calm down. It's fine," Deneus said, shoving Mort's tooth into his pocket. "We're almost done. Come over here and write your word."

Groaning loudly, the exotic beauty floated up. He seemed suddenly exhausted, his features taking on a quiet, noble quality. Mort's heart almost broke. He seemed like the type of Avarian that would probably look brave no matter what he went through or saw. "Can I have the pen?"

"Sure." Deneus handed it to Izo. "Do you want a piece of paper?"

"No, I got it." The Avarian instead took the pen and wrote directly into his palm. Then padding over, he stood in front of the Senator and Ginarsian. "Ready?"

"On the count of three," said Deneus. "One... Two... Three."

The Avarian showed them his palm.

Mort looked at the scrawled string of symbols and started a search.

Searching Error: Match Unknown.

He started an advanced search. But a few seconds later the result came back the same. He frowned at how long this was taking. Grabbing Izo's hand, he compiled and loaded each symbol separately. Still the search came back empty. He grunted and shook his head. "You got anything?"

Tearn didn't answer. Glancing over, Mort chanced a second to see what was holding him up. But Tearn didn't look stuck. In fact, he didn't seem like he was in any rush at all.

Staring at Izo, lower lip trembling, Tearn's face was radiating awe. Then, with a slow but purposeful motion, the Ginarsian reached out to gently pry Izo's hand out of the Senator's.

"I know the answer," said Tearn. "That's English for 'blue.'"

Izo smiled. "Correct."

— CHAPTER TWELVE —

Mort

Mort was excited and agitated at losing the competition for his exotic guest. True, he felt a little ridiculous, being eager and jealous over some Avarian. He was a Senator. He ate governments for breakfast and burped up their better holdings by lunch. He didn't lose unless it was on purpose, and when it was on purpose, he didn't get jealous. And yet there was something wonderfully alive and freewheeling about being near the fiery new beauty in his life. Mort could almost remember what it felt like to be young and desperate again—the struggle, the excitement, the arousal. Infuriating as it might be, there was a part of him that reveled in the thrill.

Izo was perfect. No, that wasn't it. The mysterious draw of the green-eyed youth lay in some other quality.

Mort shut his eyes and pictured his latest obsession. Wan and golden, emerald fires darting up in sharp suspicion. When his gaze locked on the Senator, steady and guarded, Mort could feel his pulse soar. Why? What was it about that expression that made Mort want to run his fingers down every inch of the Avarian's untouched body?

Ah, he realized. *It's because I know I'm not supposed to.*

That was sort of silly, wasn't it? Mort enacted hundreds of illicit policies every day: extortion and bribery; political self-dealing; more genocidal and planet destroying enactments than he could ever count. It was strange, the strength of this particular obsession. It had been years since he'd felt anything more than casual lust for anyone.

Running his hands over his jaw, Mortaco smiled at the young, untamed Avarian. It was true: Mort loved the thrill of the chase. Oftentimes more than what he caught. But he was beginning to doubt if this particular dark-haired lovely was playing hard to get. No, this Avarian was different and far rarer—he really was hard to pin down.

Mort pushed back his chair, grasped his drink, and stood. He sauntered over to the other side of the room. Green eyes froze and followed him, wary as any smaller animal in the wild watching the movements of a larger, sharp-toothed beast.

Mort smiled and stepped out of the room and onto the hanging balcony outside, a churning mist of steam rising to trap warm air within its marbled enclave. He took a long gulp of his automatically warmed drink before setting it on the balustrade next to his waist.

He looked out over the capital. His capital. And by extension, his universe. Mort was a good ruler, though many would shy away from associating his title with the term. He didn't, though. Senators were rulers—literally the people that made the rules. The only higher position was Emperor, the person who made rules through solitary might rather than influence and fear-based loyalty, and Mort had people working to get him there. They had been almost since before he was born.

The truth was, Mort decided while leaning over the balustrade, he was a good leader because he was good at figuring out what people wanted. It wasn't hard. Most people wanted money. A few wanted power. Even fewer wanted a legacy. If worse came to worst, everyone wanted their lives. But occasionally you'd meet a wonderfully rare and sweet creature who wanted nothing more in life than the chance to make something of themselves.

Mort lifted his cup and grinned before draining it. It always amused him that they weren't more specific. Though, then again, this one seemed to have his heart set on something incredibly specific...

He still remembered his first time flipping that dance theater on Salsutor. A wonderful bevy of talented and bankrupt Avarians, the performers had proven delightfully bendy and amenable to their fabulously wealthy visitor. He found himself ensnared, extending a three-day work trip ravenously week after week. His father (the gods rest him) had screamed for an explanation. When Mort tried to explain, the old man, wise beyond words, gave him the best piece of advice Mort had ever heard.

"So buy it! Get it out of your system and come home. But I swear to the gods, Mort," he'd said, his voice dropping deadly low, "you better not lose money on it."

Mort took his advice and a few months later the theater was re-opened as a VIP opera house. Available only to a select clientele of loyal and well-rewarded patrons, its profits were breathtaking.

Mort stretched his back. He looked over the city with boredom. It'd been a long time since he'd felt that way about anything— driven, obsessed, a Malforian on fire. He wondered what it would take to win the dark-haired beauty. He pulled at his Bgulvrian' suit. The youth hadn't glanced at its tell-tale insignia once. Mort looked over his shoulder. He was beginning to wonder what it would take to impress this one...and whether it was worth it.

But then in his mind's eye, he could already see it: this new Avarian standing in his room, tempting and challenging him with those eyes.

Mort ran his fingers down the inseam of his jacket. No, it would be worth it. He had an instinct for these things. It was like that blind Avarian sculptor he'd been with a few years back. He had first been wary of the attraction, unsure how a dalliance with an artist—and a blind one, no less—would fulfill anything. But it was a revelation, an Avarian with hands unlike anything he'd ever felt. He did his part—took her in, sheltered her, financed her next ten projects while loving her to his heart's content. Her premiere collection, which he helped promote and position, had sold at several thousand times its original listing. Wealthy and independent now, she still came over to relive the old days and give him first choice from her latest. Good for her. Good for him.

Mort bent down to buff out a smudge on his Driseldian reptile-skinned shoes. Was it his fault every Avarian life he touched turned to gold? And more to the point, wasn't it his obligation to touch as many lives as possible?

Other people created masterpieces from their hands or bodies. Mort's masterpieces came from his intuition and fortune. He discovered unmapped treasures, enjoyed these fresh gems for a moment, then tossed them out toward meteoric rises. It was his gift and his curse—whatever managed to catch his eye, money was soon to follow it.

Ari was his best example of this. Though he'd never admit it out loud, Ari was the single best investment Mort had ever made. Handpicked from that horribly dull Aurelian palace, the musical prodigy had been fifteen when he brought her back to IA. Since then, she'd made enough money to buy her whole planet several hundred times over.

Not that she saw much of that money. Sure, she'd tried to renegotiate her contract, doing favors for board votes, and even marrying one for a while. But Mort always found a way to get her back. Their most recent confrontation had been nasty, one of the ugliest legal battles of his life, in fact. But he subdued her in the end thanks to her mother and was unlikely to see rebellion from her again.

It was good because he needed Ari. She'd proven herself more useful and cunning than he ever had predicted. She leveraged all her perfect beauty, massive fame, and sharp mind to whatever problem she was faced with. The results stunned even Mort sometimes. Ari had proved herself dedicated and truly impressive—a perfect Avarian mate. Not that he was considering a commitment or anything. No, even perfect Ari, when you came down to it, was just another pretty blonde from Aurelia. And there were thousands of those.

Sadly, it took someone like Mort to appreciate how cheap even perfection was at the highest levels. Any laser could cut a perfect diamond; any computer could create an ideal piece of art. Perfection nowadays was like bright colors two thousand years ago: reproducible en masse and, therefore, essentially worthless. True distinction no longer lay in perfection, but in what perfection had previously represented: rarity.

And herein lay his true curse—the never-ending search for the truly rare. It was why he'd never settled down, moving endlessly between hundreds of Avarians during their white-hot prime. But nothing had felt permanent. There would always be another younger, brighter star debuting within a few months. No matter how sharp the obsession or how taut the urge, it always faded like a green light disappearing into a fog.

Mortaco turned to press his back against the balustrade, putting the city behind him to peer into the walled window at his newest fixation. He stared a long time, and it took him a moment to realize he could almost see himself in the window's reflection. Tall, handsome, and intelligent, he was a Malforian of impeccable family lineage and staggering wealth. He was certainly rare. Was it even possible to find an equal match? No, probably not. But there was plenty of fun to be had in failing.

Like the dark-haired youth inside. He could distract Mort for a while. And what more could you really ask from an Avarian? They were finite beings, burning today and snuffed out tomorrow. There was no penultimate discovery. No infinitely rare and irreplaceable gem. It was a romantic fallacy designed to confuse and anguish Malforians younger and more naive than him. He was old enough to realize now every star eventually fades.

Still, he thought to himself, gaze training slowly down this mysterious new one, *there's no harm in looking.*

"Senator, I was wondering if I could steal you?"

Mort clicked his tongue in annoyance. His drink was empty, and his would-be-date's uptight ward had followed him outside. Mort wasn't in the mood for a chat. "Do I get to steal someone else in return?"

Deneus gave him a tight smile. "This is what I wanted to discuss." He pointed to a more private corner of the balcony, away from the walled windows.

Mort moved to follow. "They going to be all right without supervision?" He gave a backward glance at the group. They were currently encouraging Izo to drop small rips of bread into their mouths as he bounced above them. The ground was littered with failed attempts. At least Mort'd get some amusement when the staff saw the mess later.

"I apologize for their uncouth behavior. Izo can be very trying with his choice of companions. For the life of me, I can barely imagine a more random or spirited bunch of hooligans. Nevertheless—they seem to make him happy."

"It's a fun group," Mort agreed. They stopped near the balcony's balustrade. "They go on misadventures together, stir up trouble, and flaunt the rules. I get it."

"You are too kind. It seems Izo is all too aware that he will soon be losing much of his freedom. As a married Avarian on his planet, certain things will be expected of him. I'm sure he's trying to soak in everything before that happens."

"Tragic. I can certainly understand his want to fit in as much fun as possible while there's time." The Senator broke into a smirk. "I'd be more than happy to help him fit in a little more."

Deneus fixed him with an indecipherable stare. "It seems we have arrived neatly at the topic of discussion."

"Let me stop you right there. You've got nothing to worry about, okay? I'm not looking for anything long term." He patted Deneus twice on the chest, hard enough to make thumping noises. "His planet will get him back in one piece, I promise."

"A most generous promise, to be sure." Deneus brushed off his chest. "But no, I'm afraid that wasn't the concern. Rather, while I'm sure Izo is undoubtedly interested in making friends of your caliber, the type of friendship I fear you're hoping to establish over drinks may be impossible."

"What? You mean intimacy?"

"I do."

Mort waved a dismissive hand. "Sex was a given. Look at him. Look at me."

"Your looks are immaterial. I was hired to protect him." Deneus's expression, already stony, took on a sharper intimation.

Mort gave the ward a dubious look. "So you took him to a private Avarian club?"

"While I admit," Deneus said, faltering, "the young master has sought new experiences while pursuing his proprietary goal, this trip was meant to function within certain unbreakable boundaries."

"Why was he so cozy with that Psegre kid?"

"That was a professional networking opportunity—"

"That ended in two guys throwing punches? Bull. Admit it: he came here to have fun. You're just trying to slow him down."

Deneus let out a long sigh. He looked back toward his ward, squinting. Then, lowering his voice, he moved closer to the Senator. "There may have been a third goal in this trip."

Mort lifted a brow. "Such as?"

"Giving Izo time to explore other...long-term romantic options."

Mort frowned. He'd assumed Izo had hired Deneus. "Who exactly do you work for?"

"I'm not at liberty to say. The truth is...there are those who've been unimpressed with the young master's prospects. Coming to IA was meant to give him time to find better ones." He shrugged. "Young Mr. Psegre, for example."

"Psegre?" Mort propped back against the barrier and laughed. "He's a baby. A nobody."

"Forgive me, Senator. But Sheost had a number of excellent qualities. He's from a good family, extremely ambitious, kind..."

"Lazy. Broke. A loser," Mort ticked off on his fingers. He smirked. "He got any other stellar qualities you want to brag about?"

Deneus stared with a blank expression. "He's one of the few Malforians on IA with good character."

The Senator's nostrils flared. "Including the wisdom not to insult his betters."

"I meant no offense," said Deneus. "I feel it only fair to explain in the plainest terms that while I have permission to encourage Izo's exploration of romantic feelings, he is strictly forbidden from acting on them."

"Naturally, but things happen." Mort smiled. "Especially over drinks."

Deneus sighed heavily. "I am afraid my entire purpose here is to make sure things do not happen. Especially over drinks."

"It's not really up to you though, is it?" He pointed to Izo. "That's a cosmic piece of naturally occurring art. You can't shield him forever."

Deneus started to argue but was cut off.

"And why would you want to?" asked Mort. "Art from nature isn't like paintings or sculptures. You can't hoard it in museums and protect it for decades. His beauty is pressing and urgent. Every moment he isn't being appreciated is another moment stolen forever."

Deneus had broken into an expression of flat disapproval. "A fascinating treatise, but entirely beside the point."

"You can reject my logic, but you can't reject the universe's. All beautiful Avarians have predetermined destinies. I'm just helping him fight the clock."

"One: I would kindly ask the Senator not to confuse his opinions with the universe's. And two," Deneus continued, "Izo's fate isn't like most Avarian's."

"Why? What makes him so special?" Mort crossed his arms and waited.

Izo's guardian looked taken aback for a moment, but he soon seemed to regain his wits. "He's engaged."

Mort tipped his head back to chuckle. "I've known Avarians that were engaged seven or eight times and still never married. Got anything else?"

"Yes," Deneus continued. "He's a virgin."

Mort shrugged. "So was everyone at one time."

"Last—he's extremely rare," said Deneus.

Mort sneered in disbelief. But as Deneus's expression held, unwavering and deadly serious, the Senator suddenly remembered the error messages from earlier that night. His embedded device couldn't place the Avarian, even equipped with infinite databanks and algorithms capable of sitting through all the universe's known information in a matter of nanoseconds.

Was it possible? After all this time, had he finally stumbled onto something one-of-a-kind?

He yanked his gaze to the mysterious Avarian. Izo was floating, drunk and laughing, as unworried and self-assured a creature as Mort had ever seen. Too self-assured. So self-assured, Mort realized with fresh eyes, that he'd been blowing off an Imperial Senator all night.

It took Mort a moment to realize how long he'd been staring. He sucked in a breath and turned sharply to Deneus. "How rare?"

The guardian shrugged. He flicked a hand at the exotic beauty with a gesture of perfect apathy. "Have you ever seen anything like him?"

— CHAPTER THIRTEEN —

Deneus

I f you'd asked him why he did it, Deneus wouldn't have been able to tell you. Sure, he could have defended it. After all, technically some of it was true. None of it could be disproven (as far as he knew). And, most importantly, it's what he needed to say to close this deal. But if you'd asked him why in that specific moment he'd decided to lie directly into the face of the most powerful person he'd ever met, he couldn't have told you. The truth was it had popped out before he'd realized he was thinking it. Like so many other elements of his work, saying what he needed to was almost muscle memory by now.

"Can't believe a Ginarsian stole my date. Now I need to find another one," the Senator declared merrily, leading their thoroughly drunken group back into the shuttle. Ever since his private discussion with Deneus, Malogue Di Mortaco had transformed into the most gracious host. He fell over himself entertaining the group and fawned over Izo's every whim. He'd even made up with Tearn.

"Tearn, you're short, but you've got game. I respect that." Throwing his hand up, the Senator gave Tearn a pat as they climbed into their seats.

Tearn beamed at Izo. "Hear that? I have game."

Izo stifled a smile as he took his seat between them. "Of course you do."

Nodding, Tearn waited for Izo to sit before patting the Avarian's knee.

The Senator threw Deneus a sidelong glance. "Are these two going to be able to keep their hands off each other? Maybe we should give them some privacy."

"Stop it," Izo deadpanned as Tearn giggled maniacally beside him.

"Don't be embarrassed," said the Senator. "I understand how couples are when they get urges. It's healthy to let these feelings out." The Senator pouted when Izo didn't respond. "You're telling me at your age, you never do anything risqué?"

Izo rolled his jaw. "As far as this conversation is concerned, no."

"I don't believe it. You're a sexual magnet, much as some might want to deny it." He shot a meaningful glance at Deneus. "Besides, I know you're lying. You probably do stuff like that all the time."

Izo laughed. "Dude, you have no idea what you're talking about."

"Oh yeah? What about your fiancé? You've never done anything with them?"

"Hanako's your fiancé?" Tearn interrupted, sobering up on the spot.

Izo's eyes went wide. He glanced at Deneus and the agent clenched his lips. He prayed the Avarian would be smart enough to go along. He internally kicked himself for forgetting to mention it to the poor surprised, creature. *Reminder to self,* he thought silently, *update the kid on his new backstory.*

"...Didn't I tell you?" the Avarian finally said, facing Tearn gently.

"I knew how much she meant to you, but—" Tearn's shoulders fell. "Izo, why wouldn't you tell me that you were getting married?"

"It never seemed like the right time?" said Izo.

"Enough about him. Back to the subject," the Senator insisted, drawing the Avarian's attention to himself again. "You're telling me you haven't had one single sexual experience with anyone but this person...?"

"Hanako," Tearn offered sadly.

Izo clenched his eyes. He seemed to be in physical pain for the moment. "Hanako and I haven't done anything like that either. So there, can we drop this?"

Deneus was doing happy backflips in his head. He could have kissed the little Avarian for his defensive answer.

"So, what I'm hearing," said the Senator, "is you need someone to show you how." The Avarian bristled, but Mort beamed. He was clearly reveling in every second of this. He put his arm around Izo's shoulders. "I'd be happy to guide you through a couple of things."

"Pass," said Izo.

"Honestly," said Tearn, lifting both arms hotly. "It wouldn't kill you to try a thing or two."

Izo's mouth fell open as far as it would go. "Tearn!"

"What? Izo, you're nineteen. As long as I've known you, you've never been with anyone. And I know you've never been with another Avarian. It's ridiculous!"

Izo shook his head, angrier than Deneus had ever seen him. "Tearn, this really isn't the time."

But Mort had his chin on his hand. He looked like he had never beheld anything so adorable. Deneus, watching the Senator's rapt expression, was seeing nothing but dollar signs.

"See? Even the short guy's on my side. It's time to loosen up. Enough! We're taking care of this tonight." The Senator hit the back wall to get the driver's attention. "Take us to a nightclub!"

"Which one, sir?" came back the driver's voice over the intercom.

"Doesn't matter," said Mortaco.

Around them they could feel a swell and dip as outside the buildings swooped around and they started heading in the opposite direction.

Izo gulped. "Where are we going?"

"Where do you think?" said the Senator. He was flashing a toothy grin. "To find you some Avarians to play with."

"By the gods, by the gods!" Came the high-pitched voice from the street. "It's him!"

Deneus sat up straighter and straighter as Avarians rushed to the shuttle's door. Senator Mortaco had instructed the driver to park a few feet off the ground outside the random club and pop the back door open. Then, swinging his head out, he'd gathered a flock of beautiful Avarians within moments. *I should have brought more business cards,* thought Deneus in amazement.

Floating into each other, the Avarians fought to get closer. Mortaco reached out to shake a few hands. "Hi, it's nice to meet you. I'm Senator Di'Mortaco."

"We know!" squealed an Aurelian in front. They were a beautiful Avarian with all the telltale marks of the famously inter-sexual species—gleaming white hair, beautiful bronze skin, and giant gilded eyes so large they looked like pools filled with gold.

"Aren't you sweet? What's your name?" the Senator asked.

"Meoimi."

"Wonderful," said Mort. He leaned his head playfully against the shuttle's door. "So tell me, Meoimi—what're you doing tonight?"

Glancing into the shuttle, Meoimi smiled demurely. "Nothing yet."

"You want to come hang out with me and my friends?"

"I'd love to!"

"Then come on in, beautiful!" The Senator laughed and turned to the others, counting. "How many here we got without dates? Four?" He turned back to the Avarians outside. "Got room for three more."

A volley of squeals answered him. He laughed and looked through the throng, pointing at his picks. "All right, let's get another Aurelian, the cute Nertian with the green shirt." He looked back. "Any requests?"

"You got any Anolituns in the group?" Glongkyle asked.

"You want fries with that?" Izo murmured miserably.

But the Senator ignored him. He searched through the crowd. "Any Anolituns?"

"On my father's side," said one slender creature with cropped blue hair and skin a soft shade of purple.

"Close enough!" Taking the last Avarian's hand, Mort ushered his final guest into the shuttle. Behind him, the door shut as the crowd outside let out deflated whines of disappointment.

But inside, the mood had risen sharply. Their guests, proud hand-selected beauties they were, huddled together and flirtatiously examined everyone in the shuttle.

Mort came up behind the Avarians to sweep them under his arms. He pointed at Izo with one finger. "I've got half a million dollars to whoever can pop this one's cherry first."

The other Avarians giggled at the exotic brunette with interest.

Izo stood. "¿Mande? That's not funny."

"It wasn't a joke," said the Senator.

"I'm starting to get real sick of your shit, chingadito." Izo whipped toward his agent. "Deneus, isn't it time we called it a night?"

Deneus frowned but wondered if maybe he wasn't right. Izo and the Senator weren't exactly getting along. They'd had an understanding in place. It was better to end things early. "My client has a point, Senator," said Deneus. "It is growing rather late. Maybe we should get drinks another time."

The Senator looked at him in amazement. "I just pulled a flock of Avarians out of thin air. Now it's time to party."

"No," said Izo. "Now it's time to take me home."

Mort dropped his arms, seeming to be at a loss. "Wait...I got it! I know how to impress you." He flopped down next to the incensed youth. "You like music?"

"No," said Izo.

"Yes, you do. And I got just the person." Eyes going blank, he seemed to be sending out a message with his internal device. "There! Now chill out. No one's going anywhere. The night's just beginning. Honey, can you go sit with him?" he asked the beautiful Aurelian still waiting next to him while pointing at Deneus.

The gorgeous creature nodded and floated up. With long curly hair and a tiny blue dress, the Aurelian alighted near to Deneus with a shy smile. "Hi," the Avarian said, extending a delicate hand before sitting. "Meoimi."

Deneus sighed and accepted the greeting while making room. "Deneus. Nice to meet you." Then he turned back to their host. "Senator, if you could please ask your driver to set down anywhere, we can find our own way back."

But the Senator was too busy dispersing Avarians around the rest of the shuttle. Within seconds he'd paired everyone except Tearn with a new companion. Encouraging the newly formed couples to get comfortable, he clapped his hands. "What do you guys think about a party on a yacht?"

Deneus immediately went to refuse. A private yacht was a terrible idea—with the ability to take them anywhere and keep them away from solid ground for weeks, it was the last place Deneus wanted to go with the Senator. He started to speak up but was drowned out by joyous sounds of the new couples and guests. Rolling his eyes, the agent glanced at Izo with concern. He wasn't sure how leaving the Avarian trapped with his suitor in an even more remote location might pan out.

"I've never been on a private yacht before," said Meoimi. Leaning forward, they cut off Deneus's view of Senator Mortaco. "Sounds fun, right?"

"I'm sure, but I'm afraid that's not the point." Deneus tried to shift in his seat so his line of vision went around the Aurelian.

But they moved and blocked him again. "Know what else I've never done?" Placing a hand on his thigh, the Aurelian locked their golden eyes onto his in a stunning beam of intent. "Been with a Malforian."

Deneus's eyebrows shot up. For a moment, he found he had no words. He could also feel a stupid look forming on his face. He was powerless to stop either.

"Is that so?" He finally managed to spit out. Clearing his throat, he sat up straighter. "That's funny. I've actually never been with an Aurelian."

The Aurelian's mouth curled wickedly.

— CHAPTER FOURTEEN —

Ari

It would probably surprise many to learn that famous pop star Ari Lumiere had been incredibly lonely as a child. She grew up in a palace, after all, the only daughter of Lyunia Lumiere. Yes, THAT Lyunia Lumiere—famous celebrated actress, defining beauty of her generation, and cultural icon worlds over. Her mother was the star of countless blockbusters and instant classics long before she gave birth to Ari or even met Ari's father. Prince Apollan, the youngest prince of Aurelia and ninth in line for the throne, could barely catch a headline before meeting her. Not that it mattered afterward. With Lyunia Lumiere on his arm, there would never again be any doubt who the luckiest and most famous prince in Aurelia was.

The pair met during a private performance for the royal family— Ari's mother on stage and her father thunderstruck in the front row with his innumerable siblings and sleepy uncles. The two were soon caught in a whirlwind romance, one that captured the attention of nearly everyone in the tri-galaxies. Their wedding a year later was a fairytale event, and their child, born Avarian like her mother, had grabbed the curiosity of even distant IA.

Ari liked to remind her mother (when they were on speaking terms) that Ari's face had always been worth more: the profits from Ari's first baby pictures alone made more money than her mother's first three movies. Not that you would've known, the way her parents fought over money. It always confused Ari. Hello? They lived in a palace.

It was a beautiful place, a penthouse hung high in a lofty tower. But with her father's time split between them and the royal family, he was seldom home. Most of the time it was just Ari and her mom...and their giant staff of servants. Chefs, maids, launderers, cleaners, drivers, guards—these were the people Ari played with as a child. Her teachers—virtuosos of singing, dancing, musical instruments, and conversation—were all too serious and busy to play.

It was sad. She held three diplomas and four degrees from the Academy of Royal Arts, yet she'd never stepped foot in the place. Ari took her lessons at home, like any royal child. Always in classes of one, she progressed quickly, a prodigy of music and language by age twelve.

But there was a deeper wellspring of talent hiding within her, waiting for a chance.

The chance came suddenly one afternoon. She was sitting at home, practicing another in a long line of exhibition dances that would never be seen, when a gardener happened by. Rather than interrupt, he encouraged her to continue, assuring her that neither the music nor her dancing would disturb him. So she had. But he'd obviously lied, because when she'd finished, she'd found him stuck to the ground, absolutely transfixed.

The next day, she gathered all the servants, sat them in the backyard, and gave her first live performance to an audience. Their reaction was revelatory.

Decades later, she'd played to countless sold-out cities and massive super-arenas so large they'd been carved into hollowed-out moons. They all faded together, but the memory of that first afternoon in her backyard burned just as bright and warm as the day it happened. She could still see and smell it—the scent of budding Aurelian Flitz blossoms, the light teal and purple color of the sky, the look of each audience member's face as they followed her every movement. Lastly, and most wonderfully of all, the sound of astonished silence as she finished, followed by an explosion of roaring applause. It was the single most wonderful moment of Ari's life...right up until she spotted her mother in the back, quaking with anger.

It was funny. Ari's mother was known for her smile. Whether it was a simple greeting, an offered hand, or the world's corniest joke, Ari's mother could always be counted on to break out into her famously picture-perfect beam of approval. In fact, Ari was pretty sure she was the only person in the world that *couldn't* make her mother smile.

"You are royalty! You don't perform for commoners."

"But you should have seen it, Momma. They loved me!"

"Of course they loved it," she spat. "Who wouldn't love watching you debase yourself?"

But the shine of that spotlight had persisted, and despite her mother's cruelest efforts, Ari discovered something about herself that day. Regardless, there was nothing she could do to convince her mother it wasn't some perverse rebellion. She was royalty. She wasn't supposed to need attention. No, what Ari needed was structure. Her mother's will had come down on her like an angry god's.

Her mother ended her dancing classes and doubled her singing, instrument, and social lessons. Lyunia had been too lenient on the child. She wasn't going to let her only daughter slip back into a tawdry profession. It would dirty everything she'd elevated them to. Ari's schedule transformed into a brutally unforgiving regimen. Every hour was carefully planned, save the five or six allotted for sleep. Even her recreational breaks were scheduled with mini-lessons on style and home decoration. Lyunia Lumiere was going to make her daughter a perfect Aurelian princess, no matter what.

She was also going to make sure Ari remained intact. With trained guards posted at every hour, she made sure Ari's every living moment was supervised.

The problem with this plan should have been obvious. Ari lost her virginity to a guard. A gentle, young, and handsome Aurelian, he was the first person to ever profess love for her. When they made love for the first time, it was tender and sweet, exactly like she knew it was supposed to be.

How her mother had found out, she'd never know.

"But Momma—he's in love with me!"

"Of course he's in love with you. You were an Aurelian Princess who WAS a virgin. But now you're just another dumb Av. Ari, how could you? To let a guard have his way with you!" Her mother fell on the couch and cried. "You're ruined. You've ruined everything now."

Two months later when Mort had shown up, she'd been happy to go.

Not that she was necessarily happy as she went with him now.

Ari Lumiere crossed her arms and tried not to go to sleep. She was propped against the Malacorp cruise liner. It was her fourth event of the night: she'd already had dinner with a CEO and attended two parties with junior Senators. She was bone tired. If she were honest, all she wanted to do was go to bed, but that's not what intergalactic pop stars on IA did over the weekend. Intergalactic pop stars were fun and glamorous and excited to screw the night away.

Ari grunted. She hadn't realized she'd shut her eyes until she'd nearly fallen over. *Ugh*, she thought, yawning loudly. *Why me?*

Ari pushed off the hull and decided to check the time on her wearable device. A gift from Mort, it was a custom Purtruvian bracelet. A prototype, it wasn't supposed to be available for another two years. But that was Mort for you. No matter how rare, how impossible, how utterly unthinkable his passing wishes, he always found a way to make it happen. The man couldn't hear the word "no." Assuming you were next to him, you never had to hear it either.

Though you might occasionally hear "Sorry I'm half an hour late to something I demanded you jump to attend," she thought while staring at the time.

Ari peered around the empty slip. Her shoulders slumped. *Why am I always waiting on him?* Ari clicked the device on her wrist angrily and set a timer to call a private shuttle to pick her up in ten minutes. She didn't care if Mort got angry. If he couldn't bother arriving on time or at least messaging her to explain himself, then Ari had better things to do. She was Ari Lumiere, goddammit. She didn't have to put up with this shit.

But then Ari could feel her curls drooping. A vision of Mort annoyed with her flashed in front of her eyes. She turned off the timer. She decided instead to kill some time by checking her face.

Flicking open the mirrored hologram, she examined the full 360-degree view of her visage. Golden curls falling in effortlessly bouncy waves; skin dewy fresh from her forehead to her lower back; cheeks and brow contoured to a laser accuracy; eyes smoldering; mouth a perfect gold. Ari pursed her lips and grinned. *Hot as a blue sun,* she thought to herself, clicking off her device.

Ari stood up straight and slapped on her best celebrity smile. This was going to be fun. She looked great. She felt great. She'd be damned if she wasn't ready to have the best night of her life.

Ari lifted her device and sent Mort another message: "Hey handsome, where are you? I'm getting lonely all alone."

Behind her, the elevator to the slip dinged open to reveal Senator Mortaco and, as usual, a gaggle of businessmen and Avarians in tow. Mort's eyes were distracted, focused on something in his embedded device. "Are you messaging me again?"

"Are you making me wait on you again?" Ari shot back.

Mort led everyone up the private dock. "Couldn't be helped. I had to pick up some more people and then—" He was cut off when the group realized who was standing at the end of the dock.

Nine ear-piercing screams shot out into the night.

A blonde Aurelian with long hair covered their mouth and crumbled to the ground. "No, no, no." Behind them, three other Avarians burst into equally inconsolable tears, fanning or grabbing each other to keep from crying more.

A short but extremely well-dressed Ginarsian kept repeating that he couldn't believe it, he just couldn't believe it. As his eyes welled with tears, the reptilian beside him, also in a fairly nice suit, saw Ari and took off running in the opposite direction.

"Must stop," moaned a giant Wuljerian, whose face was buried in her fuzzy hands.

The only other Malforian in the group, a serious and somewhat thin man, looked like he was fighting to keep it together. Pushing a shaky fist over his mouth, he managed to let out only a single, shaking sob.

Ari played with her hair and beamed in embarrassment. What could she say? Crowds loved her. Flying up, she tilted toward them. "Hello, my beautiful people! How are we doing tonight?"

"Ari, I love you!!" the blonde Aurelian screamed in a broken sob from the floor.

"I love you too!" said Ari. Landing next to them, she pulled the poor inconsolable creature into a hug. The other Avarians fell at her knees and waist too, glomming onto her like children to a fairy godmother.

She laughed and wiped away the other Aurelian's tears. "What's your name?"

"Meoimi," they cried.

Ari nodded, registering the gender-neutral name. "Why are you crying, honey?"

"I want to be just like you. I'm a singer. I came to IA to sing. But it's been really hard because no one thinks I'm Avarian or feminine enough."

A pang of sympathy hit her for a fellow Aurelian facing this type of prejudice. A naturally intersexual species, over half of all Aurelians were gender neutral. But it didn't matter how much this made perfect biological sense—other planets continued to treat non-binary Aurelians like misfits all across the universe. "I'm sorry, honey. That has to be hard."

"It is. But after meeting you, I promise I will NEVER GIVE UP!" With tears smearing down their face, the Aurelian tipped their head back to sob anew.

"Ari, I've been to six of your concerts," said a Nertian wearing green, hugging her waist. "I've seen all your movies. I bought all your albums. You're so amazing. You're...you're..." Breaking down, the poor Nertian sunk her face into her arms. "You're everything!"

"Aren't you all sweet?" said Ari.

From the back of the pack, the reptile suddenly broke out. Barreling over the Avarians, he barely managed to avoid kicking one of them in the face. "That's bullshit. Tearn and I are your biggest fans, Ari!"

The reptilian snatched the little singer by the shoulders and lifted her up in the air. For one horrifying moment, Ari had a distinct fear he was trying to kidnap her. Then Ari was able to float high and get herself free. "Of course. And you are...?"

"Glongkyle. And that's Tearn," the reptilian said, pointing at his shorter friend. "We've been following you since the beginning. We pooled our money and bought your first album together. I played it until my older brother broke it. He said you were lame, but he's a butthole. I secretly bought a second copy, and I've been listening to it—"

"I am Yula!" the Wuljerian interrupted to grab and shake Ari's hand. "You are singer! Voice like sun."

"Aww," Ari said, genuinely touched.

"I loved you in that one movie, the one that won the award for—" said Tearn.

"I'd never dreamed I'd meet her in person," moaned Meoimi from the ground.

"Is hair touched?" asked Yula.

"And your posters?" Glongkyle whistled. "Boy did I go through a lot of those—"

"ENOUGH!" said Mortaco. Pushing through the group, he picked Ari up by the waist to sling the tiny singer over his shoulder. "This is *my* date. Understand? So everyone else back off." And, carrying Ari the rest of the way up the entryway, he popped open a side hatch and led them all inside a lush black and white entry area flanked by a small floating fountain.

"Thanks," Ari whispered.

"No problem," Mort whispered back before setting her down.

"Now Ari," he said shaking his finger at her once the others had followed them on board. "I have to warn you about a certain snake in the grass. He may seem sweet, but he's an Avarian thief. He steals Avarians, Ari!"

"How horrible!" Ari gasped, picking up on their game. She flitted up and spun around to eye the guests. "And which one of these handsome monsters is the pilfering fiend?" Seeing the reptilian, who looked unmistakably nervous, Ari put her hands on her hips. "Is it this one?"

"No! See? He's already tricked you!" Whipping around, Mort pointed directly at someone behind Ari with a dramatic gesture.

"Oh no!" Ari turned to gasp at the Ginarsian behind her.

He looked at his friends with a terrified expression. "ME?!"

Then, much to the delight of everyone in the room, Ari flew up and swung overhead, scrutinizing him from every angle with adorable intensity. Finally, she paused in front of the little Ginarsian, crossed her arms, and touched one toe to the ground.

"Hmmm…" She considered him while bending low. "Now you listen here, slick. I'm not falling for any of your smooth-talking, you hear me? So you just keep it in your pants until I tell you otherwise."

The Ginarsian sputtered and nodded in agreement. He seemed nervous, but Ari was used to people stumbling over themselves around her. It was kind of sweet, actually. Ari gave him a wink. Then she floated up and turned to the dark-haired Avarian next to her target. He seemed to be eyeing Ari curiously…possibly out of pre-registered jealousy?

"Hi," she said simply, giving him nothing to work with. "How's it going?"

The other Avarian sucked in a breath. "¡Órale!" He snapped his fingers and pointed. "She's the singer from the fountain, right?"

Ari's smile withered. He couldn't be serious. There was no way. Of all her achievements—box office features, record-smashing tours, intergalactically adored albums, and hundreds of hits so chart-topping and undying she dominated entire decades of music...he remembered her as *the singer from the fountain?!*

Ari landed on the ship with an echoing thud. She'd never been so summarily dismissed in all her life. Just who the hell did he think he was? Hate emanated from her every pore. She walked over to glare directly into his stupid, ugly, jealous face. "Don't you pretend like you don't know who I am."

The other Avarian gazed at her in confusion. "I'm sorry?"

"I'm famous in places you've never even heard of. My least profitable album earns more than your whole planet every year. I could take a poop in your mouth and make you worth twice as much."

"Jeeesus, lady." The other Avarian backed up sharply. "You kiss your mother with that mouth?"

"I am so sorry. Please ignore him," the Ginarsian said, jumping in between them. "Izo's not from around here. I promise he didn't mean any offense." The Ginarsian glared at his date. "Did you, Izo?"

Izo looked over the Aurelian pop star with a look of disgust. "I didn't when I said it. Not so sure anymore."

"By the gods," said Ari. "Why don't you grow up and stop being so petty?"

"Why don't you eat my culo?" spat Izo.

"Whoa!" Mort appeared from behind them. "That's not how we make friends." Grabbing Ari around the waist again, he lifted and carried her off, the others trailing behind like children after candy.

Ari shot the brunette one last hate-filled glare before turning around in Mort's hands. "What the hell was that?"

"I don't know. They're kind of a weird couple."

"Let me guess—you've been trying to pry them apart to no avail. So naturally, you summon your resident pop star, because why would she have anything better to do. Right?"

Mort grinned at her. "Do you have anything better to do tomorrow?"

Ari sighed and set an elbow on Mort's shoulder. She tussled his silvery strands under her hand. She always liked messing with his hair. It reminded her of their early days. They'd spent entire evenings and mornings lounging together: nothing but the two of them, naked, and the view of the mountains in the distance. Those were some of her most cherished memories—the most powerful man in the universe with his head in her lap, lulling off to sleep as she stroked his hair and hummed him a sleepy song. Sure, they'd had their ups and downs. But he'd saved her. "Nothing I can't move for you," she said.

He kissed her on the cheek. "You're the best, Ari."

"Oh, I know." She looked around. "So where are we going?"

"I thought—quit it." Mort ducked his head from where she was still ruffling his hair. "I thought we could take the ship up and orbit for a bit. Soak in the stars." Mort glanced at her nervously. "That's romantic, right?"

"Sure," Ari agreed. "Don't forget, you have a meeting with the Southern Chancellors tomorrow."

Mort hissed, but then he shrugged. "I'll bump it. It'll give them a chance to see the sights."

Ari frowned deeply. The Southern Chancellors weren't exactly known for their patience. "Mort...are you going to get us stuck in a war again?"

"Nooo," the most powerful leader of the most powerful political party in the known universe responded defensively. "And besides—even if I did, I'm sure fifteen minutes with you would get us right back out of it."

"That's true," Ari said. Thinking back, she'd had a hand in soothing tensions between countless military powers. Counting just a few close calls over the last few years, Ari couldn't help tilting her head at the number. "Wow. I should be making more money."

Mort scowled. "You make plenty of money."

"No. YOU make plenty of money. I make some. I could be making more."

Mort gave her a sad frown. "Why is everything about money with you? Don't you love me for me anymore?"

"Of course," Ari agreed, hugging and kissing him on the temple. "But if I'm going to keep us out of war, I'm going to need more than your love, handsome."

"You know what? Screw it. I'll just buy stock in munitions." Giving her a long, sweet kiss, he finally set her down. They'd reached the ship's central lift. "Okay, everyone inside!" Mort said turning to the group. "We're going to the sky deck."

The group cheered and followed as the door popped open. Glancing back at her target, Ari couldn't help notice the Ginarsian still padding next to the rude Avarian from before. Ari huffed and decided to bide her time for now.

The elevator shot up, quickly passing the ship's ten stories to reach the sky deck on the top floor. It was a large, delightful space, filled with lush foliage and covered in a thick, transparent dome that gave the impression you were standing outside and taking in the heavens above, an especially impressive sight when the ship reached mid-orbit. On one side a thick grassy field rose and fell in gentle hills and pools. This area was interrupted only by a lush promenade and crisscrossing ribbons of crystal blue streams.

On the other side, a beautiful wooded area stood with trees curtaining private alcoves where all sorts of naughty things happened. Sprinkled among both were various statuary, fountains, flora, and flirty lounge areas....along with several other brazen surprises for the more adventuresome guests.

Mort gestured proudly while leading them in. "Sit anywhere. We've got drinks over here," he said, nodding to a massive bar in the nearest corner. "Pools are over there." He pointed beyond the top of the largest hill. "A very naughty forest." He gestured at the trees. "And best of all"—He pointed with both hands behind him.—"thirty separate penthouse suites, stocked and ready to go."

The group immediately began spreading out in pairs, giggling with excited anticipation. Ari, however, decided to hang back with her patron, watching and waiting for the Ginarsian and dark-haired Avarian to settle into a spot.

"You wanted me to go after the Ginarsian." She said, thinking back. "Tearn, right?"

"Sharp as always," Mort said, turning on a liquor fountain.

Ari narrowed her eyes. Tearn was laughing at something the brunette had said. The two plunked down together on a long couch. "What's with them anyway?"

Mort scoffed. "Don't get me started. All I know is they've been inseparable all night."

"Got it. Don't worry—Ari's on it."

Mort shot her a knowing grin while offering her two freshly filled cups of alcohol. "They never stood a chance."

Ari smiled, grabbed the cups from him, and went straight for the couple. "Hey, cutie. Buy you a drink?"

The rich Ginarsian in the hand-tailored Bgulvrian suit looked around in confusion. "Which one of us are you talking to?"

"You, silly!" said Ari. Sitting next to the pair, she handed one of the cups to Tearn. "You didn't think I was going to let you get away that easy, did you?"

"Did I...? Did you...?" The Ginarsian fumbled.

"What do you think of the drink?" Ari interrupted. She was used to carrying conversations when people were too stunned to speak with her. "It's pretty good, don't you think?"

Looking into the cup, the Ginarsian lifted and drank half of it with a motion like a spazzy robot. "Yes!" he answered, lowering the cup. "Excellent!"

"It's a Driseldian wine. Beautiful planet. Have you ever been? The sunsets in the eastern capitals are absolutely divine. They're the kind of sunsets that make you hot and horny, make you want to have sleep with every stranger you lay eyes on." She took an innocent sip of her drink. "You ever get that kind of feeling?"

"To sleep with every stranger I can find?" the other Avarian echoed with a disgusted look. "Not really."

Ari glared. "You should try to be less boring then. People will like you more."

"I think there's only one reason people like you, and it's between your legs," said the other Avarian with a smirk.

"Um, Izo..." Tearn yanked Izo's shoulder down to whisper something in his ear.

Izo's mouth dropped as he heard what Tearn was whispering. "Aurelians have WHAT?!"

Ari scrunched her nose at him before crossing her legs. "Anyway, I was talking to Tearn. Not you."

The Ginarsian's head swiveled slowly. "You know my name?"

"Of course. I remember all the well-dressed, interesting people I meet." Giggling, she threw her head back in a way that she knew showed the delicious line of her slender neck. Then she locked her golden eyes onto the Ginarsian, sultry intensity turned all the way up. "But you never answered me: have you ever been to Drisedlia before, Tearn?"

"Uhh... yeah, actually!" answered the nervous Ginarsian. "We've picked up some merchandise there before."

"No kidding?" the brunette asked from the other side. "Tell me neta, what kind of merchandise you pick up there, Tearn?"

"The profitable kind," said the Ginarsian.

The other Avarian narrowed his eyes. "This did not answer my question."

"Excuse me. I'm trying to talk to someone," said Tearn. "Do you mind?"

"Putting together another shipment?"

"No," Tearn answered, "but I am considering how to get rid of my last one."

"Not before it kicks your ass, hijo de la chingada."

Ari twirled a curl around her finger. She zoned out, not paying attention, nodding and smiling at anything Tearn said and hawkishly glaring at anything the Avarian brought up. This was her least favorite part of her nights: standing by as the other Avarian squabbled with their partner. Half the time she'd get lucky and the other Avarian would be so angry, they'd just get up and leave. At that point, she was nearly done—a quick stumble to the nearest room...and boom. Her night was free again.

If she could, she'd honestly have skipped the whole thing. "It's nothing personal," she'd wanted to tell those miffed Avarians. "I'm going to do them a favor. Then they're going to go do Mort a favor. It's nothing to get angry over, I promise." It was only the ugliness beforehand that made it so awkward. And why did they always feel the need to do it in front of her? It was none of her business. These things happened. Ari had personally witnessed over a hundred divorces and who knew how many broken engagements because of fights like this. What was the point? Jealousy was such a boring look for rich people.

"Oh my gosh!" Ari interrupted, thinking of a way to speed this up. "I think I left something in my room." She turned to the Ginarsian. "Tearn, can you help me look for it?"

"Sure. What did you lose?" asked the Ginarsian.

Ari laughed. "I thought empaths could read people's thoughts." She touched his shoulder. "Can't you read my mind, handsome?"

"That's not actually how it works," said Tearn. "Ginarsians can sense and guide neuro-chemical levels, but we can't..."

Ari was bored again. "What about hormone levels?" she interrupted. "Can you sense tension between two people?"

"Hmm...kind of. Hormone levels aren't as easy to pinpoint. There are a number of different biological systems in play and—"

Ari reached out and put her hand on Tearn's thigh—extremely high on his thigh. Tearn and the other Avarian looked down at the hand, confusion clear and apparent on their faces.

"Oye, Tearn," said the other Avarian. "I think she's hitting on you." He chuckled so hard he tipped back in his seat. "That suit was definitely worth the money, bro!"

Ari paused and was thrown off her game for a moment. Was he... rooting for his date? But that didn't make any sense. He was losing. She was winning. "It's sad that you think everything's so superficial, honey. Truth is, I just find Ginarsians fascinating." Turning back to Tearn, she slid her hand even higher. The confusion on his face melted, replaced by pure astonishment. "Take a guess what I'm imagining right now?" Ari waited for some slick, suggestive answer. But the Ginarsian just stared. *By the gods, this is going to take forever,* she thought to herself.

Hopping up, she started to pull on Tearn's arm. "That I want you to come with me!"

The other Avarian suddenly wasn't finding their situation nearly so amusing. "Hey!" he said, grabbing the Ginarsian's other arm. "Tearn's not going anywhere."

Ari laughed, trying to play off the whole thing as silly while also pulling harder. It was to no avail. The brunette wasn't letting go. His expression was serious though strangely more fearful than angry. How badly were these two stuck to each other? "Are you always this controlling?" huffed Ari.

Shaking his other arm to get it free, Tearn seemed to agree with her. "Izo, what the hell? Let go!"

"Do I look estupido? I'm not getting left alone on this psycho's boat." Reeling the Ginarsian in, the other Avarian lifted a leg to pry Ari off with his foot.

Ari let go. Standing back, she put her hands on her hips. She was back to square one, and worse, starting to feel ridiculous. Honestly, didn't this bitch have any sense of decorum for these things? "Why don't we let Tearn decide?"

"I'll tell you what Tearn decides," said Izo. "Tearn decides to not abandon his Avarian friend."

"Nice try...but no. I think what Tearn decides is to make a new Avarian friend." Flicking her eyes at Tearn, she winked. "A limber Avarian friend."

The brunette stared at her in disgust. Then he shook his head, his previous expression replaced with confusion. "Que demente. Aren't you supposed to be famous?"

She scoffed. She crossed her arms. She scoffed again. Then, having no response and not liking how the question made her feel, she snatched the Ginarsian's arm. "Come on, Tearn! We don't have to take this."

"Actually, Tearn has another idea," Tearn chimed in. He lifted a finger. "Why don't we all go together?"

Both Avarians sneered.

"I don't know where he's been," said Ari.

"And you knew where all those strangers in the sunset had been?"

Ari could feel her face warming up. She'd never been so insulted in her life. How dare he! She was Ari Lumiere. She was worth more than some planets. Her number one selling album had...

Ari blew out a breath. She had to center herself. This wasn't a competition. *She was Ari Lumiere.* Being the most attractive Avarian in the room was never a competition for her. She broke into a wicked grin and changed her approach. "Don't get me wrong, I love a little triangle fun as much as the next person," she said, shooting a look at Tearn, who gulped. "And as much as I might enjoy shutting this one up for a while—and I could shut you up, sweetheart. Trust me," she said to the other Avarian.

Izo shook his head. "I don't think so. I'm starting to think you aren't my type either."

"Honey, I'm everybody's type. But I also have a firm 'no boring people in my bed' rule." She looked back at Tearn. "Anyway, it's up to you, handsome. What's it going to be? Good times with Ari? Or more fights with this one?"

She grinned and waited, knowing full well it was over. There was no way the Ginarsian could refuse an offer like that, and anything the other Avarian might say to shame or argue with them would just be further proving her point: that he wasn't as much fun as her.

He seemed to realize this too as a look of resignation drifted over his features. Then, rather than continue their back and forth, he turned to his companion. "Tearn, I don't know how else to say this." He held out a hand. "Don't leave me here alone."

Ari wanted to roll her eyes, but the Ginarsian's shoulders fell. He actually seemed touched.

"You're right," said Tearn. He padded toward Izo and took the other Avarian's hand. "You need me here."

The other Avarian let out a relieved sigh. He smiled.

Ari gaped. She couldn't believe it. She'd lost? After years of prying couples apart with barely more than a smile, she'd failed? Today? After throwing herself...at a *Ginarsian*?

Ari lowered her head. *No,* she decided suddenly. She was Ari-freaking-Lumiere. She would be damned if she were ever going to let another Avarian pull focus from her. Such a possibility did not exist! She was the physical culmination of hotness. She was pure, molten sexiness personified. All sentient attention naturally resided at her feet. No. She was not losing.

She grabbed the Ginarsian, spun him around, and locked eyes with him, imagining with her full mental capacity that she really did have mesmerizing powers in her giant, golden eyes. "You know what I love most about Ginarsians, Tearn?"

"Qué hueva. Give it a rest, would you?" said the other Avarian. Perking up, he seemed to change his mind. "Actually, I want to hear this. Go ahead, blondie." He held out a hand. "What DO you love the most about Ginarsians?"

Ari glared, the precise focus of her intensity—hatred and the need to allure—swirling in her head as she tried to think of something to say. Both members of her audience were kind enough to wait. Problem was, she couldn't think of anything. Sexiest Avarian alive, and she couldn't come up with a single closing line. But how was that fair? She'd never needed one before!

Still...she had to come up with something. She was Ari. There was always another level of sensuality ready to be revealed, always another layer to be removed. But what was supposed to go here? It needed to be something subtle and sexy, mysterious yet unmistakable, tantalizing yet utterly irresistible.

Argh! She thought to herself. Why did it all have to be so damn performative? It's not like she was ever going to see any of these people again. None of this was going to matter in a few days. *And besides*, she wanted to scream, *I just want to go to bed!*

"My favorite thing about Ginarsians," she said, turning to Tearn, "is sleeping with them."

Silence followed. Then the Ginarsian turned to the brunette. "I'm sorry, Izo, but I'm going to go now."

The dark-haired Avarian raised his hands. "I get it, ese."

The Ginarsian nodded, took Ari's hand, and led her toward the penthouses as fast as his little legs could carry him.

Looking back, Ari couldn't help grinning at the other Avarian. His face was still frozen in marked confusion. *Ha!* Ari thought to herself. *That's what you get for competing with Ari Lumiere!*

— CHAPTER FIFTEEN —

Izo

Izo stared at the wide double doors that Tearn and the mean pop singer had disappeared into. He was flabbergasted beyond belief. When his agent approached a few minutes later, Izo was still staring at the door.

"Hey, how's it going?" asked Deneus. "You feeling all right?"

"Eh," Izo answered. He turned to his agent slowly. "Are Ginarsians super sexy to Aurelians for some reason?"

"No," Deneus observed Izo with confusion. "Why would you ask that?"

"¿Estás seguro? Because I think I just saw...No." Izo corrected. "I know I just saw that singer chick hit on Tearn until he gave up and finally went back to her room to sleep with her."

"Don't be ridiculous. You must have misunderstood her."

Izo's eyebrows lifted slowly. "I don't think that's possible."

"Anyway, that's not the reason I came over here. I need to give you a list of updates to your backstory."

This got Izo's attention. "Updates?"

"Just a handful of clever embellishments to help seal this deal. Nothing huge. Pretty basic." Deneus started ticking things off on his fingers. "You're a virgin. You're engaged. Your parents don't approve of your fiancé. You came to IA to break into racing. You think your parents hired me to help you, but secretly they're paying me to find you a better fiancé. You're young and in love, but a better match could steal you away, also...What else?" Deneus banged his fist into his head. "Was there a last one?" He thought hard. Then he shook his head. "Huh. Okay, I guess that's it."

Izo gaped. "¿Qué chingados? When did all this happen? And how am I supposed to remember it?"

"It doesn't matter. Don't answer questions about your past. Mort will be jealous of your fiancé, and you'll be fine. People love a mysterious Avarian. He'll eat it up and you'll be trying out for that team by morning."

"No, that's not the issue." Izo's hands flew around in confusion. Was he insane? Had he stepped into a madhouse? What the hell had happened in the last two hours? "Since when is the plan to make the Senator jealous of my pretend fiancé?"

"It's not!" The agent laughed. "It's just upping the intrigue. It's not a big deal, Izo."

"You keep saying that. Yet every time I turn around, you've got me even deeper in a pit of lies." Izo covered his face. He was seriously considering punching the man.

Deneus gave the Avarian a pat on the shoulder. "It's called marketing, kid. Get used to it."

Izo uncovered his face to stare at the agent. The fact that he thought he was being cute was just about the least cute thing Izo had ever experience in his life. "Whatever. Just don't leave me alone with him."

Deneus's face dropped to a blistering glare. "Izo, I can't babysit you all night. This is what we agreed to: in or lose, the two of you get drinks together. Remember?"

"Yeah, but I never agreed to do it on a boat, or the first night we met. Why do we have to do this right now?" Izo blew out a giant breath of air. He looked to where the looming Malforian was waiting for him across the room. Back pressed up against the bar, he smiled and waved. Izo could feel his insides shriveling. He'd never wanted to do something less in his life. He spun back to the agent. "I don't feel comfortable with this, Deneus."

"We're already here. Izo, you're a full grown Avarian. You can handle this. Plus, this is what you wanted," said the agent. "To get in a room with an interested investor."

"This isn't the sort of interest I was shooting for."

"Who cares? You're in. Please don't complicate this. Remember, I didn't want to do any of this." Deneus pushed a finger at the Earthling. "I wanted you to take pictures and drink at bars for free. You're the one that insisted on this huge, once in a lifetime shot. Guess what? It worked. Congratulations. We're here."

"Okay, but why does it have to be with that guy?" Izo crossed his arms.

"What's the problem? Talk to me." Deneus paused a beat. He seemed to be gently tapping his teeth together, a nervous tic Izo had never noticed before. "Are you worried he's going to hurt you?"

"No," said Izo honestly. "I'm worried about him being a creepy sleezeball all night."

"Yeah...see, I'm not worried about that," said Deneus.

Izo narrowed his eyes.

"Look—do you want to sleep with him?" asked the agent.

"Honestly?" Izo glanced at the big shark-shaped Senator. "I think I'd rather sleep with Tearn, and Tearn's the last person I'd sleep with."

"Great. I don't want you to sleep with him either. No offense, you don't seem like you'd be good in bed, and there's a lot of money on the line here."

Izo stiffened. He wasn't sure if he was offended or not.

"So, what do you do instead? Bob and weave. Giggle and get out. He flirts with you; you laugh and tell him to stop. He touches you." Deneus placed a hand on Izo's shoulder. "You laugh and tell him to stop. He touches you again," Deneus reached for Izo's waist.

"I hurl him through the roof."

Deneus paused. He pointed at Izo sternly. "No. You don't do that."

"Maybe *you* don't do that."

"Izo, what are you worried about? I couldn't have set this up better for our side if I'd tried. There are ten witnesses on this ship. He's a public figure. Nothing's going to happen. You're going to politely turn him down, and it's going to drive him nuts. Tomorrow morning he'll sign whatever we want."

Izo dropped his head back and groaned. "Is there any other way to do this?"

Deneus patted Izo's back. "Don't overthink it."

Izo sighed. "Okay." He felt about as excited as a ghost who'd just got the good news. "Let's get this over with I guess."

"That's the spirit!" Deneus said, rubbing his shoulders and leading them over. But then as they approached, he suddenly pulled Izo back. He stepped in front of the Earthling, back pointed squarely to the Senator. "For the record," he said, his voice going low, "you know how to handle yourself, right?"

Izo lifted an eyebrow.

Izo had grown up in the California foster care system. His mother was killed in a car crash before he could remember. His father was locked up after police caught him chaining his son to a radiator.

"He can fly!" his father had shouted in front of terrified neighbors. Izo could still remember standing in front of his house, confused but relieved, and holding a social worker's hand as his father's hateful gaze was driven off into the night. He was three, and it was the last time he'd ever lay eyes on a biological relative.

Little Izo was taken to Maclaren Hall, a sprawling, ten-acre wide foster institution filled with damaged children and broken government oversight. All he had to his name was a trash bag full of his own clothes and the knowledge that his terrible, unspeakable secret had the power to tear down his entire life.

The place was a cinderblock hell, overcrowded and under-stocked. He grew used to sleeping on the hard floor, saving napkins for use as toilet paper, and hoarding snacks on the roof. The other kids, often emotionally disturbed, were left unsupervised with the younger children for hours on end. The staff, barely supervised themselves, used physical force at almost any provocation.

Little Izo witnessed several things he didn't understand at the time, but there was also plenty he did: children hurled on the ground, slammed into walls, or dragged by their hair by adults twice their size. He absorbed these lessons quickly—the adults weren't saviors. There were no saviors here. He could still remember the surprised look on Tony Saldani's face as he crumbled to the ground, passing out cold, after everyone heard that terrible wet snap. Five-year-old Izo had shaken his head. Sure, if Tony hadn't screamed for help, the big kids might have broken his nose. But it had been the heavy-handed adult hell-bent on breaking up the fight that snapped Tony's arm in two.

Izo spent four months during his first stay. He'd later find out he was never legally allowed to spend more than thirty days. Still, four months wasn't bad. There were kids who spent years running away and getting dragged back. Over his time at Maclaren and beyond, Izo learned enough cruelty and street smarts for seven lives. It wasn't enough to look out for "bad people" and "bad moments." Any good person could turn bad. Any positive moment could turn poisonous. Izo had to be on guard at all times. Nowhere was safe. No one was harmless.

Thinking back (which he seldom did), the others must've been wary of him, too. It was during his various trips to Maclaren Hall that he first honed his skill of jumping clear of sticky situations. The other kids and staff would gossip over his ability to seemingly disappear when you swore you saw him only a second ago. This habit of vanishing, combined with his quick green eyes and silent footsteps, earned him a whispered nickname in Maclaren: *Ninjito.* The little ninja.

Eventually, he was placed in his first foster home. It was a dirty place with seven other kids and fifteen cats. Had he known the word "hoarder" then, he'd have understood a lot more about his situation...although still not why the government deemed it fit to leave him there. Instead, the three-year-old set his bag of clothes on a smelly cot (an improvement from his nights on the floor) and politely helped make a path through the boxes and magazines so his "room" could reach the bathroom.

After a year there he bounced to another foster home, and then another one, never staying anywhere for more than a year and a half. Most were fine—dingy places with too many kids and tired guardians. A few were bad. Really bad. He soon learned how to get free from the bad ones though: run away, get caught sneaking into a movie, go back to Maclaren, wait for a new assignment. Otherwise, he kept his head down, saved his snacks, and repeated the phrase "I don't feel comfortable with that" whenever the adults asked him to talk about his parents.

It was around the age of ten that Izo began running away randomly, from three homes in the span of eight months. His social worker checked for all the usual issues.

"Are they hurting you? Are they not feeding you? Did someone do something to you that you aren't supposed to talk about?"

"No," Izo said honestly.

"Then why are you running away?"

"Just because," said Izo. And it was the truth. The other boys at Maclaren could boast as many as eleven or twelve different foster homes. Izo had only lived in seven. Those were rookie numbers at his age.

The social worker, a wizened and ombre-skinned man, watched him carefully. "You flirting with chaos, son?"

Izo shrugged again. He didn't know what the question meant.

The man continued to watch him. Time seemed to pass endlessly between them. Izo could almost imagine a horde of clouds gathering and dispersing as they sat in weighty silence. Finally, the man let out a heavy breath.

"There's a lot of kids...a lot of people," he corrected himself after a moment. "Who start thinking there's no point to anything. Nothing they do matters. So out of boredom, they start tearing stuff up." He narrowed his eyes, warm and steady as the Earth. "Is that what you're doing?"

Izo picked at the fake leather arm of his chair. It was dry, cracked, and broken to bits. "Is my life worth being careful over?" he mumbled without looking up.

The man sighed and reached back to grab a yellow notebook from his bookcase. "I think I know exactly what to do with you."

Izo went back to his room expecting to get flushed to some random house or maybe sent to juvie. But instead, he caught a lucky break. Three weeks later he met an angel by the name of Ada Martinez.

Ada's house was different. Ada was different. Loving, short, and patient as the sun, she gave Izo and two other kids a real home: somewhere safe where the rules mattered, where the conse-quences were predictable and fair. Though he knew she expected a lot of him, he was never scared she'd become angry or neglectful. The house wasn't big, but it was ordered and clean. When he came home after school every day, he felt excitement rather than anxiety in his chest. At age ten, Izo hadn't known it was possible to feel that way while walking home.

And sure, Ada made him do his homework and threw a fit every time she caught him doing flips off the roof for dollars, but she was also the only person in the world who asked him "Mijo, what's wrong?" instead of yelling at him when he was upset.

Of course, this string of luck wouldn't last forever. One misun-derstanding with a highway officer and a mini-motorcycle (that didn't actually run) and boom—he was right back in the system. But her influence stuck with him, and by the time he aged out eight years later, Izo was ready to make Miss Ada proud.

Straight out of high school, he'd landed the dream job at the golf course. Tips there were great, particularly when shots everyone swore went into the rough magically appeared on the green instead. Try as they might, no one could ever prove anything hinky. The players were always together where they were supposed to be, and Izo was always far behind everyone, dealing with the bags.

Still, it wasn't enough money to save and get a place in Lake Tahoe, so Izo had lived out of his car all summer.

"Get a car. You can always live in a car," he remembered an older boy telling him in detention one day. He was right. A car was shelter you took with you. For someone like Izo, who grew up with no control over his address, a car registered in his name was the ultimate talisman of security and independence. With everything he owned packed neatly into three boxes, he'd headed out the weekend after graduation as happy and feral as a blue jay.

As a kid, Izo had always wanted to go camping. His first adult adventure was exactly that: an entire summer of camping in a giant national park. Still wearing his graduation robe like a tunic (Because, why not? He paid for it), Izo gathered with countless others to ring in the summer. On his days off there were more than enough things to do: hiking, kayaking, swimming, and flying. Best of all there were dozens of interesting strangers to try new things with, including a good-looking male and female couple one time with an expensive hotel room nearby. That holiday weekend was a lot of fun. Like, don't-bother-getting-dressed-for-three-days fun.

Most encounters weren't so fancy though. He'd always been on the lookout for secluded places to get to know someone. There were a lot of factors to consider. It had to be far enough away no one was likely to walk by, but near enough to other people that an animal or other predator wouldn't feel too confident surprising him.

One of his favorite hook-up spots was by a large electric junction box. Situated just inside the perimeter of the camp and directly next to a main road, it was surrounded by a high brick enclosure with an opening to one side and a blind corner on the opposite. The streetlamps were on the far side of the road, neither so distant you felt vulnerable, nor so close they blocked out the stars. On a clear night, you could almost see every twinkling light from inside that square brick cut out; on a full moon you could see nearly all of your partner too.

He'd gone back to that spot with weekend visitors more times than he could count. Just the sound of its powerful electric hum was enough to excite him. Those cool summer nights were the most freeing and exhilarating of his life, filled with coy introductions and subtle questions, followed by the kind of grateful, careful urgency that only standing sex could induce.

As the weeks rolled by, a group of long-term visitors soon emerged, and Izo quickly learned how to separate friends and entanglements. They were a tight-knit, friendly bunch. There was a gruff mechanic who'd look at your car for a pack of smokes; a retired LVN with a virtual pharmacy of ointments and medicine on hand; a sweet seamstress and her wife who owned a string of laundromats and who saved Izo from buying a second work polo nearly every week; best of all, there was a whole mess of interesting hippies, musicians, and weirdos to drink and joke around with after work.

But as Izo had previously learned, nothing good lasts forever, and when a rougher crowd arrived before a motorcycle rally with loud bikes and even louder jokes about the "wetback twink" in the VW, his old Maclaren habits kicked in. Sure enough, it only took a couple of days for three of them to break into his car in the middle of the night. He wasn't even surprised. He just took care of it before he moved his car to the other side of the park, tuning his radio to the local station on his way around the mountain. "Three men arrested on top of a Federal building. All three claim a flying Mexican trapped them there," the broadcaster read.

So when Deneus asked Izo if he could handle himself, the youth couldn't help but laugh.

— CHAPTER SIXTEEN —

Mort

Mort watched as the mysterious Avarian finally gave in to his guardian, his last ounce of stubborn resolve leaving him. Then, turning to face his fate, the Avarian gazed at the Senator with a dour expression. Mort couldn't help but smile and wave in return. He'd never seen anything half as cute and dejected.

He leaned over the counter to prop himself on his elbows as Deneus and the headstrong youth slowly approached. "I'm surprised to still see you here, Deneus," Mort crooned. "I'd have thought you and that nice Aurelian would have wandered off."

Deneus glared and didn't answer. Instead, he turned to his client. "Will you be all right alone?"

"Can I say no?" asked Izo.

"Try to enjoy yourself." Deneus glared at the Senator anew. "I'll be nearby."

Izo nodded and quietly bid his last and staunchest defender goodnight. Then, without looking up, he moved over to the bar.

"Aww. Perk up," said Mort. "We're going to have fun."

The youth glowered before jumping up and failing to hop into one of the floating seats hovering in front of the bar. Mort frowned at the haphazard approach. "Be careful. There's Malforian magnets in there. They require a certain finesse."

"I think I know how to sit in a chair, thanks," Izo grunted. Jumping, he struggled to clamber on top.

"I'm telling you, it's designed to—" But before he could finish the chair tilted wildly, dumping the youth out onto the floor.

Mort leaned over the bar. "You okay?"

The Avarian fumed. "I hate this planet."

Mort laughed. "Do you need help?"

"No. I just wasn't expecting it to flip over." Hoisting himself to his feet, he brushed off his pants. "What kind of pinche chair does that?"

"What kind of Avarian hits the ground when they fall?"

"Earth's luckiest Avarian, that's who!"

Mort quirked out an empathetic smile. A nerve had been struck. Not that he could blame Izo. The idea of an Avarian, the universe's most carefully crafted and graceful creations, falling flat to the ground was hilarious. The poor thing was probably mortified. "I'm sorry you fell. I can get you a different chair if you want."

Izo rolled his eyes. "No, I got it." Pressing the chair down with both hands behind his back, he quickly slid himself on top before throwing his arms out to maintain balance. The chair sprang back to its normal height, tottering all the way.

Mort smirked and clapped. Any other Avarian would have learned their lesson and floated up to alight gently atop the chair, but this one was stubborn. He had to do it his way. Mort supposed Deneus had a point after all—whatever his lineage or planet, Izo was obviously quite unique.

Mort reached behind himself to grab and begin filling two cups. "Congratulations. You managed to sit on a chair."

"*You managed to sit on a chair,*" Izo repeated in a mocking voice. He stuck out his tongue. "That's you," he said. "That's what you sound like."

"Mature as always, but let's move on." Mort finished making the drink and held it out for the Avarian. "So what made you come all the way out to IA?"

"I was kidnapped and brought here. Isn't it obvious?" Izo reached for the offered cup.

Mort pulled it back at the last moment. Eyeing the mysterious beauty, he could almost hear Deneus's lingering intimation still ringing in his ears. *Extremely rare.* "Let me take a guess: you got frustrated with life back at home, packed a bag and your two most loyal friends, left a note, and jumped at the first captain crazy enough to take you to IA." He grinned wickedly. "Something like that?"

"Sure. Why not?"

Mortaco tipped his head curiously. "No? Then what's the real story? Where are you from?"

"California. You ever heard of it?" Izo rolled his eyes. "Can I have my drink now?"

Mort pulled it to the end of the bar, more than a few lunging steps away. He glanced back with a suspicious look. "Are you really an Avarian?"

Izo glared. Then, disappearing, he reappeared in front of Mort, cup already in hand. He took a long drink before setting it on the bar again. "Sí. I am."

Mort broke into applause. It wasn't often you saw someone that could move like that. "Impressive. So you're some type of sprite, then?"

The Avarian looked at him like he was insane. "I'm a soda?"

"A sprite," Mort repeated. He blinked in confusion. "A distance racer?"

"Oh." The youth shrugged. "Guess so?"

Coy and mysterious to the end. "There is one way to find out," said Mort with a sudden thought. He broke into a challenging smile. "We ask the geneticist."

Izo drew down his brow. "You got a geneticist on board this boat?"

"No, but I have one on-call. This may come as a surprise, but you're not the first Avarian to secure a private invitation that I've had lingering questions about."

The youth considered this. "Your life's kind of weird, huh?"

"Gorgeous, you have no idea." Reaching back, Mort grabbed a clean cup to hold out in front of his guest. "Spit."

"In the glass?"

"We could gather genetic fluids in other ways...but I doubt your fiancé would approve." Mort pushed the cup closer. "Spit."

Izo glared, hocked up a loogey, and spat into the cup.

Mort grimaced. "Sexy."

The youth wiped his mouth with the back of his arm. "Always."

Opening a drawer filled with wireless read-out strips, Mort placed one into the cup before sending out a request through his embedded device. Then he set the experiment aside. "All done. In a couple of hours, we should have our answer. In the meantime..." Mort leaned over to look at the youth from a low, playful angle. "How should we entertain ourselves?"

"Why don't we talk about racing contracts? In fact, why don't you show me an example of one right now?"

Mort shook his head. "Plenty of time for that after the geneticist gets back to us. Besides, I have a better idea!" he said, clapping his hands and then offering one forward. "Why don't I give you the tour?"

Izo glared at the offered hand. "Ni madres. No, thank you."

Mort laughed. He'd never had an Avarian refuse to look around at his toys. A few had refused to play with them, but never had he met one so incurious as to resist seeing them all together. "Where's your sense of adventure?"

"I'm not interested in having adventures with you, cabrón."

Mortaco stared at the Avarian for a long time. Finally, coming up with no way to convince him to budge, he dropped his hand. He was struck by a strange, ugly feeling that he wasn't used to. It took him a second to recognize it as rejection. He didn't like it.

Mort slowly lifted his drink and went around to the front of the bar. He'd realized he needed to do something he almost never did with Avarians anymore—try.

"Worried your fiancé might hear about it?" he offered easily.

"My fiancé?" the Avarian said in confusion. A split second later he seemed to remember. "Right. My fiancé. No, my fiancé and I trust each other. It's you I don't trust."

"Me?" Mort made an offended sound in the back of his throat. "I'll have you know I'm as cuddly as a Driseldian pup...assuming you rub me the right way." Mort added, trying a lewd joke to lighten the tension. "Know what I mean?"

The Avarian made a face like he was a little disgusted and more than a little annoyed. Mort waited for the embarrassment to clear and the Avarian to laugh, even awkwardly, to clear the mood. But he never did. The silence stretched on and on until it became painful.

Mort cleared his throat. It occurred to him, quite suddenly and unexpectedly, that he was actually blowing this. He brought his cup up to his face and downed it quickly before going to refill it again. He'd never blown it with an Avarian. He'd honestly never thought it possible. And yet, here now with the single most intriguing creature he'd ever met in his life, he was coming up zero at every turn.

Mort raised his cup suddenly, knowing he needed to change directions. "We should drink to your fiancé." Izo frowned suspiciously but raised his own when he heard Mort's toast. "To the luckiest person in the universe."

"Sure," Izo agreed before taking a sip.

Elated, Mort leaned back on the bar. Finally, he'd gotten the maddening beauty to agree to something. "You like the drink?" He nodded down at the youth's cup.

"It's okay."

"Okay?" Mort said as the Avarian drank more. "Bet your beloved doesn't get you stuff this good."

Izo made a face. "Did you just say 'beloved'?"

Mort paused and realized his word choice had been a little archaic. He couldn't help wondering how it'd translated in Izo's language. "I'm not sure what word you heard, but let me assure you that my word was perfectly acceptable. Classy. Sophisticated even." Mortaco smiled as the Avarian laughed. "The kind of word we should be using far more often."

"Maybe in fairytales."

"Agreed. Hence, the perfect word for anything to do with you." The virginal creature shot him a look. But Mort was on a roll; he wasn't giving up now. He tipped closer. "How does your fiancé talk to you?"

"Why do you want to know so much about my fiancé?"

"I'm curious. I want to know what type of person lands an Avarian like you."

"The type I'm attracted to."

"Great." A beguiling smile drifted over the Senator's face. "What type would that be?"

Izo crossed his arms and sat back. He wasn't going to answer.

Mysterious to a fault. Mort shook his head in amazement. "Okay. I'll figure it out on my own." Mort tipped his head back and thought about it. "Hmmm. I'm going to guess some type of unimpressive royal—a duke, an earl, or a prince—as unpopular and boring as the planet they'll never actually rule."

"You think I'd make it with a royal?" Izo made a face.

"I can see I'm getting close," Mort grunted. "My guess is you were promised to them as a child."

"What? Eww."

"No? All right, I'll try again." He made a show of running his fingers over his jaw. "You were handpicked the second you came of age. No...there was a gathering. A royal ball where all the rarest Avarians were invited. And on that day, rows of delightful creatures came to meet the king's eldest. Many happy couples promised themselves to each other that day. But it was with heavy dismay and tragedy that the most stunning creature of all was paired with the most hideous and wretched member of the king's family." He gazed back at Izo. "Something like that?"

Izo looked at him like he was insane. "You've got quite an imagination, ese."

"Still nothing? Okay—rapid-fire: you were a handcrafted gift from the gods." Izo chuckled. Good! "You're the illicit love child of an elemental being and its resplendent Avarian mate? No? Hmm... were you a perfect flower that a callous king plucked from his garden, fell in love with, and begged a witch to restore?" Mort held up a finger. "But a misstep in the spell transformed you into your current Avarian form!"

Izo snorted. "Where the hell do you come up with this stuff?"

Mort bit his lip. Was there anything half as wonderful as that laugh? "You're just worried because I'm getting close."

"Soooo close."

"You're right. I'm getting way too metaphysical. There's a painfully obvious scientific explanation standing right there. It's so clear. I don't know why I didn't see it." He held out his hands. "You're from the future! They spliced you together in a lab! You're the perfect example of an Avarian, sent back in time to torture all of IA."

Izo snapped his fingers. "Dang it. You got me."

"I knew it." And Mort and Izo laughed.

The Senator put his drink on the bar and looked down at the untouchable being seated beside him, a beguiling creature that he'd finally made laugh. He tried to remember the last time he'd felt this happy. There was a physical ache of joy in his chest. "They did a good job," he added softly.

Izo stopped laughing. He stood up off the chair to move away. Mort didn't chase him though. He was satisfied to let the energy wax and wane between them, letting things take their course with the sweet, mysterious beauty.

When the silence had persisted for a while the Avarian suddenly turned back. "Can I ask you something actually?"

"Anything," Mort agreed. "Fame, jewels, riches. Name it—it's yours."

"What did you mean by 'quadrants' earlier?"

Senator Mortaco tried to figure out what he'd been referring to, but he had no idea. He shook his head. "Sorry?"

"Back on the shuttle," Izo explained, sitting down again. "I asked you how fast your SVS could get to another galaxy and you said 'depends on the quadrant.' What did you mean?"

"How do you remember that? That was hours ago." Mort looked at Izo curiously. "Are you into space travel or something?"

"Kind of," Izo agreed quietly. He nodded for the Malforian to answer. "But anyway—quadrants?"

Mort thought back to his celestial cartography classes. It had been years since he'd thought about any of this.

He scratched his head and stepped closer to Izo. "So the known universe isn't just above us, right? It stretches out in all directions— up, down, forward, back." The Avarian nodded. "When Malforians began exploring other galaxies, they needed a way to keep track of everything. So began the quadrant system. Our galaxy is Quadrant 1. The next two galaxies were Quadrants 2 and 3."

"Making up the tri-galaxies," Izo realized.

"Correct."

Izo considered this. "So is uncharted territory in Quadrant 4?"

"It was at first," Mort agreed. "But the more we discovered the more was added. Nowadays uncharted territory is an umbrella term. It includes anything in Quadrants 4, 5, 6, and the Southern Territories—though don't let them hear you say that," he chuckled. Lifting his gaze toward the stars, he thought it over. After a moment he headed toward the field.

"Where are you going?" asked Izo.

"Come here," Mort said, looking over his shoulder. "It's easier to show you."

Izo followed.

Mort quickly led them to the top of the tallest hill in the grassy, rolling field. "Okay," he said, looking around. They were fairly high up, floating in mid-orbit now. The stars would be easy to see at this altitude through the domed top. Checking to see there were no party stragglers left in the lounge area—there weren't—Mort cut off all the nearby lights with his embedded device. "If we lay down here we should be able to—"

"Whoa," said the Avarian, backing up sharply. He looked as cagey as an animal. "Who said anything about laying down? And why are the lights going off?"

Mort pointed up at the giant glass roof above them. "You're asking about the galaxies. I was going to show you."

Izo followed his gesture up. He gasped. "Ah chinga! Those stars are bright." Tipping his head back, he crinkled his nose in confusion. "You did that by turning off the lights?"

"Well, we're also in orbit outside the atmosphere. The light pollution up here is—"

"Orbit? We're in space? This thing's a spaceship?" The Avarian gawked at the sky above them. "I thought we were outside!"

Mort blushed. "The dome was constructed with the latest in smudge-proof technology, so...thank you. But I thought you knew? I invited you to a party on my ship." Mort inventoried the youth's expression. "What did you think I meant?"

"I thought you meant on a boat. Like a rapper."

The Senator narrowed his eyes. "Like a 'watership'?"

Izo thought this over. "So when you say *ship*, you mean *spaceship*. But when you mean *boat*, you say *watership*?"

The Senator nodded slowly. "That's what most people around the universe mean."

"Nice job translating, Tearn." Izo pressed his hands on either side of his face. He looked around again, this time a little calmer. "Okay. Standing on a spaceship. In orbit. Not in the water...or in the atmosphere." He nodded. "Got it."

"Good. May I continue?" Getting a nod, Mort knelt in the lush grass while slowly lowering the lights again. He offered the Avarian a hand. "Quadrant 1—us. Quadrant 2—the Relagian

Galaxy." He pointed above them to the swirling celestial body above.

Izo, ignoring his offered hand and followed his finger toward the sky. He was soon scowling. "Where?"

Mort chuckled. "Come here, and I'll show you."

The Avarian grumbled and dropped into a cross-legged position next to him. "Where?"

Mort scooted closer. He tried to get his face at the same height as the Avarian's, but doing so was difficult. He was much smaller than Mort. "It's right..." Mort frowned, realizing they weren't going to get very far at this angle. "Give me a second."

Relaying a couple of quick commands, he overrode the ship's autopilot to gently swing the yacht around.

"Whoa," said Izo as the stars began drifting. "Are you doing that?"

"Sure am," said Mort. He quickly pulled up a star chart to compare to the view above. He'd set the ship on an automatic orbital drift earlier, permitting it to idle anywhere remote like a lazy, unsocial behemoth. But they'd drifted out further into the Southern Hemisphere than he'd realized. He needed to head to the capital if he was going to point out each of the first four quadrants. For now, it was enough to turn the ship toward Quadrant 2.

Synching the chart in his head and with the stars up above, he laid flat on his back and pointed at the elliptical galaxy now centered above them. "Relagian Galaxy," he repeated.

Izo tilted his head back. "That fuzzy oval thing?"

Mort suppressed a grin. "Yes... the fuzzy oval thing. It contains dozens of habitable planets including Nertya, Aurelia, and Malforia's oldest and closest cousin—Cristovalia. It's the galaxy where Ari's from."

"And it's above us?" Izo asked.

Mort coughed uncomfortably. "We're talking about mapping things in space. Up and down are meaningless terms. In most universal maps, it's historically depicted to the East—the right hand of the Empire."

Izo nodded, still looking up. "And nothing in the Relagian Galaxy is considered uncharted territory?"

"No. Every planet in the Relagian system has been explored, mapped, and conquered...mostly looking for more of you guys!" Mort added with an impish grin.

Izo turned his face to the Senator. Mort could sense the Avarian's eyes narrowing to slits in the darkness. He glanced away and hurried on. "But that's ancient history. Moving on—do you see Relegia's southernmost curve?"

Izo squinted up. "Crap...I lost it."

Mort laughed. "How do you lose a whole galaxy that fast?"

The Avarian sighed. It was deep and plaintive. He plopped down onto his back with an air of defeat. "Just lucky I suppose."

Mort turned to look at his companion lying on the ground beside him. He seemed sad. "What's wrong?"

"Never mind." The youth groaned and pushed his head closer to Mort's. "Where's Relagia?"

Mort pointed up at the Relagian system again. "Fuzzy oval. See it?"

The Avarian lifted his own hand and pointed a finger to match his line of vision. "There?"

"No." Mort gently took and adjusted the Avarian's finger lower to the right spot. "There. Got it?"

When the Avarian nodded, Mort led both their fingers down to the galaxy's lowest point. "Its southern tip points directly at the Pitbian Galaxy, also known as Quadrant 3. Now Quadrant 3 holds all sorts of stuff, including Anolita and..."

"You have six fingers, dude?"

Mort paused. He let go of Izo's hand and held his own hand open. "Yeah? I'm Malforian."

The youth grabbed his hand. Turning it over, he examined it with amazement. "You guys really are aliens, huh?"

Mort turned his head to stare at the smaller creature. Because the Malforian's eyes had adjusted to the light, he could make out Izo puzzling over the mysteries of his six fingers, the youth's face a map of overcurious thirst for knowledge and life. In a flash Mort could see how it all played out—Izo returning home, shut away from the rest of the universe on some backwater planet, never to light up another room or discover another adventure. This one-of-a-kind Avarian would wither and die, his beautiful body and face erased along with his inquisitive mind. The thought broke the Senator's heart and physically took the air out of his chest.

More out of rage and rebellion than anything else, he pulled back his hand, flipped on top of the youth, and kissed him.

Izo yawned out underneath him, his spry and slender body stretching out under the Senator's as Mort held him even tighter. Izo squirmed with delicious rhythm, brushing their legs and hips together at different heights. Their kiss, surprised and sweet, rolled on until the Avarian pulled back to sound his surprise. Undeterred, Mort hungrily went to kiss at his companion's throat.

The moment electrified Mort like a lightning bolt. Mort's own desire grew rapidly as the youth breathlessly gasped out a few desperate complaints. The Senator relished the playful protest. He enjoyed this game. It was a familiar one he'd played many times with other Avarians before. Pushing both the Avarian's hands into the grass with an excitement, he clasped them together and reached down to pry the Avarian's legs apart as easily as sliding open a partially stuck door.

Then there was nothing separating them. The full exposed wonderland of the Avarian's body opened like a treasure beneath his hands. He could feel the youth trembling, his entire being shaking with anticipation. Mort breathed in, long and grateful. "It's all right," he whispered, his breath coming out hot in the place where Izo's ear met the line of his jaw. "It won't hurt." Then he took the exposed lobe between his razor-sharp teeth and bit down. The taste of blood filled his mouth, and the Avarian cried in astonishment.

Izo's knees and abdomen were twisting now, fighting to meet Mort's fingers as he searched for the quickest way to undress them both. He couldn't help himself though. Pausing only for a moment, he flicked his hand up the smaller creature's shirt, fingers flying along the slim edge of the Avarian's torso. He grunted in appreciation. The wondrous frame was exactly as smooth and svelte as he'd hoped. He wanted to stop and put his mouth on it, take every inch of the mysterious form and put it between his teeth. But first, he needed to sate a different desire.

He huffed and yanked one of the Avarian's knees around his hip. He was almost there. The latch on the Avarian's pants came open easily as his companion fought and kicked. Yanking the Avarian's hips up like a rag doll, Mort reached behind to pull Izo's designer pants down. What was revealed was an adorably soft bottom.

He was getting excited now. Within seconds he'd sink into his prize. He could almost imagine it—that moment of marked tension followed by luscious give. It was almost too much to stand. Gasping for air, he let out a mad, revving laugh. He had to give it to this one. He certainly knew how to get Mort's blood pumping.

Mort was busy pulling open his own clothes when his head suddenly snapped back. Letting go and leaning back, it took him a moment to realize he was in unimaginable pain.

Eye welling up with tears, he rubbed his palm into the spot where he'd been jabbed in the cornea. He glared down at the rude Avarian beneath him. Without thinking, he snatched and held him by the throat. "What the hell?"

Mort blinked wildly. He looked around and tried to clear his vision, but it was no use—everything was blurry. He growled and rubbed his eye again. Then, angrily rearing back, he went to make a fist.

But his brain blipped back to the others on board: Deneus with his "litigious" employers, as well as the other various witnesses. They'd probably be happy to sue a big-name Senator from IA if he punched their prize Avarian. It was with an impossible level of self-preservation that he managed to hold back the punch. Instead, he yelled into the Avarian's face. "Why the hell did you do that?"

When his vision finally cleared, he looked down and was surprised to see the beautiful face beneath him red and smeared with angry tears and snot. Mort gaped. The youth had been crying for a while.

"What are you doing?" Mort's nose wrinkled. "What's wrong?"

Izo shuddered and clenched his eyes. He let out another desperate sob. "I said stop!"

— CHAPTER SEVENTEEN —

Deneus

Deneus woke to the sounds of sharp knocking at his door. Sitting up, he looked around in confusion at the darkness. Where was he? He'd never seen the lush, two-story space, or the large, soft bed beneath him. Looking down at the naked Aurelian snoozing next to him brought the rest of the night back.

He grinned and rose. He'd finally bagged an Aurelian. Not a bad way to kill a night.

The knocking returned, sharp and more insistent than before.

"Who could that be?" asked the Aurelian sleepily, their slender arm drifting down their exposed torso to grab the covers, low on their hip, and pull them over their shoulders.

"Don't worry about it," Deneus whispered back. He leaned over the bed to kiss them on the head. "Go back to sleep."

They nodded and laid back as he padded quickly to the door. Deneus slid it open, jerking a hand up to cover his eyes at the blinding lights in the hallway outside. "Yes?" he answered groggily.

"He says he wants to call the authorities."

Blinking, Deneus slowly lowered his hand to see the Senator's angry face. Deneus dropped a foot back to take the rest of the scene in with confusion. One arm stretched high, the Senator was leaning onto it, pressing Deneus's tiny client into the wall by his throat.

Deneus gulped and looked at the dark-haired Avarian. Eyes puffy and nostrils twitching, he was bleeding from one ear and looking down at the ground, visibly trying not to tremble or cry. For a split second Deneus wanted nothing more than to quietly shut the door and chalk it all up to "other people's drama," but he wasn't quite that big an asshole.

Instead, he pulled the door wider and took one small step big enough to make the Senator back off the doorway. "Izo, are you okay?"

"He's fine."

Deneus glared. "Then why does he want the authorities?"

"I don't know," said the Senator. "Maybe that's what he was told to say at the end of the date?"

Deneus hissed. Of course. It couldn't possibly be that the rich, powerful man had lured in and attacked a helpless Avarian. No, it had to be the opposite: the money hungry Avarian must have set up and falsely accused the rich man.

Deneus wanted to punch the other Malforian but knew it wouldn't help anything at the moment. Breathing out slowly, he tried to think what "Izo's Guardian" would do.

He stood a little straighter. "Izo, come inside."

"Hang on." The Senator shoved his captive further away. Izo grimaced painfully, forced to follow the motion. "He's not going anywhere until he admits what happened," said the Senator.

"What happened?"

"Nothing!" The Senator's anger radiated down his body. He clenched his fist around Izo's throat and the Avarian clawed at his grip, trying to pull free.

"Okay," Deneus held up both hands. This was getting too real. If he wasn't insanely careful, someone was going to get hurt and from there, plain logic would be to get rid of the rest of them, land, and pretend nothing had happened.

With every fiber of his being, Deneus tried to be soothing and calm. "I get it. There was a misunderstanding. That's fine. Let's do ourselves a favor and not make it any worse."

The Senator frowned. He seemed to consider.

Deneus hurried on. "Everybody's just a little upset right now. That's all. Why don't we go to our rooms, calm down, and talk about this in the morning?"

The Senator adjusted his footing. His nervousness was suddenly bleeding through. And, in that moment, it was glaringly obvious that the Senator was scared too. "No..." Mortaco finally decided. "If I leave you two alone, you'll have fifty investigators here the second we land."

"I won't. I promise," said Deneus. Reaching to the entry table next to the door, he grabbed his device. He offered it to the man. "Take it."

Mort's lips parted. A person's device was arguably their single most valuable possession. It held all their information, all their ways of contacting the outside world. It might as well have been a digital extension of their identity and voice. Offering it to someone else, especially in a dangerous moment, was a giant show of trust.

The Senator reached for it. Deneus pulled it back. They locked eyes. "First, let him go."

The Senator's features darkened. "Not until he admits what really happened."

The Avarian, poor thing, had both eyes clamped shut and both hands wrapped around the larger hand on his throat. The Senator shook him.

"Tell him! Tell him the truth," demanded Mort. "Tell him nothing happened."

Something about his choice of words set the youth off. The Avarian opened his eyes. His expression changed. All signs of fear and self-preservation disappeared. He gazed directly at Deneus, green eyes burning brightly, the streak of blood still running down his neck. "He *tried*."

Deneus wanted to cheer. He doubted if he'd ever seen anyone half as brave. But he had to seem neutral at the moment.

The Senator huffed, and Deneus took it as good enough. "Okay," he nodded. "Sounds like we're on the same page."

"Great." Stepping between them, Mort put his back to the other Malforian and pried his hand away.

Then Deneus scooped the Avarian into his chest before anything else could happen. "Go to the bathroom. Lock yourself inside," he whispered to Izo before releasing him. Turning back to the Senator, he plastered on his best we're-all-good-here smile while leaning to block the door. "Sounds like a simple misunderstanding."

Mortaco didn't seem any happier, but he also didn't try to come in. "We'll see." He held up his hand. "Device?"

Deneus gave the Senator a meaningful frown. "You know, it doesn't look great for you if you take my device right now."

Anger rushing back, the Senator made a move to get inside.

Deneus stretched both arms out over the door. "But I give you my word as a Malforian: I will not contact anyone until I've discussed things with you first."

The Senator raged. For a moment they were locked chest to chest in the doorway. Neither pushed the other, but neither stepped away either.

"He's going to tell you a bunch of lies," Mort snarled, low and menacing. His breath was hot in Deneus's face. "He's going to make me out to be the bad guy."

"And you'll tell me your side in the morning," Deneus answered.

The Senator's nostrils flared like an animal's. And then, out of nowhere, he backed away. "Fine. Hide in here and scheme. But let me be clear." He stared Deneus down like a man heading to war. "This ship does not touch ground until this gets sorted."

Deneus nodded. "Yep."

The Senator glared over Deneus's shoulder one last time. "You scared of me too?" he bellowed at the Aurelian inside.

They jumped. "No."

"How do you feel about sleeping with Senators?"

"Great." Grabbing their clothes, they hurried to pull on their dress and meet him at the door.

The Senator offered the long-haired Aurelian his arm, which they happily took. He sneered at Deneus. "See? People like me don't need to hurt Avarians to get laid."

Deneus demurred. "Glad to hear it. Good night, Senator." He closed the door.

Putting his back against it, he finally let himself breathe. He grabbed his chest. *Shit,* he thought to himself while staring at the ceiling. *Shit, shit, shit...*

— CHAPTER EIGHTEEN —

Izo

Izo stepped back in horror at the sound of knocking on the bathroom door. With no windows or other exits, there was nowhere to go. He stared at the warm, wooden-looking barricade. It didn't strike him as terribly thick. He wondered how long it might take a Malforian to knock it down.

"Izo?" said the voice outside. "It's me, Deneus."

Izo nearly fell over in relief. He hurried to the door. "Did he leave?"

"Yeah. He left with the Aurelian. He won't be back again until morning."

"Was that all it took to get rid of him? Swapping one Avarian for another? Damn," Izo said, unlatching the door. "Should have done that earlier."

Stepping inside, Deneus's expression dropped when he took in the Avarian's injuries. Izo laughed and turned to the faucet. He still had blood dripping down his neck where the Senator had bitten him. Wiping some of it off, he turned on the water. "I don't look that bad, do I?"

Deneus's shoulders fell. "Izo, what the hell happened?"

"¿Qué crees? He wanted to, and I didn't. The problem was he was sooo much stronger." Izo laughed bitterly. How many times had he cringingly laughed at all the creepy rape jokes from Earth? He'd never particularly liked the jokes, or the people who made them for that matter, but he'd also never said anything or told them to stop. Now, it was like every joke that he'd ever heard was suddenly coming back with a vengeance.

Izo splashed the water over his neck and ear. The blood scrubbed away quickly, but more blood arrived in its place. In the sink, the water erased it efficiently, all traces disappearing from the room in a conveniently long black hole. It was loathsome to watch somehow. He looked away.

Deneus eyed him in concern. "Are you okay?"

"Of course." Izo laughed. He shrugged his shoulders high. "I don't normally tell rape jokes," he said, remembering another. "But I guess it got forced on me!"

Deneus's face broke into a grimace. He shifted away.

Izo smiled sarcastically. "What? Am I making you uncomfortable?"

"Stop it," said Deneus.

Izo covered his mouth, but a sob escaped anyway. He turned his back. He didn't want Deneus to see this. His entire body clenched with anger and self-hatred. He was suddenly aware how cold the room was—the top of his shirt had gotten wet from the water.

Deneus moved forward to hug him, but Izo shot out a hand to stop his advance and shook his head. Deneus moved back.

Izo wiped his eyes, shook out his arms, and tried to laugh it off. But in the mirror, his eyes were red and glassy.

You crying, bro?

He grunted angrily at the mirror. He shook his head harder. He was fine. He was tough. He was a full-grown person. He needed to stop.

Stop it...

Izo swallowed hard. He wasn't going to do this. He was fine. He wasn't a child. He wasn't going to cry. Children cried. Children were small and helpless and were allowed to cry because there was nothing else they could do. Izo was an adult.

Stop it…

The youth slammed his fist into the wall before scrubbing wetness from his cheeks. Laughter suddenly burst out of his chest. He didn't know why he was laughing. It was like a muscle memory. He tried to stop but couldn't. It was out of his control. What had happened wasn't funny.

But like so many other things in his life, it was too scary not to laugh at.

He managed to cover his face before imploding. It all came out a confused mixture of angry laughter and snarky weeping. And why shouldn't it? It was a sad, cruel joke. Of everything else that he'd lost control of lately, why should this be any different?

"Stop it," he said, pausing long enough to push this final taunt out of his head. He had no idea why they kept coming. He really wished they'd stop. "That's what she said."

Izo smiled at Deneus's horrified look before dropping into a ball on the ground.

"It's going to be okay." Deneus bent down to wrap the youth in a hug. "I'm sorry about what happened, but I swear it's going to be all right."

Izo nodded. He sniffed and pulled out of the embrace. "Thanks."

"Is there anything I can do?"

Izo rested his back against the sink. He took a long, shaky breath to steady himself. Then he waved around the room. "Want to try getting us out of here?"

"Working on that."

"Okay." Izo said. "In that case, I think I just want to get some sleep."

Deneus nodded. "Of course. As soon as you tell me what happened we can—"

"No. Absolutely not. I'm sorry, but no." Izo scratched his arm. "I don't think I can relive that shit right now. It's too soon, it's too real, it's—" He looked around the room and tried not to cry. "It doesn't even feel like it's over."

"I know. I get it, and I'm sorry. But people are going to ask what you told me after you got back. If you didn't tell me anything, even if you had a good reason, his defense will jump all over that. Trust me." Deneus shook his head with a depressed, faraway look. "I've seen them throw out cases for less."

Izo hugged himself. His hand latched onto his bicep. He flexed it, feeling it inflate and go solid under his fingertips and palm. It made him feel better; stronger.

But then his mind flashed back to how useless his strength had been.

He let go of his bicep. "Do I have to?" He wasn't sure he was ready to admit it happened at all.

"No," said Deneus, "but it helps him if you don't."

Izo hung his head.

Mort

Mort continued flipping through documents. The mysterious Avarian's real backstory was spotty, short, and strange, but he was slowly putting it together. He'd seemingly arrived on IA for the first time the morning before and immediately broken out into some sort of chasing game in the spaceport with his friends. Leaving a trail of destruction in their wake, they'd left to go shopping at a low-end designer store. After hacking into the company's private customer data, Mort had maddeningly confirmed once again there were no naked photos of the wily creature to find anywhere in the known universe.

He shook his head in frustration and continued sifting through Deneus's files. A talent agent in real life, his clients' files had revealed many interesting questions. It seemed more than a few of Deneus's long-term clients were coming up as missing persons. An interesting pattern, to be sure, but not the information Mort was looking for. No, the only file that had anything to do with the mysterious beauty contained almost zero leads: no last name, no birthdate, no mailing address, no government identification codes of any kind. For all intents and purposes, it appeared as if the Avarian had walked into Deneus' office the morning before, given him his first name, and the two had been thick as thieves ever since. The only new clue, if it could be called that, was one word listed under the "Employment Sought" section-

Racer.

Mort grunted. This was getting ridiculous. In this modern era of techno-tracking and mass digital footprinting, how could there be so little information? How was that possible? Somewhere in the back of his head, his worst fears alighted with cruel merriment. What if the youth was really a rival's asset? He could easily have been sent by another Board Member of Malacorp, hell-bent on publicly humiliating him with a scandal and staging a coup. Or, worse, what if it'd been planned by a political rival? Maybe that Psegre kid? Or even another government? What if he'd just left a loaded gun for the Southern Chancellors waiting with a handler in the other room?

Mort grabbed his head. "Who are you?" he gritted out between clenched teeth.

Next to him, the naked Aurelian from earlier, Meoimi, gasped awake. They sat up and backed away sharply. "What's he doing?!"

Ari sighed from the other side of the frightened Avarian. Also still naked, Ari glanced up from her prone position. "Don't worry about it. He's looking up stuff on his embedded device."

"He's doing what?" Meoimi's gaze trained up and down his frozen form. They cringed and pulled the blankets up to cover their chest. They looked like they'd rather be anywhere else.

Mort grinned and didn't respond. Far larger than either of the Avarians, butt naked, and staring blankly ahead at nothing, he must have looked like some sort of giant, dead-eyed android waiting to power on and tear them to shreds.

"Embedded device," Ari repeated with a yawn into her hand. She pointed at her temple. "He's doing work on the computer in his head."

"Oh." The taller Aurelian sank back onto the headboard, relieved. "I forgot people could get those."

"They're crazy expensive," Ari agreed sleepily. She threw an arm over the other Aurelian, curling to nuzzle herself against Meoimi's still covered breasts. Meoimi relaxed and allowed themself to be drawn back into the warm comfort of Ari's dainty arms.

Little surprise. Ari's job was ironing out wrinkles. Leaving Deneus's room with his new Avarian companion, Mort had begun sensing the tall Aurelian's immediate hesitation and regret. In fairness, it was probably easy to assume another Avarian had exaggerated a simple misunderstanding...until you found yourself suddenly alone with the accused.

Terrified at the possibility of a second incident, Mort had made a beeline for Ari's room. Ari could smooth things over. Ari could always smooth things over. Sure enough, the moment the famous singer had popped out into the hallway—peppy, flirty, and trust-worthy as a best friend—the other Aurelian had relaxed. Relaxed so much, he was pretty sure (with some Grade A coaxing from Ari) Meoimi had tried a couple of things for the first time in his sprawling Master Suite.

"You don't hear about them often, but lots of people have embedded devices," Ari explained, uncovering Meoimi's chest to give their nearest nipple a sweet and endearing kiss. "The news doesn't even mention them anymore, but if you ever start dating politicians and tycoons, you'll see them a lot."

"I see," said Meoimi. Then, lifting Ari's face, they pressed a finger against the singer's mouth. "I didn't know that."

Ari took the finger gently between her teeth. She stared up into the other Aurelian's features with smoldering intent. Then she let the finger go, instead nuzzling her head down on the taller Avarian's shoulder. "Everything's fine. Go back to sleep."

Mort blinked. He hadn't realized he'd paused to watch. "Do that again."

Ari flicked open one gold eye long enough to shoot him an impish smirk. "You go to sleep, too. You're spending way too much time on this. It's turning into an obsession. It's beneath you."

Mort growled. "You want to talk about beneath me? Who slept with a Ginarsian tonight?"

"On whose orders, jackass? Oh, and thanks for mentioning he was broke, by the way. I had to figure that out afterward while looking at his jacket on the ground. The thing was a complete knock off. It didn't even have an inner lining!" Sticking her tongue out in disgust, she suddenly sat up. "Ugh. I need to go brush my teeth."

"You didn't brush your teeth before? Holy shit, Ari," Mort yelled at the Avarian's back as she floated to the bathroom. "We kissed!"

"Relax," the singer called out from the bathroom. "I didn't do anything gross."

"You forget that I know what that means. You gave him the Ari special. You know what the Ari special is, don't you?" he said, grinning at the other Avarian. He made a jerking motion near his face.

"You better not be making fun of me," Ari warned. "And again—who told me to?!"

"Nobody told you to do anything. I say 'distract a guy.' You hear 'jump in bed.'" Mort laughed. "That's your problem."

Ari came out of the bathroom, hands on her hips. She pointed at the door. "You realize I don't have to be here?"

Mort bit his lip. She was right—he did still want her there. "Hey, how's your mom doing?"

"Her...mom?" the other Avarian turned to the famous pop star with the even more famously deceased mother in rapt confusion. "I thought she died?"

"She did. He's being a jerk." Glaring at Mort, Ari shut her mouth, his off-hand comment snapping off her rebellious streak as fast as turning off a light switch. And why wouldn't it? Even a hint at the truth about her mother always put Ari back in her place. Just in case, Mort continued to watch her like a hawk for any further sign of Avarian attitude, but there was none. Floating up, Ari dropped into his bed without another sound.

Mort frowned over the tiny Aurelian's form, fuming at her show of defiance. He was unsure he'd cut it down in a fully satisfactory manner. After killing the lights and laying back, he decided to leave it alone. They could always discuss things later at home when they didn't have an audience. Besides, he had more pressing issues.

Mort dove back into the databases in his head, tearing through files for any sign at all of the mysterious Avarian. Nothing existed from more than three days ago.

"I will figure you out," Mort muttered to a picture of the youth stuck in his peripheral. Pulled from the club's surveillance footage, it was the exact moment Izo had looked up at him for the first time—confused, concerned, and utterly adorable. "I'm not giving up."

In the background, a new message popped up. Pulling it forward, he realized it was another in a long line of genetic read-outs from Dr. Gujklydolen, his on-call geneticist. Ready to brush it off, he happened to glance at its title. Written in giant font and in all red, it consisted of only two words: Gravity Sprite.

Mort opened the message and began perusing. By the time he finished reading the long scientific report, his other two guests were snoozing peacefully. Three hours had flown by.

Mort sat up and messaged his favorite attorney. Then, thinking better of it, he canceled that and messaged his head attorney instead. This, after all, wasn't the time for bringing in friends.

He rose from his bed and stretched. Then, cutting on his shower with a quick command, he padded to the bathroom. He needed to get cleaned up. It was going to be a busy day.

— CHAPTER NINETEEN —

Ari

Ari waited until she heard Mort's bathroom door click shut. Then she snapped her eyes open. It was late. Later then she would have hoped. *Oh well,* she thought to herself. There was never a good time to get this type of news.

She leaned down to gently shake the other Aurelian awake. "Hey, sleepyhead. How are you feeling?"

Meoimi sighed long and slow. They were awake but refusing to open their eyes. "Good." They shivered, pulled the covers closer to their body, and shifted away.

Ari leaned in to tug the covers away from Meoimi's arm and back. She kissed the exposed skin of their shoulder, a move she knew was annoyingly effective at rousing someone after years of being "gently" awoken by horny lovers. "That was pretty fun last night," she whispered. "You seemed like you really enjoyed yourself with Mort and that other Malforian. What was his name? Deneus?"

Meoimi yawned. "Yeah."

Ari clicked her teeth together. She'd been trained too well at veiled, diplomatic conversation. She was having a hard time getting to the point. "Ever done anything like that before?"

"Not really."

Ari pressed a perfectly shaped finger to her brow. *Oh, screw it,* she thought to herself. *Just say the damn thing and get it over with.* "Two Malforians in one night." She nodded awkwardly, trying not to seem judgmental. "That's really something."

The Aurelian huffed and pulled their covers closer. "Guess so."

Ari waited. After a moment she loudly cleared her throat. "I say again—two Malforians in one night." She wanted to snap her fingers at the sleepy creature. "Sex. With both of them. Two Malforians. In one night."

The other Avarian gasped loudly, sat up straight, and covered their mouth, golden eyes looking like they were about to roll right out of their head. "Oh shit!"

There it is, thought Ari with relief.

Meoimi looked down at their stomach. Their expression was of unspeakable horror. "Is it necessarily...could they have—?"

"It might not have been an egg and seed, so it may not be viable," explained Ari calmly. "It could be two hits of sperm or two sets of eggs. If it was, you're fine. Either way, there's no point in worrying until you can take a test. Call your doctor and make an appointment—"

"Doctor?! I don't have a doctor," spat Meoimi. "I've been on IA for six months. I don't even have my own place yet."

Ari nodded. "It's fine. Call a clinic. There are free ones that offer—"

"What am I going to do?" Meoimi moaned, interrupting. "My parents are going to kill me. They told me not to come to IA. They said it was a waste of time, that I was getting in way over my head and that—"

They didn't finish their sentence. They were looking at the closed bathroom door where the Senator had just disappeared. They had a strange look on their face, half-dazed, half thinking, like a dreamer figuring out there were parts of this mystical world that maybe they'd be able to command.

Ari looked at Meoimi, looked at the door, and sucked in a breath so loud it sounded like the sound of smashing glass. She shoved the other Aurelian in the chest as hard as she could, knocking them clear off the bed and into the next wall. It had been a reaction so harsh and vicious, it surprised Ari too.

"Don't tell him. Don't threaten him. Don't even think it when you're around him." Ari scratched out low and hissing. It was a noise so desperate and ugly, she didn't recognize her own voice. "He will take over, and you will never get your life back."

Meoimi gazed up from the ground in confusion.

— CHAPTER TWENTY —

Deneus

Deneus awoke to the cool, quiet sounds of the enormous cruiser orbiting around him. He was in a large, stately bedroom decked out in warm wooden colors and creamy lush furnishings, lying on the softest couch he'd ever felt. His thin jacket was spread over his arms in a makeshift cover. It was dark and, outside their huge panel window, a thin blue ring was beginning to circle the soft curve of IA's horizon below.

Deneus blinked and looked around in confusion. It took a moment for the events of the night before to come back to him—the club, the fight, the Senator and, finally, the attack.

He sat up and checked on his client. Izo, still sound asleep, was lying on the bed across from the couch, huddled under the covers like they were a magic cloak of protection. Deneus smiled and decided to let the Avarian sleep. He'd had a long night.

Deneus stood and quietly stretched. His back whined in agony and he silently cursed himself for being stupid and gallant. Chivalry was a young person's imperative, not unlike sleeping on couches, no matter how soft. He would have woken the Avarian and demanded they switch if only he'd been a little bit more of an asshole.

Deneus instead swapped the couch for the chair nearest the door and tried to figure out what the hell they were going to do next.

Izo's story had been rough but, sadly, nowhere near the worst he'd heard. As he'd listened, nodding and gently pressing the Avarian on, he could have kicked himself for never getting any formal instruction on this stuff. Disclosure training was important, especially in his field. But at the end of the day, who had the time? Of course, now he would have traded anything to be there instead of here.

Deneus sighed and rubbed his face. The Senator said he wouldn't dock until everything had been sorted. It was kind of a good sign. Deneus had lived his whole life on IA. He knew the difference between veiled threats and promises of violence. A veiled threat was a calculation, a purposeful weighing of what needed to be said versus what needed to be ambiguous enough for attorneys to quibble over later. A promise was scarier. It meant, for whatever reason, the speaker wasn't worried about you going to the authorities.

That, combined with the fact that the Senator had brought Izo back—these were all good signs. Thus far, he was respecting their legal rights. Knowing what he did about men like the Senator, Deneus knew this probably had an expiration, though.

Izo mumbled something in his sleep. Looking down at the small Avarian, snoozing bane of his existence, Deneus couldn't help breaking out into a cheeky smile. *Who knew you'd be so much trouble?*

A moment later the Avarian's brow drew down. He twitched and his mouth stretched into a grimace. Then he muttered something unintelligible, his half-formed sounds coming out as tiny whines. Sweat beaded on his brow. After a few tries, his sounds finally came together enough for Deneus's translator to register.

He was mumbling the word "no" over and over.

Deneus jerked up and hurried to the bed. "Hey," he said shaking the Avarian. "Izo."

Izo opened his eyes, saw Deneus, and jerked back. "Shit."

"It's okay—it's me. You're having a nightmare."

Izo sniffed and looked around. He covered his eyes and hissed at the light. "Why does my head hurt?"

Deneus frowned with concern. The sunrise, streaming into the window in a bright golden wave, was well underway now. He reached over to shutter it out with an automatic dimmer. "Better?"

"Yeah." Izo nodded and groaned. "¿Qué hora es? What time is it?"

"Early. No one else will be up for hours. Go back to sleep."

"No, I'm up," the Avarian said, shaking his head and sitting up straight. "What were you doing?"

Deneus blew all the air out of his cheeks. "Figuring out our next move."

"Yeah?" The Avarian stretched and yawned. He pushed himself back against the headboard. "Hit me."

"I think we have a pretty good case. There are multiple people that saw us leave together, lots of witnesses can confirm your discomfort and his aggressiveness. You were alone in a public place and, ultimately, your only reason for being here was professional. All in all..." Deneus shrugged. "We could be looking at some real money."

"Money?" The Avarian blinked in confusion. "Deneus, I don't want his money. I want him behind bars."

Deneus snorted. "Yeah, and I want a shower full of Aurelians to greet me every morning, but it's never going to happen. Less than one percent of sexual assault charges end in conviction, kid, and what you described last night wasn't sexual assault. It's closer to sexual battery, which his PR team and attorneys will downplay to sexual misconduct."

Izo's mouth dropped. "Are you kidding? You're saying he didn't do anything wrong?"

"Of course he did. He's disgusting. I'd smash in his face with a chair leg if I could get away with it. What I'm saying is these cases are notoriously difficult to win. You have to prove you did everything Avarian-ly possible to make him stop."

"I did do everything. It didn't matter." Izo scratched his ear. It had scabbed over a little since last night. Deneus imagined it must still be sensitive to touch. "It was scary."

"I know. Trust me, I believe you. But other people are going to have questions. Like—" Deneus paused. He didn't want to say it. He'd hate himself if he said it.

Izo narrowed his eyes. "Like what?"

Deneus wiped his hand across his face. He would be IA's biggest rape apologist if he said it, but he had to anyway. It was right there, melting away their case like a thousand burning suns. "Look, I'm on your side," he started. "It's no excuse. What he did was disgusting. It doesn't matter what you did or didn't do. You were very clear. You said 'stop' and he should have stopped."

"But...?"

Deneus hissed with discomfort. "There are some people—not me—" he noted again quickly, "—who might wonder why you didn't tuck and cover."

Izo stared at him like he'd grown an extra head. "What?"

"Again," Deneus hurried on, "we're not talking about me. I would never think that. If an Avarian is uncomfortable and communicates that discomfort in any way, it is absolutely the responsibility of the other party to—"

"Deneus, stop," Izo interrupted. "I'm literally asking: what is 'tuck and cover'?"

"You know." Deneus put his hands over his head and rolled his body into a tight ball. "The signal."

The Avarian's sharp green eyes traced over Deneus blankly. "What signal?"

"The universal sign that an Avarian wants you to stop? Goes back millennia? Is referenced in most ancient myths? Hello? Any of this ringing a bell?" He tilted his head at the youth. "It means 'stop.'"

"And 'stop' doesn't mean 'stop'?"

"Sure. But this means 'stop' more. Everybody knows if an Avarian 'tucks and covers' they're scared. Which is important because"—He waved a hand at Izo.—"you tend to be smaller than other species. Anyway, how do you not know this? This is stuff we all learn in middle school: if an Avarian 'tucks and covers,' you have to stop. Never go to the Southern Provinces when you're expecting; don't sleep with two Malforians without strong contraceptives, don't push an Avarian who's curled into a ball. Speaking of," he said, suddenly thinking to ask, "what birth control are you on?"

"Birth control?" Izo made a face. "I'm not on birth control, dude."

"Don't laugh. He could have gotten you pregnant. It's rare, but there are cases where a Malforian has impregnated someone alone." Deneus shook his head with disgust. It wasn't the most pleasant topic in the universe, but it was biologically possible for the double fertilization of one donor to create a viable specimen. Was it distasteful and grotesque, like incest? Oh yeah. But it was biologically possible, nonetheless. Regardless of how society might look at it, the idea of hosting an Imperial Senator's child? Deneus shivered at the thought. That was a problem more than a little out of his league.

The Avarian let out a pitying laugh. Deneus looked up in confusion. The youth seemed to think something was funny. What it was the Malforian couldn't imagine. "What? Why are you laughing?"

"Dude, I can't get pregnant. I'm a boy," said Izo. He pointed at his face. "I'm male. I have a dick."

"Okay?" Deneus shook his head. "You can still get pregnant, Izo. He's Malforian."

"What?" Izo stuck out his tongue to one side and made a silly face. "What are you saying? Malforians can get dudes pregnant?"

"Malforians can get anyone pregnant."

Izo's silly face froze. He looked a little sick. "That's not funny."

"I wasn't trying to be."

The youth opened his mouth, but then he seemed to glitch out for a moment. Trapped in Izo's wide, horrified gaze, it took Deneus a second to realize the Avarian wasn't actually looking at him. No,

Deneus was more incidentally sitting nearby at the exact moment the youth's mind become lodged up against this horrific new realization.

Deneus looked around the room as he waited for Izo to come back to reality. He shifted in his seat. Finally, he leaned in to gently wave his hand in front of his client's eyes. "Would you like some water?"

Izo breathed in sharply, seeming to reboot. "Malforians can get dudes pregnant? Like..." His eyes seemed to go blank and he looked like he was going to pass out, but then suddenly he was back. "Like with a baby?"

"That's what pregnant means."

"But...but-but... how?" The Avarian looked like even asking the question caused him physical pain. "I don't have..." He gestured at his stomach. "What about a womb?"

"Malforians don't use wombs. We never have."

"But...eggs!" the youth cried. "I don't have eggs. How can he impregnate an egg that isn't there?"

"Because he has the eggs. He could put them in you. Then he could fertilize the eggs himself, or another Malforian could come along and do the job." Deneus looked at Izo strangely. "You don't know this?"

"But..." The Avarian looked down at his stomach as if it had personally contrived to torture him. "There's no room for a baby!"

"Exactly—hence my worry about birth control. Most Avarians don't have half a chance going full term with a Malforian child."

"Malforian child," Izo repeated. His face was filled with horror. "I could have an alien child growing inside me?"

Deneus looked around the room. "Yes, that's what I've been trying to tell you! Seriously, this is news to you? I promise you, they covered all this stuff in school."

That seemed to snap the Avarian out of it. He chuckled and rubbed a hand down his face. He seemed incredibly tired all of the sudden. "Guess I was absent that day."

"And a few other ones too: Malforian reproduction, tuck and cover, wearable devices…I'm starting to wonder where the hell you went to school." Deneus laughed. "Shit! You didn't even know about Ari."

Deneus's smile froze. Izo didn't know about Ari. How was that possible? There were species with no written language that knew about Ari. There were planets so far away and so seldom traveled that their entire solar system might share one intergalactic spaceport, but even they'd heard of Ari. It was *Ari*.

Deneus gazed slowly at Izo and suddenly saw his undocumented client with the mysterious face, zero cultural knowledge, and inexplicable talent in a different light. He stood away from the bed. "Izo, where are you from exactly?"

The kid flopped onto his back with a groan. "Can we do this later? I just found out my near-miss last night was with a way bigger bullet." He covered his eyes with one arm and let out a whining noise. "I haven't even had breakfast."

Deneus went around the bed to stand in front of the Avarian. "Answer the question, Izo."

"Leave it alone, Deneus."

He furrowed his brow as he watched the Avarian. There was a part of him that considered letting it go, but he couldn't. He wasn't that type of person. He kicked the bed hard.

"They abducted me, okay?" Izo blurted. Deneus' eyes widened. Izo hadn't uncovered his. "They took me from my planet, which is in the middle of nowhere, and no one can take me back except them because nobody else knows where it is. There. You happy? You feel better? Now you know." Izo sighed. "I swear to God, this has been the longest fucking day…"

Deneus had dropped back a step. He was looking at the door. "They kidnapped you?"

"Glongkyle and Tearn." Izo took a long, deep breath—first in through his mouth then out through his nose. "They were going by Earth, and I guess they spotted me while I was flying. All I know is I was heading to work when I hear this behind me. Next thing I knew I woke up in a locked room that it never got bright outside. After a couple of weeks, they did something to me, my ears hurt, and I could understand what they were saying. They said if I ever wanted to see Earth again, I'd go with them to IA and help them make money." Izo uncovered his eyes to glare at Deneus. "This whole scamming a Senator into getting me on a race team? That's been a decidedly recent development though."

Deneus nodded with calm understanding, even as the room seemed to fold in on itself. His client, the same undocumented Avarian currently embroiled in a sexual battery scandal with a high-ranking politician, was also the unquestionable victim of intergalactic trafficking. *Great.*

Deneus pursed his lips. "So that's it? You need to close this deal with the Senator so they'll finally take you home?"

"Pretty much." Izo stared up at the ceiling. Lying on his back, young, trapped, all alone and lost on the other side of the universe, Deneus wondered if he'd ever seen anything half as pathetic or vulnerable. "Any suggestions?"

Deneus lifted an eyebrow. He was considering their options when a notification sounded from his device. Looking down, he was surprised to see the sender. "It's a message from the Senator's head of council," he mumbled. Opening it, he could feel his eyes growing wider as he read.

"What's it say?" The Avarian asked. He rolled off his back to look at the device.

But Deneus just shook his head. It must be some sort of mistake.

"Well?" the Avarian insisted. "What's he want?"

Deneus dropped his wrist. He couldn't believe it. It didn't make sense. Or maybe it did?

"He wants to go over your racing contract."

"There he is!" Raising a hand, the Senator waved Deneus over to the long, wide table where he and another older, wider, and infinitely more serious Malforian waited. "Grab some food," he commanded.

It'd been an hour since getting the truth from Izo, followed by the invitation from the Senator. He still had no idea what he was going to do about any of this. He'd considered cutting and running about a dozen times, but every time the guilt from leaving the kid high and dry stopped him. For now, he was just going through the motions, keeping up the status quo. Once they all got safely off the ship, he'd figure out his next move. Probably.

Deneus crossed the long dining room while keeping his face flat. He was doing his best not to look around or seem impressed, but it wasn't easy. The room held a luminous natural decor, flowers, and greenery strewn everywhere, low enough to leave the views unobstructed. The only accents of any height, aside from the high-backed chairs, were a few dozen statues depicting naked Avarians in various states of sultry submission.

But the two most impressive features of the room were its location on the ship and the architect's choice of building material. The room, shaped like a giant platter, was situated at the bottom of the massive cruiser. Its floors and walls, seamlessly connected without so much as a crease, were made of one continuous piece of crystal-clear glass. The powerful combination left Deneus feeling like he was floating weightlessly above the majestic Imperial Mountains trailing for miles down below.

Reaching the banquet table filled with food, he casually grabbed a few choice samples from the lavish spread before heading to where the Senator and his companion waited for him.

"The Avarian didn't come?" the mystery Malforian asked.

Deneus cleared his throat briskly before settling in a few seats down from the Senator. "I'm afraid my client was feeling out of sorts this morning. He sends his regards."

"That's fine. It'll just be us—Malforian to Malforian. Speaking of, this is my Senior Head of Legal Counsel," said the Senator. Seated at the end of the table, the rising sun at his back, the Senator nodded to the attorney on his left.

"Nice to meet you," said Deneus.

"So, what are we going to do about this problem of ours?" The Senator speared a piece of fruit from his plate and took a bite. He chewed it slowly and smiled.

Deneus cleared his throat. "I had a few ideas that I hoped both parties would find suitable."

"I'm sure you did. You're really good at finding solutions for everyone, aren't you?" Mort responded merrily. Something about the joy in his tone gave Deneus pause. "And that is the central question, isn't it? Finding something that makes everyone happy. Especially when there are so many big, moving pieces to consider. You've got me, you, your client's whole career, your bottom line, your ability to ever work in this town again—"

"Your political reputation just before an election," Deneus added curtly.

Mort paused. He grinned slowly. "You know who we should ask about this?" Spearing another piece of food, he pointed it at Deneus. "Your old friend, Tasdid."

Deneus's eyes widened. His blood went cold.

"You remember Tasdid, right?" the Senator continued. "You must. You and he go way back. It's funny, being such a big part of the Malforian mob, you'd think I would have met him before. But no—this morning was the first time he and I had ever spoken. Interesting guy, though."

"Very," agreed the Senator's attorney.

"Had a lot of great stories about you," Mort pointed out.

"I don't—" Deneus started.

"You know, he was surprised to find out you were still representing clients," the Senator continued easily. "It was his understanding that when you'd been let go of your old job, you'd lost your agent's license—which makes it a little difficult to represent anyone. Doesn't it?"

"Makes it fraud," agreed the attorney.

"Which was interesting to learn. But you know what was even more interesting? How you lost your license in the first place."

Deneus sucked in a shaky breath and tried to think of something to say. When he opened his mouth, nothing came out.

"Seems you used to work for a big-time agency and things were going well. But they could have been better, especially for someone as ambitious and impatient as you. So you took out a few bets on some up and comers you knew about, and you did pretty well at first. Then you got greedy. Next thing you knew, you owed Tasdid and his friends more money than you could ever hope to pay back. In fact, it was more money than you could make regular payments on...even with your big-time job! So, after kicking the shit out of you every few months for a year, Tasdid came up with a better solution."

Mort turned and laughed at his attorney. "You have to admit—it was genius! Tasdid skipped right to the heart of the matter."

The Senator turned to Deneus. "You remember his solution, don't you?"

Deneus winced and stared at the ground. He couldn't have looked someone in the eye at that moment if his life had depended on it.

"It was simple," continued the Senator happily. "A fresh-faced Avarian from a big-name company goes for a lot of money in certain circles. Best of all, Tasdid never actually asked, and you never actually agreed. When a couple of dozen of your clients went on interviews they never returned from, everyone at your company could honestly say they had no idea what happened to them."

Mort tossed his hands up. "It was a perfect solution. Your big-name company got to keep its big name. Tasdid made more than enough money off some high-end Avarians. You magically found yourself with no more payments due. Happy endings all around!"

Deneus was pretty sure he was going to throw up.

Mort paused to cut off another piece from his steak. "But, hilariously enough, you couldn't leave well enough alone, could you?" Snatching the bite into his mouth, the Senator beamed as he chewed. "You just had to stick your nose back in."

Deneus let out a breath he'd been secretly holding in for months. This was it. This was the moment he'd been waiting for. Everything would finally cave in.

Why had he done it? It would have been the easiest thing in the world to leave well enough alone. The loan was clear. He never had to see Tasdid or any of his goons ever again. He could have changed planets. Changed names. Started over. But those twenty-six missing faces haunted him, and even if it technically had nothing to do with him, he couldn't live with himself.

He blinked and stared. The room had sucked back a couple of feet, and he was beginning to feel like a brain floating inside his own body. The windows of his eyes had shrunk back, and everything had taken on a wildly unreal feeling. It occurred to him that all living beings were puppets filled with little more than electricity and water.

"So what did you do?" the Senator continued. "Set up shop in the slimy part of town, exactly like everyone who thought you were guilty expected you to. But what no one realized is you were purposely hiring Tasdid's scouts, undercutting his business at the source. And it was easy to do! Tasdid's scouts are simple creatures. You pay them more; they come to you first. But you weren't just stealing his Avarians, were you? You were gathering intel—how Tasdid collects Avarians, where he ships them out, where they're headed to. You even managed to reverse engineer some of his sales. You figured out clients, prices, dates of delivery, everything. More than enough to hand over to an investigator.

"Of course, that's the problem. When we broke into your office last night, you still had documentation of all this! You haven't handed over anything!" Mort laughed and held out both hands. "You realize you actually look like the mastermind at this point? I'm honestly tempted to turn you in just out of the sheer hilarity of pinning all this on you. I mean, come on! How funny is that? You, rotting away in prison for the rest of your life, having accomplished nothing but gathering enough evidence to frame yourself?" Mort tipped back and fell into peels of raucous laughter.

But then the Senator shook his head and clapped his hands, instantly sober again. "What am I saying? How could I even consider denying Tasdid the joy of getting his hands on you one last time? Especially with all your history together, and after he was so helpful to me yesterday."

"He was extremely helpful," agreed the attorney.

"You know how I hate to disappoint new friends. That's the problem with making too many friends: you can't keep them all happy." Leaning back, Mort rested his hands behind his head. "Can you keep all of yours happy, Deneus?"

"What do you want?" said Deneus.

The Senator bent his head low to look him in the eye. "Is he taking a tone with me?"

The attorney scrutinized Deneus. "He can't be. He isn't that dumb."

"That's what I would have thought," said the Senator.

Deneus glanced back and forth between them. He'd never seen two people more in their element, like birds returning to the sky or deep ocean fish returning to the depths they were born in. He dropped his head down slowly. When he finally spoke again it was much quieter. "Just tell me what you want."

"I want you to vanish," said the Senator. "I want all of you to vanish, in fact. I want every obstacle between me and that Gravity Sprite to wither up and—"

"Gravity Sprite?" said Deneus. He gazed at him in confusion.

The Senator paused. His eyes scanned Deneus's expression, digitally analyzing him, no doubt. After a moment he frowned. "You didn't know?"

Deneus blinked. No. It was impossible. The Senator was delusional. They were no Gravity Sprites walking around anymore, much less into his office on a weekday.

Deneus turned to the attorney, waiting for some sign that he was placating his client and wanted Deneus to play along. The attorney looked straight at him and nodded.

"The genetic results were very clear," the attorney said. "The genes are a little muddled, but he's a Gravity Sprite."

Deneus shook his head. No. He couldn't believe it. It was impossible. Being threatened with murder or extortion? Sure. He lived on IA. That made sense. But the idea that he'd been joking with the universe's only living Gravity Sprite a few minutes ago? Absurd. "You're crazy. He can't be." He pointed at himself. "I'd know."

The Senator eyed him for a long time. Then he sat up, curious. "How much do you actually know about him, Deneus?"

Deneus huffed out a laugh. Then his mind jumped back to Izo's explanation of his origins, and the humor slowly drained off his face.

He was taken from an uncharted planet...no one else on his planet could fly...they've been kidnapping Avarians for years...they took him from the other side of the universe ...no one else on his planet could fly...

Gravity Sprites can hop between planets.

Deneus shook his head. No. It was ridiculous. If Izo was a Gravity Sprite, why bring him to an agent like himself looking for random investors? It would have been the single stupidest approach imaginable. It made no sense unless—

Deneus gasped. *They didn't know.*

None of them knew.

Deneus grabbed his forehead slowly. The morons had kidnapped the universe's rarest Avarian and let Deneus wave it at the single most dangerous Malforian alive...and they didn't even know it. He pinched his eyes shut. They were so completely screwed.

The Senator chuckled at Deneus's reaction. Then he continued eating. "Lighten up. There's a chance you'll live through this." He grinned and took another bite. "A small one. But a chance."

The last living Gravity Sprite. The kid was a walking science experiment. The applications to physics alone...a shiver ran down

Deneus's spine. He glared at the man so casually eating across the table. "What are you going to do with him?"

Mort made a face. "Don't look at me like that. You want to hear my big, evil plan?" He lifted both arms to drop onto the table loudly. "I want to make him happy."

Deneus squinted. "What?"

"I know. It's unthinkable, right? I like someone and want them to like me back. Yes, it feels a little weird admitting it out loud, but there it is. I want him to stay here with me. That's it. At this point, I'd do just about anything. Kill you. Kill the crew." He shrugged and lifted another bite to his mouth. "I've done worse for less."

Deneus tried to gulp, but his mouth was too dry to swallow.

The Senator searched the agent's face curiously. His expression was eerily void of malice or anger. It was almost childlike. "So anyway, are you going to help me, or do I have no use for you?"

— CHAPTER TWENTY-ONE —

Izo

Izo gazed at the seemingly never-ending hallway. A whine pulled at his throat as sweat poured off his brow. "When will this nightmare end?"

Commissioner Wruit, a snide Malforian, glanced sharply at Senator Mortaco. "This is your pro athlete, Mort?"

The Senator dismissed this. "He didn't get much to eat this morning."

"Does he ever?" countered the commissioner with a concerned glance at Izo.

"Trust me, his food intake will be the last thing on your mind," Mort replied. Turning to Deneus, he gave Izo's agent a seething command. "You want to take care of this?"

Deneus rotated toward the Avarian like a robot. "Izo, this is your big moment. The walk is just a little further. Can you hang in there?"

Izo nodded. Deneus was right. Everything was finally coming together.

The Senator, completely caught over a barrel by Izo's wizard of an agent, had caved to everything they wanted. It had honestly been embarrassing. The man had agreed to all their demands!

Izo's signing bonus (more money that Tearn or Glongkyle had ever seen) had paid for all Izo's training, team and racing expenses, and even for stuff Izo wouldn't have thought of, like board certification and medical insurance. Some of it was a little overkill—payment schedules for a publicist and living expenses—but he supposed anything he didn't use wouldn't matter.

Point being, he was almost home free! All the boring, official crap had been signed. He was so close to getting the money and going back to Earth, he could taste it. The only contingency now was an official speed recording to be performed by a sports registrar. In this case, the Commissioner of Avarian Racing himself, who happened to be one of the Senator's old school chums.

At the time, Izo had been glad for any excuse to finally get off the god-forsaken yacht. But now, dragging himself through the backend of some ridiculously famous stadium Tearn couldn't stop blathering about, Izo was convinced he was going to die on the planet anyway.

And why? Because of all the ridiculous, worst possible times to come down with something, it had to be now. Sore, exhausted, and with a needling headache biting into his right eye, Izo couldn't remember the last time he'd felt this miserable or sick.

He dug three fingers into his brow and kept moving. It was weird; the room didn't even feel hot, and yet he was sweating. In fact, he was a little cold.

"Izo, are you all right?" asked Tearn.

Izo smiled down at the big black reflective eyes, shining at him with concern. Tearn was always so worried about him. "I'm fine." He gave him two thumbs up and an encouraging smile before losing his sense of balance and veering left.

Wruit shot up an eyebrow. "Is he drunk?"

"On the need for speed," insisted Izo, trying to save face. "Just show me a field and I'll blow your mind. Or...hey!" Stopping dead in his tracks, he gestured at the never-ending hallway. "Why don't we do it right here?!" Dropping into a starting position, he pointed at the Commissioner. "Just tell me when to go."

"What the hell, fly-by?" hissed Glongkyle.

"No, it's perfect. I'll do a lap and then I can go...lie down..." Izo tipped over, falling onto his side. He was suddenly struggling for breath. He motioned desperately around himself. "It's a really big area. Can't you, like, measure it later?" But now that he was finally on the ground, the prospect of hauling himself back up to his full height suddenly felt impossible.

Wruit leveled the Senator with a look so sneering it hurt Izo's feelings. "Wow. You really know how to pick 'em, Mort."

"Can he meet us on the field?" the Senator asked Commissioner Wruit.

Rolling his eyes, the man stiffened, and his eyes went blank. A second later a door ahead of them popped open. "There. He can hop over a balcony and wait for us below."

Izo gasped and snapped through the door. He burst out an open veranda before anyone could answer.

As he floated into the central stadium's arena, he paused to take it in.

The Avarian racing stadium was huge. It was as wide as a football field, as tall as a skyscraper, and furnished with rows of stadium-style seats, like arenas on Earth. In front of the lower levels were dozens of suspended fields and obstacle courses. At first glance some of the courses seemed incredibly simple— long-floating lines arranged in perfectly straight racing strips; a cone-shaped track that slowly spun downwards into tighter and tighter circles. Izo could easily imagine how similar these events would look to Earth's foot or even car races. But some of the tracks were substantially more complex. Shifting and compressing through endless physical iterations, these colorful 3-D tracks seemed hellbent on contorting through every geometric path available in a dizzying display of dynamic twists, turns, and pitches. Izo shuddered to imagine what type of chimera-like racer could survive winding through one of those at top speeds.

Izo turned his face higher to inspect the upper half of the arena. Toward the top, the seats were set in a sharper pitch and repeated in sixteen balconied stacks. There were no floating racetracks up here though. Instead, giant floating jumbotrons hung like oversized dice every few hundred feet, offering a clearer view of the action down below, no doubt. But as you got higher, even these screens became smaller and less frequent, until the top dozen rows offered nothing but a bird's eye view of what must have looked like racing dots near the ground and a distant visage of a screen roughly the size of a minivan.

Izo was musing at the inherently punitive nature of purchasing seats on the upper levels, when a wave of tiredness hit him and he dropped down to the floor like a crippled helicopter. Landing hard and tripping backwards, he landed butt-first onto the gelatinous ground with happy surprise. He laughed and fell back against it, the floor rippling out in waves from beneath his back. The surface was wonderful. It bypassed every pain and ache to cradle his tired bones. Izo rolled onto his stomach and tucked his face into his arms, surrounding himself in sweet, cool darkness. He sighed, happier and more content than he'd been in weeks. An instant slumber lulled him into a soft and tender embrace.

After what felt like barely a moment later, the others' voices drifted into hearing range. Izo licked his chapped lips and didn't move. The tickle at the back of his throat had been replaced by a scratchy, winter-fresh feeling. His headache had cranked up three octaves.

Izo coughed and groaned. He didn't look up. "That was quick."

He wrapped his arms tighter around his face. The stupid room had gotten colder too.

"Your shirt's riding up," the Senator said behind him. "I can see most of your back."

Izo flipped him off over his head. A moment later a large hand traveled up his side. He whipped around into a seated position. "What the hell?"

The Senator was bent down on one knee, very close. Izo could smell his skin, the scent reminding him of the night before, the time spent during their struggle. The smell made him nauseous, like the idea of eating pizza dropped on a bathroom floor.

The offending hand still hung between them. Over his head, the Senator watched him intently. "You need to be more careful to cover yourself from now on."

Izo opened his mouth, but words wouldn't come. His gaze fell away. Mort was too close, and Yula was too far. It didn't matter anyway. It was a small thing, not worth the fight. They were nearly done. A little while longer, and he'd never have to see this man again. Izo clenched his jaw and kept his burning humiliation locked deep inside.

The Senator stood, the difference between their size plain. "Let me help you up," he said, reaching a hand down. It was a sudden and unexpected kindness. It was almost...protective? It unnerved Izo in a way he couldn't quite place.

"Bro, I can fly. I don't need help getting up."

"Suit yourself."

"Thanks. I will." Izo shot a derisive expression for Deneus, his agent, to share. When he turned in his agent's direction though, Deneus wasn't watching him. In fact, gaze firmly locked on his device, Deneus seemed to be purposefully looking anywhere but at Izo.

Mort followed Izo's gaze. "Do you need something from him?"

"No. I'm fine." Izo hauled himself up and moved around the Senator. There was a weird prickling on the back of his neck, but he didn't know what to do with it. He hurried for Commissioner Wruit.

"Not to be rude, but can we move this along?" asked Izo.

"As soon as the other racer gets here," said the Commissioner.

"Other racer?" said Izo.

"The one this tryout was originally for." Wruit gave Senator Mortaco a pointed look.

"Trust me," said the Senator. "You're going to want to see this."

"That's what you said to me at five this morning." The Commissioner looked at Izo with skepticism. "So far all I see is a skinny Avarian that needs to see a doctor."

"You have to see beneath the surface to the mysterious and splendid creature that lurks below." Mortaco waved his hands over Izo to finish his point.

Izo sneezed so hard his head flew forward and he zipped back a couple of feet. When he landed, he sniffed and groaned. A large glob of dark green snot had appeared on the top of his right arm. He looked around the wide arena desperately. He didn't know where to wipe it. "Does someone have a tissue?"

The Commissioner glared, first at him and then the Senator.

"What's going on?" interrupted a confused voice from behind them.

"Graydith, you're here," said Wruit. "Thank you for agreeing to this at the last minute."

Izo turned, saw the newcomer's face, and busted out laughing. It was one of the rude, purple-skinned people from the club! "Hey dude, wassup? Where's your hot cousin and her friend?"

Shorter than Izo by an inch and sporting a beautiful mess of short dark blue curls, the other racer eyed Izo with confusion. When recognition hit, he gasped. "You're the jerk from the club!"

"Yeah, I am!" Izo began walking toward him. He felt relieved to see another Avarian in the arena, which was strange. Before a few days ago he'd never seen another Avarian in his life. He threw his arms open for a hug. "You ever find another table, dude?"

"What the hell is going on? THIS is the sprinter you want me to race?" Graydith said while backing away from Izo's hug. "My times are easily good enough to get on the team. I was told this was a formality. I've already met with Coach Staydle. We worked out a training schedule. I was told I was a shoo-in for the Cups."

"Coach Staydle is still very excited to welcome you," said the Commissioner. "This changes nothing. We added an unranked contender to try out for a completely different position. This has nothing to do with you."

The purple-skinned Avarian narrowed his eyes. He inspected Izo. "What's your race?"

Izo stopped trying to get a hug. "I'm Mexican-American, but I don't know what that has to do with—" Before he could finish his sentence he broke out in another fit of coughing.

The other Avarian crossed his hands. "No. Nuts to this. I didn't work this hard and make it this far to get out on the track with someone this tore up. If we go out there and he cuts into me or loses focus, he could hurt us both."

"Or worse—he could beat you," said Glongkyle. Lifting an eyebrow, he leaned his face forward in an expression of open challenge. "Bet that'd be pretty embarrassing, huh?"

The Anolitun racer glowered. Eventually, he shook his head. "Fine. Screw it. But if he runs into me and explodes, I won't be held liable."

Izo started to laugh until Glongkyle said, "Agreed," behind him.

"Wait, what?" said Izo. But the others were already pointing him to the starting blocks.

"It's fine. Just don't touch him mid-race, okay?" said Tearn.

"Sure," said Izo, unsure. Turning, he snapped onto the starting block nearest the Anolitun. But as he reached it, he gasped and nearly staggered to the ground. He was suddenly lightheaded. Grabbing the railing attached to one side, he held on to stop from doubling over. For a sick, tipping moment it took everything inside him not to fall on his hands and knees and blow chunks everywhere.

"Racers, take your marks," said the Commissioner.

Izo eyed him desperately. It took a second to realize he was gesturing for Izo to hunker down. Once the Earthling complied, he continued. "When you hear the siren, fly as quickly as you can across the red line." He pointed to a wide red line at the opposite end of the field. "Any questions?"

"Can I touch down anywhere across the red?" asked Izo. He had a feeling this one was going to go wide.

"Yes." The Commissioner glanced at the Senator. "Should I be surprised he doesn't know that, Mort?"

"Don't have to know things to be a racer, Wruit—just have to be fast." The Senator gave a confident nod. "Don't worry. This is going to blow you away."

"I tremble with anticipation," said the Commissioner. He turned to the starting blocks. "Racers ready! Starting in five... four..."

Izo turned his gaze to the other end of the field. He focused on pulling the invisible rubber bands connecting him to the red line. In a moment he would release himself and charge forward. One snapping leap and this would all be over. Tearn and Glongkyle would get their money and Izo would finally be headed back home.

"Three... two..."

Izo could feel his feet and fingertips digging into the ground. The invisible rubber bands that pulled him were beginning to thicken. For a moment he was almost convinced the light was turning a darker shade of red.

"One."

The siren sounded. Izo snapped forward and lightning struck, a surgically bright light slicing into his vision with a sound like shotgun fire.

Izo screamed, lost his balance, and tumbled into the gelatinous floor. He rolled, bounced, and bruised his shoulder while spinning across what felt like most of the field. He only managed to slow himself by slowly spreading his limbs. Once settled, he lay on his back in a sad, broken heap directly in front of everyone. Above him, the sound of rolling thunder continued to reverberate and echo throughout the giant space.

Commissioner Wruit turned to the Senator. He lifted a brow. "A majestic creature, to be sure."

Mortaco scowled.

Izo slowly lifted a hand. "I'm okay." Then he set it back down on his chest. His heart was thundering like a racehorse.

The Anolitun racer touched down beside him. "What the hell was that?"

"*What the hell was that?*" Izo repeated, sitting up with a jerky motion. "What the hell are you—Raiden!?"

"I'm an Electric Sprite," said Graydith. "What the hell did you think?"

Unable to make himself fly for the moment, Izo spun and awkwardly lifted himself off the floor, butt first. "I didn't think you were about to fart out a lightning bolt. GODDAMN! I was standing right next to you. I could have been killed."

"Izo, Anolituns use electricity to fly," explained Tearn. He pointed at Izo's opponent. "He's extremely fast. High amounts of speed require high amounts of energy."

"As do high amounts of patience," said Commissioner Wruit. Grey Malforian hand pressed up against his temple, he looked ready for a nap. "Is there any way we could wrap this up?"

Izo agreed and snapped himself to the starting block again with a nervous and somewhat more appreciative look at his opponent. He was starting to think he should've given them the table when they'd met back in the club.

Not that it mattered now. As he reached the starting block, he began hacking a dozen burning coughs before finally catching his breath again. A strange feeling bubbled up in his stomach. He couldn't tell if he was ill or anxious. His headache was rebounding with a vengeance too. As he knelt, he could feel his body complaining and desperate for rest. His body felt strangely delicate as he tried to brace himself for the bright light and loud noise again. He wasn't sure he could take another tumble like the previous one.

"Ready!" said the Commissioner. "Starting in five... four... three... two... one..."

The siren sounded and Izo snapped across the field. Ignoring the lightning, he embraced the wind at his face, threw his arms back, and let himself relish in the free abandon. Was there anything better in the world than flying? Free as a bird, he left his throttle wide open and thundered across the field like a human cannon-ball. All too soon, the other side loomed, and he was forced to pull back and land.

Dropping to the ground with a couple of skipping hops, he grinned at the Anolitun before snapping to where everyone had gathered to review their times.

"How about that?" he asked with a proud smile. But no one else was smiling. In fact, neither Deneus, Tearn, nor Glongkyle could look him in the eye.

"Very fast!" said Yula, clapping.

"It was all right," Tearn agreed gently.

"Izo, what the hell?" Glongkyle jabbed a clawed finger into his chest. "That Anolitun just wiped the floor with you."

Izo gawked at the purple-skinned Avarian. "How fast are you, dude?"

The Anolitun grinned. He shrugged in faux humility. "I'm only the second fastest in my family."

"We know." The Commissioner gave a simpering look to the Senator. "That's how we knew you'd be a great fit."

Mortaco cleared his throat. "He's just warming up. Izo, a word?"

Taking him by the arm, the Senator led Izo a few meters away from everyone else. He looked back to the others with a smile pleading for forgiveness. Then he turned to rake Izo with a blistering glare. "What the hell are you doing?"

Izo swallowed. He was trying to clear a dry, burning sensation in the back of his throat. "Nothing. Catching my breath."

"You realize how important this is, right?" The Senator leaned over the youth. He stared. The heat off Mort's glare could have melted a block of ice. "You need to do this well."

Izo stilled under the heavy weight of the Malforian's disappointment. At the other end of the field, Glongkyle and Tearn noticed the youth's distress and sat up straighter. Izo could sense them staring at him, begging him, willing him to hurry up and get this over with.

Izo looked down at his palms. He was begging himself too.

"Is there some reason you're having difficulty?" The Senator turned to look across the field. "Is it because you're Avarian? Is it too difficult for you to understand?"

Izo sneered with offense. He'd never expected to be insulted like that. Hearing it so blunt and direct, it was almost funny. He tipped his head back to look at the man. "I got this, cabrón. Just back off and let me do my thing."

The Senator studied him. Then he jerked his eyes away and shrugged toward the starting line. "Good. Get it done."

Izo forced himself over to the starting blocks. He'd somehow never felt heavier, and yet somehow disconnected from his body. By the time he reached the block, his head was throbbing and he wanted nothing more than to curl up in a bed. Izo steeled himself, knelt, and tried to concentrate on the far side of the field. For some reason, his goal was growing blurry.

Izo blinked, shook his head, and demanded his eyes refocus, but it was no use. He physically couldn't see the other side of the field. A sudden wave of weakness knocked him out of his kneeling position and onto his butt.

The Electric Sprite snickered.

"I'm fine," Izo insisted.

He swallowed back a wall of nausea and ignored the sweat dripping off his chin. The Senator was right; he had to do this. But his headache was doing weird stuff to his vision which, in turn, was throwing off his balance.

He shook his head and yanked himself back into position. To keep himself standing he attached a rubber band to the ceiling and hung himself on it like a marionette—but he could tell it wasn't strong. One brusque motion and he'd snap and fall. He tried not to think about that, concentrating instead on the far side of the field instead.

The truth was he didn't have a chance. This was futile. He could already see it—the siren sounding one last time...Izo starting, clumsy and slow off the block...a soaring leap that hit a hiccup mid-flight...a downward spiral that he couldn't pull out of in time...a crash...a spin...a crumpled heap...and finally, the Senator's displeased expression.

Where would that leave his return to Earth? Glongkyle had threatened to leave him behind and find another Avarian if he couldn't make enough money. Maybe Izo could convince them to give him a little more time?

It took Izo a long time to realize he was falling again. After hitting the floor, it took him even longer to figure out who was lifting and trying to rouse him with heavy, lumbering motions...

"Stop," Izo whined in annoyance. The worried Wuljerian shook him like a rag doll and the motion, while well-intentioned, did nothing to help soothe his shattered equilibrium. The room spun and reeled. A new wave of dizziness hit him.

He did his best to shake off his furry friend. "Yula, I'm awake."

"Izo is sick. Izo must stop."

"I can't see." Izo pulled himself out of Yula's grasp and onto a heap on the floor, but the Wuljerian snatched him from behind.

Izo tried to bat the furry arms away but it was as useless as it had ever been. He was engulfed in an endless fuzzy hug.

"I'm all right," he said patting the giant's arms. "Yula, I'm okay."

"What the hell is this?" the Senator asked Deneus with an expression of rank disgust. Yula's protective growl gave him his answer, and all three Malforians moved further away.

The Wuljerian turned to Glongkyle and Tearn. The two had finally gotten off their asses and were approaching quickly. "Izo is sick," she insisted. "Sick must quit."

Izo dropped his head. This was the most anyone had worried about him in a very long time.

"Izo's fine. He just needs a little encouragement," Tearn said. He reached out to grab the youth's arm, his expression softening into a familiar calm and soothing pattern. Something from deep within Izo's tired subconscious flickered up in agreement. The muscles in his arm jerked instinctually for the Ginarsian like a starving man reaching toward the smell of food.

Yula yanked the Earthling away. "Izo not fine," she said, holding him higher and decidedly more sideways than Izo might have preferred. "Izo must rest."

"Yula, calm down," said Tearn.

"Yula is calm," said Yula.

"People are waiting," Glongkyle hissed.

"People can wait," agreed Yula.

"Look, if he ever wants to see home again, he needs to suck it up, fly right, and knock the snark off this Anolitun," said Glongkyle.

For once, Izo agreed with Glongkyle.

Yula shook her wooly head. "Home must wait."

"No, Yula. Home can't wait." Izo smiled at the large, gentle alien. "It's okay. I just needed a second. I'm fine now."

Yula hugged the Avarian tighter. Desperation and concern dug trenches into her features. "Yula protect Izo."

Izo hugged her back for a moment. "What are you protecting me from?"

Yula glared at the Senator. "Malforian."

"He's not the problem," said Izo. He gave Yula a noogie. "This is something I have to do. One quick race, then we all head back to Earth." He shot a look at Glongkyle. "Right?"

The Strungian nodded, first at Izo, then Yula, and finally Tearn. "As soon as the checks clear."

Yula seemed to relax at this. "And Wookie practice?" She remembered, turning to Izo.

Izo laughed. "Every day."

Yula set Izo on his feet and stepped back gingerly, her furry paw kept pressed against the youth's shoulder to steady him. Tearn approached to slide his stubby palm up and down Izo's forearm. A rush of wondrous comfort flooded the Earthling. It was as if the entire top half of his body had suddenly been dipped in warm water. His green eyes looked to Tearn's, and he could feel the color coming back into his face. Somehow, despite his illness, he was suddenly as charged as a stick of dynamite.

Tearn took a step back. For a moment he looked tired, but then seemed to shake it off. He patted Izo's arm. "Good luck."

Then they all shrank back.

Izo closed his eyes as the Commissioner began counting down. It felt great to shut out the light. He realized he didn't need it anyway; all he needed was to focus on the subtle pull coming from the other side of the field. In fact, he could already feel where he'd snagged the rubber bands before. Manipulating them gently had proven ineffective. Gritting his teeth, he grabbed onto the bands and hauled them in with every fiber of his unseen powers.

Within seconds a massive cord had gathered between him and the red line across the field, a singular connection stretching into a blistering density.

Yet still, he thickened the band. Why? Because screw it. Soon he could feel the space around him beginning to bend, something that had never happened before. He pulled even harder, the invisible rubber bands beginning to feel more like a tube-shaped hole. Somewhere deep down, he let out a silent long whistle. Whatever this was, it was going to be a doozy.

Raising his chin, Izo opened his eyes just as the siren sounded. Then he let go.

The cord anchoring him to the opposite side of the field snapped, and he soared, caught like a kite in a hurricane. A flash of light shattered and the visible spectrum exploded. The three dimensions of his spoken universe disappeared. He could feel it just beyond the edges of his arms, like a breeze outside of a jacket. Behind him, there was a crackle of stilted brightness and it took him a moment to realize it was the beginning of a white flash.

Of course! He was moving through the shortcut in the middle of space! He giggled and wanted to kick himself. He couldn't believe how dumb he'd been, going the long way through the dimensions his whole life like a moron.

Shifting forward, he immediately stopped. There was something wrong; the proportions were off. When he moved forward, he expected the ground to stay the same distance away. But instead, all the edges of things were moving at irregular angles. Had he been on the ground he could have misjudged the depth of a single step by an inch or a mile.

Luckily, he was midair and there was an invisible trail to follow—the path he'd carved into the other end of the field. Pulling too hard, he'd accidentally ripped the path away from the first three dimensions, like pulling masking tape away from a wall and across the center of a room. Without using his sight, he could follow the path of the tape and reach the other end far faster, even if he had no idea what "direction" the tape was going.

Izo shut his eyes and moved along the middle path, giggling as he swam through it like a fish.

Landing on the ground at the other end of the field, he opened his eyes. Everything was still distorted. Izo screwed up his face and tried to figure out how to get everything to go "flat" again. A moment later, some reflexive effect shifted his perception. Dimension and space fell into their normal and orderly, if slower, places in the universe. Behind him, an image of lightning stuttered.

Smiling, Izo's last thought before passing out was that the Senator could eat a butt.

— CHAPTER TWENTY-TWO —

Mort

Izo's eyes fluttered slowly. The Senator, noticing, shifted closer to take the Avarian's hand, but it turned out to be a false alarm. A few moments later, the strange and lovely creature sighed and relaxed back against his fluffy covers. Mort smiled and returned to his reading.

They'd been like this for days, the Avarian blipping in and out of near-consciousness as Mort held a never-ending bedside vigil. The Southern Chancellors had finally left, no doubt half ready to dash all their carefully crafted plans of Imperial treason out the door, but it was no matter. Truth was, they needed him more than he needed them, and there wasn't anywhere he'd rather be than watching over his broken Gravity Sprite.

Mort knelt next to the bed to look down at Izo's face. Paler than normal, it had grown gaunt in the corners of his jaw and the hollow of his throat. His cheeks were flushed pink in a low-grade fever. Mort's chest tightened. He'd never seen anything half so sweet or fragile. Grabbing a limp hand, he couldn't help but hold it to his lips. There'd never been another Avarian like this in his house. There probably wouldn't ever be again.

Mort gently tucked Izo's hand under the covers again. His heart soared as he pulled the sheets higher, the compassion at caring for his Gravity Sprite so strong it overwhelmed him like a physical pain. A flash of fear hit him. What if, now that he'd finally found this one, perfect companion, this singular discovery, this irreplaceable creature whose value and measure would never diminish—he lost it? No. He wasn't going to think about that. He was going to keep Izo safe and nearby no matter what it took. Harbored securely in his home, he had procured the single most precious Avarian alive. He wasn't going to let this go wrong. He'd rearrange the universe and everything in his life if need be. Everything was going to work.

Mort fell back into his chair slowly. He would be gentle, gallant, and kind. He would be a protector, a confidante, and a fortress. Eventually, he would become a lover. Until then, he would be patient. He would protect and support his Gravity Sprite. He would treat Izo better than any other Avarian in existence, because Izo was better than any other Avarian in existence. He was it. He was the one.

Yes, this was the only thing that made sense. Gone was the funny green-eyed curiosity that had caught Mort's attention and could maybe tickle his interest for a week or two. Since then the mysterious, dark-haired youth had bloomed and revealed himself as something entirely different. Something special. It was only natural to react differently. The way he felt for Izo now was deeper than desire, larger than love, and purer than obsession. This was... commitment.

Mort brushed his fingers against his own jaw. Wow. He never thought he'd so much as think the word. And yet, there it was. Mort was dedicated. No matter what it took or how long he had to wait, he was going to see this through. And then everything would finally be perfect.

Izo opened his eyes. The Senator, noticing the Avarian finally awake, sat forward. He smiled. "There he is."

Izo looked around the bed. Large and ornate, it dwarfed him like he was a flower in a forest. He blinked slowly in confusion. "Where am I?" Izo asked, wheezing roughly. His voice was raw and weak.

"You're safe. You're in my home."

Izo looked around the room. He didn't look especially happy about the location. Mort peered behind himself in confusion. The room was a wide and airy space, the second largest guest room in the estate. The green walls, vaulted twenty feet high, had been modified to match a lighter shade of Izo's eyes. Tall Malforian furnishings lined the room in tasteful gleaming black. Mort hissed. "The furniture is probably too big for you. Don't worry though. I'll have someone take measurements as soon as—"

He stopped short when he saw the Avarian's expression. Izo wasn't glaring at the furniture, but the walls. Mort glimpsed back again and it hit him—the room's decorations. Six large etchings, three on each side of the room, were smiling down on them from a ten-foot height. Engraved in black and gold, each was derived from a classic Malforian myth and showcased a study in ideal Avarian form. The Avarians in them, splendid and nubile, were poised in various states of floating allure. The collection was from a single master, an old family favorite, and represented a small fortune. For some reason, the Avarian seemed repulsed by them.

"Is everything all right?"

The Avarian looked away with disgust. "Where am I?" he rasped again.

"I already told you," said the Senator. "You're in my home."

"Why?" Izo asked. He was coughing and struggling to sit up.

"Take it easy." The Senator moved forward to help. Lifting the Avarian gently, he moved him back against the top of the bed. Mort was rewarded with a fresh if somewhat feeble glare. He moved away. "You're very sick. I don't know how much you remember, but you ripped a hole in the space-time continuum before losing consciousness. You've been out cold for four days."

"How long?" asked Izo. Before Mort could reply, a rolling succession of painful wet coughs seized the youth and proceeded to kick his ass for the next minute straight. Mort could only sit back and wait. A little while later, when Izo glanced up with a mouth full of phlegm, Mort reached down to hand him a marble bucket off the ground.

He held it up for Izo to spit into. The Avarian hocked up everything in his throat. Moving to return the bucket to the floor, Mort paused as Izo placed a hand on the bucket's edge, then cleared his nasal cavities into it, too. By the time he released the bucket, his breathing sounded much clearer. Swallowing gingerly, Izo lay back against the top of the bed, an unmistakable look of pain and fresh exhaustion on his face.

The Senator placed the bucket back on the ground. "Does it hurt?"

Izo nodded and cleared his throat again. Based on his expression, you would have thought he was swallowing fire. Mort frowned. It might be a long time before his Gravity Sprite could breathe or speak normally again. The Senator gazed sadly at the wretched youth. "I never should have made you finish that race."

Izo started to respond but broke into another fit of coughing. The Senator stood to soothe the Avarian's chest and support his neck. "Don't try to talk. Save your strength."

Izo shot him a tiny, withering glare, but he was clearly too miserable to fight. Mort could feel the small shivers radiating out of his core and the way his limbs jerked when he moved them, no doubt aching in brittle soreness. The pink on his cheeks and forehead had also grown darker. When Mort reached to brush the area, it was decidedly warmer to the touch. He frowned and reached under the Avarian's chin for his neck.

Izo shifted his face despondently. "Quit it," he rasped.

The Senator sighed and turned in the opposite direction to mix a soothing medicinal powder and fever reducer into a small cup of water. The fine powder dissolved easily. "I know I'm not your favorite person right now, but you still need my help." Stirring the drink a few times, he held it up to the Avarian's mouth. "Drink this. It'll help your throat."

Izo grunted in annoyance and shut his eyes instead. He looked like he wanted nothing more than to slip back into the painless oblivion of sleep again. Mort couldn't allow that, not until he got some liquids and medicine into the youth's system. The Senator waited another moment, then grabbed a slender shoulder to gently shake.

Izo made a whining noise. "Leave me alone."

"I will after you drink this." Grasping the back of his head, the Senator held the cup to his Gravity Sprite's lips. Izo tried to lift his arms to fight, but couldn't seem to manage. After a few moments, he gave up. Dropping his head against Mort's hand, he forced down a couple of swallows.

The Senator smoothed the Gravity Sprite's temple with one thumb before moving the drink away. Then, tipping the Avarian back, he gently replaced him against the pillows. "Better?"

Izo cleared his throat but didn't answer. It took Mort a moment to realize that though open, the Avarian's eyes were staring blankly ahead, seeing nothing. He was clearly too tired to register most things happening, much less answer questions. He looked as limp and listless as a pile of cut flowers in the sun. Mort smiled and poked him in the cheek with one finger.

Izo glanced up vacantly. "Hmm?"

"How does your throat feel?"

Izo swallowed and nodded. Opening his mouth, a rush of tiredness grabbed him—a side effect of the quick-acting medicine, no doubt. Eyes fluttering shut, his head lolled to one side. Mort reached out just in time to catch and cradle the youth's skull. He chuckled and petted the Avarian's damp forehead before gently lifting his Gravity Sprite's body to slip him more soundly into the covers.

Mort sat back and dimmed the lights from his embedded device. A cool easiness seemed to fill the room. After a moment, he decided to lower the temperature of the room and Izo's pillows as well. He was rewarded with a peaceful sigh of contentment as Izo turned to relax his face against the pillow on his right. It probably felt great on his warm cheeks. Mort beamed.

Mort leaned down to smooth away a few hairs that had fallen forward over his Gravity Sprite's eyes. "You really are a handful, you know that?" he told the sleeping creature. "But it doesn't matter. I'm not going anywhere. And you know why?" He leaned down to rest his chin next to his beloved. "Because you're worth it."

Izo shivered. His brow seemed to draw down in deep unease and dismay. He looked like he might be starting to have a nightmare. "We were at a store," Izo mumbled. He was trying to pry his lips apart, but they seemed to be half welded shut. "I didn't want to wear a dress…"

The Senator smiled and didn't respond.

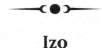

Izo

Izo tried to remember what was going on. He'd been looking for something in the dark. Had it been raining? He remembered the sound of lightning cracking above. It had filled him with hopelessness. At some point, he thought he heard someone ask him a question. Was it Tearn? Where was Tearn?

He could feel the Senator watching him as he slept. It unnerved him beyond words. A curl of nausea hit the miserable teen. He groaned. "Don't."

There was a long silence. "I'm not going anywhere," said the Senator.

Izo hadn't realized he'd fallen asleep again until he felt the bed shift. He cracked an eye. There was a hazy figure floating above him, lifting his torso to arrange him on a platter. Izo jerked away like he'd been burnt by fire, but the Senator just shushed him and repainted his face before packing him into a box filled with pillows.

Izo whined and wanted to cry. He didn't want to be alone with this man. He didn't want to be drifting in and out knowing Mort was nearby. But his half-sleeping consciousness blipped in and out of reality like a broken time machine. Memories, dreams, and the present splintered around each other in a kaleidoscopic explosion. He needed to snap out of it and get somewhere safe. Somewhere alone. Somewhere closer to home.

But his limbs wouldn't move.

The Senator let out an angry breath. He was kneeling on the ground next to Izo. Elbows propped on the edge of the shrine, his hands were steepled in supplication. "Don't do that." He warned in a voice like a lion's roar. "Don't run away from me."

Izo turned his shoulder to roll in the opposite direction, but the motion drew another wave of hammers from the sky. They plummeted down to beat the air out of his chest.

— CHAPTER TWENTY-THREE —

Izo

Some unknown period of time later, Izo opened his eyes. Vision coming into focus, he looked around. It was mid-morning, and there was a wonderful freshness in the air. Izo breathed in and stretched. A deep, healing yawn broke through to fill his lungs with cool, crisp oxygen. By the time he dropped his arms to the bed, he felt a million times better. He'd never been so grateful to not feel like shit, even if he had no idea where he was at the moment.

Wait, I do know where I am, he thought to himself. *I'm in the Senator's house.* Gazing around, he took in the large room. Bigger than a penthouse, it was tall and filled with fancy furniture and the single largest bed he'd ever seen. In the far corner, a floating table and a bunch of chairs led to a balcony outside. In the opposite direction he spotted what looked to be a decent-sized bathroom. The pictures on the wall were a little weird, but overall it was a pretty swanky spot. *Not bad.*

Izo nodded in appreciation, but then he frowned. *Wait. Why am I in the Senator's house?*

Appreciation for his new digs disappearing, Izo was filled with a wild sense of discomfort. It wasn't the first time he'd awoken to an entirely new set of circumstances. He knew enough by now to sense when something was weird in a way that people probably wouldn't openly admit. This whole situation was distinctly starting to feel like one of those times.

Izo spun his head and spotted the Senator a few feet away. Arms crossed at his chest, the large Malforian was sound asleep, hard face tipped dreamily to one side. His clothes were disheveled; he'd been wearing them since the day before. Feet crossed in front, he'd kicked off his shoes and left them sprawled on the ground between the two of them.

Izo scowled at the sleeping monster. He could vaguely remember the Senator watching over him the entire time. It was a weird feeling: ninety-seven percent pissed, but three percent begrudgingly grateful. It was like if Dracula saved you from falling off a cliff. Sure, you were a dick if you didn't say thank you, but you were wise to pay attention every time he looked hungry.

Truth was Izo hadn't felt safe in months. Maybe it was something about being abducted by aliens and forced into intergalactic extortion, but lately, it had been hard to get a reading on his emotional freak-out meter. Everything was terrible. His psychological "togetherness" felt like an ever-tenuous autumn twig ready to snap at the slightest pressure. And that was fine. He was used to it. But it hadn't left him a lot of range to assess new events.

He knew he didn't like the idea that they'd technically spent the night together, but he also had a sense this wasn't actually the biggest issue. Oh well. He'd figure out what he was supposed to be angry over later.

"Hey—tall, dark, and creepy." He leaned forward to snap his fingers loudly. "Why the fuck am I in your house?"

Jerking awake, the Senator glanced over at Izo. He grunted. "Good morning to you too, sunshine. I take it we're feeling better after being selflessly saved and nurtured back to health by a benevolent, good-looking leader of politics and industry."

Izo held up a hand. "Save the self-congratulation for later. I have questions."

"No, really, it's fine," grumbled Mort while rolling his eyes. "Your gratitude is more than enough."

"Why did you bring me here?"

The Senator stretched languidly. "You were sick. What was I supposed to do?"

"Take me to—oh, I don't know—a hospital?"

"I took you to my private estate instead. You're welcome."

"No welcome. Normal people take others to a hospital, not back to private estates. This isn't some eighteenth-century gothic story where the villain sneaks the helpless damsel back to his castle in the mountains."

Mort considered this. "But...the mountains would be safer."

"The mountains are remote. They're only safer for the villain."

"It doesn't matter if they're remote. The damsel can fly."

"Not if she's sick, asshole!"

Mort frowned and sat up. "Look, I couldn't go to a hospital; I had an unresponsive, supposedly extinct Avarian with no records, zero vaccinations, and half of every disease known to sentient-kind. Do you have any idea how many viruses you had running through your system? What did you do, lick every door handle on the way out of the spaceport?"

Izo thought back to the table at the spaceport cafeteria, how he'd slammed his hands down on it and eaten afterward. "No." He shook his head and turned to swing his legs over the side of the bed. "And that's beside the point. I don't care how sick I was," he continued, moving to stand. "This isn't an appropriate way to help people—" But before Izo could finish his sentence, his legs, weak as limp noodles, buckled beneath him. With a surprised yelp, the youth dropped to the floor like a pile of wet laundry.

The Senator looked down between his legs at the helpless Avarian laying at his feet, face as stern and distant as a god's. "Did you want to finish that thought?"

Reaching out for the edge of the bed, Izo tried to pull himself up, but he was too weak. He glowered sullenly and hated everything. "Would you just get down here?"

Mort stooped next to the Avarian. "Are you all right?"

"I'm fine. I just—" Izo paused as he was suddenly caught under his knees and back to be lifted against the Senator's chest. Stunned at the motion, he threw his arms around Mort's neck before thinking better of it and shifted his grip hold onto one shoulder. Humiliated at being scooped up like a pet, he turned to the Senator, fighting to hold some semblance of dignity on his face. "Didn't spend long debating how to do that, did you?"

Mort stood solidly beneath him. "It's the easiest way to pick someone up."

"Congratulations, Hercules. You want to put me down?"

"You want to say 'thank you' for once in your life?"

"Not especially." Twisting away, Izo swung out of the Malforian's hands like a cat insisting to be let down. The Senator had little choice but to quickly follow suit and lower him onto the bed again.

"Did you hurt anything when you fell?" Moving forward, Mort gently grasped Izo's nearest leg to slide up his pant cuff and examine it.

Izo frowned, noticing the white and loose-fitting fabric for the first time. It was the same material as his shirt. He didn't remember putting either on. He glowered anew. "Did you change my clothes while I was sleeping?"

"Yeah, but only after getting a couple of dozen naked pictures," Mort mumbled. He turned Izo's ankle, examining it with concern. "Is this supposed to bend in multiple directions?"

Izo smacked the hand away.

The Malforian paused long enough to take in Izo's blistering glare. He lifted his hands above his head. "I'm kidding. The medical emergency team cut off your clothes while checking your organs for damage. I don't remember who gave you these. Someone on the staff, probably."

"They cut off my shirt?" Izo grabbed his head and groaned. "Do you have any idea what I went through to find a shirt like that?

This is bullshit." He pointed angrily at the Senator. "Someone owes me a new shirt, ese."

"I called specialists in the middle of the night. They worked around the clock for days. They had to run clinical adverse reaction tests on every drop of medicine they gave you. I consulted and put under contract the three foremost forensic geneticists in the universe. It was literally millions of dollars' worth of healthcare."

"Okay. You guys need socialized healthcare too." Izo shrugged. "What's that got to do with my shirt?"

Mort stared in amazement. "You really are a pain in the ass."

Izo tsked. "Don't worry. You won't have to deal with me for long." He looked away and scratched his arm. "Speaking of, where were Tearn, Glongkyle, and Yula during all this?"

The Senator looked confused. "Who?"

"The other aliens I was with. You don't remember? There was a short grey one with big black eyes," Izo said, indicating Tearn's size with his hand. "A big fluffy one that could crush a car, and a scaly green asshole."

"Oh, those guys. I don't know. They bounced as soon as the cops showed up."

"They bounced?" Izo's heart skipped a beat. He blinked a few times. "Where did they bounce?"

"Couldn't say. The second everyone figured out we had the universe's only Gravity Sprite lying on the floor, people had a lot of questions. They didn't seem to like that."

"The universe's only what?" Izo shook his head. He was saying "What?" way too many times. "Back up. Where are Tearn, Yula, and Glongkyle now?"

"I told you—I don't know. They skipped town. The authorities tried to catch them at the spaceport, but it was too late. They disappeared before anyone could figure out what was going on."

Izo tried to come up with another question but was having a hard time. There was suddenly a loud rushing noise in his head. It was like the sound that came on a TV or radio before blaring static.

He tried to shake it off. "I don't understand. What does that mean? Where did they go?"

The Senator looked at him like he was crazy. "How would I know that? They didn't leave a letter. Hell, I don't even think they waited to refuel. That was six days ago. They could be anywhere by now."

"No." Izo shook his head. "I thought they were waiting for the racing check. Did you pay them?"

"Of course not."

"Then why did they leave without me?"

"I'm assuming because they didn't want to explain kidnapping the universe's only known Gravity Sprite."

"Why do you keep using that word?!" The rushing noise was growing louder. "What the hell is a Gravity Sprite?"

Now it was Mort's turn to look lost. "It's exactly what it sounds like—an Avarian capable of moving incredible distances using gravity. Gravity. Sprite." He pointed to Izo. "You."

Izo made a disgusted face. "I don't use gravity to fly. I use..." Izo thought back to how he usually explained it. "Invisible rubber bands."

Mort grinned and covered his mouth. "I've never heard gravity explained quite like that before...but sure. Anyway, the tests all came back positive. You're half Gravity Sprite on your mother's side. The only known example in the universe." He tipped his head, a look of curious affection spreading over his features. "You really didn't know either?"

"That all the doctors on IA are loco? No." Izo shook his head. "This still doesn't explain why the others left."

"Doesn't it? They got caught abducting the only member of a species previously thought extinct. People had questions. They didn't feel like answering. They left."

"No, no, no." The sense of tensile fear he'd been feeling ever since waking up was growing more and more splintered by the second. "You don't understand. I need them to get back to Earth. We have to find them. I need to get home."

Mort held out his arms. "I'm all ears. I'd love to catch those guys, but it's probably not going to happen. And it doesn't matter. You're a Gravity Sprite, Izo. Earth was never really your home."

The air left the room. "What do you mean? Of course Earth is my home."

"Not really. Gravity Sprites can travel between planets," explained the Senator calmly. Though he was seated only a few feet away, his voice seemed to be coming from a very long distance. "Your kind was discovering new worlds before inter-planetary travel was ever invented. You don't have a native world. You're a descendant of the cosmos, not Earth."

Izo reeled. "But I was born on Earth."

The Senator shrugged. "And now you live on IA."

"But I'm still going back to Earth. It's my home. It's where I belong."

Mort shook his head. He stood to sit next to Izo on the bed. Reaching down, he gently took the Earthling's hand. When he looked into Izo's eyes, it was with a look filled with sorrow. "Not anymore."

Izo opened his mouth but nothing came out. To his horror, he realized the air still hadn't returned to the room. He gasped to try to find some but couldn't. The sound in his ears had suddenly risen to an all-out pounding. He moved to turn away from the feeling, but there was only more of the terrible planet waiting in every direction. There was no escaping. He had nowhere to go.

"It's going to be okay." The Senator shushed the Avarian while pulling him into a hug. He rubbed Izo's back and spoke plaintively, like a person trying to coax a puppy out of hiding. "I'm going to take care of you. You're going to be safe here. No one's ever going to hurt you again."

Izo suddenly started to laugh. This wasn't real! He wasn't stuck on IA. This was some sort of prank. Glongkyle—of course! He was messing with him for being a butt. They hadn't actually left him halfway across the universe with some random psycho. They were coming back. They just had to be jerks about it first. That's all.

Izo grinned at the silly joke. Everything was fine. It was weird though—quite to the contrary, the room was beginning to shrink and tilt around him. His laughter continued, harder than before, even as he suddenly started feeling very dizzy and small. He gasped between chuckles but couldn't seem to get any air.

The Senator frowned down at him. He paused to pull back from their hug and survey the youth. "Are you okay?"

Was that a joke? Izo laughed even harder. He smacked his thighs with both his palms. He'd never laughed so hard in all of his life. But now his chest was tightening and he still couldn't get a breath in. Tears poured out of his eyes. His hands and feet were starting to feel cold.

The Senator grasped his face. He stared into Izo's eyes, dead serious. "You're having a panic attack."

Izo shook his head and struggled to move away, but the Senator just held him closer. His heart was pounding in his chest like a hammer, and the rushing noise had turned into a painful boom. It was also getting harder and harder to see. Eyes racing back and forth, Izo reached out to claw at the larger being holding him back.

The Senator blocked him, pushing him onto his back awkwardly. "Why are you fighting me?"

Izo lifted his legs and kicked Mort in the chest as hard as he could. The strike landed with no physical reaction. The Senator looked down at the pair of feet pressed against his chest with a frown.

Izo cried in frustration and struggled to get further away, but the Malforian grabbed him and flipped him like a floor mat. Gasping on his stomach, Izo tried to get up, but a vortex of fear was sitting on his back. Panic crashed over him, and he shivered like a dying fish.

The Senator hopped off the bed and yanked Izo to the edge of it by both his legs. Once there, he jammed a knee onto Izo's thigh, holding him in place. Then he reached back to the floating nightstand. "Hang on. I have something for this."

Izo couldn't answer. He was too busy struggling to get air, but there was none in the room. He spotted an open window in the far wall. If he could fly out of it, he could leave the terrible room and get back to the spaceport. At the spaceport, he could find a way home. He grunted and reached for it with his invisible cords, but his powers were barely a flicker in his chest.

His pulse pounded in his ears like giants playing the drums. His fingers and lips tingled sharply. A pit of cold darkness started to close in at the edge of his vision.

The Senator made a victorious noise. Then, turning Izo over again, he climbed atop his middle, smooshing his arms against his sides. Izo watched helplessly with wide, roving eyes. He was alone in the house of his attacker. He was smaller by half, weaker by days, and no one even knew he was here. If the Senator wanted to hurt him, what was he going to do at this point? Part of him begged his limbs to fight anyway, begged his mouth to say something, anything, make any type of noise. Instead, he just froze. Prayed for it to end. The reality was too much. Mort, like every other Malforian on the planet, was a monster compared to him. It wasn't any use. He might as well be fighting off a bear.

And then, just like that, the Senator flicked open the blue cone's lid. Lifting Izo's sleeve, he jabbed the shell-shocked youth in the top of one arm. Izo hiccupped and jerked away, but Mort just hushed him and held the cone fast.

Izo's heart rate slowed. The fog around his head lifted. His eyes widened in amazement. A warm, calming sensation radiated through his body from the spot where the cone had stabbed him. His shoulders relaxed and he was finally able to pause, blink, and take a long, slow breath. Outside, he could suddenly hear the wind rustling in the trees, and everything of the horror shit-show from moments before had been completely replaced with a light and easy-going soberness.

He tilted his head at the Senator, still hovering astride him. "What the fuck was that?"

"That's my line." The Senator sighed and pulled the cone out of Izo's arm. Shifting over, he sat next to the youth. "This is your newest prescription medication." He held it up for Izo to see. "One click for a small panic attack. Two for a big one." Grabbing Izo's hand, he placed it in the youth's palm. "Take it. That's yours now."

Izo stared at the cone. "Since when do I need panic attack medicine?"

The Senator pushed a thumb into his brow. "Since that Ginarsian best friend of yours started juicing you with empath waves every time they needed you to calm down."

Izo thought back. "Tearn was forcing me to calm down?"

"Yeah," said the Senator. "I'm sure it came in real handy while abducting Avarians. Problem is he's been doing it to you for months, and now your neurochemistry's all fucked up. We'll probably be dealing with it for years." He breathed out angrily. After a moment, he glanced down at Izo. "How are you feeling now?"

"Okay." He mulled this over. The difference was staggering, which was strange because nothing had changed. He was still completely fucked. He just didn't feel worried about it anymore. He narrowed his eyes. "Why do I feel okay with all this?"

"The medicine is telling you to."

Izo nodded sagely. "It's lying."

The Malforian made a disapproving noise, but he smiled. "The chemicals are helping you cope with everything."

Izo nodded at this too. "You're also lying to me."

The Malforian's hand reached for Izo's. A mask of tenderness had appeared on his hard, shark-like features. "I'm also trying to help you cope."

Izo bristled at the intimate touch. He quickly sat up and moved away. Once far enough, he turned back. "Appreciate the meds, Chief, but you should go."

The Senator nodded and climbed off the bed. "You're probably right." Standing, he started for the door. "I'll be downstairs if you need anything."

"Thanks," Izo said, wanting him to go.

This show of gratitude, although casual and meager, was immediately met with a pleased smile. Izo realized he'd been right not to kowtow earlier. Mort's look of sheer self-satisfaction and victory was easily the most stomach-turning thing he'd ever seen. You'd have thought Izo'd handed over a month's worth of lunch money.

"You're welcome. I'll be back to check on you in a bit."

Izo dropped his gaze and didn't answer.

The Senator paused as he reached the door. He turned back. "You know, I realize I'm probably not your favorite person right now, but I want you to know I really do care about you. I'm not going to let anything happen to you. I'm going to take care of everything, and we're going to figure this out."

"Okay."

"I mean it—everything's going to be all right."

The youth closed his eyes at these words. An ugly memory flew through his mind, but he nodded and smiled through it. "You're right."

The Senator nodded and patted the door twice. "Well, try to get some rest." Then, lowering the lights, he gently shut the door behind him.

Izo crawled to the top of the bed and dropped his head back against the alien bedframe. He stared up into the dim grey darkness surrounding him.

"Everything's going to be all right," he repeated mildly. He was amazed at how flat his emotions remained even as his memories and thoughts kicked like broncos in his head. "That's what Tearn always used to say."

— CHAPTER TWENTY-FOUR —

Izo

I zo woke, saw the lush, green bedroom, and remembered his life was gone.

The Earthling groaned. He reached up and tried to rub out what felt like a pit in his chest. It didn't work. The pit was deeper than skin. His frowned and looked around the room sadly. He didn't want to cry when he felt this scared. Curling up on one side, he covered his face with his hands.

No, he decided suddenly, sitting up and sniffing instead. He wiped his eyes and yanked off his covers. He wasn't going to cry— at the very least, he wasn't going to cry in *this freaking room.*

The youth looked around for an exit. At one end of the room was a pair of glass-paneled doors, thrown open, with two green curtains left loosely rustling in the breeze. A tertiary glance revealed a high drop, followed by beautiful but steep mountainous terrain below. Sure, he could fly, but he'd also thought he could stand when his ass had unexpectedly greeted the floor the last time he got up.

Izo turned to the other side of the long room. There stood the inside facing door, the one the Senator had left through. It was tall and looked heavy and might be locked, but it was also his only real option.

Izo screwed his face up and swung his feet to the ground in the direction of the inner door. Then, ginger as a little old man, he tried standing.

A wall of weakness hit him and a spinning sensation forced him down again. His light-headedness verging into nausea, he waited for what felt like an eternity for his vision to clear.

Eventually, it did. Swallowing a mouthful of thick saliva, Izo told himself to just take it slow. Grabbing the bed banister like a lifeline, he slowly shifted up onto his feet. His balance was off, and his legs tried their best to buckle underneath him. After a few test-runs, he finally figured it out, leaning, straight-legged, against the wall. As long as he could avoid tipping too far forward or back, he might be able to remain upright.

Izo slid a few steps along the wall without falling. He grinned. *I totally got this.* Leaving the accursed bed behind, he began the long journey across the room and toward the door, accidentally knocking his statue over to smash on the floor as he passed.

"Lo siento," he said to the pile of broken glass, "pero eres siniestro."

His goal loomed. A giant portal, tall and silver, it stretched from the ground all the way to the top of the fifteen-foot-high vaulted ceilings above. As he finally shuffled up to its massive foot, he silently gave it a little pat, looked up with a friendly smile, and begged, "Please be cool?"

Izo held his breath and pushed. He was in luck! The door swung open with a click as easily as a magnetized cabinet.

Hugging the threshold, he peeked out. Outside was a long stone hallway, filled with bronze columns and strange, lewd statues that floated and twirled. Ten identical doors were spaced out at different distances on both sides, including his.

Izo turned to look down the opposite side of the hall and was met with a strange intersection.

It was an impressive design—a wide, circular mezzanine with a gaping drop, dark stairways connecting floors above and below. At its top was a dizzying marble-dome with intricate designs depicting raunchy scenes of floating people doing unspeakable things.

Izo scowled and turned his gaze down to the bottom half of the massive structure.

Punctuated with enormous art installations—either curved to follow its walls, or free-floating in the central opening—the masculine design was conspicuous. Brassy browns and bronzed golds were interrupted only by spots of espresso details: a round of exposed beams, an arrangement of tufted club chairs. It looked like a cigar room in Willy Wonka's house, if Willy Wonka had decided to build a seven-story-tall cigar room in the center of his home. Part foyer, part basilica, it struck Izo as something designed more for exhibit than living.

He was still looking around in stilted amazement when an angry voice cut in from behind him.

"What the hell do you think you're doing?"

Izo's eyes widened. He turned to look at the source of the sound. What he found, he never would have anticipated.

Behind him, the tiny, mean singer from Mort's ship stomped up the hall like an angry (if somewhat small), curly-headed torpedo. *Oh shit, not her again.*

"Take your sick, uncharted ass back to bed."

Instinctually moving away, Izo tried his best to hurry around the mezzanine. He knew he wouldn't get far, but he was hoping the next hallway might have something he could use as a weapon.

"Don't you run away from me," the blonde said, speeding her approach. "Get back to bed!"

"It's fine!" Izo singsonged over his shoulder. "I'm feeling much better now, gracias."

"I don't give a flying shit how you feel. Some of us work for a living. I can't have you smearing who-knows-what undiscovered diseases up and down our shared spaces. Now go to your room until you've been cleared by someone with a medical license."

"Mind your own business, Skipper."

"News flash: this hall is my business. Do you see this?" she asked, spinning to gesture at everything around them. "This is the Avarian Wing. I am Queen Supreme of this place. Everything comes through me. You want to live here, bitch? You do what I say. And I say to take your disease-ridden ass back to bed before I do it for you."

Izo gritted his teeth. He whirled on her. "Fuck. You."

Ari flitted higher. "Excuse me?"

"I have been abducted by aliens. I have been locked in a spaceship for months. I have been drugged and dragged, kicking and screaming, all the way across the fucking universe to get dumped here and left to die alone. I have been blackmailed, lied to, stolen from, assaulted, and chemically manipulated in ways"—Izo threw his hands up and nearly fell off the wall.—"I still don't understand. But this," Izo said, glowering down at her, "this is the fucking line. This is where I put my foot down."

He took a shuffling step forward, anger radiating off his body and face. "Fuck you. It will be a cold day in hell before I ever take an order from a nasty, black-hearted, puta-bitch like you." Then, rearing back, he screamed so loud he hurt his own throat. "SO BACK OFF, TINKERBELL!"

Ari's face went tight. She glared. She shook with rage and then, almost before either of them knew what happened, she'd jerked up and smacked the youth on the head.

Izo blinked. The strike, while not exactly heavy, had left a decided sting. Izo inclined his head at the tiny female. She was easily thirty percent smaller than him. "Did you just hit me?"

Ari flitted higher, clearly a little embarrassed but determined to hide it. "I'm sorry, but you were being very rude and—"

Licking his hand, Izo smeared it across her cheek.

Ari's mouth dropped like a stone. She smacked him on the head again. Izo maturely responded by leaning forward to spit in her face. Ari, equally a picture of maturity at this point, floated high and began beating at Izo's head and shoulders like a drummer keeping time.

Izo grunted and wrapped his arms around his head while leaning against the wall. "I don't want to hit you," he said, swiping at her and missing. "Miss Ada told me never to hit anyone smaller than me, and I don't want to disappoint her. But I have made exceptions before, you bug-eyed bitch!"

"My eyes are my best feature," Ari said, flitting back far enough to drop a none-too-soft kick to his stomach.

Izo reached out, swiped, and missed again. It was slowly occurring to him that despite his bigger size, he might not fair too well in his current state. "Does that pumpkin-head make you gorgeous too?" He laughed when she made a high, offended noise. "That's right! Your head's too big for your body. You look like a bobble headed Barbie, if they replaced the top half with a globe."

"Aurelians have big brains, you street trash!" she yelled. "We're known for high social acumen and artistic skill. This big head could read ten languages and play thirty instruments by the time I was your age."

"Oh yeah? Were two of them the Malforian meat whistle and the Ginarsian skin flute?"

She looked at him in confusion as her translator took a moment to catch up. As her huge gold eyes began slowly widening, Izo was able to break into a shit-eating smirk at the exact moment she seemed to catch his meaning.

The pop star touched down to the ground, and there was something slightly altered about her aura that told Izo he needed to run now.

Turning, Izo shuffled down the wall like he'd never shuffled before. Before he could even get six feet away, Ari had leapt onto his back to trounce him with an attack so vicious, mean, and angry, he was left wondering if she wasn't part banshee.

"Don't you ever sneer at me!" Ari screeched, ripping and pounding at his head and back. "I'm one of the best-selling recording artists alive! I have the highest-grossing live act of all time! I am a living fucking legend! DO YOU HEAR ME?"

Izo grunted, cursed, and tried to duck through the veritable slap-n-scratch tornado currently nailed to his back. When she added a volley of hard kicks in for good measure, Izo abandoned all defenses and did the only thing he could think of: fling the two of them onto the ground to try to pin the singer's arms at her sides.

Tumbling to the ground, for one magical second Ari was too surprised to attack. Izo seized on that singular moment, grabbing the Aurelian's arms to pin against her tiny body. As he began holding her in place he realized, much to his dismay, how many levels of strength she'd been holding back.

Grunting, Ari immediately broke one arm free. Izo fought to snatch it back but was instead greeted with a heavy blow to his ear.

"Ow!" He cringed his shoulder up as his hearing rang painfully. "Use your words, gaddammit!"

But Ari was done talking. Rearing back, she smashed the same tiny fist into the side of his head over and over again. It stung more than hurt—he'd had his ass kicked worse than this before—but he was getting seriously annoyed. Try as he might to be patient, Izo found it harder and harder not to sock the smaller alien girl in the face. Knowing he had to stick by his morals no matter how far away Earth might be, Izo instead grabbed and pulled on the first thing his free hand could find—a hefty chunk of the pop singer's hair. Miss Ada would've never approved of hair-pulling, but she also never met an Aurelian.

Ari gasped and froze. "Not the hair!"

"Okay," Izo agreed. "We're just going to calmly—"

But before he could finish explaining what they were going to calmly do, Ari reached up and clamped her tiny, claw-like fingers around his jaw and nose.

Izo tried to pull away, but the only way to do that was to let go of her hair. Twisting his face, he managed to get a nail nearly lodged into his nostril. It was no use. They were at a stalemate.

"Shit," whispered Izo. "Estamos de la chingada."

"You are la chingada," said Ari.

Izo frowned. "No soy la chingada. Soy el chingón."

Ari grunted. Her nails twisted harder into his face.

Izo yanked her hair. "You better knock it off. You're about to be bald, Polly Pocket."

Ari glowered as her translator explained the reference. "You're making fun of my size?" She laughed in a way that genuinely hurt Izo's feelings. "You got abducted by a Ginarsian, sweetheart!"

The teen's shoulders dropped precipitously. "That's not funny."

"You're not funny."

Cursing and gently hurting each other, they were locked like that for longer than Izo would have liked to admit when a throat-clearing sound suddenly came from behind them.

Eyes widening, they both looked in the direction of the noise.

Mort and another Malforian, both wearing surprised expressions, were gathered at the top of the nearby stairs.

The slimmer of the two, slightly shorter and with narrower features, looked over at the Senator with a smirking expression. Izo felt like he'd seen him before. "Well, that didn't take long."

"Shut up, Lrasa," mumbled the Senator. He peered at the Avarians in confusion. "Ari, what are you doing?"

"Nothing." Then, grabbing Izo's waist close, Ari hopped up and spun the two of them around to switch positions and rise above him in an arched-back straddle. It was a move so quick and polished it reminded him of something from a pro-wrestling show.

"We were discussing household policy." Gazing down at Izo, Ari cocked her head to the side like an adorable but overly intense kitten. "Weren't we, cutie?"

"Sure," Izo agreed lamely.

Ari beamed up at her audience. "See? We're all good. No worries."

"Okay..." the Senator said, eyes still dancing over the two of them with concern. "Just be gentle with him. He's still on the mend."

"Aww…" Ari said, wagging her body back and forth in a way that made Izo, still beneath her, feel very confused. "What? Worried about little ol' me?"

"Ari, I'll give you a million dollars to kiss him right now," said the other Malforian, Lrasa.

"Ew," Ari said with a snarky expression. "I don't know where he's been."

"Do you ever know where the stuff you kiss has been?" countered Lrasa

Ari sat back on the Earthling's hips. She crossed her arms. "Suck my Aurelian dick, Lrasa."

Izo sulked and tried to think through his options, but it was no use. Ari was smaller than him, and that's all there was to it. Even if Izo was sick, even if Ari was a pixie-like monster with tiny, clawed fingers and devastating elbows, even if the bigger person could barely stand and the smaller person was meaner than a rattlesnake and twice as dangerous—it made no difference! Miss Ada's rules were Miss Ada's rules, as hard and unbreakable as the rules of physics.

"I'd be happy to," retorted Lrasa at Ari's crude comment from earlier. "But you'll have to float a little higher than normal tonight."

Izo's eyes went big as saucers. His head shot up to gaze at the blonde. "You're Avarian." He pointed at her. "You can be as tall as you want!"

Ari looked at the Earthling like he was crazy. "Huh?"

But Izo had already broke out into a simpering grin. A switch had flipped and Izo finally saw the truth. She was Avarian. He was Avarian. Midair, everyone was on even ground. Logic re-asserted, his bruises and scrapes screamed for vengeance, and Izo cackled for what was about to come. "Oh—it's on now."

Then, bringing in an arm, Izo cracked the blonde across the face with a wildly unrestrained backhand.

She squealed in surprise while crumpling sideways to the floor.

"Shiiit," said Lrasa, covering his mouth. "I didn't think Avarians could do that!"

A split second later as Ari was on her feet. Flipping her hair back, she wiped a line of blood off her mouth before locking eyes with Izo. All rules were clearly suspended.

Ari hurtled herself forward, rocketing the two of them high into the nearest wall with a resounding slam, followed by a clatter as they fell into a heap to the floor.

"Whoa!" Izo heard the Senator call. "Lrasa, help me split them up!"

"Do I look crazy? I'm not getting in the middle of that," protested Lrasa, backing up instead—and just in time, too. Izo and Ari slammed into, and then began rolling across, the ground barely an inch from where he'd been standing.

Catching up to the heap, Mort grabbed Ari and yanked her off before the Aurelian could do any more damage.

"Enough!" the Senator shouted. Setting the singer down, he planted himself between the two. "Ari: we've talked about this before, and you will not treat one of my guests like this. Particularly one...from so far away from home."

"And Izo," he said, spinning on the youth with an expression that reminded the youth of a teacher he'd hated in middle school. "Ari has more connections and business experience than anyone. You want to be a racer? You are going to need her."

Izo glared and stuck his tongue out at the blonde.

"So guess what?" Mort continued, shaking them both. "The two of you are going to be civil to each other—not because you like each other. Not because you respect each other." He glared back and forth between them. "You'll do it because every time you hold an event together, you'll get paid ten times as much." The Senator's gaze settled on the singer. "Okay?"

Ari blew out an angry breath. "Whatever."

The Senator turned to Izo. "Okay?"

Izo scowled at the ground. He couldn't believe it. Even when trying at full force, the tiny bitch had held her own. Hell, she'd cleaned the hallway with him. His jaw twitched with fury and abject humiliation. The fact that he knew these feelings were mostly consistent with machismo pride did nothing to ease the sting.

"Okay?" The Senator repeated, jostling the incapacitated Avarian with his foot.

Izo glared up at her from the ground. "Slut."

"Mutt!" Ari yelled. Rearing back, she went to lunge at the Gravity Sprite again.

"Lrasa!" the Senator bellowed and struggled to pull the two apart.

But Lrasa was laughing so hard he'd fallen over. "You know, Mort," he chuckled, holding his stomach while hunched up against the wall. "Up until this exact moment, I'd always been a tiny bit jealous of you."

— CHAPTER TWENTY-FIVE —

Ari

Ari stumbled into her room just as the first rays of the morning sun began peeking up over the mountains. Covering her eyes, she thought back and tried to remember the last time she'd felt so *tired*.

Her new album's big reveal with Mort's last-minute stand-in had proved exhausting, as she knew it would, but what could she have done? The asshole had left her searching for a date at the last possible second. She obviously couldn't have made him go, and she just as obviously couldn't have gone alone. And sure, she had a roster of back-ups to call, but they all knew when they were doing her a favor, which meant they all knew the deal.

She'd tried to pick someone esteemed and older, but as was often the case with all her "biggest fans," the Malforian had proved to possess the libido of a Senator half his age as well as the pathetic clinginess of a small child. It had been enough to make her wonder if she shouldn't have just taken Lrasa or some other routine Sword member. They tended to treat her (and most Avarians) like a second-rate form of depraved entertainment, but at least their dismissiveness tended to go hand-in-hand with letting her go home early. After all, there was nothing so boring to the rich and powerful as spending too much time with a familiar pretty face.

Dragging herself across her room and to her windows, Ari supposed there would always be someone who found her shiny and new. It was both a hazard and a benefit of the job. There was no way to meet the entire Mountain, much less the trail of foreign diplomats and high-ranking officials that popped by throughout the years. There would always be someone left still yearning for her as this perfect, unattainable, untouched Avarian. And poor little Ari was cursed to run into them one by one, these enraptured admirers who'd watched and longed from a distance until, when their turn finally did come around, they spent the night drawing out the agony, like a tantalizing self-torture, talking for too long, undressing too slowly, straining to temper their love-making, fighting to savor all of her luscious benevolence as they struggled to both embrace and stretch time, an ill-fated paradox if ever there was one.

Mmm! It was enough to nearly get her going again. But for now, she needed to rest, particularly before she had to get up and possibly do it all over again tomorrow.

Ari grunted in effort while slamming her shutters closed. Then, sailing high toward her bed, she touched down, yanked off her dress, and finally dropped into her sheets to fall into an exhausted sleep.

Several hours later the pleasant trills from one of her favorite hit songs began pouring in from her bedroom console, gently rousing her awake. Rubbing her eyes, she couldn't help smiling at the golden sunlight gently pooling in as the shutters slowly re-opened, bouncing light playfully across her favorite place on the Mountain. Taking in a deep breath and enjoying the soft aroma of her flower infused pillow, she slowly began gathering enough energy to start the day. At first it was a losing battle amidst the cool softness of her downy coverlet, but musings on the different types of breakfasts she could afford to indulge in broke through this languid mindset.

"A fresh madrilian, two bites of thake, and..." Ari scanned her mind for the best weekend indulgence that wouldn't completely wreck her caloric count for the day. "A crinkle roll with shaved sucra-legraun, mmm..." Her mouth was watering by the time she sat up and tapped her bed's central console to call the kitchen.

"Good morning," she chirped pleasantly. "I would like to request breakfast for room—"

"I know which room, Ari," replied a smiling voice.

"Zokie, is that you?" Ari always flirted with Zokie mercilessly and, as a result, was able to keep all sorts of sweet treats off her dietary record. She usually had to wait until the work week to catch him, though. "I didn't know you were going to be here this weekend!"

"Yeah. With the big party coming up, they've got everyone on prep."

Of course. Mort was holding a private get together to introduce everyone to his latest discovery, the bedraggled, dark-haired cretin across the hall. Slated as a small, "intimate" gathering, this would no doubt be crawling with over a hundred of the richest, most powerful Malforians on the Mountain. "Ahh, makes sense. I'm sorry you lost your weekend."

"That's all right. I get to see my favorite singer." Ari couldn't help but smile at this. She loved Zokie. "So, what can I get you?"

"I woke up with this wild craving for something sweet."

"No kidding?" Zokie deadpanned in good humor. "Ari Lumiere after something sweet first thing in the morning? Who would have guessed it!"

"Ha ha, very cute. So, can you hook me up?"

Ari heard a sigh coming from the other end of the line. "I don't know, beautiful. It's really jumping in here. There's people every-where. I don't think I can sneak anything out without anybody seeing."

"And here I thought we were friends," she pouted. When he didn't respond, she suddenly had a new idea. "You know," she said, drawing herself up close to the speaker, "if I had something sweet and delicious to look forward to, I might get so caught up thinking about it, I'd forget to do anything else until you get here. Like get out of bed." A wicked smile curled the edge of her mouth. "Or get dressed."

She could hear Zokie shifting closer to the speaker on his end. When he spoke again, it was lower and huskier. "You're not dressed yet?"

"Nooo," Ari purred quietly. "I was so tired last night, I just threw my clothes off and fell into bed." Ari drew her feet up and down the covers, letting the soft rustle of her legs sliding over the fabric drift into the speaker. "And I'm always so tired first thing in the morning. I don't think I could move a muscle. Zokie-eeeee," Ari whined sensually. "Won't you please come up here with something warm and delicious to help wake me up?"

Zokie swallowed hard. "I'll figure something out. What do you want?"

"A sucra-legraun glazed crinkle roll and my usual."

"Okay. I'll be up in twenty. Just...stay exactly where you are."

"You're the best." Ari cooed before ending the call. Yawning one more time and giving her shoulders a good stretch, she hopped up and took a running leap out of bed, twirling to grab her favorite gauzy robe off the back of a chair as she went. If she only had twenty minutes, she'd need to get her face on fast.

Sailing across her sitting area, she landed near the front of the room at her five-mirrored vanity, the single most ornate and organized space in her place. Floating daintily just above the chair (as her mother always taught her), she immediately began scrubbing and rinsing her face before pulling out her anti-aging kit to lay out the tools and carefully sterilize them.

She hated sticking the skinny needles into the problem areas around her eyes and mouth, but she hated letting someone else do it more. Her doctors had a funny way of acting towards her ever since she slept with that one Dr. Jajurut, and she preferred to avoid them except in emergencies, which she'd explained to Dr. Pittrin, her psychiatrist. Dr. Pittrin had been sweet enough to give her a waiver for the supplies and to secure enough classes for Ari to learn how to administer them herself. So, really, she was incredibly lucky to be doing this, which she kept repeating as she pricked herself over a dozen times to situate the semi-permanent gel into the fine crevices in her skin. Working quickly, she soon finished and was happily putting everything away for another week.

Done with that, she was moving onto her foundation when she heard the telltale click and rustle of someone coming into her room. "Just a minute!" she called out, pulling a face projector onto her neck while glancing at her clock. *That was fast.*

"Have you seen the new one?" came Senator Mortaco's unexpected voice. "He keeps sneaking out of his room, and I can never find him when I need him."

Ari held in a groan and pulled off the projector, the vision of her pre-made face disappearing in the mirror. "Maybe if you stopped barging into places unannounced, he'd feel more comfortable staying in his room."

Mort waved this off while hunching down to look under her furniture. "He's got to be around here somewhere."

"Well, he's not in here." Tapping her mirror console, she prompted her first level of colors to rise and unfold itself over her vanity, revealing all her favorite base shades and brushes.

Huffing, Mort rose to put his hands on his hips while looking around the room in confusion. Then he squinted over at her. "You going somewhere? I thought you had the day off."

She glanced at him in the mirror. "I'm going dress hunting. What do you care?"

He stuck his tongue in his cheek as if considering something. "You want to take him with you?"

Ari's eyes went huge. "Uh, how about 'Fuck no. How dare you?' You blew me off last night, and now you want me to take your homeless, broke-ass, weird-ass obsession shopping on one of my only days off? Go fuck yourself."

"Come onnnn," said Mort. "He needs someone to take him around. Show him the ropes."

"Okay—get him a tour guide. Why are you asking me? In case you haven't noticed, he and I kind of hate each other."

Mort shrugged this off. "He hates everything."

"You're kidding!" Ari gasped. "Now I'm super excited to spend the day with him!

Mort crossed his arms, but a playful grin danced across his face. "Now Ari, is this any way to talk to your number one corporate sponsor?"

"Are you still my number one? Because I didn't remember signing up for someone that leaves me stuck taking whatever horny, bottom-feeding Senator has nothing better to do out on a weekend night."

"Aw, Ari. Don't be mad," Mort said, beginning to saunter closer. "I didn't know you were going to miss me so much."

"I never get a chance to miss you. I'm too busy cleaning up after you."

Mort came up from behind her, his warmth hitting her back like a revved up engine. The fingers of one hand began tracing over her shoulder and neck, feeling along the lines of her clavicle and throat with insistent curiosity. She was suddenly reminded of the fact she was naked under her satiny robe.

She *humphed* and tipped her face away.

Mort leaned down to pout at her in the mirror. "I really am sorry."

"Sorry isn't going to get me back my album reveal or erase the all-nighter I had to pull with that ancient, groping—"

"Shh," Mort shushed, brushing a thumb over her lips and the rest of his hand under her jaw. "Come on. Let's make up."

"Uh-uh, no you don't," Ari said, soaring out of the chair to turn and float above him, eyes full of fire. "I don't need to make up for anything. I am not the one that messed up. I am not the one always asking for last minute favors! I am not the one that agreed to this event months ago! I'm not the one who stood me up because you'd rather sit around slobbering over some uninterested, uncharted nobody who—"

"But he's a—" Mort stopped and tapped a finger against his teeth. "He's a virgin! On IA!"

Ari squinted in suspicion. Mort didn't usually get nervous about things involving Avarians. He'd definitely been about to say something else, but it wasn't worth arguing over. If he didn't want to tell her, nothing she could say would make him. "That's not good enough! Now either you're going to promise to never do this again, or...the next time you call, I'm going to be busy for the next five years!"

"Okay, okay." Mort held up his hands, his eyes making clear he was loving every second of her fiery show of force. "I was going to offer you this extra touring stipend to make up for last night," he said, reaching into a pocket and pulling out a thin black packet, "but if you're really that angry with me, I should probably just go…" Putting it back, he turned towards the door.

"Don't you dare!" said Ari. Dropping fast, she pushed the larger Malforian into the nearest chair to straddle him and begin digging through his pockets. "I knew you wouldn't come in here empty-handed."

Mort laughed as the tiny blonde continued flipping through the half a dozen pockets on his left side before starting in on the other. It occurred to her he'd likely chosen the outfit on purpose to mess with her.

"Mm, have you checked the front of the pants? I think there might be something interesting there."

Ari looked up at him with a sly grin. "No, that's a whole other endowment I need to take care of."

"Want to take care of it first?"

Ari stopped searching, an easy smile coming over her face. "I thought you'd be tired from all your virgin drooling last night."

"Who, him? No, I only saw him for a second last night. Like I said, he hates everything. Which is why I need someone wonderful, sparkly, and beautiful like *you*," he said, poking her on the nose. "To show both of us a little love."

Ari rolled her eyes. "You really want me to take him shopping?"

"Just for a few hours while I go take care of a couple of things. Show him the sights, spend some money, talk about how great life on IA is." Sitting up, he adjusted to a more comfortable position in the chair. "It'll fly by. Next thing you know, you two will be best of friends."

"I don't know that I want to be best friends with someone that hates everything."

"It'll be fine," Mort said, reaching down to pull open her robe. "Just don't lose him."

— CHAPTER TWENTY-SIX —

Izo

I zo slid on his stomach out the tiny crack he'd made in Ari's door and into the hallway. Outside, he carefully rolled onto his back and raised one foot to gently press her door closed behind him. Then, finally free of the lusty alien boudoir inside, he grabbed his chest and let out a giant breath. That was close. He thought he was going to be trapped there the entire time that...well never mind. He was just glad he was free.

He looked upside down at the Senator's tall Avarian hallway. It occurred to him for the first time that all the doors went clear up the ceiling, an easy fifteen-foot height. Malforians were tall, but even Mort was dwarfed by these massive entryways. Maybe there were Avarians even taller than Malforians? If there were, he hadn't seen any around yet.

The sounds of groaning and thumping oozed in from the door beside him. Izo grimaced and rolled away onto his feet. He wanted nothing more than to leave the house and never return, but it made no sense to flee while they were still waiting for the authorities to get back to them on Tearn, Glongkyle, and Yula. In a way it felt ridiculous waiting around in the predator's playhouse, but with the *Atrox*'s navigation system still his only link to Earth, there didn't seem to be much point in doing anything else. The irony of the very thing he'd been trapped on and hated for so long suddenly being the one thing he was waiting and begging to return to wasn't lost on him, and Izo found himself in the strange position of both dreading and dying to see Glongkyle.

Izo's snooping around the hallway had led to the discovery of three things. One, that Mort went through Avarian house guests like people with allergies went through tissues. Two, that other than his own the only rooms never locked belonged to Mort's other two permanent house guests, Ari and a tall, mean dancer named Zusy. And three, Ari tended to be out most nights.

Solution? He'd been sneaking into Ari's room to sleep on her couch and/or hide in her massive three-story closet. He'd basically been living there for the last couple of days. He was surprised how great it worked, too. The singer was gone most of the time and, besides magically sprouting food or the Senator visiting every couple of hours, his room had nothing going on anyway.

Speaking of, he supposed he should head back, though he didn't really feel like it. But where else was there to go? He'd already wandered around the Senator's mansion several times, memorizing exit routes and figuring out where the food came from. He didn't really want to be in the house at all, but he also had nowhere else to go. Plus, Mort was basically keeping to his word to leave Izo be, even if he did have a bad habit of bursting in at any time like he owned the place—which he did, but it was still creepy. Lying awake for hours, Izo'd wrestled with the idea of leaving almost every night, but the fear of missing a new development had held him back so far.

Izo turned and for the first time noticed a skinny, short man with pink skin pushing a floating gold box. He glanced over the man curiously and wondered what type of alien he was. He was approaching from the central staircase, and he had a wide face and an even wider smile.

"Good morning, gorgeous!" the man said, tipping his head at Izo. "You happen to know if Ari's in?"

Izo looked over his chipper expression of approval and sneered. "Yeah. She's a little busy with the big guy, though."

The short man gave him a confused look. "The big guy?"

"The Senator."

The man looked at her door, even more confused. "I didn't think she was taking visitors yet."

Ohhh, he's the guy from the kitchen, Izo realized. He gave the man a knowing look. "I think he came down to help wake her up too, buddy."

"Oh, well, um…awesome." He stared at the door with a crestfallen expression. "This is her breakfast anyway, whenever she wants it." He pushed the box to the left of the entrance.

"I'll let her know." Izo went back to trying to decide if he should return to his room or just leave the house and any chance of ever finding Earth again, but the man didn't leave. Instead, he stood there for a minute, looking Izo over with a curious expression.

"Do you need something?" Izo asked.

"Are you one of the Senator's house guests?"

"I guess. Why?"

The man shrugged. "Seen a lot of you guys around here. Wouldn't have pegged you for his type."

"Oh. Well, thanks." Izo grinned and mused over this fact happily.

"You're just kind of wiry and sullen-looking. No offense. The Senator usually likes friendlier Avarians with a little more energy. Maybe you could, you know, try a little bit harder," the man moved a pink-hand toward Izo's face. "Put a little more into it?"

Izo's initial pleasure withered. He glared balefully at the man. "You're no Casanova either, dude."

"Yeah, but I'm a cook."

"Then why don't you go fucking cook something?"

The man tipped his head back sharply, clearly offended. "Why don't you go sit on a Malforian?"

"I would, but I'm busy arguing with a goddamn cook!"

The man shook his head in disgust. "Whatever. Just let Ari know Zokie was here."

"Zokie's an asshole, left you some food. Got it." Izo said, knocking into the gold box with his hip hard enough to make the cover clank.

The man's eyes went wide. He pointed a short, angry finger at the youth. "You better pray you didn't mess anything up."

"It's fine. Fuck off," said Izo.

"Yeah, backatcha. Don't ever ask for nothing special from the kitchen!" And with one final glare, he stomped off.

Izo turned back to face his room. "He seemed nice."

"Who seemed nice?"

Izo whirled around and found himself inches away from Senator Mortaco's wide chest. He slowly looked up. "Wazzup, Chief?"

"I've been looking for you." The Senator appraised him carefully. "What are you doing out here?"

"Nothing. I was just—" Izo waved his hand flippantly as his brain fired blanks. "Making friends. Loving life." *Debating whether to run away, stay, or end it all.*

"That's good. Sounds like you're feeling better." He flashed the little Earthling a wickedly benevolent grin. "Ari was thinking maybe the two of you could hang today. Get to know each other and get a chance to get out of the house. Right, Ari?" He turned to look at the singer, who was still getting ready at her giant makeup desk.

Ari waved back without looking up. "Right. I'm looking forward to it."

Mort nodded and turned back to Izo. "What do you think? And don't worry—I'll pay for everything."

"I didn't ask you to."

Mort tilted his head. "You didn't have to." Smiling, he chucked Izo on the arm lightly. "Paid outings are just another of the great perks to living here!"

Izo glanced around Mort's shoulder at the blonde. She was holding a tiny silver pen connected to her makeup desk by a long, skinny tube. With laser-equipped accuracy, she seemed to be painting her face...the exact same shade as her face.

Izo frowned with distaste. "Sure," he said slowly. "Sounds like a blast."

— CHAPTER TWENTY-SEVEN —

Ari

Ari should have been having a wonderful time making her way through the lusciously opulent studios of all her favorite designers. This was fashion pre-season, almost a religious holiday to her, after all. These were the sacred fountainheads during their most sacrosanct time, where she went to renew her spirit, clear her mind, and both be filled and fill others with inspiration and intent, her pilgrimage to the mad geniuses, mischievous gods, and kingmakers of fashion, art, and reality.

She'd grown up surrounded by creatives. Virtually everyone on Aurelia prided themselves on taste and good form. She'd been raised in and among it, both an artist and a muse, on stage, in the sewing room, on the canvas. Many of her oldest friends (and more than a few of her mother's) still traipsed the halls of the Studios in the Sky—the bundle of floating ateliers in IA's most prominent fashion district—so these yearly visits were also a mini homecoming, a good week of holiday rest before beginning the massive headache that was planning whatever sold out, intergalactic concert tour had already been scheduled without her say so.

Or at least, it was supposed to be. Instead, she was stuck babysitting the universe's rudest, most boring Avarian alive—outside of Zusy. (Zusy was the worst.) She was trying to greet all her old friends, get introduced and familiar with the new breakouts, and quicken the hearts of all the chief designers. Instead she was confusing the hell out of everyone! She could almost feel him, like an awkward weight around her neck, pulling focus and dragging down the party. *Who is this?* She could see their eyes begging every time they glanced at him. *No one,* she wanted to tell them, point blank. *He's just some stubborn Avarian that Mort's obsessed with for no reason.*

"Are we done yet?" Izo asked, interrupting her thoughts. "I'm thirsty."

Ari turned to glare daggers at the homeless little cretin. She pointed slowly at the far wall. "No. And if you ask again, we'll go straight home and won't get anything to eat or drink afterwards. Now go stand over there and be quiet."

Izo crossed his arms and snapped to the other side of the room.

Ari forced on a fake smile and returned her attention to the Aurelian in front of her, Senior Designer Azli Elisure. A divine gift from the gods draped in lengths of slinky purple, they were the chief mastermind behind all Bgulvria's latest sensations, and one of the only people in fashion who could move the needle virtually whenever they pleased. "I apologize for him," said Ari. "Please, go on."

"There isn't much more to say. I'm telling you, the entire ide is a mess," said Azli.

Ari smirked. "You always say that, my dear. And it's always a revelation."

Azli flicked their golden eyes high to the ceiling, sighed, and pulled up the sketch on their giant, floating drafting table. Flicking a hand over it, they averted their gaze mournfully. "You'd think I'd be used to the chaos and unshakeable fear by now, wouldn't you?"

"It's lovely," insisted Ari.

Azli coughed out a bitter laugh. "You're an angel and one of my best friends, but you're also a shameless fucking liar. It's horrible!" Azli flung both arms at the design as if wild, urgent motions would somehow make it magically disappear. "It's the worst thing I've ever made. It's the worst thing anyone's ever made. I'm telling you, I'm done. I'm chucking the whole concept. It's worthless. I have no idea how to fix it."

Ari looked down at the digital sketch again and suppressed a frown. They were right, of course: there was something intrinsically wrong with the design. It was a lovely sketch, an elegant crescendo of ruffles draping over the faceless model in a regal array. But it didn't work. It wasn't the color—the shade was a deep purpling-fuchsia dotted with ecstatic bursts of shimmering white. It had energy. It *was* energy, both a study and an exhibition, the creator's vision clear as the early morning sun.

And yet...it just didn't work.

Ari pursed her lips. She tipped her head. "Maybe with different hair and shoes?"

Beside her, Azli took a deep breath before pulling a long drag from their medicinal vaporizer. The ensuing puff of medicinal smoke smelled of sweet Aurelian fritz blossoms as its heady constitution numbed her nose.

Ari sniffed. "Well, if anyone can figure it out, I know it's you."

Azli sighed and moved away. "Of course, you're right. I just need to give it time. You're an angel, and dear, and I don't know what I'd do without you. Let me show you the other things I'm working on." Azli slinked away from their enormous drafting table to lead Ari deeper into the workshop, toward the textiles in the back. "There's a new fabric we're coming out with. It's going to revolutionize everything. No one will be able to get their hands on it, and it's going to drive them all absolutely mad—"

"Not giving away trade secrets, are we?" came a sudden Malforian voice from behind the two of them.

Azli and Ari twirled around into none other than CEO of Bgulvria himself—Senator Jrinsin Pynalt. Head of the massive fashion empire, he'd taken the family company from one illustrious line and expanded it to a veritable legion of all the best names. Bgulvria, Rurjin, Pradnai—he owned half the studios floating outside.

"Senator Pynalt, how lovely to see you!" Flitting high, Ari kissed the Malforian several times with bubbling affection. "How have you been?"

"Busy, per usual," he said, taking the kisses genially. "I see we're looking divine as a goddess and curious as a goddess's daughter."

"Also, per usual," said Ari with a sly grin.

But the Malforian wasn't grinning back. "Hmm," he answered simply, eyeing both her and the designer. "So, what's the occasion?"

"Oh, nothing," said Ari innocently. "You know me. Any excuse to go out and blow money."

"Ah, but the things for sale are in the showroom and salons out front. You seem to have wandered into our private workshop and studio," said Senator Pynalt. "I'm afraid the things back here won't be available for ages. Maybe never, if the competition gets a hold of them first," he added with a meaningful glance at Azli.

Azli looked down at the ground. "I was just showing her my new master closet. Got the whole thing blown out and remodeled last month. It cost a fortune, but it had to be done. Great art requires great muses and plenty of space. Don't you agree?"

"Of course, but great art also requires savvy business if it's to keep the artist fed and buying new closets."

Azli's face tipped back as if they disagreed, but they didn't reply. Instead, Azli turned to Ari. "Maybe it is best if you go. It would seem I have a Mountain's worth of work to do. Lucky me."

Ari nodded in sympathy and bid her friend goodbye before watching them turn and go. Then she whirled on the Senator. "Are you honestly kicking me out right now?"

Pynalt grinned down at her, easy and dismissive. "Are you honestly pretending you weren't about to hit every other Studio in the Sky the second you left this one? Ari, you know I adore you, but you do this every year—you flit around, bat your eyes, and walk out of here with every design secret in the universe."

"Yes, before my big tours, where I help showcase and sell them all over the universe."

"On your timeline. Not on ours."

Ari glared while working her jaw to one side. Then she shrugged. "Fine. You don't ever have to worry about me wearing any of your clothes ever again."

"Ari..." he said with a tsk. "We both know you don't mean that. You're throwing a fit because you didn't get your little insider's scoop—but you were never supposed to, and you know it. Don't make a scene."

"Trust me, there will be no Ari scenes today or any other day. You want me out? Done." Spinning, she started for the door.

She didn't get far. Snatching the little Aurelian by the arm, the Senator held her aloft easily.

"Let me go!"

"You need to slow down," Pynalt said calmly. "I know you're under a lot of stress right now, but you're beginning to lose focus and—"

"Dude, she said to let go."

Ari's head spun toward Izo. Behaving and quiet for once, she'd almost forgotten he was there. Approaching with both hands raised, he shook his head at the Malforian. "Let's just keep our hands to ourselves. Okay, bud?"

Senator Pynalt looked at Ari in confusion. "Who the hell is this?"

"He's a friend." She shook her head in annoyance. "He's new in town and just moved into the house. Mort asked me to..."

"This is Mort's new guest?" Turning to Izo, his eyes immediately began searching over the youth's features.

He's running a scan? Ari wondered to herself. *Why is he running a—*

The Senator tilted his head. "It really is true," he whispered, the words pouring out in unconscious amazement, nearly too low for her translator to pick up. He grinned, instantly entranced, gaze lighting up as it played up and down Izo's figure curiously. "Mort, what have you found now?"

Ari frowned. She looked back at Izo in confusion. What the hell was going on?

She had no freaking idea, but it didn't take long for her to grasp the gist of it. When she turned back to Pynalt it was with a dazzling new smile. "Well, you know I had to bring him out to meet everyone on the down low. We were hoping to get a jump on next season for him as well, but if you really don't trust us to be here—"

"It's not a matter of trust. We trust you completely," said Senator Pynalt. "We just don't have anything ready for the public yet. You know how it is," he said, waving his hands around at the building. "It's all concept and mockups right now."

"I love mockups! They're easier to have tailored later," Ari insisted. When it was clear this wasn't working, she broke out a coy pout. "Please? Couldn't we have just a tiny look?" She nodded her head at Izo. "To welcome the new guest?"

The Senator glanced at Izo. He smiled despite himself but shook his head. "I'm sorry, but I'm going to have to insist. Come back in a few weeks. I'll have something personally prepared for both of you," he said, holding a hand out to Izo. "I promise."

"You're not really going to let both of us walk out of here without taking off our clothes even once, are you?" Turning her body, she pointed her shoulder directly at Izo. His eyebrows shot up as he looked over at her. If looks could kill, Izo would have leveled her on the spot. But Ari just held her pose.

The Senator hesitated and glanced between them. He seemed almost in physical pain at the dilemma. Letting out a quick breath, he finally gave a little shake of his head. "I suppose one tiny fitting never hurt anyone."

"See? Now was that so hard?" Ari asked happily. Turning to Izo, she grinned. "I told you this was the best place for—"

But before she could finish, the other Avarian had disappeared. Behind them a doorway at the end of a long hallway flew open with a bang.

Ari bit the inside of her cheek. Then she smiled awkwardly. "Excuse me for a moment."

Ari flew across the sparkling reflecting pool under the studios. Wide and flat, it was a giant circle spread out evenly beneath the entire district, reflecting the studios back up at themselves with gleaming, watery precision. Izo floated over it slowly, gaze down, shoulders hunched. Ari, immediately spotting the miserable wretch, flew at him at full speed, marring the studio's reflections in her wake.

"What the hell?" she said, reaching back to shove him in one shoulder. "I was almost in!"

"Funny, I'm pretty sure that guy was thinking the same thing," Izo said, shoving her back.

Ari dropped her mouth in confusion. "What are you talking about?"

"I'm talking about you throwing me out on the table like a pornographic ace up your sleeve!"

"Ace up my sleeve? I have no idea what you're saying right now," said Ari. "All I did was remind him that you'd be changing clothes if he let us try something on. It's the truth, isn't it? Is it really that big of a deal?"

"If he thinks you're offering a free show—yes!"

Ari rolled her eyes. "By the gods, would you stop being so dramatic? My own mother used to suggest way worse all the time right in front of me. Hell, she all but advertised my virginity to the highest bidder for years. All I did back there was..." Ari shrugged and looked at her nails. "Finesse things a little bit."

Izo's lip curled in disgust. "Call it what you like. Just don't ever use me to 'finesse' anything ever again."

"You act like I promised him we'd take turns finishing him off. It wasn't that big a deal; it's just a little harmless flirting. It's building up people's confidence, being positive and fun! You should try it sometime." She folded her arms slowly. "You might make more friends."

Izo crossed his own arms. "And get better food for breakfast."

Ari squinted in confusion. "Breakfast?" Then her eyes went wide as she remembered her conversation with Zokie that morning. "You little creep! You were hiding in my room?"

"I wasn't perving on you or anything," Izo explained quickly. "I...a lot of stuff has happened. Anyway, that's not what we're talking about. You want to walk around like the patron saint of sluts? Fine. I couldn't care less. I just don't want people thinking I'm a part of the giggle-and-bounce club too. So go finesse whoever you want. Just do it on your own time."

Ari grabbed her head. "You are such a fucking hypocrite! We're living with the same man—rent free! You're surviving off giggle-and-bounce too, honey. We're not that different. And even if we are—so what? I should be more like you? Uptight and unpleasant all the time? Make up your mind! Are you high and mighty, or lost and pitiful? Because this half-and-half is getting old. Seriously, either find somewhere else to go, or figure out how to fit in here."

Izo dropped back a step, and even Ari winced. In the long silence that followed, the echo of her words reverberated over the gleaming waters, bouncing and growing, different phrases high-lighting and looming in ugliness. Finally, Izo gave a nod, a single, furious acknowledgement. "You know what? You're right." The air whooshed and the water sprayed in every direction as he once again disappeared from view.

Ari sighed and wiped the water off her face. "How does he keep doing that!?"

"I'm Izo. I'm so special and sad. I'm the *only* Avarian that's ever missed home before." Ari snickered and finished her drink. "Well, good riddance to you. Don't trip on your way out of the galaxy, bitch!"

She waved for the waiter, a lovely Cristovalian male with an interesting smile, to bring her another. She'd stopped into one of her favorite Aurelian cafés to grab a quick lunch. Or, more accurately, to grab two or three drinks while pushing food around her plate. So far, the plan had worked like a charm.

Her device went off. She looked down at it and groaned. Mort was calling to check in on his weird little obsession, no doubt. She considered blowing him off. It wouldn't be the first time or the last. But no, she still hadn't cleared the stipend from earlier that morning. Rolling her eyes, she clicked her device to take the call.

"Ari, where the fuck is Izo?"

"Good morning to you too," she huffed. Throwing out her arms, she shrugged. "I don't know what to tell you, okay? We got in a fight, he got his feelings hurt, he took off. I knew this would happen. He doesn't like me and I don't like him. I don't know what you want me to do."

"I want you to find my fucking Gravity Sprite."

"How? He's an Avarian. He could be anywhere by now. In case you hadn't noticed, it's kind of a big planet." She shrugged and continued pushing food around her plate. "Honestly, I don't even understand what your deal is. This obsession with him is creepy as fuck, not to mention incredibly beneath you—"

"Ari, shut the fuck up," said Mort, "and listen to the words coming out of my mouth. I need you. To find. My Gravity Sprite."

Ari's brow drew down deeply. "Your...what?"

Mort cleared his throat and didn't respond.

It took her far too long to figure out she hadn't misheard him. Izo was a Gravity Sprite. She winced and covered her forehead. Of course he was. It made so much sense. This was the last piece of the puzzle: the obsession, the protectiveness, that weird moment with Senator Pynalt. Mort was up to something, and the other Malforians were picking up on it. There were probably already whispers all over the Mountain. How could she be so stupid? Of course Izo was a fucking Gravity Sprite, the only one of his kind in the universe. And of course Mort had found him, rescued him, and brought him into his house.

And of course—Ari realized with no small amount of pain—she had lost him.

Ari clamped her eyes shut. She held her device closer to her face. Mort's steely silence hung in the air like an invisible black hole, widening by the minute and swallowing every hint of warmth or light in the universe. She tried to force her mouth to form words, but her voice felt as tiny and fragile as a thread of glass. "I—" She stopped and swallowed back the bile in her throat. "Mort, I didn't know."

"I'm sorry?" She could almost hear him bending his ear to whatever speaker he was using on the other end. The motion would be relaxed and utterly furious. "I didn't quite catch that."

Ari's mouth trembled. Of course that wasn't what he wanted to hear right now. Ari sucked in a shaky breath and made herself nod. "I said I'm going to find him right now."

"Good. And once you do, I think the two of you should have a long talk. This silly feud between you two has gone on long enough. Don't you agree?"

"Yes."

"Good. Because he's important to me. If something happened to him, it would be like..." Mort considered for a moment. "Well, I think it'd be like if something happened to your mom. You know? That'd be really upsetting. Right?"

Ari opened her mouth lamely. "Yes. It would."

"And I don't want *you* to be upset, which is why I know you don't want *me* to be upset."

Ari covered her mouth to keep from breaking into tears. Her hand quivered over her lips. "Mort, please—"

"Shh," Mort cooed over the line. "Calm down. Everything's going to be all right. You're going to look around for a little bit and you're going to find him. Maybe start to the north, okay?"

Ari nodded in relief. Her hand fluttered to brush a single tear out of her eye. "Of course."

"Good. But first you're going to calm down, because we don't want to upset *him* either, do we? No, of course not," Mort answered for her.

She nodded. His voice had taken on that precise, condescending tone that Ari knew all too well. He didn't want to hear anything except what he'd already said. "You're going to do a great job, and everything's going to be fine. Right?"

"Of course."

"Good," said Mort, but there was still an angry pause in his voice like he wasn't satisfied yet, like he might still need to make things clearer. Everything in her body wanted to jump in and beg him that things were already clear—he didn't need to do anything else. But he hated it when she babbled, and she didn't know what he wanted to hear yet.

"So," he said finally, the tiny space for her to land as clearly marked as if he'd been guiding her in with batons. "What are we going to do?"

Ari nodded gratefully. "Find him. Make friends. Get him home."

Approval warmed his voice. "Good girl."

— CHAPTER TWENTY-EIGHT —

Izo

Izo glared up at the Fountain and tried to figure out what he wanted to do next. All around him the figurines of the universe's most important Avarians spun in lovely concentric circles through the air. They were beautiful and frozen in perfect poses. The crowds shouldered in, one by one, to get closer to them.

Izo turned away from the Fountain. An entire alien world greeted him, filled with magical floating shops and staggering buildings. He could go anywhere. Do anything. He was free as a leaf on the wind.

Except no, he wasn't, was he? Leaves had predetermined paths and outside forces affecting their momentum. Leaves followed the wind. Izo wasn't free like a leaf on the wind. He was free like a leaf on the ground.

He sat down on the edge of the Fountain. Around him the street was glutted with tourists taking in the shops. He vaguely recognized it as the first place Tearn and Glongkyle had brought him after arriving. Back then, he'd been too busy worrying about how to get back to Earth and combatting Tearn's subtle come-ons to really pay attention to the place. It was nice, bouncing with energy and joy. You could feel the excitement pouring off people. Everyone here had plans. Sure, some of them were probably lost and penniless and alone. But they knew what direction they were heading.

Izo squinted up at the sky. It was a greener shade of blue than the sky on Earth. He'd never noticed that before.

He tisked and looked away from it. There was a heavy feeling in his chest that he couldn't quite put his finger on. He pushed it down. As a child he'd learned that heavy feelings in your chest had a bad habit of whispering ugly things to your head, like *nobody wants you* and *you'll always be alone.* The best bet was always to ignore them, take your mind off things, and find something else to do.

Only problem was...Izo couldn't think of anything else to do.

Ari

Ari let out a sigh of relief. She'd found the Gravity Sprite despondently leaning over a fountain two blocks up. His bright green eyes were low and far away, and his shoulders hunched in as if he'd been ducking to hide from someone and then forgotten to straighten again.

Floating over next to him, Ari waited and watched the fountain toss water into the air. It took her a moment to realize it was Ara's Fountain, the same one she'd dedicated a statue to years before during her first intergalactic tour. Gosh, how many decades had it been? It felt like a lifetime had passed since that young, bright-eyed girl had been standing here, smiling into the sunlight.

It took a long time for Izo to finally notice her. Searching her face, he narrowed his eyes at her visage. "Ari?"

"It's me," she confirmed. She pointed at the face projector slung around her neck, a spare she kept for public outings. "I needed to go incognito out here."

"You look weird with straight hair."

Ari laughed. The face projector was set on a pretty, albeit utterly forgettable, Aurelian visage with dull eyes, an ashen complexion and dark, stringy hair that fell past her shoulders. "I used to wear it straight every day as a girl."

"Hmm." The Gravity Sprite nodded and looked away.

Ari glanced down at her feet. She couldn't think of anything to say to the Gravity Sprite. In perfect honesty, they had nothing in common and liked even less about each other. She had a terrible feeling small talk with him was going to be torture. She blew out a breath and decided to skip it for now. "Look. I owe you an apology. I was mad, and I took it too far. Of course you're still adjusting to things here. It's not your fault. IA can be a lot. What I said back there was completely uncalled for, and I'm sorry."

Izo looked over at her curiously. "You're being nice all the sudden." He glanced around. "Are you planning to murder me or something?"

"No," said Ari. "I just know I can be a bitch when I want to."

Izo gave a begrudging nod. "I wasn't exactly being a prince."

"So are we cool?" Ari asked, point blank.

Izo nodded and didn't say anything more. Ari took this as a good sign, but not one of full confidence either. It made sense. Bridges weren't built in a day, and friendships took more than one apology. She'd need to offer him something else, something bigger. She tried to think what it could be, when it hit her—the most natural thing in the world.

Clapping her hands loudly, she beamed at him. "Great! Because I still have full reign on Mort's credit for the rest of the day, and we haven't bought *you* anything extravagant yet."

Izo smirked. "Well...there is this one place around here I kind of liked."

Seemi

Seemi was having the most boring day of his entire life. It was mid-morning and there was absolutely no one in the store. Worse, tourist season was in full swing, meaning if sales didn't pick up soon, he was going to be stuck restocking their entire inventory for the third time that year.

He shook his head and looked around for something to pair with the tiny black Camiyen dress that'd just come in. High at the neck, it was cut in at the shoulders, leaving yards of billowy material to drape low on the mannequin's arms. Grabbing a deep blue Camiyen scarf from the same collection, he held it against the floating mannequin's waist. *No, that's not quite right,* he realized with a frown. Although the colors matched beautifully, and he was sure it would be darling on almost anyone, it was a little too predictable, particularly for a piece from an Aurelian designer. Setting it aside, he reached for a chunky silver belt instead.

It was a weirdly bold choice for such an elegant ensemble, but he tried it anyway. Fastening it at the waist, he floated back. It was surprisingly fetching. There was something about the soft draping and bold reflective metal that caught the eye and held it with confidence. It was weird, but it knew it, and didn't care. Seemi folded his arms in pride.

"That's him! That's the guy I met my first day on IA," said an excited voice behind him. "Come to think of it, I think I met you that day too... Jesus that was a long day."

"Well, it is a big planet, so the days are longer than most places—"

"THE DAYS ARE LONGER ON IA?!"

Seemi turned. Closer to the front of the store, two customers were arguing while heading up the middle aisle, one waving at him in unexplained excitement.

Seemi floated back in confusion. He recognized one of them, but he wasn't sure from where. It took him a moment to place the face, but once he did, it all came back in a rush. "You're that Avarian who came in here with the Strungian a few weeks back."

"Yeah, I am!" Holding out his hand, the youth grabbed and shook Seemi's fingers enthusiastically, a gesture that Seemi found bewildering but tried to be gracious about anyway.

"Name's Izo, don't know if you remember. Man, you don't know how happy I am to see you. How have you been?"

Seemi shrugged. "Same old, same old. What about you? How's IA been treating you?"

Izo blew out a long breath. "Hoooo, boy. Where to start?"

Seemi looked down at Izo's outfit, a thin white top with a pair of black pants, both bearing the distinctive Pradnia emblems. He let out an impressed whistle. "Well, you're certainly dressed better than last time. You were wearing the same jumpsuit as a Strungian and a Wuljerian...and swimming in it, too!"

"I'm borrowing from people a little closer to my size now. Speaking of, this is my new roommate, Ari."

"Nice to meet you, Ari," said Seemi to the other Avarian. Also Aurelian, she was wearing a face-projector with a rather plain selection on it. Seemi smiled and greeted her warmly but couldn't help being a little confused. He'd seen a lot of people use face-projectors to improve their looks. But the visage on this projector seemed...boring? He couldn't understand spending gods-know how much money to have everyone look at *that* face all day. "I must say, you're also something of an improvement. The last time he was here, he had this creepy little Ginarsian following him everywhere."

Izo laughed. "That's hilarious! You know, Ari actually—"

Before he could finish explaining what Ari had actually done, his friend smashed him in the ribs with an elbow. Izo grunted and hunched over.

Ari broke into a beaming smile. "This is awkward, but I actually need to charge this for a few minutes." She said pointing at her face projector. "Would you mind shutting the store for a little bit?"

Seemi's eyes went wide at the request. "You want me to...close the store?"

Reaching up, the other Avarian hit the button to cut off the projection. Blinking a few times, the bland face disappeared and was replaced with the single most famous visage in the universe.

Shaking her hair out with her fingers, Ari Lumiere beamed at the stunned store clerk. "Only if it's not too much trouble."

Ari

Ari was having the time of her life and feeling far less anxious about Mort. Which was good because, well, Mort was Mort, and Mort wasn't going to change. What could change was her outlook, though, and sitting in the empty store, glass of wine in hand, with a line of Imperial credit as wide as the Malforian sky, her outlook was pretty bright.

She was also having a fun time getting to know Seemi, the delightful clerk who was apparently Izo's oldest friend on IA (go figure). After shuttering the store and ordering snacks and Vitruvian wine, he'd cranked up the music and let Izo physically try on everything by JepaGult, the darling new wunderkind designer from Anolita (another go figure).

"This is it! This is the shirt!" Izo announced happily. Coming out of the fitting room, he floated out and spun proudly in the air, the garment's tapered hem and loose-fitting hood flaring into the air as he went. He strutted and preened at his own reflection beaming live from a camera embedded into the side of the towering digital sales screen. "Is it just me, or do I even look taller in this thing?"

Ari covered her mouth to hold in a laugh. The screen was zoomed in, displaying the Gravity Sprite at almost 130% his normal size. But if looking bigger was the way he felt more confident about himself, who was she to argue?

"Well, I can see why you were so obsessed with it. You look incredibly handsome. Suave, even," she said, pouring herself a little more wine. Then, nodding at Seemi, she pointed the top of her glass at the happy Gravity Sprite before taking another sip. "We'll take it. One in every color you've got."

"That sounds wonderful, but it's actually a limited-edition piece," said Seemi. He shrugged. "Color-morph comes standard with it."

Ari nearly spit out her drink. She turned to the Gravity Sprite, still preening and flexing his muscles at his reflection. "Izo, you were wearing a limit-edition color-morphing piece the night you met Mort, and you chose to wear it in black?"

"What?" said Izo in confusion. "It looks good in black."

"I can't decide if that makes him more or less original," Ari told Seemi.

"Black has been popular on Anolita recently," Seemi offered.

And with Gravity Sprites, too. She turned her face away to hide behind her drink. Truth was, she was still having a hard time wrapping her head around it. Izo was a Gravity Sprite. No, that wasn't quite right. Izo was THE Gravity Sprite—the only one of his kind in the known universe. Her entire life Ari had been a famous curiosity, first due to her parents, then her looks, and eventually her talent. Izo was going to be famous for his...genes.

On her worst days she'd often wondered if maybe she should just quit it all—give up the "Ari" persona, cancel every appearance, event, and performance from now until the end of time, and finally just call it a day. Her legions of fans would hound her for a while, and she'd probably get requests to present awards and give out exclusives for the rest of her life. But things would eventually quiet down once a new superstar came along. It was a simple fact of life she both feared and looked forward to.

She wasn't sure how that was supposed to work with Izo, though. Had he simply remained an interesting curiosity on some random planet, it probably wouldn't have been a big deal. A few experts would have been called in to test and confirm his lineage, a couple hundred articles would have circled the news feeds, and that probably would have been it.

But now that he was on IA, living with Mort? This was something different. This was taking an unquestionable oddity and setting it alongside a titan. There was a larger story here, one even she had questions about. How had Mort figured out Izo's ancestry? How had Izo's kidnappers figured it out? Most importantly, what was Mort planning to do with the Gravity Sprite now?

"Is everything okay?"

Ari glanced up at the shopkeeper. She'd accidentally let her expression drop into one of concern. Shaking her head, she broke into her neutral celebrity smile. "Forgive me, I've got a lot on my mind. Tour coming up. Promos to shoot. You know how it is."

"Not really," said Seemi. He gestured around the store. "This is pretty much it for me."

Ari nodded and surveyed the store. It was a cute little place, though a touch too crowded for her tastes. She certainly understood the instinct to pack the shelves, though. At this price point, you weren't trying to give people a sense of relaxation, quality, and leisure. You were just trying to catch their eye.

She glanced over at an arrangement of floating mannequins nearby. One was wearing a delicate black dress with a wide, silver belt latched around the waist. She pointed at it curiously. "That's interesting. Who designed that?"

"The dress is a Camiyen."

"And the belt?"

"Uhh, I don't really know." Rising, Seemi floated over to the outfit to check the belt's label. "Apparently it's Driseldian."

Ari tipped her head curiously. "They didn't come from the same designer?"

"No. I actually put them together myself."

"Really?" She looked at the pairing again. It was interesting. Surprising even. The two pieces were so different, virtual opposites of each other on the fashion spectrum. They shouldn't have worked together, and yet somehow she couldn't imagine anything more perfect. On a whim, she pulled up Azli's design from earlier to cast on the screen in front of Izo.

"Hey!" Izo said, angrily. "I was looking at that!"

"Hush, child," Ari snapped back. Turning back to Seemi, she smiled genially. "Tell me, Seemi—what do you think of this dress?"

Seemi appraised it quickly before nodding in automated polite-ness. "It's beautiful. I love the color."

"Cut the shit, honey," Ari said, her voice dropping dangerously low. "I already know it's fucked up beyond all hope. I just need to know if you can see it too."

Seemi angled his head at the sketch. He let out a deep sigh. "Well...the proportions are all wrong. They're trying to accent the neck and shoulders, but the bunching of the fabric is too much. It'd probably look good on a Cristovalian or a Malforian, but it'd swallow an Aurelian whole. I'd also get rid of the tufts here," he said, pointing to a pile of ruffles near the shoulders. "The color really is amazing—it'd bring out your eyes and skin tone beauti-fully. But the textures are going to distract from the waist, which is one of your best features." He turned back to her, eyes going sharp and focused as he followed the lines of her figure. "On you, I'd do everything I could to streamline it for a sleeker silhouette, pick a focal point near the middle and simplify everything else."

Ari lifted her eyebrows. It would seem their little Gravity Sprite had great taste in friends. Who would have guessed?

Tapping her device, Ari pulled up her contacts. "I have a friend named Azli Elisure who would love to talk to you. Would you be available later this week?"

Seemi's eyes widened. "Azli Elisure... you don't mean Azli from—"

"The Senior Designer at Bgulvrian? I do." Ari laughed when she saw the horror-stricken look on the other Aurelian's face. "Don't worry! They're an old friend."

"That would be amazing, but I'm just a day manager," said Seemi. "I'm not qualified to—"

"Tell people how they'll look in a design no matter their shape?" Ari gave Seemi a knowing grin. "Don't downplay yourself, honey. You've honed skills more valuable than you know. It's just a matter of putting yourself in a place that values them." Ari blinked and held in a frown. She'd accidentally lectured herself too.

Seemi shook his head. "Wow. Thank you. This is amazing. I don't know what to say—"

Ari reached out to squeeze his arm. "Don't mention a thing. It's my pleasure." And it really was. If the Gravity Sprite's one and only friend on IA could be uprooted and replanted directly into her favorite design-studio, her friendship with Izo would probably become a lot easier to schedule.

"Good. I'm glad we settled that." Smiling, Ari turned back to the Gravity Sprite. "So, what else are we going to buy?"

"Eh, I'm good."

Ari coughed out a laugh. "Are you kidding me? I have access to Mort's credit line all day. That thing's more infinite than infinity itself. Take that off. Pick out something else."

Izo shrugged. "This was the only thing I was looking for."

"Don't be ridiculous. You have no clothes! Winter season is coming up. If you like this designer, go ahead and stock up. I promise you, it's not a big deal. Mort understands you need to get some things if you're going to live here with him."

"Except I'm not going to live here with him. I'm going home any day now."

Ari stopped. The Gravity Sprite was glaring at her like she was trying to convince him his entire religion was wrong. For whatever reason, this clearly wasn't something he was open to debating. She broke into her easiest, most agreeable smile. "Of course. Good point."

Nodding, Izo turned away. "I'm going to change back into my clothes. Then we can get out of here."

"Maybe we can get something to eat?" she offered quickly.

"Sure," said Izo.

Turning back to Seemi, Ari broke into an embarrassed smile. "Sorry about that. I would have liked to have picked up a little more today, but he can be a little stubborn about weird things sometimes."

"It's fine. I picked up on the fact that he's a little different from most people before."

Honey, you have no idea, Ari thought to herself. Tipping her head to one side, she reached out and tapped the clerk on the leg. "Hey. What do you think about him though? Like, really?"

Seemi glanced at the fitting room where Izo had disappeared. He seemed to be considering the question. "He doesn't want what most people want."

Ari pulled back. "What do you mean? What does he want?"

"I don't know," said Seemi. "I just know it's different than most people."

Ari turned to where Seemi was looking. *Yeah,* she realized. *He's probably right.*

— CHAPTER TWENTY-NINE —

Izo

Izo was laying in his bed and picking his nose, enjoying the peace and quiet while he still could. Tonight was the night of the big party and he already knew the Senator would be down soon to assail the distraught and hapless Earthling with his worst nightmare of torture and madness: introducing him to more Malforians.

From what Izo had gathered from eavesdropping over the last few weeks, Mort's house parties were enough to make Gatsby blush. Izo, already exhausted from avoiding Mort's other Avarian guests and staff (who didn't like him for some reason), wanted nothing more than to hide in his room for the rest of the night and let the sounds of decadent chaos lull him to sleep from a safe and unmolested distance.

But, as it had been made clear by Ari and Mort, hiding in your room forever was not appropriate behavior for a future professional athlete—particularly one staying with a Senator.

Izo scratched his arm, sat up, and decided to mess with his latest drawing. He'd been working on a new image of Earth and was struggling to remember where to put South America's eastern shoreline. Pulling his pile of pictures onto his lap, he began by making a line with his finger from the tip of Florida. That was a good place to start, right? But as he dipped down and started to put his pen to paper, he frowned and decided to check it against his other pictures of Earth first.

Izo carefully flipped through his pile of loose pictures. Brightly colored and alarmingly thin, he'd seen them wrapped around a shipment of Ari's home-delivered clothes one day while hiding in her room. Snatching them immediately, he realized with no amount of excitement that it was the closest thing to paper he'd seen since arriving on the planet. Best of all, he wouldn't owe Mort anything extra by taking them.

Ari, the ever-gracious host, seemed unsurprised when he'd asked her if he could keep them. Beaming sweetly, she'd simply shrugged and asked if there was any other trash around her room that he wanted. He'd told her no. But he'd let her know if he saw something.

The pile of pictures was a giant mess, but he'd protected them like his last sip of water in a desert. After all, these pages were the only thing in the nearest three galaxies (or more?) that he could actually read. They held all his most important musings, memories, and knowledge he knew would be useful later: Earth's position in the solar system; the shape of the Milky Way; a list of places he'd go with Hanako as soon as he got home.

Flipping through the pages, he let his eyes drift over some of his other drawings. Still confident he'd be going home soon, he'd taken time since getting the pile of papers to sketch out some of the more interesting people he'd met: the hot male store clerk who'd zapped him for grabbing his arm; the floating octopus guy with his dozens of limbs; the sweet Malforian from the club who'd come to his rescue (at least at first) and punched his butthole of a friend.

Izo paused on a particularly suggestive drawing. Looking around the room nervously, he settled in a little lower before gazing down at it again. It was his only nude picture, and the drawing he'd spent the most time on too. Surrounded by swirling shapes and flowers, in the center was a careful depiction of the mean Anolitun female he'd run into at Mort's club. Izo gulped while remembering back. Truth was, of all the attractive species he'd met (and there'd been a few), Anolituns had by far made the strongest impression on him. And who could blame him? It was as if every member of their species had been personally modeled after Scarlett Johansson.

On Earth, his attraction to certain people had always hit differently depending on their characteristics. With more toned and athletic partners, the desire was often raw and sexual, a heated animal magnetism drawn out by the urge to compete, spar, and conquer (or be conquered). With softer, more demure partners, the sexual attraction was more romantic, almost mystical, an overwhelming rush of woozy-eyed devotion, like the moment after his big date with Jasmine where goes Aladdin swooping through the clouds with a big, dumb grin on his face. The Anolitun from the club, despite their short interaction, had somehow managed to tick both these boxes for him.

Izo brushed a thumb over the drawing. It was his only piece of "porn," and a pretty tame one at that. But he would have protected it with his life.

He sighed and eventually moved on to the next page. There it was, the thing he'd been looking for this whole time: Earth. His home planet. His Kansas. His wherever the hell Odysseus was from.

Lately, he dreamed about going home almost every night, about speaking with Hanako, and explaining everything to her in hushed tones until, like a person holding their breath in a pool, he was forced back up to the surface world. In these dreams he could almost feel IA waiting nearby to drag him back into reality again, where the sky was too green and all the doors were too tall. Night after night it was the same dream: her confused face, and him trying to tell her everything as fast as he could.

He always stumbled over that explanation. It was a weird thing to summarize, this event that had separated them so soundly. He never quite found the words, but it didn't matter. By the end of the dream, she understood what he was trying to say: that he had to go when he woke up, but he was coming back. Then they'd be a family, just like he always promised.

Izo cringed at the wording of that thought. It was no small thing that everyone on IA still believed he was engaged to her. It'd been a smart lie for Deneus to tell the Senator, stalling and averting Mort's advances until the contracts were signed and money exchanged. But after Tearn, Yula, and Glongkyle disappeared with said money and the only known navigation system containing Earth's coordinates—it had left Izo in the awkward position of being the only person on the planet that knew he wasn't actually an engaged virgin. Like, at all.

Then again, it might have been better than the alternative. The Senator, overbearing predator of Avarians he was, had proven surprisingly respectful of Izo's "honor" while letting him stay in his house. Izo had to give it to Deneus—that one perfect lie had bought more time and space than he ever could have predicted. He wished he could let Deneus know he appreciated it, even if he didn't appreciate how he'd disappeared at the same time as everyone else.

Izo grunted. Regardless, it had been a smart call to lie about Hanako, but it also kind of sucked that everyone on the planet thought he was engaged to his little sister.

Or rather, soon to be little sister, assuming he could get back to Earth in time.

Izo made a face and tried to do the math in his head. He knew he'd spent three months on Glongkyle's ship and roughly one month on IA so far. Hanako had been twelve when he'd left Earth, but she'd had a birthday coming up, so she'd probably be thirteen by now. That gave him roughly five years to find a way back to Earth, get a place, and adopt her before she aged out of the system like he had.

Izo thought harder. The adoption process took at least a year. He'd need to find not only a place to live, but a job and a car too.

Factoring all that in, he probably had...three years to find his homeworld again. Izo nodded. Yeah, that was plenty of time.

Izo glanced over at his window. Outside, the Malforian sky had faded into blue-green dusk and the stars were shining dimly, as remote and mysterious as the myriad worlds that obeyed and followed them like little cosmic ducklings. He wondered if maybe hot-headed and solitary Hanako wasn't staring at the same set of stars from the opposite direction. He liked to imagine she was. In that way, Earth wasn't so impossibly lost, like a single diamond misplaced on a shimmering beach. No, Earth wasn't lost—it was on the other side of a couple of stars which weren't even that close together. He would get home again.

It was like Hanako had told him years before: Izo was a superhero. And superheroes always found their way home. He just didn't know where his way home was yet.

A knock sounded at the door.

Izo looked up sharply. "Yes?"

The Senator entered. A shiver ran down Izo's spine at the ease with which the Malforian strolled into the youth's room. Silver hair down, he was dressed in black pants, a thin white shirt, and a red alien cape that clasped over one shoulder and draped across his chest. He stood at the edge of Izo's bed, towering over the youth's back. He gazed at the pile of papers curiously. "What are you drawing?"

Izo stifled a cough. He hated the sense of dread and vulnerability that always filled him when he was around the Senator, but he hated the idea of showing it even more. "What do you want?"

"Don't do that—don't pretend," said Mort. "You know exactly what I want."

Izo twisted around to search the Senator's face. It was as intense and inscrutable as a vampire's. The youth slowly rotated off his stomach to sit on his bottom with his legs crossed underneath. He pulled his papers into his lap. "Which would be?"

The Senator stared. His cold black eyes focused like laser-accurate weapons on the object of his attention. Then he broke out in a silly smile. He plopped down on the bed. "Come to the party."

Izo floated off the bed. "No thanks."

"Why not?" The Senator leaned back onto one elbow. "Give me one good reason."

"Because I don't want to. Because your friends are creepy. Because you're creepy. Because you and your friends are creepier when you're around each other."

Mort flicked his gaze around the room. "You still don't have anything to wear, do you?"

"That—" Izo paused. It was true. Besides his designer hoodie which he wore virtually every day without fail, he had nothing except the alien pajamas he'd been given to meander around the house in while recovering. "That has nothing to do with it," Izo finished.

"I told you to buy some clothes when you went out with Ari. What did you think that jaunt was for?"

Izo shook his head. "Keep your money and your friends to yourself."

"This room is depressing. You can't tell there's a person living here." Mort peered around the empty space. "Is anything in this room yours besides that shirt?"

Izo didn't have to look. There wasn't anything else. "Makes it easy to pack."

The Senator sighed. He focused on Izo again, squinting at the stack of papers in his hands. "What is that?"

Izo pulled the papers closer. "Nothing. Don't look at it."

The Senator gave him a pointed look and stood. One large, six-fingered hand reached to grab Izo's shoulder. The Earthling floated to one side to avoid him. "I understand that Gravity Sprites are solitary creatures. You need time alone, and I'm usually happy to oblige."

Izo gritted his teeth. This was a recent development, using his genetics as an excuse for his behavior. Though it did sometimes work in Izo's favor, it never failed to feel dehumanizing, like being turned into an animal whose temperament and personality were being cataloged for its companionship rating. Could his distrust of alien strangers have anything to do with the group of extra-terrestrials that abducted and abandoned him? No, there must be something up with his genes.

"But you can't hide in your room forever," the Senator continued. "There are some very important, very busy people who took precious time out of their week to come and meet with you. The least you could do is give them an hour."

Izo nodded in agreement. "Pass."

"I know it seems like a lot, but I need you to try and be social. I'm a very public figure. If you're going to be a part of my life, your privacy flies out the window." His lips cracked into a wide grin. "Do you see what I did there?"

Izo knit his brow.

"No?" Mort waited. He searched Izo's face. "I said privacy 'flies out the window.'"

"Oh. Because I'm Avarian. Hilarious. Mira, I know we've been over this, but let's review." Izo clapped his hands. "You and I? We're not a thing. We're never going to be a thing. I am not a part of your life, public or private. I'm crashing here for the time being because it beats living under an alien bridge." Izo titled his head. "I mean...I'm assuming."

The Senator's expression had grown annoyed and flat. "How generous of you."

"I'm not saying I don't appreciate everything you've done for me. I do. But I'm also not going to any of your weird parties so you can show me off. Sorry, but that's just not my jam. So, have a good night," Izo said, gesturing toward the exit. "And please shut the door on your way out."

Mort looked over his shoulder at the door. He squinted at it and looked back at Izo. "I think you mean *my* door."

"Of course," Izo agreed naturally. He gestured again. "Please shut *your* door on your way out."

The Senator bobbed his head a few times in begrudging resignation. He lifted his shoulders in defeat. "You're right. I can't make you go."

Izo narrowed his eyes at the answer. He didn't trust it.

"You are an independent creature, free to do whatever he wants," the Senator continued. "Sure, I took you in, fed you, clothed you, nursed you back to health, and sheltered you all out of the kindness of my heart—"

"But that doesn't mean I owe you anything in return," Izo finished.

The Senator peered down at the smaller being. Izo matched his gaze. Neither budged an inch. A heavy cloud filled with the silence of a thousand unsaid things floated between them. Finally, the Senator smiled and dropped his gaze. "Of course."

Izo squinted warily. "Okay... good."

"If you don't mind, I did want to clear up one thing before going though."

"What is it?"

The Senator's eye flashed with mischievous energy. "I was wondering if you'd really stopped to consider...THIS!"

Mort snatched Izo's pile of papers.

Izo shouted and flew to get them back, but it was too late—the massive creature had folded them into his chest with both his giant arms. Izo darted up and tried to pull Mort's arms apart, but the Senator tucked his head and rolled like a log across Izo's bed before finally landing in an awkward heap on the ground.

Izo followed, dropping hard kicks and elbows into the Senator's sides and arms, all while Mort made the slowest and clumsiest escape possible. Try as the Earthling might, it was no use. No matter how fast or hard the Avarian threw himself at the beast— some movements faster than the eye could see—it was like beating at a boulder with a straw.

Izo grunted in frustration as the Senator made it out the door. "Puta madre!"

"Language!" Mort scolded. Izo grinned smugly. Ever since Tearn had disappeared, he knew no one on the planet could understand his Spanish and that the Senator hated it. Pointing a finger at Izo, Mort gave him a warning look. "If you ever want to see these again, you'll be downstairs at the party within the hour."

"I'm not going to that stupid party."

"Fine. Then I'll destroy these."

Izo crossed his arms. "You wouldn't dare."

Mort gave the Gravity Sprite a sad smile. "Izo," he tutted with cloying sympathy. And he was right—they both knew he would.

Izo stole a concerned look at the papers. They held countless hours of work and careful recall that he might never fully remember again. They were easily the most important thing on the planet to him. He was on the cusp of genuinely begging for them back but bit his lip at the last moment. The big jerk wouldn't give in, and he'd just enjoy Izo's pleading the whole time. Changing tactics, the Earthling motioned around his room with exaggerated humor. "You said it yourself. I have nothing to wear!"

"So go borrow something from Ari. Everyone else does." The Senator began striding backward down the hallway in large, confident steps. "Remember, you have one hour. Otherwise they're gone forever."

Izo watched the Senator leave with clenched fists, cursing his tiny body and trying to think of some way out of this. He was thinking so hard, in fact, he didn't notice the others who'd gathered in the hallway behind him.

"By the gods, did we actually spot Mort's infamous pet virgin?" said Zusy, voice as calm and self-assured as a snake's.

"I was starting to think he was a myth," came a second, less recognizable voice from behind. "Do you think we'll get a prize for spotting it in the wild?"

"Don't be silly," answered Zusy.

Izo turned to the Cristovalian dancer sauntering up the hallway. Zusy was seven feet tall, grey-skinned, and willowy. She looked like a cross between a Malforian and a super model. According to Ari, Cristovalians were the oldest and closest cousins to IA's ruling species.

She grinned at her new friend, a random Anolitun with a mean smirk. "Everyone knows you have to hold down a virgin to get its prize."

Izo gritted his teeth. Behind her, a whole group of floating foes gathered in the hallway. Mixed-gender and mixed-species, Mort's orchestra of assorted Avarian houseguests never failed to make his day worse. Over the past month, it had been amazing how any combination of them—and Mort went through a lot of Avarians—could always somehow find it in their hearts to band together and torture him specifically. Had they held a meeting? Did they have a newsletter? It honestly boggled the mind. He tried being friendly. He tried to ignore them. Eventually, he'd even tried punching one or two. Nothing worked. Their undying hatred of him was like a freaking religion.

Zusy, the only regular besides Ari who had been in the house longer than Izo, was the worst. She was as calculating and mean as she was drop-dead gorgeous. The first day they'd met, Izo had caught himself nervously asking her about living in the house. Sensing his weakness, the dancer had zeroed in on tormenting him endlessly ever since. The other Avarians, never ones to miss out on a dog pile apparently, had gleefully joined in.

Zipping around the giant female and the others, Izo snapped himself into Ari's room at the other end of the hall. Door perpetually open, Ari gasped when Izo appeared suddenly beside her.

"Shit!" She yelled, dropping a laser-enabled make-up brush. "What the hell do you want?"

"The others are being mean to me again."

Rolling her half-finished eyes, Ari turned in her chair and shouted into the hallway. "What the hell? Don't you have anything better to do than pick on some goofy, homeless boy?"

"Why are you protecting him? He's an ungrateful, whiny brat," Zusy complained. "He's only here because he needs a place to stay. He doesn't even like the Senator. Goodness knows he's said so himself a hundred times. He's taking advantage of Mort, Ari. He's a leech and everyone knows it."

"So? Isn't that Mort's problem? If he wants to house twenty ungrateful bitches, what business is that of yours?" Ari turned to continue coloring her eyes. "It's his house, Zusy."

"Exactly. It is his house. And everyone staying here should be appreciative." She narrowed her eyes at Ari. "Or do you not agree?"

Ari's eyes found Zusy's in the mirror. She put her tongue in her cheek. "Don't you start. You think I don't know you're only accusing Izo of exactly what you don't want people accusing you of?" Ari tipped her head and smiled slowly. It somehow reminded Izo of Seemi for a moment. "Please. You're not as subtle or smart as you think you are, Zusy."

The blood rose to Zusy's cheeks. She crossed her long, slender arms. "I'm not trying to be smart, Ari. I think anyone with even a hint of genuine devotion would be hurt seeing Mort exploited like this. But maybe that's just me." Zusy shrugged. "Maybe I'm just more sensitive and loyal than most Avarians."

"Bitch, no you didn't." Ari threw down her makeup brush.

Oh shit, thought Izo. *This just got real.*

Zusy held out her hands innocently. She looked around at the other Avarians. "What? What did I say?"

But they didn't get the chance to answer her because before anyone could move, Ari had sailed into the air, and attached herself to the towering Avarian to begin hitting her point blank on the head. "Don't you ever accuse me of being disloyal! I was supporting Mort and his career before you ever left your fleabag planet. I am his first, his second, and his LAST resort. You do not question me! I will set your life on fire and pose for pictures in the ashes."

Zusy screamed and tried to pry Ari away as Izo laughed and cheered the Aurelian on. After two final kicks, Ari relented and let the big, grey Avarian go.

The Cristovalian shot to the door, angry tears streaking down her cheeks as she grabbed and hung off the frame. "Why are you defending him?!"

"Why are you attacking him? Oh wait, I know why: because you think it improves your station." Racing to the door, Ari shrieked at the Cristovalian, who quickly fled. "You're not a hero, Zusy! You're just another asshole getting off on exclusion."

"Yeah! ¡Chupa mi ano!" yelled Izo, following Ari to scream out the door also.

"Izo, language!" said Ari over her shoulder.

"Right. Sorry." Izo agreed before turning back. "Eat my ass!"

With a disapproving glare, she flicked her fingers at the others still gathered outside her room. And it worked. Like an annoyed command from the universe's cutest fairy-godmother, the others dispersed instantly.

Izo tipped his head against the inside of Ari's door in relief. "Thank god we're friends now."

Ari sneered. "We're not friends. My friends are rich." Then, floating back to her giant vanity, she picked up a brush to finish her face. "You just happen to be a little less annoying than the rest of them."

Izo shrugged. He padded across Ari's massive corner room to her seating area. Painted in a soft blue, it was unquestionably the best room in the hall. Two stories tall and fixed with wall-to-wall gold-framed windows on two sides, it featured a lofted sitting area with no attached staircase, a living area trimmed in gold, and a complete dining area with an oversized table and seating for eight in creamy whites and blues. With every piece of furniture fitted on braided strings of precious metal and tufts of creamy cushion, it'd originally struck Izo as an elven studio-loft.

The Earthling flopped down on her couch before looking back at her. She was wearing the tiniest white dress Izo had ever seen. It looked like she'd pulled a white lily from the ground and stepped into its petals. Working on the bottom line of her lip, she was posed daintily above a seat barely bigger than Izo's hand. Here was another funny thing about Ari he'd recently realized: the Aurelian never fully rested her weight on anything. Whether eating, walking, or getting ready, she was constantly hovering.

Her big eyes flicked higher in the mirror as she sensed his attention. "What?"

Izo was still staring at the dress. His stomach clenched with unease. "I need to borrow something to wear to the party," he said.

"I thought you didn't want to go?"

Izo pursed his lips. "Mort made me an offer I couldn't refuse—returning my own stuff."

Ari made a uniquely Aurelian growling noise. Half-adorable rumble, half-terrifying growl, Izo had never been able to replicate it. "This is why I told you to get your own stuff. Who's going to pay me back if you rip or lose something?"

"No tengo feria. I'm broke, you know that."

"Not my problem. Ask Mort for another line of credit and fucking buy something this time."

"You know I don't want to do that." Izo rolled off the couch and onto his knees. "Please, Ari? I just need one outfit for an hour."

Ari considered the kneeling youth in her mirror. Her mouth flicked to one side in a sharp and cheeky grin. Izo felt a chill run up his spine. "Fine, but you're doing a live shopping event with me right before the tour."

"Deal." Izo had no idea what he was agreeing to, but he was desperate. "Whatever you want."

Ari laughed with malicious glee. "Ari Nation is going to love you!"

"Ari Nation?" Izo blanched. "What's Ari Nation?"

"Nothing you need to worry about today." Finishing her lips, she threw down her brush, which magically floated back into its holder, before flicking her head at her closet's entrance. "Let's go find you an outfit."

Izo gulped and followed. She led him into her master bathroom and attached closet. Three stories tall, it was almost more sanctuary than wardrobe. Zipping into the middle of the first floor's ceiling, they hurried to the second story where Ari's wide array of fashion was housed.

"How long do we have?" asked Ari as she floated in front of her clothes.

"He gave me an hour to get ready."

Ari groaned and moved faster. "That's barely enough time to do anything! Izo, you'll be a complete disaster in front of everyone!"

Izo gazed around at the armada of small, sparkly outfits. He sighed. "That is pretty on-brand for me."

— CHAPTER THIRTY —

Ari

You are going to look so chic in this," Ari said, holding the long, plush sweater to her body. Emerald green and made of fine Dreseldian fibers, it was softer than a newborn flying seal and twice as cuddly.

It reminded her of her own youth on Aurelia, passing the endless hours locked away in their family apartment with her favorite hobby—stealing into her mother's closet to touch and admire her gowns. Cut from the finest fabrics around the universe (gifts from Ari's uncles and other admirers), her mother's dresses were handmade, wildly glamorous affairs befitting a famous royal. This sweater was even the same shade as Ari's favorite gown—her mother's green and white wedding dress.

Ari hummed one of her early hits while spinning softly in the air with it. "No offense," she sighed, "but I might kill you and steal this to wear myself."

"Better yet," said Izo, his voice muffled from inside her shower, "you take the outfit and steal my papers back, and I won't bother going to the party at all."

Ari frowned. Izo was still joking that he might not go. Now that he'd agreed, no-showing wouldn't be acceptable to the big man downstairs.

The Aurelian singer landed hard on the ground. She tossed the sweater toward a free-floating pedestal near the middle of her master bathroom. The pedestal, a state-of-the-art piece of fashion tech all the rage two years ago, stood near the main entrance to pull and magnetically suspend any hanging outfit with the flick of her wrist. It was like a fashion summoning altar, and she'd demanded Mort install it the second she'd laid eyes on the prototype.

But even her favorite structural extravagance couldn't put her in a better mood at the moment. Izo was vexing her, and before an important social gathering no less!

"Avarians don't cancel social events without good reason, Izo."

"Do they ever lie about having a good reason?"

"No," she said flatly. Flitting forward, she banged on the side of her jewel-encrusted shower door. "And they don't take this long in the shower, either!"

"Calm down, your highness. We still have thirty minutes."

"Tell me you're joking. That's barely enough time to contour and put on an eye!"

"Or—and here's a crazy thought," said Izo, "what if we don't put a bunch of goop on my face?"

Ari glowered. Was this her destiny now? All her precious moments before big events—press outings, fundraisers, awards— doomed to be wasted arguing with this child?

She understood he was unused to their customs, but he was a public figure now. Everyone at this level, Malforian to Ginarsian, used facial coloring for big events. Ari sailed across the room to stand in front of the shower. Lifting her wearable device, she went into the settings and turned on the one selection she knew would speed him up faster than anything. Then she floated back onto her bathroom lounger and waited.

It took him barely a minute to notice.

"What in the hell? ARI!" Izo yelled. She could hear him stumbling around in the shower. "Why is all my pinche hair coming out?"

"Don't worry!" She called out merrily, holding in laughter. "It's designed to only remove body hair. Stay in the water a few more minutes and it'll wipe everything away itself."

Izo yowled and slapped the water off. A second later, the shower door swung open and a very annoyed, very naked Gravity Sprite was revealed in all his angry, hairless glory. "I happen to like my body hair!"

"Oh? I didn't think you'd miss the little you had." Ari held up her hands. "I'm sorry!" She pointed at the shower. "That's how I always have it set."

Izo lifted an arm to look at one of his armpits. Smooth as a flying seal's bottom. He glared at her anew. "Mentirosa. You did this on purpose."

"I swear I didn't!" she lied. "Anyway, we don't have time for this. Dry off. You have to get ready."

But Izo wasn't done yet. Looking over his chest with a mournful sadness, he caught sight of his privates. He gestured angrily at them. "Puta madre, I've got no hair on my balls. I look like I'm thirteen."

Ari lifted a brow. This certainly wasn't true. After a month of a carefully curated diet and nutrition, the scrawny and half-starved stray who'd arrived in Mort's house was long gone, replaced by a healthy, young-bodied Avarian, just as lithe and compact as any carbon-based person she'd ever seen. Not that all this healthy youthfulness had amounted to anything. His sex-life was still as dry as a desert wasteland.

"Don't talk to me about your balls. Your balls are stupid as shit. Why are they on the outside?" said Ari. *Last Gravity Sprite in the universe and he's got all his genetic material stored in a pair of squishy bags.*

"Where the hell am I supposed to keep them?"

"On the inside, duh!"

Izo looked at her like she was crazy. Ari returned the expression. After a minute both seemed to realize they were at an impasse.

"Whatever," said Izo. "Can you hand me a towel? Inside or not, they're about to freeze off over here."

Ari reached back and tossed him a towel. *Yeah, because they're on the outside.* But she didn't say anything. Instead, she glanced at her device again. She hissed. Feet soaring off the chaise, she arced behind him and began pushing him toward the top of the bathroom. "Enough! We have to go."

Dragging them straight up, she led him into her attached wardrobe overhead. Two stories tall and directly above her bathroom, it was designed by one of the top Avarian-friendly architects in the tri-galaxies.

She hurried them to the far wall where her larger face and hair stations were housed. "Sit down!"

Ari sent the youth a flying robe while pushing him toward the makeup station. Flitting next to the floor-to-ceiling mirror behind the station, she quickly synced up her wearable device. "We're going to a party, so the lighting will be mellow," she said mostly to herself while reaching down to adjust the room's backlit hue.

"You base make-up around lighting?" Izo asked.

Ari wanted to roll her eyes. *Do you base make-up around lighting? I don't know—do you base music around time? Or spices on flavor?*

But she didn't have time to explain how dumb he sounded. Instead, she mashed a finger over the younger Avarian's lips. "I'll throw something stylish but simple together. We'll have to pray no one takes pictures." Ari pushed her finger in harder as her subject began to speak again. "Quiet," she warned.

Izo stilled under her deadly serious glare.

Ari took a deep breath and floated off the ground. She centered herself in front of Izo's face, her eyes flashing back and forth as she mapped out the Earthling's every feature and facial line. Her brain silently analyzed the fastest ways to contour slenderness, symmetry, and youthful vibrancy while using Izo's favorite masculine color: green.

Cocking her head to one side, Ari flicked a finger to summon her floating, refrigerated cosmetic stand.

Twenty minutes later Ari floated to one side to finally let Izo look in the mirror. "Whoa!" the Gravity Sprite said, moving his face back and forth. "That's cool."

He was the picture of Avarian youth. Knowing his preference for warrior looks, she'd given him a stronger eyebrow and a streak of green across the cheeks, both of which he would think looked "tough" even though she knew it was incidentally the fashion of the time.

His nose and lips she'd left alone, neither highlighting nor hiding since she'd known he'd throw a fit. His eyes she'd also barely touched, giving him a simple green line that accentuated his eye color. It was a bold statement, the exact universal shade symbolizing pre-budding and virginity.

Not that Izo needed to know that.

The thing she was most proud of, though, was the contouring around his chin. She remembered the accidental conversation that had led to it. Doing his makeup for a team photographer who'd shown up out of the blue, she'd been admiring the shape of his face once they eventually stopped quarrelling.

"You have such a nice jawline," she'd complimented as he squirmed in the chair in front of her. "And the cutest little chin!" she'd added, giving it a playful pat with her brush.

"Thanks," he'd mumbled. "I guess it's never been very strong or square."

The comment had surprised her, and she'd changed brushes and outfitted him with a stronger, "squarer" jaw on the spot. He'd been astounded, truly impressed, and genuinely grateful. For some ridiculous reason, she'd decided to add it again.

"Niiiiice," Izo crooned back in the present moment. Grasping his powerful new jaw, he turned his face to check himself out. "On Earth we call this dashing."

Ari dropped her brushes into their swirling cleaner with a chuckle. Sure, it took a little longer and the effect was so subtle that almost no one ever noticed it, but it gave Izo a happy little boost of confidence. Wasn't that the point of all this?

Then she glanced at her wearable device and cursed. They had ten minutes. Ari flicked her wrist to summon the outfit from the pedestal below. As it flew into one hand, she yanked Izo up with the other. "Get up, Prince Dashing! You have to get dressed."

"Calm down," Izo said, taking the long black pants. Pulling the magnetic riser off the top, he bent low and began stepping into them one foot at a time. The pants were tighter than expected and he immediately snagged his foot.

"Mierda," he said, hopping on one leg. "How do you—"

"Are you stepping on my pants? Those are Bgulvrian, you oaf!"

"Ari, I'm stuck," said Izo.

"So fly, dumbass!"

It never failed to amaze the tiny pop singer how many times she had to remind the Gravity Sprite that he could fly. Shoving Izo into the air by his butt, Ari managed to yank and tug him into her tiny slacks, smoothing and adjusting its skin adhering fabric as they went.

"Done," she said, gasping for breath. "Now pull on the top. And don't forget to—"

Izo jerked his head through the tiny head hole. "Forget to what?" he asked, fishing his arms through.

Forget to unzip it first, she thought to herself. A headache was lighting up her temple. "Nothing," she said out loud.

Ari dropped to her hands and knees to crawl to the spot where she'd hidden the only pair of shoes she'd ever lend the Gravity Sprite—an ancient pair of hideous boots with size-morphing technology. She'd let him borrow them during their outing and, as if the fates themselves had spoken, the shoe's software had glitched and gotten stuck in his exact foot size.

She handed him the shoes. "Here."

"Hey! It's my favorite green boots." Izo plopped down to pull them on, gazing happily at his feet. "Man, do these things fit great."

"Doesn't matter—they're mine," said Ari. She turned to kneel more gracefully on the ground. "If you lose or ruin them, I'll clean the hallway with your face again."

Izo's body went rigid. As Ari well knew, their fight in the hallway was one of the Gravity Sprite's more touchy subjects.

"That fight didn't count," said Izo. "I was sick. I could barely stand."

"Sure as hell couldn't stand afterwards either," Ari mumbled, looking away. She pretended to adjust her hair.

Izo glared at her sharply. "You want to go again, Tinkerbell?"

Ari smirked and kissed him on the nose. "I would, but I don't have time to fix your face twice. Anyway, come on! It's time for the best part."

Jumping up, she soared through the hole in the ceiling to the last and most expensive floor of her closet. In fact, she was pretty sure it was the most expensive room in the house.

Over the years, Ari living with Mort and Mort inviting various Avarians into their home had led to a number of ugly fights. Many had no foreseeable end. Mort wasn't going to apologize for his lifestyle and interests. He also wasn't going to let Ari leave no matter how much his life choices hurt her.

What formed was a hellscape of a relationship, a sharp and dangerous place where no one was safe to relax. Every square inch was filled with pitfalls, all leading to the same set of painful, never-ending impasses. But over the tops of these pits a few rickety bridges had been erected, jittery compromises that allowed them to move about confidently enough as long as they didn't look down.

Virtually the first of their mad house compromises was their arrangement for Ari's wardrobe. All her collections were curated and hand-chosen for being only the latest, most cutting-edge and flawless pieces. Mort, on the other hand, often picked whatever gaudy thing caught his eye: ridiculous, over-the-top garments that rose and fell in popularity as sharply as the Mountain from which he sprang. Since Ari's tastes tended toward things that were ninety-eight percent sure to be classics, it was little surprise that the more random Avarians seemed to waltz into Mort's house, the more Ari's stuff seemed to walk out of her closet.

Hell, she almost couldn't blame them. Given the choice between taking something from a famously vengeful Senator and a famously adorable pop star, who wouldn't choose her stuff? Nonetheless, it had been a sore subject and a barely-masked proxy to a much larger fight.

In the end, they'd compromised—Mort would finance her ever-expanding wardrobe and she would open it (within reason) to his guests. Every year she'd pushed herself to the edge, outfitting all of Mort's Avarians in the absolute pinnacle of style and taste. And every year her budget had gone up until, one day, Mort had unknowingly equipped the captive singer with a wardrobe worth more than most armies.

Landing on the third floor, she clapped her hands under her chin. A proud, un-ending smile had spread across her face as she gazed at her collection.

Seventy shelves of handheld clutches. Twenty-two columns covered in shoulder bags. Fourteen drawers filled with quilted and leather Minaudières. Sixteen shelves, all positioned at eye-level, with the absolute latest in day bags. A section for flap bags, satchels, buckets, and slings. There was even a small area dedicated to vintage saddlebags in case they made a comeback again.

All together the room housed over twelve hundred name-brand options. Ari's collection was worth enough money to get her and whoever else she wanted across the universe and safely settled for life. The best part? Ari was slowly sneaking them out of the house, and tonight, she had the perfect reason to set aside two.

"So, which ones should we take?" she asked. Her voice had gone low and sultry as her fingers played over some of her favorites.

Izo eyed the collection with a frown. "It's just a house party, right? Do I need a purse?"

Ari whipped around on him like he'd mentioned how young her mother looked. "Are you trying to piss me off?"

"I don't have anything I need to bring with me and I'm only going to be there for an hour. What do I need a purse for?"

"Purses aren't for things, they're for...ugh!" Ari pushed a finger into her temple. They didn't have time for this.

She stomped up to the clutches and grabbed a silver Pradnai. She turned and shoved it into his hands. Small and encrusted with antique jewels, it was worth more than six months' rent on most planets.

Izo turned it over dubiously. "Does it have a strap or...?"

"No, so you need to be extra careful to keep track of it." She put her hands on her hips, challenging him in the low tone she'd figured out always worked. "Think you can handle that, genius?"

"Psshh." Izo put the purse under his arm. "I got this."

— CHAPTER THIRTY-ONE —

Ari

Thirty minutes later, Ari and Izo arrived at Mort's gathering, Aurelian in front, Earthling behind her. Situated beneath the main floor, the gathering was in Mort's grotto, a multi-leveled space filled with floating pools that spilled into each other through a series of streams and waterfalls.

Backlit in a dreamy glow, all its waters were shallow, crystal clear, and synchronized to gently lap against the wall in a way that Ari knew for a fact had been programmed to seem sexual. Situated amidst these were the main events—black seating arrangements attached to floating white platforms. The attendees lifted in small groups, Mort's guests were safe to drift about the room in a free-floating kaleidoscope of lofty, drunken power.

Ari and Izo approached the nearest platform as it drifted by the room's grand entryway. They were greeted by the whole gaggle of Mort's current roster of Avarian houseguests. Gathered in a kittenish sprawl, they waved Mort's guests inside with a show of lithesome playfulness.

Zusy saw Izo and made a gagging noise. "By the gods, who invited the virgin?"

"Wow. Look at that. Don't see stuff like this on Earth," said Izo with an impressed tut.

"What?" Zusy broke into a cruel smile. "Running water? Indoor electricity?"

Izo circled his hand at the mixed-gender group. "Whore smorgasbord."

Zusy rolled her eyes and ignored him to greet the next set of guests. Ari shot Izo a look as they passed deeper into the room. "You want to lay off with that stuff?"

"What?"

"We're at a party. They're not doing anything wrong by flirting with people. They're having fun, okay? Why are you being an asshole?"

Izo gaped in confusion. "Me? They started it."

Ari growled and turned away. Determined to ignore him, she tried to search the party for familiar faces, but their surroundings made it hard. Everyone there was moving forward and over to catch a look at them—or, more accurately, at Izo—which made it difficult to see around the first couple of groups.

Ari gave up and headed deeper inside, Izo following close behind her like a stray. It occurred to her they must have made for a funny pair—Ari in her teensy white party number and Izo nearly covered head to toe in black and green. Not that it seemed to matter to the mesmerized crowd. She could have wrapped him in twelve layers and he'd still have stolen the spotlight. He couldn't seem to help it. The Gravity Sprite naturally drew attention towards him like a full moon pulling at the tides.

"There's the one we've all been waiting for!" said a guest stepping in front of them.

Ari laughed. It was Senator Bryckturn, CEO of Ari's record label and a Senior Sword member. Floating up, Ari greeted him warmly, hugging and kissing him on both cheeks. "Senator, how wonderful to run into you! I didn't know you were coming."

"I wasn't planning to. Goodness knows I hate these little get-togethers of Mort's. But I broke down when I heard we'd finally be able to lay eyes on this new mysterious guest of his. Hello there," he said to Izo. "I've heard a lot of whispering about you, not that it did you any justice."

Izo held up a hand. "Reel it in, chief."

"Izo!" said Ari. "Behave."

"It's fine," said Bryckturn. But as his gaze settled back on the youth, it took on a duskier shade. "Mort warned us his new Avarian could be a bit feisty."

"Ah. So, he also mentioned the inside-out thing?" said Izo.

Bryckturn's head tilted in curiosity. "The what?"

"The thing all people from Earth can do? Flip a person inside-out? Don't worry; it's totally safe," said Izo. His feet split wide and he dropped into a lower stance. A rhythm erupted from his limbs as he raised his hands, swirling them in mystical circles. "Try to hold perfectly still, though."

The man sputtered, backed up, and left.

Izo rose to his full height and grinned at Ari. "Earth Kung Fu. Gets 'em every time."

Ari smacked him on his nearest ear. "That was the CEO of my record label, you moron." But she already knew he wouldn't care, so she skipped ahead a few steps. "Izo, can you please use your brain for once? We are surrounded by some of the most powerful and well-connected Swords in the tri-galaxies. This is our support team. Would it kill you to act normal for once?"

Izo rubbed his ear and glared at the shorter Avarian. "I am acting normal. These guys are the ones acting like they got free tickets to the zoo. Yeah, I'm talking about you!" Izo roared at another handful of people watching them.

Ari grabbed the Gravity Sprite and pulled him farther to one side. "Izo, I'm serious. I have an album to promote. Mort has his election coming up. I guarantee your flying-race team is going to need money for something eventually."

"So? I haven't even joined it yet."

Ari sighed. "I need you not to embarrass us. There are over three hundred of the universe's best connections in this room. Your job is to make friends, not run everyone off." She narrowed her eyes. "Promise you'll be good?"

"I promise to be good...won't say what I'll be good at, though..." he mumbled, voice dropping sadly at the end.

"What was that?" snapped Ari.

"Nothing. Let's look for Mort." Floating up, he tried to search the room. "The sooner I can get my pictures back, the sooner I can get out of here."

Ari nodded. On that, they could agree. Also flitting up, she began searching for any sign of Mort among the floating platforms. There was also a chance he could be mingling on the bottom level. She floated lower with confusion. "You want to try the ground or air first?"

Izo followed her closer to the ground and was about to respond when he was interrupted by someone snatching him from the air. Scrambling, he was lucky enough to stop the person before they could pull him completely onto the ground. But the ploy had still worked—holding Izo as hard as he could, Lrasa, Mort's best friend, had wrapped the Gravity Sprite into an inescapable hug.

"Gotcha," said Lrasa. He squeezed the Avarian tighter as Izo struggled and failed to lift them both into the air. "Good evening, gorgeous."

"Let go," Izo grunted.

"Never. I caught you fair and square," said Lrasa. He draped his chin onto Izo's shoulder. "You belong to me now."

Ari ground her teeth. Of all Mort's friends, Lrasa was by far the most annoying. He competed with Mort like his life depended on it, sneered at every Avarian alive, and had done the one thing that could make Ari hate someone faster than comparing her to her mother—slept with her and made fun of her for it afterward.

"Let him go, or I'll tell Mort you're harassing his new favorite," said Ari.

"Aww. You going to run and tell master on me?" Lrasa said.

Ari glared at the arrogant Malforian. Tall and stronger than either of them, he was clearly basking in his element. Crossing her arms, she wavered between getting Mort and trying to handle this herself.

Lrasa took her delay as a victory. Beaming, he pressed his mouth into Izo's ear. "I'll make you a deal. Give me a kiss, and I'll let you go."

"Better idea," said Izo. And with a quick and purposeful move, he slammed himself down onto both of Lrasa's feet before rebounding the top of his head into the underside of Lrasa's chin.

Ari burst out with surprised laughter as Lrasa grunted and fell back, his butt hitting the ground as he grabbed his jaw. He rubbed while glaring at Izo with cold grey eyes. "That was rude. Your master should have trained you to behave better."

"Shut up, Lrasa," said Ari. Standing alongside Izo, she floated up to lean a shoulder on the Gravity Sprite. Together they stared down at the felled butthole of a politician. "We don't have time for this. Do you know where Mort is?"

Lrasa seemed to consider whether to help them. "I know exactly where our evil overlord is scheming. And I will tell you," he said, turning to Izo, "in exchange for that kiss you promised me."

"I'd rather fuck myself with a pinecone, vato."

"Interesting." Lrasa hopped to his feet. "So the next question is— what's a pinecone? More importantly, can you fashion a life-sized costume of one?" When Izo rolled his eyes and didn't respond, Lrasa broke out into a victorious leer.

"Cut the shit, Lrasa," said Ari. "Tell us where Mort is, or I'll tell everyone here what you really like to do in bed."

Lrasa waved her down. "Put away the big guns. I lied. I don't actually know where Mort is. All I know is I was told to stall this Avarian. I was happy to oblige, naturally." Lrasa threw an arm around the Gravity Sprite's shoulders. "Heck, it might just be my new favorite pastime."

Izo knocked Lrasa's arms clear. "Stall me for what?"

Before Lrasa could answer, a loud noise cut in from overhead, drawing everyone's attention. Izo, Lrasa, and Ari looked up simultaneously. Floating on an especially large platform near the center of the room, Mort stood nodding and greeting his guests from safe inside a velvety white balustrade.

"Good evening. I hope everyone is enjoying themselves," he started. All around the room his voice was subtly reproduced by a speaker within every platform, giving each attendee the impression he was speaking at voice level personally to them.

"Thank you all for being here," he continued. "I know this invitation was last minute and that several of you have traveled great distances to attend this little showcase. But I promise your exertions will not be for nothing."

"What's he up to?" Izo whispered to Ari.

"Don't know," answered Ari honestly.

"As many of you know," Mort continued, "for most of my life I've been an avid fan and devoted supporter of rare talent. During that time, I've learned that singularity isn't something you can put a price on—but it is something you can categorically examine. There are, in fact, three essential categories which give value to any curiosity: rarity, authenticity..." He paused to grin. "And condition."

A whisper of salacious snickers rippled through the room. Ari glanced nervously at Izo, who looked like he was smelling something rotten.

"Why are these the central elements?" Mort broke from the center of the platform, meandering to speak to the left side of the room. "The reasons are simple—the rarer something is, the higher its demand and, therefore, value. The more authentic, the better its quality. The more pristine its condition, the better its care. The presence of these qualities will make almost any item inherently more valuable. The item itself is almost immaterial. Of course," he said with a meaningful glance at the left side of the room "it doesn't hurt if the object in question is also fun to look at."

The left side chuckled with approval.

"Our ancient ancestors understood this better than anyone," Mort continued after the laughter abated. The crowd visibly straightened at this reference to their history, widening their shoulders and lifting their faces. You could almost feel them swelling with dignity at the mere mention of their proud roots.

"Those ancestors spent centuries charting the universe, mapping and exploring everything in their path. One of their chief pastimes, as we know, lay in discovering and returning with the uncommon individuals. Over time, they perfected ways of not only bringing their discoveries back, but in cultivating them here as well.

"It was later generations that would lose their way by trying to improve upon these methods while failing to correct what they wrongly assumed was a problem with the old ways. They created clones, which quickly fell out of fashion. Why? Because they never realized the importance of two of the characteristics. First, as soon as a clone is possible, its rarity comes into question. Second, that there's no authenticity to be had in a clone.

"Now is a clone's condition unassailable? Of course," Mort admitted, opening his hands. "But this is only because clones are created in laboratories and factories, under the most clinical conditions imaginable. What emerged from their labs were manufactured beings. There was nothing natural or genuine about them. No, far rarer and more valuable is something raw and unprocessed, cultivated and matured lightyears away from any lab or scheming scientist...no offense, Dr. Gujklydolen."

The group laughed as Mort nodded down at the renowned geneticist and Sword-member. Chuckling, the foremost representative of his field nodded with good humor and humility. Ari realized with no small amount of amazement that Dr. Gujklydolen's platform was actually occupied with fifteen of the universe's most prominent experts on genes and biology.

In fact, looking around the room, it suddenly hit her that there were several groupings like this: Senator Wruit, the Commissioner of Avarian racing, was seated with twelve of the highest-ranking executives in Avarians sports. Senator Hreisn, a board member of one of the biggest tech conglomerates, was seated with several other tech giants. Three platforms were filled with major media heads. All around the room, dozens of the most powerful titans in all walks of life were gathered purposely by specialty, the seemingly innocent gathering representing an absolutely staggering cross-section of the Imperial elite.

As she turned back toward Mort, her hand drifted over her mouth as she realized who he'd chosen to sit with him. *Of course,* she gasped. *The twins.* Biggest gossips in the universe, the twins were some of the oldest, richest, most trusted Malforians on the Mountain. Anything the twins witnessed first-hand was gospel fact, plain and simple. No one would dare question their word. He couldn't have picked a more perfect or unassailable pair of mouthpieces.

Ari shifted her eyes back to Mort. *When did you plan all this?*

"They tried cloning and cultivating rare discoveries in the wild," Mort continued to his audience. He was now slowly crossing back and forth, tracing his lofty stage like an excited storyteller. Which he was: he was telling them the story of themselves.

"But their arrogance and machinations smacked of artifice. After centuries of failure, they finally gave up when the truth had become too painful to ignore—that there simply is no way to artificially create rarity. It was a contradiction from the start.

"Tonight, standing here, I can confidently tell you I've accidentally corrected their error. Tonight, I offer you a glimpse of something truly rare, something those ancestors, ambitious as they were, could only dreamed about. This rarity is unlike anything we've ever seen, more singular and valuable than anything any Malforian has ever laid eyes on, in fact. This remarkable gem was plucked from antiquity and hidden away from time, preserved in a natural state for thousands of years inside an undiscovered galaxy. I must admit, I cannot claim to have any hand in having found him. No, fate dropped him into my life, an unexpected and miraculous twist of destiny."

He stopped walking suddenly. His gaze grew low and far away. He seemed to be reflecting on something, regathering his thoughts, and surveying the people. A hush fell over the crowd. He caught several individuals' eyes for brief, unprotected moments. He seemed to be weighing whether he could trust them, gathering assurance from individual members while working up the nerve to truly speak from within his heart. They played directly into it. No one in the room daring to move a muscle. They were like an audience of onlookers scared of frightening away a rare animal sighting.

"Like most of you here," Mort started slowly, still connecting with them, one by one, "I've grown accustomed to an extremely high set of privileges that came with my station in life. The things most spend whole generations struggling to attain—safety, comfort, luxury, influence—have always been utterly common-place for me."

He paused again, his voice and gaze growing fainter. "What I intend to present to you tonight is commonplace to absolutely no one." He gave a nod of self-affirmation, as if to say to both himself and the world that *yes, this is exactly what I want to say. This is the real, un-bared truth.* Looking up, he smiled at his audience. "Least of all to me."

The crowd held its breath. You could almost feel their veneration and excitement filling the room with approval. If it'd been physically possible for everyone in the room to reach out and hug him, they would have.

Mort took a deep breath. He held out a hand. "Dearest friends and esteemed colleagues. Tonight I offer you, for your delight and utter amazement—the last living Gravity Sprite in the universe."

All around them the lights cut off. At the same time three single beams of light clicked on to shine at Izo. The light, too sudden and bright for him, blinded the surprised youth who, hissing loudly, ducked behind one hand.

The crowd gasped and broke into peals of applause.

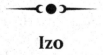

Izo

Eyes slowly adjusting, Izo lowered his hand. He glanced at the crowd nervously, unsure whether to be ready for some sort of titanic, alien stampede. But no one approached him. In fact, no one even seemed to adjust in their seats. Like perfectly well-behaved theater guests, they seemed satisfied to simply watch and whisper to each other.

Izo's gaze flicked up to Senator Mortaco. He was still standing proud and tall, one hand held out like a ringmaster presenting his next act. Izo gave him a red-hot stink eye. He'd never wanted to murder anyone half as much in his life.

The party-goers' applause eventually died down. After a few seconds of punctuated silence, it became abundantly clear the audience was waiting for him to do something. Every stubborn muscle in his body wanted to scream, flip them all off, and hit a backflip on his way out. But there was still the matter of his drawings, homeworld and pornographic alike.

Izo moved forward to get clear of the lights. Then, taking a few running steps in, he took off for Mort's platform.

The crowd gasped at his speed, clapping with unexpected joy at his accidental performance. Izo clenched his face in burning humiliation while hugging the outside edge of the platform. Ducking his head and his shoulders, he tried to make himself disappear. "Do you still have them?" he whispered.

"I do." Mort smiled and opened a doorway on the side of the platform. "You'll get them back in one hour, starting now."

Izo blew out an annoyed breath and floated into the doorway.

— CHAPTER THIRTY-TWO —

Izo

Izo was no closer to getting to Earth than the day he'd stepped off the *Atrox Killboard*. He still had no idea how he was going to get home, or if hanging around the creepy Senator's house was actually helping or hurting his chances at this point. But there was one thing he knew for sure: with the possible exception of Ari, he did not like a single person in this room.

He tried to shake it off and look bigger, but that was no easy task while sitting in an overly-large couch surrounded by the ninety-eight percent Malforian demographic. Mort's platform, arranged in a square, was a little less intimidating than the room of curious strangers. With Mort and Lrasa on either side of him and Ari on the other side of Mort's friend, the platform held on its opposite end only two people Izo didn't recognize—a pair of nearly identical Malforians, both slightly older and stuffier than the two playboy Senators. If worse came to worst, he supposed there'd only be four apex aliens against the lost teenager from Earth and the universe's smallest intersexual pop star.

Izo leaned over to the Senator. "If I promise to never sass you again, can I go back to my room?"

"Like I'm going to take that deal," the Senator whispered back. He patted Izo on the shoulder. "Relax. The twins came all this way to meet you. They just want to ask a couple of questions and get to know you a little. That's all."

"That is, unless more is on the table," laughed the larger of the two twins. Heavyset and indistinguishable in the face from the Malforian beside him except for a slightly larger frame, Izo got the distinct feeling he enjoyed creeping out Avarians. "You come face to face with a once-in-lifetime beauty, you take whatever interactions you can get. Don't you, dear sister?"

"Behave yourself, Bvoscar," chided his companion. Tall and pale, she wore her long silvery hair in thin braids. In a gleaming red ensemble and a big hat, she was the fanciest Malforian Izo had ever seen.

Fawning at him, she let out a squee. "I just can't get over it, Mort! It's like looking at something straight out of a fairytale. He's so little and cute!"

Izo made a face. "I'm five foot eight, lady."

"Is that large on your planet?" she asked.

"It's... not short for a Chicano."

"Will he get any larger than this?" Bvoscar asked Mort.

The Senator shook his head. "Males from his planet reach full height just after puberty. He may grow a bit more, but most stop between the age of eighteen and twenty."

"How old are you now?" the female twin asked Izo.

"Nineteen." He turned to Mort. "But I could always be a late bloomer."

Mort laughed. "Of course, you could. And anyway, it doesn't matter. He can fly; he can be as big as he wants."

"Exactly," Izo agreed, glaring around the platform. "And I'll fly up and pee on the next person that calls me short."

Mort held out a hand to Izo with a flat expression. "Speaking of, not to disappoint you, Tig, but I assure you though he may seem fairytale-like from a distance, in person there's nothing particularly mystical about him. He's just a normal Avarian who happens to be the only one of his kind. Please, don't feel the need to put on airs around him. Ask him whatever you'd like. He may be rude or sarcastic, but..." He shrugged. "I can also promise he won't hold back."

"All right. I have a question for him," said the female, Tig. Sitting forward, she smiled warmly. "We've all been hearing rumors you're joining the Imperial racing team. Any truth to that?"

"I guess I technically tried out and qualified." Izo gave a noncommittal lift of his shoulders. "Might as well give it a shot."

Tig frowned. She glanced at Mort. "Are we not serious or excited about this?"

"Of course we are," answered Mort, handing Izo a drink. "He's being bashful. Tomorrow is his first day of practice. He's going to be amazing." The Senator mussed Izo's hair. "The head coach says his try out time had one of the best off-the-block accelerations in the tri-galaxy."

"And my last run broke the fourth wall," said Izo.

Mort smiled in embarrassment at the twins. "That's not exactly what happened...but everyone who attended in person agreed it was certainly a sight to see. The coach was very eager to get him started as soon as she reviewed his times."

"Good! We look forward to seeing him in action as well. I know everyone is very curious to find out what he can do," said Bvoscar.

"As a Gravity Sprite, I'm sure you'll be a natural," Tig said to Izo.

Izo shrugged in agreement while taking a sip of his drink. His eyes widened—it was surprisingly good, smooth and bubbly with just a touch of melon flavor. He looked down at it, impressed. "What's this called?"

"That's called 'the good stuff,' and you're going to get used to it living here, my boy," Bvoscar chuckled before turning back to Mort. "Speaking of living here," said Bvoscar, his voice suddenly dropping with insinuation, "It's come to our attention that this lovely creature has been staying with you already for...what? A whole month now?"

"A couple of weeks," said Izo.

"It's been almost a month," agreed the Senator.

"Mhmm," said Bvoscar. "And during all that time together you and your supposedly virginal guest here never..." Bvoscar pointed between them and grinned.

Izo narrowed his eyes.

The Senator smirked and covered his mouth. "Why whatever are you accusing me of?"

Bvoscar tipped his head affectionately. "Nothing untoward, my dear boy! You know I've adored you ever since you were small."

"And, likewise, I've always admired and been honest with both of you," said Mort.

Bvoscar broke into an even wider sharky grin. His age showed plainly the deep-set wrinkles of an expression often used. "Of course, of course! But you have to realize I still have eyes in my head. A person says they have a nineteen-year-old, one-of-a-kind virgin living in their home...particularly one who looks like that..." Bvoscar's gaze slid slowly down the Earthling. "You can't help but wonder."

Izo sneered and started to stand.

"You can stop wondering," Mort said, holding out a hand to stop him. "There's nothing between Izo and I. And it wasn't from lack of interest or trying, let me assure you. I was simply too late; Izo's already been spoken for," said Mort.

"Even so, you're telling me there haven't been any midnight mistakes? No run-ins in the hallway? No drinks after dinner or accidental wanderings onto the same patio late at night? Really? Not even once?" A cool smile played across Bvoscar's face. "You honestly expect the Mountain to believe that, Mort?"

"The Mountain can believe what it wants. It's immaterial." The Senator spread his arms over his head with ease. "I'm here purely as his protector and sponsor. There has not now or ever been anything romantic between us. If you don't believe me: ask him." He gestured at Izo.

Izo quickly decided now wasn't the time to disclose anything personal. "It's not like that. I'm just here until I figure out how to get home."

"Hmm." Bvoscar threw a look to his twin. "What do you think, Tig?"

Tig's shark-eye flashed between Izo and the Senator. "I think Izo's very sweet, and Mort has always been a perfect gentleman."

"True, but how does that answer my question, dear sister?"

"I think it means they aren't going to answer your question, dear brother."

"Ah. I see." Bvoscar nodded knowingly. "Very good, then."

Mort chuckled and shook his head. Izo folded his arms and did his best to set the place on fire with his mind. He would have gladly burned himself too if it would have taken the rest of them down with him.

"Well, I know the truth, even if these two are too precious to admit it," said Lrasa, cutting in rudely. "I have it on very good authority that Izo likes sex. In fact," he said, turning to the youth, "he told me so himself the very first night we met."

Izo stared in confusion. He had no idea what the shorter Senator was talking about. Then it suddenly hit him like a thunderbolt. He snapped his fingers and pointed. "You were the other guy at the club that night!"

Lrasa's mouth dropped open. Beside him, Mort snorted and nearly fell forward, he was laughing so hard.

The smaller Senator searched Izo's face with pain. "You didn't remember me until now? Izo, I've visited you twice a week since you moved in."

The Earthling grimaced. He hadn't put it together.

"Don't feel bad, Izo," Ari said, touching her hair and not looking at any of them. "No one can seem to remember Lrasa at election time either."

At this, the twins threw their heads back and roared with laughter.

"I would be angry at you, but I'm just amazed your mouth isn't too full to talk," Lrasa said, snapping at Ari.

"Watch it," the Senator told his friend.

"Speaking of watching it…" Ari suddenly sat forward to glare at the Earthling. "Izo, where's my purse?"

Izo froze. He looked down at his side. The purse wasn't there. His head swiveled as he searched the immediate area, but the stupid bag was nowhere to be found. He looked up at Ari with an embarrassed expression.

Ari's eyebrow drifted up. "Well?"

"It was just here. I—I'll look for it." Izo floated off the chair and toward the nearest platform below.

"Have you seen a purse lying around? It's silver and shiny," Izo asked hopefully. The group smiled in sympathy but shook their heads. Izo scanned the area. Even with every eye in the room resting on him, he could still feel the Aurelian singer burning holes into the back of his head. He looked up at her sheepishly. "Maybe it fell after I sat?"

Ari turned her angry expression toward the Senator. Izo took the opportunity to zip left and right near the ground below. His movements were drawing attention and whispers from around the room, but it felt more important to keep the mean singer from attacking him again.

"This is why I hate lending things to your house guests," the singer told the Senator, her voice somehow echoing all around the room. "They're always losing my stuff. The fabric on that piece had some of the rarest and most delicate natural fibers in the universe. They say they'll take care of it, but deep down they don't care because they know it's not theirs."

"He obviously didn't mean to misplace it," said the Senator. He shouted down to where the Gravity Sprite was still floating and trying to peer between people. "Izo, do you remember where you saw it last?"

Izo shook his head up at the platform. "I know I had it when I arrived."

"Then it's got to be around here somewhere. We'll find it. Come back," said the Senator, waving him up. He glanced sharply at Ari. "It's not a big deal."

Izo zipped back to the platform and frowned sheepishly at the blonde. "I'm sorry. I didn't mean to lose it. I'll buy you another one."

Ari tsked. "It's not *my* money you're wasting."

"Exactly, so there's nothing for Izo to apologize for." The Senator gave the Earthling an encouraging pat on the back as he climbed into his seat again.

"I'd be happy to punish him if you don't want to," said Lrasa from Mort's other side. "Sometimes a strong, loving hand is exactly what a young Avarian needs."

Izo flipped him the bird.

"No one's punishing anyone. It was an honest mistake." Sitting back, the Senator placed an arm around both of Izo's shoulders. "When I took him in, I swore to help and support him. That means supporting his mistakes too."

Izo's face pinched. "Huh?"

"No one give it another thought," the Senator shushed everyone. "As long as he's here, he doesn't have to worry about anything. It doesn't matter how big or small; I'll take care of it." He gave the Gravity Sprite a reassuring squeeze. "You're protected here."

"Makes you wonder why he wants to leave and get several million lightyears away," whispered Lrasa to Tig.

"He doesn't want to leave," snapped Mort. "He misses home. It's different."

Lrasa shrugged. "I'm sure that's what I'd tell you in his place too."

The Senator gave his friend a look like he was almost ready to push him off the platform.

"Speaking of missing things, I understand the agent is still unaccounted for?" asked Tig. She shook her head in confusion. "That part I didn't understand. Was he a part of the kidnapping too?"

"I told him about the kidnapping at the end, right before he disappeared," said Izo. Thinking it over, he frowned. *Maybe it did make sense that Deneus left after all.* He sighed and looked down. "He didn't know anything when it all started."

The Senator held out a finger. "We can't be entirely sure what he did and didn't know; he disappeared before anyone could ask him."

"I know when he found out. I'm the one who told him." Izo turned back to the twins. "Deneus didn't know what was going on. He was a good guy."

"Then why disappear? Why avoid the authorities?" asked Bvoscar.

"I—I don't know," answered Izo honestly. "Maybe he was scared of being accused along with everyone else?"

"Or maybe he had something to hide from everyone else," whispered Bvoscar to Tig.

Tig nodded with a knowing look. "There were rumors he was working with the Malforian mob."

"I heard he was tangled up in Avarian trafficking," agreed Bvoscar.

"What? No," said Izo. "Deneus would never do anything like that. He tried to protect me."

"The truth is," the Senator said, holding out a hand between Izo and the twins, "we simply don't know. The investigation is ongoing at this point, and there's been nothing conclusive. Unfortunately, we'll just have to wait to see if anyone can find him to understand what he was thinking. What we do know, in the meantime, is Izo's kidnappers are gone, and he's finally safe."

"Mort's right," Tig told her brother. "Izo's safety is the most important thing here."

"Mmm, quite right," said Bvoscar.

Turning to Izo, Tig broke into a charitable smile. It was so sweet and demoralizing, you would have thought she'd heard he was being dissected later that night. "Tell me, do you miss your fiancé and home world?"

"Y-yes," said Izo, awkwardly. "I miss Earth and Hanako a lot."

Tig nodded in rapturous sympathy. She looked half ready to break into tears. "You poor, sweet thing! I couldn't believe it when I heard what happened to you. It's absolutely heartbreaking. I don't know how you've endured, to have no idea where the love of your life or your home planet is? It's unimaginable!"

"It's a terrible thing to lose your birth planet," agreed Mort. "Sadly, neither Izo nor his fiancé knows where the other is. When Izo's kidnappers took him, they did it suddenly and without warning." He turned to Izo. "The two of them were planning to start a family too. Weren't you?"

Izo shifted uncomfortably in his seat. "That's kind of private."

"Completely understandable. I'm sure it would take a while for a heart to heal and open itself to anyone else," the Senator said with a meaningful glance at Lrasa. "Anyone with half-a-brain could easily understand that."

"I don't know. Ari seems to bounce between lovers pretty fast," said Lrasa.

"Some don't take as long as others," replied the singer.

"Is that an invitation?" asked Lrasa. "Because I could kill ten minutes."

"Would you two stop it? We're talking about Izo." Tig turned back to the Earthling. "Tell us, was your fiancé also a Gravity Sprite?"

"Hmm? No." Izo shook his head. "Hanako isn't Avarian."

The Senator cleared his throat. Tig had begun to frown deeply, and her brother had broken into a matching look of arch disapproval. Izo looked back and forth between the three of them. "Did I say something wrong?"

"I would think so. You realize pairing with a non-Avarian makes it more difficult to pass on the Gravity Sprite gene, correct?" said Bvoscar.

"I wouldn't really know," said Izo.

"And aren't you only half-Avarian yourself?" asked Tig hotly.

"Yeah, but—" Izo blinked. "Wait, how do you know that?"

"How sure are we about him going back to this long-lost female from his planet?" asked Tig, turning on Mort. "Because while I certainly understand how he feels and of course anyone should be free to choose love if they really want, isn't maintaining the species an important element to consider as well?"

"Well-said," agreed Bvoscar.

"After all, finding the right match for any Avarian is an incredibly touchy matter. For someone like a Gravity Sprite, I'd think careful forethought would be even more important." She turned on Izo. "Be honest, how much did you really consider the repercussions of this engagement?" Her eyes glowed with intensity. "It affects more than just you, after all."

"Maybe," said Izo. "But it sure as hell doesn't affect you or anyone else—"

"He was in love," interrupted Mort. "He didn't have to think it through or consider the repercussions because love isn't about making smart choices. Or doing what makes sense in the long run. It's about finding a certain feeling with someone. Regardless, now isn't the time to chastise him about his past. Even if we don't agree with his earlier decisions, I'm sure we can sympathize with his plight. None of this was his fault. He's suffered a great and profound loss, and it's going to take some time to get over it." He patted Izo's back. "I for one am happy to support him no matter what."

All around the room, whispers of genial agreement seemed to sweep through the other platforms. Izo looked around in confusion. Several of the Malforians present had turned to glance sadly at him. None seemed more distressed than Tig, though. "Of course, you're right, Mort. I shouldn't be angry with him. I can't imagine losing my first love and my home world."

"Birth world," corrected Mort.

"Yes," said Tig. Sitting up, she smiled brightly at Izo. "I'm sorry if I got too involved. It's just—I already adore you so much! Please forgive me. I only mean well."

"I think we're all feeling a little over-protective of him at the moment. No surprise there though—he's a genuine find. You're a lucky Malforian, Mort. I've never been so delightfully impressed or jealous in my life."

"You're too kind," said the Senator.

"Anything he needs, you let us know," said Bvoscar.

"And please come and visit us soon," said Tig to Izo. "We want you to feel nothing but welcome in your new home."

Izo scratched his arm. "Thanks, but this isn't permanent. Earth didn't disappear. I'm still going back. It's still home."

"That's right." Mort ruffled the Earthling's hair before turning to the twins. "He's been gradually working through it. But it's not easy. It's been a lot to process."

"There's nothing to process," said Izo. From all around him people in the room seemed to be sadly disagreeing with soft whispers. Izo sat up and wanted to argue with them, but Mort held him down by one shoulder.

"I think he was just taken from home so suddenly, and his kidnappers had been promising to take him back for so long... I don't think there was ever any time to grieve." Mort continued. "But he's shown a lot of fortitude by trying to start over—"

"I don't need to start over," insisted Izo. "I'm going back to Earth!"

"Izo, why don't we go upstairs?" offered Ari. Her expression was as pliant and gentle as a kindergarten teacher's. "It's getting late. You still have to get up for practice tomorrow."

"No," said Izo. "I'm not tired and I—"

"That's probably for the best," Mort agreed with Ari. He turned to the Earthling. "Thank you for coming. I know you were nervous about it. I'll see you tomorrow after work." Then, returning to the twins, he left Ari to pull Izo up from his seat and towards the platform's door. "This is why the Mountain's support for the Swords is so deeply appreciated," continued the Senator. "It's for finding and protecting rare talents just like Izo all around the universe."

"Of course," agreed Bvoscar.

"Let's go," said Ari, pushing Izo toward the platform's door as it neared the ground.

"I said I'm not tired!" insisted Izo. All around them the room echoed with fawning laughter at his show of apparently adorable defiance. Izo glared up furiously in multiple directions. But it only seemed to make their pandering sympathy worse. Unable to think of any way to make them stop, he eventually buckled and let Ari nudge him off the platform and toward the room's exit. In honesty, he didn't actually want to stay.

"I'm just so glad you found him instead of someone else, Mort," said Tig from behind them. Their voices had already begun rising into the air again.

— CHAPTER THIRTY-THREE —

Izo

I zo woke with a start. He'd been having that dream where he couldn't fly again. He stared up at Ari's ornate, gold and blue ceiling, his heart rate surging. He placed his hand on his chest and tried to make it slow, but his breath was speeding faster. He could already feel his focus narrowing.

Mierda.

He blinked and tried to convince himself the feeling wasn't real, but a haunting unease had already filled his body—pins and needles in his limbs, a sickly tingle covering his skin. He couldn't catch his breath. The air in the room was too thin. The edges of his vision began to blur. He told himself to calm down, that he was fine, but it was no use. This was no dream. It was real: he was trapped, and there was no air.

His skin broke out in prickling sweat as his mind raced with fear. He had to escape. He had to get back to Earth. But he was lost, alone, and had never been so far away from home. There was nothing he could do. There was nowhere to go. He had waded in too far and now he was trapped here forever.

The icy reality of his existence crashed over him like physical pain. He grimaced and rolled on his side. Clumsy hands knocked into Ari's things, priceless figurines and curios, as he clawed for the only thing that could help him—his medicine.

Once he finally had a hold of it, a terrifying new problem shook him: he didn't know how to take it. Someone had always been around to help him, and he still hadn't learned how to use the alien cone. Twisting its top with a spastic motion, he stabbed himself repeatedly to no avail. He huffed and tried again until his arm burned from over a dozen pinpricks, but it was no use. A well of cold desperation and grief sprang up and swallowed him whole.

Ari shifted up in the bed beside him. She was virtually naked, a gauzy blue nightgown revealing much of her gold body. She glared over one shoulder. "Not again," she groaned, her voice thick with drowsiness.

Izo clenched his eyes and fought to breathe.

Ari hurried to his side. Nimble fingers took the alien contraption from Izo's grip. She twisted the top through two clicks and popped it away.

The first hit of relief felt like plunging into cool water after stumbling through an arid desert for days. Izo breathed out slowly. It was going to be all right. His muscles screamed where he'd likely stabbed them to shreds, but he didn't care. Help was on the way. Everything was fine. Swallowing hard, he let himself drift back to sleep.

Sometime later he opened his eyes to the sounds of Ari getting ready for the day.

There was a gentle glow about the room. The sunlight was warm and golden; the air was crisp and fresh. Everything had gained a subtle, brighter quality to it.

Gazing around, Izo smiled and sat up. It was amazing how much better he felt. *Alien meds: can't beat 'em!*

He happened to glance down at the top of his arm and hissed. A fresh coat of bright red cuts and lesions had been added to an already colorful canvas of ugly bruises and scabs. Oh well. It was nothing a good shower and breakfast couldn't make him forget.

He leaned back against Ari's headboard. "Were you planning to shower first?" he called out loudly.

A moment later a highly annoyed Aurelian appeared at the mouth of her massive bathroom-closet. "Better yet, why don't we shower at the same time?" She pointed at her door. "I imagine yours works fine, don't you?"

Izo shrugged. "Your shower is nicer."

"That's not the point and you know it. You can't keep hiding over here and using my stuff all the time. You're a full-grown Avarian; you have your own room."

"It's just a shower. I'm already here."

"Is it?" She floated closer. "You realize you haven't gotten showered, changed, or slept once in your own room since getting better? Seriously—what the hell is up with that?"

"I don't know." Izo blew off the question. He didn't like the way it made him feel. "You have better stuff than me."

"Bullshit. You know what I think it is?" Ari pointed a shoe at him. "I think you're scared of being alone in your room."

Izo made a farting noise. "I'm not scared of being alone in there. I chill in there by myself all the time."

"Yeah, to color and avoid people. But anything scary—changing clothes, showering, sleeping—you run over here and hide behind me!"

"I'm not hiding behind anything, estupida. I just like it over here. It's more comfortable. It's prettier. Plus, you can't argue with the view." He arched an eyebrow at the tiny singer.

Ari smirked. "Is this you trying to hit on me?"

Izo tipped his jaw up confidently. "Is this you pretending it isn't working?"

Ari pursed her lips. She floated forward, eyeing him up and down. Her expression had broken into a distinctly curious look. "Do you want it to work?"

Izo's pulse jumped in his throat. He hadn't expected her to reciprocate so fast. A split second later his hornier instincts kicked in. He raised both hands behind his head and tried to do his best impression of bedroom eyes. "I'm game if you are."

The corner of her mouth pulled in interest. She floated smoothly across the room. He expected her to pause at the end of the bed. Instead, she arced up to hover just above him. The motion surprised him, and he found himself sitting up awkwardly.

She lifted both eyebrows once he'd settled. "Up for a round right now?"

Izo fought to keep his face flat. As much time as they'd spent together over the last few weeks—showering, dressing, and even sleeping in the same bed—he'd thought of her more like a dormitory roommate than a potential partner. But the reality was, there was a tension between them, even if he'd ignored it for the most part, and the thought of having a little bouncy fun had crossed his mind more than once.

Still, facing the real act was a little different. "Would it be a big deal if we did?"

"It's just sex." Floating nearer, she began undoing her top from the front. "I'm a little curious about the whole Gravity Sprite thing."

"I am a fascinating specimen," Izo agreed while staring into the middle of her small and perfect golden breasts.

The Aurelian bobbed down to straddle his lap, and the two quickly began pulling away at their clothes and adjusting their angle. It wasn't the first time Izo'd been approached with quick, meaningless sex, or been with a person he was pretty sure could teach him a thing or two—there'd been one guy visiting from the Bay area who'd nearly made him fly. He knew the general run down and was excited to finally learn more about a fellow Avarian.

But as he went to grab the back of her neck and kiss her, he paused. What would it mean if this went well? Would she expect him to date her? He grabbed her hands to stop her as she went to pull her shirt off completely.

She looked up at him curiously. "What?"

"To be clear," said Izo. "This isn't going to make things weird, right? We're not going to fall in love or anything?"

Ari's hands slowly went up to cover her mouth and chest. She looked at him like he was the most adorable thing she's ever witnessed. "You think we're going to fall in love, Izo? Awwwww... how freaking cute are you?"

Izo rolled his eyes.

She shook her head at him sadly. "No, Izo. I don't think we're going to fall in love if we have sex together. If anything, I'm expecting to be let down a little bit. No offense."

Izo frowned. He was highly offended. "This is your pillow talk?"

Ari wrapped her arms behind his neck. "Relax. We live across the hall from each other. It's convenient and fun. That's all."

Izo relaxed into her embrace. "Ari, in case no one's ever said it before—you are the single coolest person in the universe."

"Thanks. Now shut up and kiss me."

Izo nodded and obeyed. The kiss was sweet and easy, and below it, he could feel her teacup breasts press against his chest with a warm tenderness that almost made him ache in his abdomen. Behind her he trailed his hands slowly, first down her curly hair and lightly over her neck to slide down her back along the gentle lines of her shoulder blades. As he brought his hands forward to grasp her waist, she giggled and jumped at an accidentally discovered ticklish spot. They paused to smile and press their foreheads together before continuing.

After a few minutes the skin to skin contact and subtle, heady pressure had left Izo a little dizzy. Closing his eyes, he pulled back to lick his lips. They tasted like hers. "I've never done this with anyone who could fly before."

She ran her fingers down the side of his face affectionately. "That's okay."

Izo leaned his face into the touch like an abandoned animal. "How does it work?"

"Simple." Taking his hands, she guided them to grasp tightly onto her hips. "You grab me here. Then you show me what you want."

Eyes still closed, Izo made a noise that was half laugh, half grateful prayer. Pulling her closer, he realized with no small amount of gratitude that she was maneuvering weightlessly under his fingers.

Replacing her arms around his neck, Ari spread her thighs wider and began rocking in a gentle rhythm on top of his lap. "Just relax."

Izo let out a long breath. He was imagining doing this not only this morning, but every morning for the foreseeable future. *Maybe living here wouldn't be the worst thing after all...* he caught himself thinking.

He was getting close when she suddenly pressed her mouth against his ear. "I almost forgot," she whispered. "My publicist is supposed to meet me here in a little bit. So we have to hurry."

Izo's eyes snapped open. They flew to her door. "Could someone walk in?"

"No, the door's locked, but I don't want to make her wait." Her hand snaked up the back of his neck to gently knot into his hair. She was beginning to move more and more encouragingly now. "We should still have twenty minutes. That sound like something you can manage?"

Izo wasn't listening to her anymore. He was surveying her door. It was tall and lined with swirling gold bars over a blue brocaded base. It seemed strong enough...in theory. But the visage of a far larger creature suddenly busting through it kept interrupting his thoughts. Below his chin, his body was beginning to falter. "Could Mort walk in on us?"

The Aurelian grunted, eyes shut, still trying to continue. "Mort? Of course. It's his house." She tapped her temple, recalling the Senator's embedded device. "He has the key to every place in here."

Izo's stomach filled with a deep and swirling unease. All interest in finishing fled him. He couldn't have performed if there were ten naked Aris in the room. His nose filled with the heat of an incredibly frustrated groan that he refused to vocalize. He was done. This was over.

Placing a hand flatly between the Aurelian's exposed breasts, he gently pushed her off and away from him.

Ari's eyes blinked open in anger. "What the heck are you doing?" Surveying his face, her heat abated, and a look of confusion replaced it. She frowned sadly. "What's wrong?"

Izo tried to think of an answer that didn't seem pathetic. "Nothing. I was just...we're such good friends. You know? I don't want to mess that up."

Ari narrowed her eyes. "If you don't think I'm sexy, just say so!"

"That's not it." He scratched his arm and stared at her floor. "I just don't feel comfortable with it. I thought I did, but...I don't." Izo sighed, before looking at her angrily. "I'm sorry, okay? I shouldn't have tried to start anything. Can we move on?"

But Ari wasn't ready to drop it. She studied him, seeming to read something in his face while slowly putting things together. After a few seconds, her gaze flicked over to the door. "Are you scared Mort's going to walk in on us?"

Izo winced, then laughed. Turning on his side, he quickly began crawling away from her. "Where are you getting that? That's crazy. I'm not scared of him."

"It's okay if you are. I love the guy, but honestly?" She paused in consideration. "He's kind of scary."

"Not to me. No one scares me. No, the truth is, I'm just not that into this. I thought I was, but as it turns out, I'm not." He flipped his feet around to climb off her bed. "It's nothing personal. You're very pretty, but I don't see you that way. I thought I did, but oh well." Standing upright, he turned to give her an apologetic shrug. "Sorry for wasting your time."

Ari blew out two cheekfuls of air while re-buttoning part of her shirt. "All right," she agreed. Floating up, she crossed the room to her main make-up counter and hovered above a seat to continue getting ready. "Whatever you say, Izo."

Izo stood by awkwardly, unsatisfied with her pliant tone but unsure what to do about it. "Besides," he added, breaking into a suave expression, "I'd hate to make you choose between us."

"Choose between who?"

He pointed at himself. "Me and Mort."

Ari's eyes bugged out at him. Then she burst out laughing like a seagull. Izo frowned as she clasped her chest and tipped back in her seat. She laughed so hard one of her boobies fell out of her still mostly unbuttoned shirt.

Three minutes later, she finally pulled herself upright enough to adjust herself and her clothes. "Oh, sweetheart. You think I'd leave Mort...for you?" She gave him a look so sweet and patronizing it hurt his feelings. "You're even more adorable than I thought."

"Why? You think I'm too weak? Look at this thigh," he said, slapping the top of one leg. "That's pure power right there."

Ari was too busy doing her makeup to look at him. "Izo, you're very cute, and, as it turns out, I don't completely hate having you around. But I barely know you and, no offense, what I have seen I haven't been impressed by. If I was going to leave Mort, it'd be for someone who had it more together than me, not less."

"You need someone to take care of you? I can do that." Izo leaned against her bedpost. "I can take care of you all night long, Mamacita." Ari flicked her eyes at him, her bed, then him again. She seemed vaguely embarrassed. As he stood under the weight of her expression, his smile faded slowly. He straightened off her bedpost. "Anyway, that's not the point. You got loyalty problems."

The Aurelian rolled her eyes. "What is with Avarians accusing me of that lately?"

"Because they know the truth! Deep down, you'd choose a Malforian over an Avarian any day of the week. That's some real internalized bullshit."

Ari leaned forward to apply cream to her face. "Don't get me wrong—I'll gladly take down Lrasa or any of Mort's friends.

They're assholes. But if you think I'm taking sides with you over Mort, you've lost your gods damn mind."

"Traitor!"

"Hey, at least I'm giving you a heads up. Mort and I are welded together at the side. You might as well try to pull the tri-galaxies apart."

"La Malinche," Izo insisted.

Ari rolled her eyes. "Why are you still using that weird language? No one can understand you; you sound like a crazy person. Go get it translated and uploaded in the database. I can give you someone to contact. It doesn't take long."

"Some words don't have translations." Izo looked down at his feet, remembering Tearn's language lessons on the ship. The memories of the little Ginarsian were not welcome. "Like Malinche—it's not a word. It's the story of a traitor woman."

Ari picked up a brush to start her eyes. "What kind of traitor?"

Izo sighed. "Malinche was a Nahua Princess in ancient Mexico. Her father died, and her mother remarried a different ruler. When Malinche's mother gave birth to her new husband's son, her mother was worried the new child's inheritance would be at risk. So she faked her daughter's death and sold Malinche to slave traders."

"And I thought my mom was mean," said Ari.

Izo smiled. "Malinche was bought by some Maya on the eastern coast of Mexico. She was clever and learned the language of her captors. A few years later when Cortés and his conquistadors conquered the Maya, Malinche and nineteen other women were given to the Spanish as part of a peace offering. At first, Malinche was given to a random captain. But Cortés saw her secret power and took her back for himself."

Ari glanced up sharply at this part of the story. She seemed intrigued. "She had a secret power?"

"Malinche spoke both western and central Maya—the language of her captors and the language of her family. Cortés already had an interpreter for the western Maya, but if he wanted to conquer the Aztec Empire, he needed someone that spoke the central dialect."

Ari pursed her lips. "How does this make her a traitor?"

"Hang on, I'm getting to it. Malinche was a translator for Cortés—they literally called her his 'tongue.' But she was more than that. She was a guide for the Spanish, served as their strategist and political schemer who helped flip her people to side with the Spanish against the Aztecs. She's the most evil villain in Mexican history. It was because she turned her back on her people that an entire civilization was erased."

Ari chuckled. "Good for her!" Then she continued doing her makeup.

"What?" Izo blinked. "What the hell do you mean 'good for her'?" He could feel the heat rising into his face. "Hundreds of thousands of people were slaughtered because of her. Countless more were enslaved to the Spanish."

"Didn't it all start because she was sold into slavery?"

"Yeah, but...that's not the point. She betrayed her people."

"What people?" scoffed Ari. "The people that sold her to protect a baby's inheritance? Or the people that lost a battle and gave her away as a peace offering? And for that matter..." Ari placed a finger on her chin. "Why is she the one being blamed? You said all these other groups were flipping sides to join Cortés. Wasn't that a way bigger piece of him winning?"

"Exactly," said Izo. "She convinced them to turn on the Aztecs."

"She made them turn on their own government?" Ari lifted an eyebrow. "There was no other reason they didn't like the Aztecs?"

Izo scowled. "Would you listen, woman? You're not listening. She tricked them! She tricked them into helping the Spanish."

"Fine. Let's assume that's true. You're telling me a captive slave convinces a bunch of groups to help Cortés, and they were all confused. But when Cortés convinces a slave girl to help him, she was purposefully malicious?" Ari shook her head. "They're either both at fault or neither."

"You don't know the full story. She was a skilled communicator. She was known for her intelligence and diplomacy."

"Hmmph." Ari said over her shoulder. "Sounds like they sold the wrong person."

"She was a whore!" Izo continued. "A traitorous whore who joined the Europeans."

"Whose fault was that?" Ari put down a brush and looked at him sharply. "And a traitor? Are you kidding me? Who did she owe loyalty to? Her family? Her people?"

"You're supposed to be loyal to your people! To your ancestors!"

"Your ancestors don't know you! They're a bunch of dead strangers."

"That's not the point... Mira, how are you not getting this?" Izo slapped the back of one hand into the palm of the other. She handed all of Mexico to the Spanish."

Ari copied his gesture and rhythm. "All of Mexico handed her to the Spanish first."

Izo's mouth dropped. He was confused. He needed to think. Waving her off angrily, he turned his back.

Ari went back to doing her hair. "I'll be honest, I don't care. It's your story. Maybe you're telling it wrong. Maybe I'm just not getting it. All I know is if someone sold me into slavery, I couldn't care less about their Empire. Hell, I'd probably help end it too. I just hope this Mexico place learned their lesson and stopped treating their Avarians like shit." Finished, she stood to survey herself. "Turns out they couldn't afford to lose some of them."

"She wasn't Avarian, and that's not the point of the story." The Earthling scowled and wrapped his arms around himself. "You *would* defend her. You are such a Malinche. Every weekend Mort points you at another pile of beds, and every weekend you get to work. And you know what the saddest part is?" Izo laughed, hard and fake. "You chose this! You left a palace and came here on purpose to—"

The sound of the smack registered before the pain on his cheek. Surprised, Izo moved away from her. In his hand, he cradled his stinging face.

Ari's face was a hideous mask of anger verging on tears. "Don't you dare pretend you know anything about me. You don't know shit. So just shut your mouth." She closed her eyes, breathed out, and pointed at the door. "And stay the hell out of my room from now on."

— CHAPTER THIRTY-FOUR —

Izo

A few hours later, freshly showered and wearing a pair of green workout clothes, Izo stepped out of the Senator's private shuttle. It was early morning. All around him the sounds of the alien capital were coming to life, racing by with the upbeat pulse of an entire ecosystem bursting with purpose and drive. In front of him, the capital's Avarian Athletic Training Center shone like a freshly sharp and jagged jewel.

Powerful and sharp, the building stood before him like a metal structure caught mid-disaster, careening and tearing in mass catastrophe toward the sky. A monument to the chaos and beauty of unfiltered momentum, its designer must have chosen this thesis to capture the energy inherent to all Avarian sports. Izo had to admit it was one of the strangest buildings he had ever seen, and also one of the most beautiful.

Izo went inside the massive entryway and straight in the direction of what he'd been assured was the Avarian racing wing. He walked under the approving watch of thousands of honors and awards hung proudly within its hallowed halls. It was official: this holy shrine to elite athleticism would actually be his regular haunt.

Izo saw the tall double doors that led to the practice field and felt a surge of anticipation under his skin, like a happy twitch in a dog's hide. Unable to stop himself, he snapped forward, yanked the doors open, and stepped into where he hoped would be where he spent the majority of whatever time he had left on IA.

It was the biggest thing he'd ever seen. Laid over a vertical landscape, the practice field stretched up thousands of meters in the air, like half a dozen football stadiums stacked end to end. From this massive central column branched off another dozen smaller fields in stacked alcoves.

Padding out into the field, Izo couldn't help taking a couple of gleeful bounces on the springy surface, like a happy kid on a trampoline. Gelatinous and squishy, it reminded him of a bouncy house but with a far softer give. Waving ripples dispersed around him with every heavy motion.

Izo continued to bounce until he reached a full-on jumping celebration. Throwing down his bag, he dropped hard onto his back, giggled, and finally stared up solemnly at what might as well have been his very own universe. Breathing in the musky scent of sweat, feet, and cleaner, he let out an adoring sigh.

Izo sat up with a contented smile, let his eyes focus, and immediately dropped flat on his back to avoid another Avarian zooming at his head.

"Hi!" said the green-skinned Avarian with a streak of bright orange hair. "Are you our new teammate?"

"I am," said Izo, watching him from his position on the floor. Squinting, he felt like maybe he recognized him from somewhere. "Hey, have we met before?"

Lifting into a spinning arc, the Avarian flung himself up and landed with one foot on either side of Izo. He was tall as the Earthling, as thin as a reed, and covered in dark hunter-green skin. Handsome and lithe, he leaned his head to peer down at Izo curiously. "Maybe. Did you go the Imperial Sports Academy for school?"

"I did not." Izo presented his hand to the green Avarian, who helped pull him to his feet. The two athletes tried to place the other. "Did I slam into the back of you at the spaceport?"

"Maybe. Do you slam into the back of people a lot?"

"It's like a medium amount? Anyway, the name's Izo. Nice to meet you."

Ignoring the offered handshake, the Avarian tipped back and began whipping around Izo in impossibly quick circles. "Ruefin. I'm a Nertian Wind Sprite. You?"

Izo spun around, trying to follow the Nertian's movements. It wasn't much use. "Earthling Gravity Sprite."

Ruefin stopped on a dime. He whistled with a high-pitched noise that sounded exactly like the wind through the trees. "Wow. Sounds rare."

"It is. Thanks."

"They said you didn't have much racing experience." Ruefin cocked his head to one side. "Is that true?"

"Uhh," Izo tried to think of the best way to answer. "I'm mostly self-taught."

"Leave him alone, Ruefin," interjected a second Avarian. Large and Malforian, the other racer wore their silver hair in a long hairdo similar to a braid. Flying the same as any Avarian, the big alien swooped toward them. "You're going to scare him off."

"Me? You're bigger than a building, Imana."

"We're on my planet. I'm normal-sized for a female on this planet. You're the tiny freaks of nature," said Imana.

Ruefin shook his head mildly and touched her arm. "Big girls have to learn to control their tempers, Imana."

The Malforian female lunged just in time for the orange-haired Avarian to dive back and swoop away. She followed, hot on his trail, but a maddening showcase of impossibly fast circles kept her at bay. Within seconds the two were thundering up the arena's heights to chase after each other.

Izo chuckled while watching their high-flying antics. He was starting to think there might be a small silver lining to spending time on IA after all. All around him, a multitude of other Avarians had begun drifting onto the practice field. He introduced himself to all of them and quickly concluded he didn't have a hope of remembering all their names or species. But they seemed cool, friendly, and most excitingly, incredibly strong.

Behind Izo, two doors slammed open loudly, drawing his—and everyone's—attention. When he turned to the noise, he was a little annoyed. But as soon as he saw who was there, he broke into a smile.

It was the female Anolitun from the club!

"Table Girl?!" Izo threw his arms open and began walking toward her. He looked the female up and down before letting out a low, appreciative grunt. "Girl, you look even better than I remember!"

She smirked. Then, with a flash of light and a sound like shotgun fire, she appeared directly in his face. Izo stumbled back, stunned and half-blind, and fell onto his butt. The Anolitun advanced rapidly, crackling fingers of electricity dancing off her body in white-hot arcs. Izo, seeing little choice, scrambled to move away in a reverse crab walk. She followed with an intense and playful look, bearing down at him from on high.

"My cousin mentioned you were a spaz about lightning."

Izo gaped at her from his spot on the ground. "Who?"

"You don't remember?" She narrowed her eyes dangerously. "It wasn't that long ago. You and my cousin had a race to see who would make the team. You lost, shacked up with your rich boyfriend, and magically ended up with his spot anyway."

Behind her, Ruefin and Imana had stopped chasing each other to land and watch. "Oh shit," said Ruefin quietly. "You're the guy Tobith's been talking about."

"That's right! Everybody come and see the guy that slept his way onto an Imperial racing team!" She spread her hands for everyone to see. To Izo's horror more people had begun floating closer in curiosity. "Come and hear his triumphant story!"

Izo started to respond but his hand slipped awkwardly on the soft ground behind him. Wrenching his wrist, he stumbled back to land softly on his ass.

He grabbed his wrist with a hiss of pain. He still wasn't used to the flooring yet and the sudden shift had caught him off guard. He rubbed the place where his tendon had stretched painfully. Luckily, the damage didn't seem to be permanent. He shook it out a few times before looking up again. By the time he did, over twenty people had casually gathered nearby.

He took a deep breath and stood. "You need to get your facts straight before you start accusing people. I didn't sleep with anyone to get here."

"You moved in with the Mountain's most famous sugar daddy and expect us to believe it had nothing to do with landing a spot on IA's most exclusive racing team?" She tilted her head. "How stupid do you think we are?"

"Stupid enough to forget that I beat your cousin."

"One time. You beat him *one time* out of three and had to get emergency medical attention afterwards," she said.

"So....?" Izo blinked angrily. He needed to come up with more words. "That last run was epic. I smoked him. I was so fast he couldn't even see me."

"Funny. According to him, you couldn't even make it across the field your first run, he ate you alive on the second one, and the last one almost killed you. Not that it mattered. They were going to keep going until you finally won." She crossed her arms. "Guess the rules are a little different when you're doing it with a Senator."

Izo clenched his hands. "I'm not doing anything with him! I earned this spot. My last run had one of the best accelerations—"

"Ohhh, I never said you didn't earn it," Tobith interrupted. "I'm sure you did. I'm sure you probably did more for your spot than anyone else here." Her golden-purple eyes sized him up with crackling insinuation. "I just don't think it had to do with racing."

Izo seethed. His heart pounded in his chest. He wanted to say something but could barely string together a sentence, so he snapped toward her face instead. "I don't know what your cousin told you, but I wiped the floor with him. I beat him by ninety percent of the field."

"If that's true, why was there no official time? And why did you magically feel the need to move in with your boyfriend the second the race was over—"

"It had nothing to do with that. He's not my boyfriend!"

"He's not your boyfriend, but you're living together?"

"It's just until..." Izo waved his arms. "I figure some stuff out."

Tobith nodded. Her gaze had settled into ugly confidence, the kind that said she didn't really need any more information—she had come to her conclusion already. "You're not the only one figuring stuff out, honey."

Izo gritted his teeth. What could he do? She'd made up her mind. Making a *pshh* noise, he turned away.

Tobith jeered with mean triumph behind him.

"By the gods, would you give it a rest?" interrupted another Avarian. Slight and covered in grey skin, she was shorter than Zusy but clearly the same species.

Floating next to Tobith, she stretched with an annoyed expression. "So he slept with a Sword. Big deal. Those guys are built on corruption. As soon as his boyfriend gets bored, they'll kick him off the team and bring your cousin back."

Izo turned to the new Avarian. "Excuse me?"

She shrugged but didn't respond.

"That's not good enough, Cadenza," Tobith said, ignoring Izo to respond to the grey Avarian. "The Cups are in a year. Graydith can't afford to lose months while we placate some Senator's himbo. This is a place for professionals, not for bored Avarians to work out and play athlete."

"No one's playing anything," Izo said, stepping closer to Tobith. His prior fear of being electrocuted was somehow far less important than what he needed to say. "You don't know the first thing about me."

"I don't need to. I know an opportunistic Avarian when I see one," said Tobith.

"Yeah," agreed Cadenza with an eye roll. "They're usually the one surrounded by unearned stuff."

Izo turned to jump at this new tormentor when he realized what was behind her—the rest of the team, nodding their heads in agreement.

The Earthling snapped off the floor sharply. He glared at the rest of the team as they floated in small groups to stretch. "Screw this. Keep your stupid spot. I never wanted to be on this team anyway."

The groups murmured to one another rather than respond. Based on their glances and tones, they seemed vaguely amused by his outburst. Izo turned to rush the double doors and leave the practice arena. Behind him, he heard Tobith ask, "What was his problem?" followed by a chorus of laughter.

Izo ignored her and picked up speed. The hallway, so welcome and inviting only minutes ago, flew by in a furious rage. Within seconds he was out the front doors and fleeing the building entirely.

Outside, the chaos of the rising capital greeted him, jagged outlines catching the light and trapping it in isolated triangles. It was a fearful visage, a place where peaks and valleys flooded your senses, a sharp, metallic jungle flanked by ice-capped mountains as far as the eye could see.

A feeling of smallness overwhelmed him. He shuddered and looked away.

He snapped up to retreat into the sky. Alone and exposed, a looming sense of vulnerability struck him, so he descended to the practice arena's rooftop instead. For a moment, he was too upset to do anything except pace like a chained animal. Thoughts and emotions swirled too fast to process, and he found himself angrily kicking at pieces of broken sticks and gravel that had traveled onto the roof in the wind. They skittered across the floor with unexpected sounds. Izo groaned. Nothing here happened the way he expected.

He grabbed his face. He wasn't supposed to be here. He didn't fit in. On Earth, he was a freaking superhero. Here he was small and ill-adapted, a fragile creature of negligible resilience that the planet kicked around as it pleased. He wasn't okay. He'd finally turned eighteen and escaped being shoved around as a kid, but now he was right back to being helpless again. He couldn't take it. He'd worked too hard. He wanted to do something, fight back, rip it all down.

But how do you change an entire planet?

He felt so angry and helpless he wanted to puke.

Above IA's city and mountains, the sky was an expanse of green-blue. He gritted his teeth at it. Why should he be stuck here, feeling small and alone while Glongkyle, Yula, and Tearn were free to roam the infinite universe, sailing through the stars with his Earth and moon? He reached down, picked up a rock, and hurled it at the sky. It arced up and fell to the ground below.

"Hey douchebags," Izo yelled. "Where are you?" He threw his arms open and waited. "It's been over a month!"

He kicked a pile of littered foliage trapped against the rooftop's short border wall. The mess of discolored leaves burst into a skittering cloud. "I did what you wanted. I held up my end. I'm supposed to be heading home right now. Instead, I'm stuck here getting bullied by a bunch of flying Tinkerbells." He grunted. "Glongkyle would probably be loving this right now. You'd tell me to suck it up, right? Well, I did! And now I'm done. You hear me? I'm done!"

He paused to catch his breath. There was a spot on the ground in front of him that was suddenly fascinating. Staring blankly, he let his eyes roam, absorbing the random shapes and patterns in its grainy, static image. He didn't know how long it was before he looked up into the sky again, but by the time he did a small cluster of clouds had formed above him.

He glared at the clouds. His anger surged inside him like an electric storm. It wasn't fair. After everything they'd put him through, he couldn't believe they'd just abandoned him.

"You promised you weren't going to leave me!" he shouted. "Maybe it was naive to trust you, but I did. I had no choice. You knew that, and you let me. Hell, you used it! You used my hope. It was the only thing I had left, and you used it against me. It's bullshit." Izo scrubbed his eyes with the heels of his palms. "You guys are bullshit!"

His expression broke and his head dropped low. He tried not to cry. "Maybe I could have done better. Been less of a pain in the ass. But I had no idea what I was doing. Plus, everything went wrong— how was that my fault? And why am I the only one paying for it? Sure, I could have been smoother. Reacted a little smarter. Wore the stupid dress."

He snorted. He'd forgotten about the dress. His sleeve came up to wipe his face. "That's it, isn't it? It all comes back to the dress. This was your final way of getting back at me. Well, you know what—fine. Glongkyle, you win! I'll wear a freaking dress. You hear me? I'll wear it the whole way back to Earth if you want. And I'll take care of it too!"

He laughed hard and painfully. "I'll clean it. I'll iron it. I'll hang it up at night. Whatever it takes, just as long as you guys—" He dropped his face into his hand. It took him a few stomping hops to shake the deluge of frustration off.

The truth was, he didn't care anymore. All pride and anger were gone. Nothing else mattered except getting back to Earth. "I'll do whatever it takes. I'll get you twice as much money and...three times as many pop stars, Tearn!" He was laughing again now, but the sound was coming out thick. He pushed through.

"Come on!" he shouted at the sky. "It'll be great. We'll get the team back together. I have some new ideas for hustling Avarian races and lifting alien tech at clubs. There's still a shitload of money to make here! But you gotta come back. You can't—" His face broke and he was suddenly crying all alone on a rooftop. "You can't just leave me here," he finished into his palms.

Izo wept quietly into his hands. The sound of the humming city was kind enough to conceal the noise. When he finally looked up at the sky again, it was with child-like repentance. "I'm sorry. I'll do better. I'll do whatever you guys want. But you have to come back, okay?" When nothing but silence answered back, he let out a sudden shrieking yalp. "NOW!"

And then, without warning, the clouds suddenly parted. A spacecraft appeared out of nowhere to drop rapidly from out of the heavens. Descending fast, it came to settle almost exactly at eye-level.

Izo stared and was too scared to breathe, for fear the ship might disappear as suddenly as it had arrived. Hands still pressed together in front of his face, he stood before it in stunned wonder. It wasn't the *Atrox Killboard*, Glongkyle's piece of shit bucket of bolts. This was a sleek and expensive marvel of alien engineering, a swept-back bullet whose hull dazzled in the sun in gun-metal silver.

Its bow rotated silently to turn and glance back at him through a long black windshield.

Izo chanced a movement, wiping the wetness from his cheeks before stepping closer. The ship didn't disappear. His pulse drummed loudly in his ears as he watched the stunning spacecraft continue to rotate effortlessly on a pin. It's face spinning away, it turned to reveal its left flank, a sheer silver surface catching the sunlight and blinding his eyes with a flash of white. Its side now fully perpendicular, it finally stopped to hover silently in the air.

Then, out of a seamless stretch of hull, the outline of a doorway appeared. The cutout deepened until an entire slab of carved metal slid out of the way with a pressurized hiss. A white mist rushed out and the door disappeared revealing a shadowy expanse.

Inside the darkness, a figure appeared, a large, hulking outline covered in fur.

Izo leaned forward with a gulp. "Yula?"

A big Wuljerian with white fur stepped out of the shadow. He or she was wearing an Imperial outfit. It wasn't Yula. It was a local security guard.

The Wuljerian peered at Izo in confusion. "Why Avarian here?"

Izo dropped back. There was a tangible pain in his chest. He'd never felt so disappointed or stupid in all his life. Still, it wasn't the guard's fault. He forced on a fake smile and waved. "Hi. Sorry. I was, uh…hired to clean the roof."

"They hired Avarian?" asked the guard.

Izo widened his eyes at the guard in unspeakable frustration, but after a moment he pushed it down. "Yeah, and they wanted it finished by the end of the day. So..." He motioned for the guard to go. "Thanks for checking in."

The Wuljerian frowned but turned to go back inside. "Okay. Be careful."

Izo watched the hatch slowly shut. A minute later the ship floated up a few feet before departing. Izo was again left standing on the roof alone.

Spotting a shaded area on the ground, the Earthling threw himself into it. "I hope you jerks are having fun."

— CHAPTER THIRTY-FIVE —

Tobith

I couldn't care less if someone is a virgin," explained Tobith. She buoyed up to grab both her feet and stretch her back. "What I can't stand is the lying. How stupid does he think we are? You move in with a Sword member and expect us to believe you're... what? Sitting in a corner reading poetry together every night?"

"Maybe he's not lying. Maybe they do stuff besides sex," said Cadenza.

"And that makes it better? It's still trading sexual acts for favors, and it still makes him way more successful as a whore than a racer," snapped Tobith.

"I heard a rumor he's dumb. Someone saw him at this big, fancy party and supposedly he kept losing his stuff. He was walking around asking people if they'd seen his purse and his shoes. He seemed genuinely surprised to learn your cousin was pushed off the team. Maybe he really didn't realize what his boyfriend was doing?" offered Cadenza.

Tobith thought about it, but then she shook her head. "But why lie about being together?"

"Maybe the Senator told him to?" said Ruefin.

"Or maybe he's so dumb, he doesn't realize they're having sex," offered Cadenza.

Tobith burst out laughing. "How dumb would you have to be…" She covered her face and squealed. "Can you imagine? *Senator, I'm so glad we've decided to wait. I know you have to inspect my virginity every night,*" she said in a high-pitched voice, pretending to be the Gravity Sprite. *"But do you have to inspect it so hard!?"*

"Hush, baby," Cadenza answered in a low, lascivious voice. "*I'm almost done inspecting you.*" Together the two of them laughed and laughed.

"You guys want to lay off?" interrupted Ruefin. "It was his first day. You didn't even let him set his stuff down before you ripped his face off."

"One: you've got to be tough if you're going to make it in this town, honey. Two: he didn't seem to feel bad when he ran my cousin off." Tobith shrugged.

Ruefin shook his head and continued to stretch. "Whatever. I still think it was shitty."

"ALL RIGHT MORONS—HUDDLE UP!"

Tobith cringed and tried not to hug her head. Shrill and loud beyond description, Coach Staydle's voice at full volume was the spoken equivalent of having the inside of your ears scraped out by blunt objects.

The team gathered in straight, floating lines across the field. Coach Staydle, tiny, pink skinned Azarian that she was, glared at them with deep red eyes. "GOOD MORNING, TEAM," she bellowed, sending everyone cringing back again. "I hope you got plenty of rest this weekend because we're going to have a lot of fun this week."

Tobith shared a nauseous glance with Cadenza, who was parked further back with the other mid-length racers. Everyone knew what it meant when the Coach said they were going to have "fun."

"We've got a new team member starting today. We're very excited to see what he can do…" She paused to search the group. "Wait, where is he? Did he not arrive yet?"

"He left already," came Ruefin's voice from beside Tobith's. "Someone ran him off."

Tobith swiveled her head to glare at the other sprite. He met her look with an expression as dry and bored as a tree. Clearly, he wasn't over how she'd treated their newest member.

Tobith turned to meet Coach Staydle's gaze. She peered at Tobith with barely contained fury.

Coach lifted a hand in question. "You want to tell me what the hell he's talking about?"

Tobith shrugged. "It's not my fault. I didn't realize he'd be so sensitive."

"That wasn't really my question." Coach Staydle moseyed directly in front of her target. Tobith wanted to fly back but knew she couldn't. The arena, now filled with all but one of their contracted racers, had gone as silent as a mortuary. "Where is he?"

"I don't know. He got upset and left." Tobith pointed at the door. "He didn't say where he was going."

One of Coach Staydle's tiny red eyes went wide. The other one narrowed with such trembling ferocity it nearly shut. "Are you telling me that on the very first day we were slated to welcome the only living Gravity Sprite in existence, you managed to lose him… BEFORE PRACTICE STARTED????"

Tobith and Ruefin both grunted and bobbed lower, the full blast of the Coach's volume slamming through them with almost sensory-obliterating intensity.

"I'm sorry! I'll find him." Straightening from her cringing position, Tobith moved toward the front doors as far as she could without seeming disrespectful. "I'll bring him back."

"You'd better." Clenching her hands, Coach Staydle snarled from her position in front of the team. "If you don't, you'll be doing ten extra laps every day, Missy."

Tobith staggered and nearly fell to the ground. "Ten?!"

"Ten," repeated Coach Staydle. "Or you can hurry up and find him. Either way," she said, turning back to the others, "you have an hour."

"Coach, can I help her find him?" asked Ruefin while raising a hand.

"Sure," said Coach Staydle, moving on. "The rest of you, GET IN POSITION. We're doing five hundred up-downs."

The team groaned loudly in response.

Where the hell are you?! Tobith thought. She and Ruefin had searched everywhere for the over-dramatic Gravity Sprite and couldn't find him. Together they'd hunted over every square inch of the complex, the surrounding park, and the nearest fifteen blocks. After over a half an hour of searching, he was still nowhere to be found.

Tobith watched Ruefin waft high in the air above the arena. He turned in a whirling circle. "Which way do you think he might have gone?"

"How should I know? He's a Gravity Sprite. In his last run against my cousin, he accelerated 60,000 lengths per second. He could be basically anywhere."

Ruefin grinned while continuing to search. "You looked up his time?"

"Of course. We're going to be in the same races. You didn't?"

Ruefin laughed without answering and kept moving.

Tobith decided to ignore him and instead tried to take a guess which direction the rookie might have gone, but it was no use. She didn't know anything about him. In fact, virtually the only thing she did know was he was new to the place.

She grabbed at her forehead, but her fingers ran into a mess of hair. Tobith groaned. She was so stressed out her hair was beginning to lift in the rising static pouring off her skin. She'd love to go downstairs to grab a headband from her locker, but they didn't have time. Dashing left, then right, she gaped helplessly at the rows of packed streets shooting off in every direction in front of the building. *This is pointless!*

A high-pitched whistling noise drew Tobith's attention back toward the arena. Darting back, she stopped next to Ruefin, who was still floating high over the building. "What?"

With a short nod upward, he drew her attention to a small compressor near the back of the complex's roof.

She turned toward it and froze. There was the Gravity Sprite. Seated in profile, he was facing away and hadn't spotted them yet. He was curled into a ball and hiding in a shadow, knees folded in front with his arms propped on top. His gaze was low, long, and unseeing. As she watched, he wiped his cheek with the back of one arm before returning it to rest on his knee again. He continued staring ahead. There was a layer of snot smeared into the back of his sleeve.

Ruefin began sliding forward, but Tobith snatched his arm and stopped him. He looked at her curiously.

"Don't," she said in a whisper. In her mind she was remembering the last time she'd been so overwhelmed she had to leave and take a moment to collect herself. The idea of another person walking in on her, much less one of the people who'd caused it, was almost too painful to imagine.

Tobith eased the two of them down onto the roof silently. Then, cupping her hands around her mouth, she began crossing with loud, thumping steps. Ruefin, picking up on the idea, soon followed.

"Here rookie, rookie, rookie!" They called out in the opposite direction of where he was. "Where are you? Hey rook—where you at?"

There was a skittering noise as the Gravity Sprite darted away from his hiding spot. Tobith gasped. Had he fled again? She hissed and regretted her civility; who knew how long it might take to chase the distance racer down now?

But luck was in her favor. Rather than leaving, he'd simply hidden behind a taller electro-magnetic generator, which Ruefin quickly spotted and pointed out. The two continued to call and look around in the wrong direction, giving him whatever time he needed.

After another few minutes the Gravity Sprite appeared around the corner. His expression was annoyed, but his eyes were disheveled and red. He seemed hell-bent on ignoring it, though. The two teammates played along.

"What do you want?" He tipped his head in confusion as he glared at her and then Ruefin. "And what's wrong with her hair?"

Ruefin snorted.

"You're what's wrong with my hair!" said Tobith. "We've been busting our butts looking for you for the last half hour. Congratulations on your scene, by the way. You've been here five minutes and you're already the biggest diva on the team."

"I told you—I don't want to be on your stupid team. Your cousin can have his spot back. Tell him I wish him the best."

"It's too late for that!" said Tobith.

"He already moved back to Anolitun and joined their team," explained Ruefin.

The rookie made a *tsking* noise while looking down. "Shit. I didn't know that."

Tobith worked her jaw to one side. He really did seem sorry about what happened. "What's done is done. It's no one's fault," she said. When the rookie looked up at her questioningly, she rolled her eyes. "Whatever. It's over. So knock it off and come to practice. You're already late. Coach is going to be pissed if you make her wait even longer."

But Izo shook his head. "No. I can't go back there."

"Why the hell not?" said Tobith.

"Why the hell do you think?" said Izo.

Tobith could feel the static rising in her chest again. "Look, I'm sorry if we hurt your fragile little Avarian feelings. Everyone gets razzed their first day. It's not a big deal. You'll have to learn to be a tougher Avarian if you're going to make it in this town."

"Oh yeah? How's this for tough? You can take the team and your weak apology and shove them both up your asses." His eyes were bulging in seriousness. "Leave me the hell alone and go away." The electricity in Tobith's veins was surging now. "Look here, rook. Coach said if I didn't come downstairs with you, I have to do laps. And since a lap for a sprite means circling the continent, I'm not failing her." She jerked herself high in the air. "Now, I don't care if we have to drag you kicking and screaming, your skinny butt's going downstairs with us."

"You can try, but I promise it's going to take something a lot bigger than the two of you to drag me somewhere I don't want to go," said the Gravity Sprite. "All that's going to happen is you'll tire yourself out chasing me, and then have to do your laps anyway. Better cut your losses now."

Ruefin glanced at her with a knowing look. Izo didn't seem like he was bluffing.

Tobith tried to come up with some other way to get him downstairs. She had nothing. "Excuse me for not greeting you with gold plates and Tmipian pies, your highness. It was your first day! Everybody gets razzed on their first day. Suck it up, buttercup. It's not personal!"

Izo shook his head in disgust. Then, extending the back of one finger at her, he turned and snapped back to his spot behind the generator without another word.

Ruefin shot Tobith an exasperated look. "That went about as well as I thought it would."

She clenched both her fists so hard an electric pop sounded off the top of her back. They could try storming downstairs and explaining that they'd found him, but he simply refused to come back. She already knew Coach Staydle wouldn't accept this, though. Worse, the Gravity Sprite might move again in the meantime and the whole thing would start over.

Tobith scrubbed her face with the heels of her hands. Wrenching herself into the ground with a booming *thud*, she stalked stiffly around the generator.

The Gravity Sprite had resumed his position on the ground. Both hands covered his eyes. When he heard her coming, he shook his head and didn't look up. "Mira," he said. His voice was low and plaintive. It surprised her. "I don't feel like fighting with anyone right now. Just leave me alone."

Ruefin, who'd followed slowly behind Tobith, scrutinized her warily. Her storming anger quickly dissipated under his cool gaze. She scratched her temple and finally tossed her hands high. "I don't know what your problem is. I already apologized, okay? If you're still pissed at me, fine. But that's no reason to keep the team and Coach Staydle waiting."

"It's got nothing to do with you," said Izo.

"Oh." Tobith remembered the tears she'd spotted earlier. She'd assumed it was because of what she and Cadenza had said downstairs. Now that she wasn't on the defensive, she was suddenly flailing. "So...what's wrong?"

Izo coughed out a bitter laugh before leveling her with a harsh glare. "You think I'm going to talk to you about it?"

Ruefin pointed around the area. "I don't see anyone else here."

The rookie shifted his glare to Ruefin. After a moment his hostile expression slid away into one of begrudging vulnerability. "You promise not to joke later?"

"Of course. Avarian swear." Ruefin lifted a hand and splayed his fingers in the accompanying gesture of the super-secret-promise-sign all Avarian children learned to do when they were younger. Then he sat down beside Izo. "Talk to us."

Izo peered at them with marked distrust. Then he shrugged. "Whatever. It's stupid anyway. I don't know how to talk about it."

"Just say what you're thinking about," encouraged Ruefin.

"I was thinking about these shape-sorting toys I used to play with as a kid."

"Okay..." Tobith said, gingerly taking a seat on his other side. "What about them?"

Izo hid his mouth behind his knee. "I was thinking about how they had these cut-outs, and the blocks that came with the toy were supposed to fit into those cut-outs. Every cut-out was meant to have a matching block: the stars fit into the star hole, the squares fit into the square hole. Everything had a place."

"Sure." She glanced at Ruefin. He looked as confused as she felt. What kind of crappy toys did they give to Avarians on the rookie's planet?

"I could never get it to work as a kid," Izo continued. "I remember sitting in daycare and spending hours on this one toy, trying to get it to work. But it didn't. I thought the problem was me. I'd seen these toys on TV and in movies. I knew how they were supposed to work, but this one didn't: the rectangles were too wide, or the heart was too steep, or I'd have an extra oval that didn't go anywhere at all. Used to drive me nuts. You know?"

Tobith nodded.

The rookie pursed his mouth. "I finally figured it out around the time I turned nine. Most of the toys in state-run daycares were donated. People only donated the toys that they had no use for. We were getting mismatched sets: either the toy didn't have its blocks anymore, or worse, it had been paired random blocks to clear out the area. Either way, by the time they got to us, they were never going to fit together anymore. They were mismatched toys." He made a sad noise. "We were mismatched kids."

Tobith considered his story. As everyone in the Tri-galaxies would soon know, he was the only living Gravity Sprite in existence. At first glance, it seemed like a good thing—he was the chosen Avarian, born instantly into an everlasting celebrity. Who could ask for more? But she could also see it from another perspective.

She chose her next few words carefully. "So...you don't want to be mismatched?"

"I don't think I want to be an Avarian."

Tobith and Ruefin's eyes widened and found each other immediately. She almost moved for her device. A statement like that was borderline a confession of self-harm, something they were contractually bound to report if they ever heard on the field. But she held off for the moment.

"Are you thinking about killing yourself?" Ruefin asked plainly.

"I'm thinking…" Izo dropped his knees into a criss-cross shape. "I'm thinking this whole thing sucks. And I know that sounds childish, but it's the truth. There are so many different kinds of people out there. Strungians have claws and tails. Wuljerians are nearly indestructible. Malforians are basically the top of the food chain. Even Ginarsians have their own special thing, the little dickwads." He snatched a piece of a stick and skipped it across the roof in a fit of surging rage, and Tobith figured out what felt so familiar about him. *He'd fit right in on Anolitun!*

"I know it sounds dumb," he continued, "but I don't know if I like being born this way. And I hate feeling like that. I used to look forward to messing with it as a kid, getting faster and figuring the whole flying thing out. Now that I understand what it means, I'm starting to wonder if being Avarian is worth it. Even if I went home and wasn't treated like an Avarian anymore, I'd still know what it promises for me and my kids one day. That doesn't go away."

Ruefin gave him a sympathetic bump with his shoulder. "I get it. I know how some people think about us. They think we're like…" he trailed off, reaching for the best analogy.

"Teacups," said Tobith. "At best we're something special and delicate that needs constant watching. At worst we're something out-of-fashion, damaged, and worthless. Whichever side you fall into, you're stuck because—let's be honest—how many uses are there for teacups?"

Behind Izo, Ruefin nodded sagely. "Yeah," he agreed.

"Hmm," agreed Izo. His voice was muffled. At some point, he'd started hugging his knees tightly again.

Tobith frowned. She knew there was more to this speech, but she didn't know what. Truth was she'd also been struggling with her own identity since moving to IA. On Anolitun she'd been tough, quick, and scrappy. Not that anything had necessarily changed about her. No, it was the way she was viewed that had shifted.

Maybe that was the question: which is more important? Which defines you more: what you think about yourself, or what other people see? Which was more real? Which had more authority? There wasn't one answer. It was an ongoing tension. Every day both sides gained and gave up ground: a concession here, a victory there. It wasn't something that ever ended. Tobith, like everyone, fought to remain self-complete. It wasn't easy. Sometimes you did need to change things about yourself, to adapt to your environment or grow as a person. As an Avarian, like everyone else, the idea that she was growing or adapting in a predetermined way scared the living shit out of her.

But that didn't mean she could stop growing.

She stared at the floor. There were some days she wondered if it wouldn't be easier to just walk on the ground all the time. Then she narrowed her eyes. "Nuts to that. I'm proud to be an Avarian."

"Huh?" said Izo. Ruefin watched her skeptically.

"We can fly! We have irreproducible magic. We have powers. Sure, we may not be big, but we're powerful. We're marvels of evolution. Hell, we're the gatekeepers of Avarian evolution. Other creatures have cool abilities, but by the gods, ours are freaking awesome!" She could feel the other two rallying beside her. "Being Avarian doesn't suck. IA sucks. Being Avarian is awesome!"

Izo and Ruefin cheered.

Tobith jumped to her feet. "So screw IA, and screw anyone else that thinks like them. They're morons!"

"They don't know the first thing about us!" agreed Izo.

Tobith paused. How she'd treated him that morning suddenly came back full force. "And I'm sorry too." She gazed down at the still seated Gravity Sprite. "It wasn't okay to come at you like that. I didn't even give you a chance. Truth was, I was doing the same thing. I was treating you based on an idea. I wasn't seeing you as a real person. I'm sorry."

"Thanks." Izo scratched his arm. "Out of curiosity, what did you guys think about me before I got here?"

"Honestly?" Tobith blew out a giant breath of air. "I thought you were just a publicity stunt the coach signed up for."

"¿Qué? I assumed you were going to say a princess or something." He beetled his brow. "You thought I was a publicity stunt?"

"IA's got their Imperial election next year. It's going to decide the Emperor for the next ten years. The Sword's frontrunner just so happens to find the last living Gravity Sprite and sponsor him for the Imperial team?" Tobith shrugged her shoulders. "It all seemed a little convenient."

"Emperor for the next ten years? ¿La neta?" Izo said turning to Ruefin with surprise. "That's what the election is for?"

Tobith's mouth dropped slightly. "You didn't know that?"

"Uh uh," said Izo.

"Aren't you living with a candidate?" asked Ruefin.

The Gravity Sprite wasn't paying attention anymore; his thoughts had moved on to something else. He bit his lip, his eyes distant. "I guess it's easy to make shitty assumptions about other people when you don't know their full story." He clicked his tongue. "I need to apologize to Ari."

"Ari?" Tobith's mind jumped straight to the megastar singer, but he obviously couldn't mean her. Though, then again, he did live with a sitting Senator.

"It's fine." He glanced over at Ruefin, seeming to come back to the moment. "Does the coach really make the distance racers circle the continent every time we get in trouble?"

"She does, and it totally sucks for you guys!" responded Ruefin with a laugh.

"It's not fair," complained Tobith. "The distance racers get all the worst punishments. I swear that woman loves torturing us. It's like—I get it. Technically I can move sixty-eight million lengths per hour. That doesn't mean it's how I want to spend a whole hour!"

"Sixty-eight million lengths? ¡No manches!" But then he seemed to consider this. "Wait. How many miles are in a length?"

Tobith's mouth dropped. *Is he kidding me?* A gleam of electric fury surged in her chest. It took everything within her to stay calm. "Please. Tell me. You're joking."

He shrugged his shoulders up. "What?"

Tobith pinched the bridge of her nose. "Please tell me they didn't replace my cousin with a racer that *doesn't even know how long a length is?*"

"Not this again." Izo clicked his tongue in annoyance and waved her off. "Calm down, Sparky. You'll mess up your hair again."

Ruefin snorted and covered his mouth.

"I just need to figure out the conversion of miles to lengths. Then I'll be fine."

Tobith looked at Ruefin for help. "What the hell is a mile?!"

Izo opened his mouth. But his eyes went wide before he could say anything. He seemed to be realizing something terrible. "Oh shit." His head dropped to his chest. "I'm never going to know how fast I am."

Tobith was on her own thing now. "This is such typical Sword bullshit. They replace a real Anolitun racer with decades of training and more than a dozen track records with—no offense— some stupid, hot moron that no one's ever heard of and—"

"Oh, give it a rest! I beat your cousin fair and square and—wait." Izo blinked at her a few times. "You think I'm hot?"

Behind Izo, Ruefin's jaw dropped open as he realized what had happened. He stared at her with gleeful shock. Tobith froze. She could feel her face flushing in purpling crimson as she looked at the two of them. "I-I didn't say that."

"You did. Just now," said Izo.

"Right in front of him and everything," added Ruefin with a bemused shake of his head.

"No. That's not—" Tobith's eye twitched. She failed to suppress a look of mortified terror. "I said he was stupid. I said he was a moron."

"Close," Ruefin agreed. "You said he was a stupid, *hot* moron."

"Yeah...but..." Tobith furrowed her brow. "It wasn't a compliment. I was insulting him. I'm saying he's vapid and shallow!"

"No duh, cause you think he's hot."

"It's a classic over-correcting bully move!"

The two grabbed each other, tipped back, and laughed so hard tears started coming out of the edges of their eyes.

"It makes sense! This is why you were so mean to me! You've been pissed at this 'idea of me' for a month but then in walks this hot Latin papi and you have no idea what to do with yourself." Izo leaned his head in disappointment. "Pobrecita—this is no way for you to express these feelings."

"I don't have feelings for you. And I wasn't being mean." She could feel her hair rising again. "Everyone gets razzed on their first day!"

The freshly minted best friends laughed even harder.

"Okay. You guys win," Izo stood. "I'm definitely staying on this team now." He winked at her. "Honestly, I'm kind of looking forward to it."

Tobith glowered. "Who would think you're hot? You're skinny as a rail! A Ginarsian has more muscles than you."

"I'll have you know this is a natural swimmer's build," said Izo.

"Swimmer's build?" Tobith shook her head in confusion. "I don't know what that means. Anolituns don't swim. It's against our religion. All I know is—"

"Swimming is against your religion?" Izo looked at Ruefin in confusion. "It's an inherently amoral act."

"All I know is—" Tobith repeated. "You're not hot. You look as weak as an infant and twice as dumb. How many times have you even worked out in the last few months?"

"Excuse you." Izo made an offended face. "I've been a little busy getting kidnapped and dragged across the universe, okay?"

Tobith rolled her eyes. "Yeah, we got a real top of the line athlete. By the gods, you're not going to make it halfway around a distance track."

"Want to bet?" said Izo.

"With you? Hell yes." Tobith nodded at the mountains beyond the city. "First one to the peak and back wins."

"You're on!" said Izo. He turned to Ruefin. "You think I can beat her. Right?"

Ruefin gave Izo a pinched smile. He clapped the Gravity Sprite on the back. "Let's just get out there and have some fun."

"Screw you guys. I'm fast goddammit. I'll prove it."

"Great," said Tobith. The two sprites stood and moved to the edge of the building to take their marks. "Ruefin, say when," said Tobith.

"Do you have any idea how much trouble we're going to get in?" hissed the Wind Sprite.

"Just count us down," said Tobith.

"Get ready to eat my dust, same as your cousin," Izo said, bending lower. Then he straightened sheepishly. "Actually, can we only race to the Mountain? I may need help finding this place on the way back."

Ruefin and Tobith shared a knowing glance. "Of course," said Tobith.

"Thanks." Izo knelt beside her.

Ruefin sighed and lifted an arm. "We go in five... four..."

Tobith began gathering static inertia like a lightning rod. All around her charged ions linked together in invisible networks. Giant crackles of electricity danced off her shoulders and arms. Out of the corner of her eye, she could see the rookie focusing on the Mountains in the distance. She could have sworn the area around him was beginning to look redder.

"Three...two...GO!" shouted Ruefin.

Tobith cracked into the sky and the two sentient rockets devoured the horizon together.

— CHAPTER THIRTY-SIX —

Mort

Senator Mortaco was growing ever sicker of the endlessly ribbing "banter" of his fellow Sword members. They were in the Sword's Senior Member Wing, deep in the capital's Legislative Rotunda. They'd been in the same meeting for hours.

They were surrounded by the most cutting-edge technology and luxurious trappings in the universe—Driseldian leather seats, Malforian magnetic marble, gold wood paneling brought all the way from Aurelia—yet they'd somehow managed to get less done than teenagers put together on a school project. It didn't matter how many times Mort tried to get them on topic. The week after his big party, they only had one thing on their minds: Avarians.

"You're saying to get an Avarian in bed, you should treat them like shit?" asked Senator Bryckturn.

"No," said Lrasa. "What I'm saying is Avarians are biological powerhouses of sexual attraction. And they know it."

"No argument there," agreed Senator Psegre, the eldest son of his family, "but I still don't understand how pissing a person off makes them horny."

"That's because you don't understand how the sexual market-place works. Think about it," said Lrasa. "Avarians naturally have higher sexual value than other species, right? Yet Avarians, like everyone else, want to mate with someone of an even higher sexual value than themselves. The first step in any mating ritual is to compare your sexual value to a potential mate. What are the classic signs of sexual value? Age, status, wealth, looks," he said, ticking them off on his fingers. "But what's the sexiest quality of all?"

Psegre thought about it. "Being good at sex?"

"No!" said Lrasa. "Confidence."

Mortaco rolled his eyes but knew better than to interrupt his childhood chum. It would only prolong Lrasa's idiocy.

"Confidence takes everything you already have and maximizes it. Likewise, lowering the confidence of any Avarian automatically diminishes their value. Conclusion: your sexual value goes up; theirs goes down. You are then within an appropriate range for mating."

"And this actually works?" asked Senator Hriesn, wearing the same shoes he'd worn last week—he was clearly slipping. Not that Mort could fault him. His family's I.C.O. had taken a dive since the Shields passed the bill that penalized big companies for ignoring inspections. His company, known for cutting corners when it came to environmental and citizens' rights issues, had lost nearly thirty percent of its net worth over the last month.

"Works on Ari," Lrasa assured them.

"Pshhh, Ari doesn't count," said Bryckturn. "That Aurelian is a double-edged sword of pride and self-loathing."

"There are some holes that just can't be filled," Senator Hriesn agreed sadly.

"Yeah… but she's got plenty that can. Am I right?" Lrasa grinned proudly around the room.

Mort rubbed his eye and didn't respond.

Senator Psegre noticed this. "You're being suspiciously quiet, Mort. What about you and that mysterious new Avarian living with you?" He laughed. "You know my little brother keeps asking me about him, right?"

"Yeah," said Bryckturn. "How are you planning to pop the seal with the hottest new virgin on the Mountain?"

"Assuming you still can," sneered Lrasa.

Mort huffed out a stifled laugh. "I think Lrasa is a moron and Avarians aren't nearly as stupid as Lrasa wishes they were, which is ironic because they probably wish he was a little smarter. More to the point, Izo is my guest. Nothing more."

"Gods! You're really starting to bum me out. Our 'Great and Golden Leader' can't even close the deal with an Avarian already living with him." Lrasa shook his head in disgust. "Makes me question the direction of the whole Sword party."

"It's understandable. He was abducted and brought here against his will. He's been free of his kidnappers for barely a month," said Bryckturn.

"For heaven's sake, Lrasa—he lost his planet. He lost his first love. When Sheost met him, he was still being used by those people," agreed Psegre. "Mort's just trying to help him out. The last thing he'd want is someone trying to nail him right now."

"Whatever you guys need to tell yourselves," said Lrasa. "If he were living with me, I'd have cashed in on some of that goodwill by now."

"Enough," Mort said. His tone had been annoyed and serious, surprising even himself for a moment.

Lrasa straightened in his seat. Beside him the others went silent too, watching warily. Mort pursed his lips and wondered if he'd need to beat them down to move on. They seemed to be wondering the same. Before he could decide, a notification popped up in his peripheral vision. It was encrypted—in other words, it was important.

Mort rose from his seat at the front of the conference table. "Excuse me for a moment. I need to check on something." The others nodded, almost seeming to look relieved—except Lrasa. Eyes stubbornly down, he rocked from side to side, pouting.

Mort went to stand behind his friend. He looked to the others before clapping a hand loudly on Lrasa's shoulder. "Please forgive my absence. I won't be gone long." He smiled with apology at them. "To the Mountain."

"To the Sword," the others agreed.

Mort nodded at them with approval. Then his gaze dropped to Lrasa. He hadn't said the callback. Still seated under Mort's palm, he'd instead looked away. This, as everyone in the room knew, simply wouldn't do.

With a barely perceptible change of pressure, Mort began slowly squeezing his oldest friend's shoulder. Lrasa flinched under his fingers but otherwise didn't make an outward reaction. The two of them stood there, silently battling under the plain view of their fellow Sword Senators. Lrasa didn't try to get away or fight. He knew better than that. And so Mort simply held him there and continued, squeezing harder and harder until his grip was surely leaving bruises, grinding muscle into bone.

Below his fingers, he could feel Lrasa beginning to cringe at the pain. His attitude and stubborn demeanor slowly melted away. Mort squeezed even harder.

"To the Sword," Lrasa finally spat quietly.

Mort smiled and let go. Patting Lrasa's hair, he gave his colleagues—who looked wildly uncomfortable all of a sudden—a ruthlessly unencumbered smile over the back of his best friend's head. Then he simply turned and strode to the back of the Sword conference room where he kept his private office.

Once inside, he shut the door behind him and opened the encrypted notification. It was an alarm—his Gravity Sprite had just left the city.

Mort's brow drew down. His skin went clammy. He pulled up a live satellite feed and loaded Izo's image into it. Within seconds the all-seeing program had located the one-of-a-kind Avarian. Turning to the nearest castable device, a mirrored decoration, Mort sent the live video feed onto its screen.

An image of Izo hanging onto the top of a tree flickered into view. Sweat poured off his face. He was clearly out of breath.

Gasping, he waved someone off while trying to hang on to the tree for dear life.

Mort's mouth twisted in pain. For a moment he wondered if something had happened and Izo was running from someone. He was just beginning to pull up the contacts for his security team when, soaring in at full tilt, a beautiful Anolitun female came into view. Flashing by at impossible speeds, she was harassed and poked at Izo who, in turn, tried to swipe back at her. A moment later a green Nertian showed up to chase her off.

Mort frowned in confusion. It seemed...playful?

Still, this was over 500 lengths outside of the city, deep within the wild forest ranges that surrounded and covered the capital's mountains. The oxygen would be lower there, and he was worried about his Gravity Sprite. The numerous stress tests they'd run while Izo was in his medically induced coma all pointed to the same thing: he needed a good amount of oxygen to survive, which had made what should have been a mild illness much worse. They'd run multiple scenarios several times over the four days they kept him unconscious. As a Gravity Sprite, theoretically capable of traveling between planets, one of Mort's main questions was exactly how much oxygen Izo needed.

Mort shook his head with worry. "Where are you going?" he whispered to the image.

He quickly summoned and cast out a second feed, a wide-angle shot of a half topographical, half political map with cities and elevations shown. Triangulating Izo's path from his last known position, he let the algorithms go to work predicting his destination. But the results made no sense. There weren't even any tiny mountain villages in that direction. Was he planning to hide in the woods? If so, with what supplies? From what Mort could tell, he had nothing but the clothes on his back and his mysterious new friends.

Mort paused to watch as his Gravity Sprite snap off the tree to catch up with the other two. The three of them tore across the sky, skimming the landscape and twisting between hills. Izo flew beneath the Anolitun and Nertain before flipping onto his back. He smiling and joked with both of them, winding back and forth in a leisurely pace. Then, with a little wink, he suddenly dashed ahead. The Nertian took off after him. The purple Anolitun, not to be outdone, decelerated, charged herself, and exploded forward with an electric burst.

Mort gasped. "You're not running away. You're racing each other." Touching the screen, he felt a surge of love, protection, and relief fill his chest like a swath of cool water.

He fell into the nearest chair. There was nothing to worry about. His precious Gravity Sprite, whom he had so many plans for, wasn't going anywhere. No, Izo would soon be back at home— one-of-a-kind, perfect, and secure.

Mort let out a sigh. His fingers rubbed his temple where a tension headache had started to form. He decided to give up and pump some pain medicine into his system. The tiny implant near his spine went to work, releasing chemicals directly into his vertebral arteries.

The effect was nearly instantaneous. He stopped rubbing his head. Remembering that he also needed to return to the world's most annoying meeting, he decided to crank up his anti-anxiety medication too. He'd already far exceeded his daily dosage. His weekly dose too, for that matter. But he wasn't worried. He could always fire the psychiatrist if she refused to play ball.

He crossed his legs and waited. It would take a few minutes for his brain to absorb the psychoactive drug. Then he'd be ready for anything. In the meantime, he flipped through a couple of local feeds and notifications sitting in his peripheral. There was another protest in the Relegian System: they were still pissed about their water. The Southern Chancellors had enacted another medical law; it would only affect Avarians, though. Aurelia was holding their annual memorial for Ari's mom. Ha! If only they knew.

He stopped skimming to fully open one interesting piece of information. It was a new intergalactic poll, just published that morning, pitting him against Senator Waldrud, the leader of the

Shields. Mort was winning, of course, but it was by a slightly larger margin than he was used to.

He skipped down to the demographic area with interest. His base hadn't grown or shrunk (they never grew or shrank), but his results with undecided voters were up. Curious, he searched for the underlying data. He found it in a sequestered report, protected from view due to citizen privacy concerns. Mort easily bypassed its protocols and opened it.

His eyes went wide. It seemed people all over the tri-galaxies were finding him more "trustworthy," "generous," and "kind" than they had before. Some weren't sure where they'd gained this opinion. They just felt it instinctually. But many knew exactly why their assessment had changed. Sixty-five percent of participants who admitted to changing their choice from previous polls mentioned the term "Gravity Sprite" in their self-reported explanations.

He smiled, feeling much better now. Maybe it was the chemically enhanced self-assurance; maybe it was the good news that all his plans were working exactly as designed. Who could say? All he knew was he was on top of the world. He could do anything. He could have anything. There was nothing in the universe beyond his reach.

Clicking over to the secret, encoded portion of his brain, he dug for his favorite piece of illicitly acquired data. It was hidden in the invisible partition of a secret file stored locally in his embedded unit. Inaccessible from anywhere but in his head, it was locked with a 10^{56} encryption. Launching the decryption, he leaned back in his chair and waited.

It was funny, Lrasa with his silly games. The man honestly thought confidence gave you power. How stupid could you get? Control gave you power. For that matter, control gave you confidence. Controlling an Avarian wasn't some mystical science. It was the same way you controlled anyone. You took the time to listen to them. You figured out what they wanted. You let them pour all their hopes and dreams out in perfect, starry-eyed detail. Then, when you finally understood what made them tick—fame, love, family, money—you used it as leverage. Lrasa thought he could use compliments and attention as leverage. What a joke.

The program finished decrypting the file. He opened it. In his mind's eye, Mort surveyed the spinning planet. The recording's resolution was terrible, and it blipped out every few seconds as it reloaded. Surveying it, he had to admit it was sort of pretty, this funny little blue and green marble hidden in the middle of nowhere. When Izo told people he was from uncharted territory, he certainly hadn't been lying.

Next to the recording was the planet's full report: size, solar calendar, water-to-land ratio, atmospheric composition. There was even an attachment to the original language which, thanks to the hastily signed contracts of Izo's abductors, he now had full legal ownership of. Most importantly, at the bottom of the file was the one piece of information he knew his stubborn little Gravity Sprite would do anything for: the only known coordinates to Earth.

Mortaco closed the file and stood. He took a moment to stretch his shoulders and neck before returning to the meeting. What had he even been worried about? His Gravity Sprite wasn't going anywhere.

— CHAPTER THIRTY-SEVEN —

Glongkyle

Miles above and unbeknownst to anyone, Glongkyle was slowly being roused out of traumatic hibernation by an insistent alarm.

Glongkyle didn't know this yet, of course. He was still asleep: trapped in a deep and ungenerous state of barely functioning homeostasis. But the ship was growing warmer, flooded by the stored energy gathered from the light of distant stars for the last two weeks. It wasn't much energy, and the warmth wouldn't last long, as Glongkyle knew when he initially programmed it, but it would last long enough for him to send a mayday signal to whatever ship had happened to drift within range.

Glongkyle didn't remember this yet though. His reptilian brain was still restoring the majority of his neural synapses, naturally severed two weeks ago to save electricity for his super-cooled body.

His dreams were like a baby's—unfettered by living experience or memory, the free-floating stimulus of pure wonder. But as the temperature rose and his cells continued to thaw and resume their functions, his memories reconnected in a confused jumble of pressing scenes set in no particular order. Details slowly sharpened and came fully into view. At the same time a subtle cloud of rage-filled grief painted his pre-conscious visions....

"Take my ship; I'll trade you," the Senator had said. A hazy image of his smile stretched and grew, filling Glongkyle's mind like the ridge of a storm cloud. "It's untraceable and fully stocked. You can party there for weeks without anyone being the wiser...

"What's going on?" Glongkyle scanned the blaring read-outs in confusion. "Does this thing have power or not?" His veins turned cold, and his bones filled with a heaviness that ached like regret...

"Can't leave Izo," Yula had whined. She'd pulled back on Glongkyle's insistent grasp, fighting almost the whole way as they trudged down the private dock toward the state-of-the-art space cruiser.

"He'll be fine," Glongkyle insisted. "We'll be back before he knows it...

"The coordinates to Earth are gone," Tearn said, staring at his device from the captain's seat next to Glongkyle.

"Are you sure?"

"I just got an alert from the *Atrox*. It says there was a breach on the ship." Tearn flipped through the updates, his expression flashing through higher and higher levels of stunned disbelief. "Everything's been downloaded and erased." When he'd finally met Glongkyle's gaze again, he was radiating fear like a clear and lucid bell. "Someone took all our data, but they were looking for the coordinates to Izo's planet."

Glongkyle's eyes snapped open in the present. The console's alarm was the loudest and most piercing thing he'd ever heard. It sliced through his sleep-addled brain like a laser. He struggled to move his paralyzed body. The cold blood in his veins felt like super-chilled molasses, and it took every bit of concentration to painfully begin clenching and unclenching his fingers.

Slowly, the need to turn off the alarm, signal the nearby ship, and, most importantly, get back at that gods damned Senator filled him with focus.

Ripping his limbs through stilted motions of trembling facility, he managed to re-awaken his muscles and begin moving again. First, he needed to get to the console. His eyes struggled to search the nearly pitch-black cabin. But the subtle nuance between dark surfaces and darker shadows eventually came into focus and the outlines of walls and terminals filled his vision with ghostly supposition.

He was strapped to the hull by a sleeping bag attached to the wall. Reaching for the eject button at his back, he sank an over-ly-long claw into its recessed opening to engage the hydraulic release. A moment later he was floating in zero gravity.

He pushed off the wall toward the console, following the sound of the alarm. The room was darker and colder than the coldest spot on any planet...exactly like the inky black void surrounding him. It had been the height of arrogance to assume that any of these thin metal shells could ever have hoped to keep him safe amongst the endless depths. Out here was the Kingdom of Nothing, Death's chief domain, where even demons and ghosts dared not venture, a quintessentially indifferent realm where all warmth, light, and benevolence fled to huddle together in tight, naturally concentric circles.

Glongkyle inched forward toward the ship's console, his every motion filling his brittle limbs with unspeakable pain. He'd antici-pated this and placed his sleeping perch only a few feet away from his goal. Reaching it, he sat as gingerly as he could and hit the button to turn off the alarm.

He read the console. The gathered energy levels were dismally low, barely recharged a half a percent. He glanced at the date. Two weeks since his last awakening. He considered checking his location but decided against it. He could see clearly from the windshield that it wouldn't be good news. Instead, he focused on triangulating the passing ship that had set everything off. It was close—barely 150,000 lengths away. But a quick calculation of available energy showed the distress signal would only reach

100,000 lengths though. There was a chance that the other ship would steer closer. But it was just as likely that it wouldn't.

Glongkyle sent the distress signal anyway, cutting the heaters and rerouting their energy to boost the signal an extra 15,000 lengths. He had no choice. There was no telling when or if another ship would ever come this close again. Then, resetting the alarm and confirming his charging protocols, he reached down to grab a collection of food and water he'd left under the console.

The cold was re-advancing quickly. He hurried to hydrate before the water turned solid. The food was terrible, barely edible now from repeated exposure to frost-burn and thawing. He managed to force down a few pieces, the unused muscles in his jaw crying with agony at every chew.

Consciousness offered the worst parts of his existence now, but these were also the only moments he could act, meager as his choices were. The internal temperature continued to drop on the console's analog thermometer. He watched it with bitter joy. In just a few precious minutes he'd strap himself back in and return to a place no pain could reach. He bit off another piece of food. The outermost layer splintered into ice crystals in his mouth. He chewed and swallowed blankly before replacing the food and drink with relief. It was finally time to go back to sleep.

He was rising from his chair and turning to swing for his sleeping-bag when a glimpse of Tearn's frozen corpse snagged his peripheral. He cringed away. Still buckled loosely in the cockpit's backseat, Tearn's body floated loosely off the chair, arms wrapped around his legs in a permanently miserable huddle that, unfortunately, surrounded his seat belt and effectively frozen him in place.

Tearn had taken forever to die of the cold, his tiny body adapted well for the low oxygen levels but poorly for the temperature. Waves of fearful panic had rung out of his brain endlessly like the screams of a scared child. For Glongkyle, it had been torture beyond words. Nowhere on the ship had been far enough away to escape it—Tearn's psychic mortal terror reached every freezing inch of the ship. And, selfish reptile he was, Glongkyle at some point found himself wishing Tearn would just get it over with.

It wasn't until the ringing began to weaken that Glongkyle realized his mistake. Tearn's horrified emotives, while hideous, meant Glongkyle wasn't alone yet. As they quieted, he realized he would be though—utterly and irreversibly so. Regretting every wasted moment, he rushed to get back to his best friend, the one person who'd been there for him since they were kids.

He'd made it in time, grabbing Tearn's hand and holding him a little while longer as Tearn shivered against the cold. And when Tearn eventually stopped shivering and his breathing stilled, Glongkyle had held him for a long time after.

I keep forgetting to move you. Covering his eyes with one claw, Glongkyle pushed down an endless well of emotions he didn't have enough time to parse. It was too late to do anything now. Floating back to his sleeping-bag, he apologized silently. *I'll move you next to Yula next time I get up,* he promised. *You two can keep each other company.*

Had he thought of it at the time, he might have insisted Tearn go down to where Yula was to begin with while he was still alive. But of course, that would have been morbid.

Bigger than them and warm-blooded, the initial drop of oxygen had hit her the hardest.

After only two days in the dying ship, Glongkyle had noticed Yula's coordination problems. And sure, everyone was terrified and hurried, desperate to restore life in what had essentially become a giant metal coffin, but Yula's degradation had been especially pronounced. She'd crashed into walls with half-mad clawing, tearing into circuit breakers to rearrange fuses. But it was no use. With every percentage drop in oxygen, her motions grew increasingly spastic and unpredictable.

Glongkyle didn't know how long Yula'd been hiding her convulsions, but by the time they finally witnessed one, a lot of things suddenly made sense. The pink around her mouth wasn't a result of sensitivity to the cold; it was from her jaw snapping closed on her tongue. And the ear-splitting noises that ripped through the ship in random waves weren't unfamiliar systems failing or the metal freezing and contracting; they were Yula's semi-conscious cries of pain.

The convulsions continued at random, each seeming to drain a little more from the big, furry Wuljerian. The last time they found her, she had hidden deep within the ship, foaming out the mouth, thick bubbled saliva pink from where she'd gnawed on her tongue one last time. They'd tried to rouse her, but she hadn't stirred. Her final expression through matted fur would be a snarling grimace. It was horrible. It wasn't anything like what Yula looked like.

Not that anyone would notice any time soon.

The cold-resistant reptile settled into his sleeping bag and looked away from Tearn. He didn't want to think about either of them at the moment. He didn't want to think about...this. So instead, he turned his mind to the one beautiful thing he could still see. Spinning and dimly shining, she was centered in the far side of the ship's shuttle bay window.

The dark side of IA floated on, her majestic face lit up in nighttime jewels, decked to the nines in shimmering golds and whites, as magnificent and miraculous a mirage as ever he'd seen.

As a child, he'd watched movies set in the capital. By adulthood, he'd memorized most of her storied landmarks. The planet had taken on a life and meaning of her own. She wasn't just where dreams happened—she was where everything important happened.

Glongkyle tipped his head lower and closed his eyes. In his mind the planet soared toward him, growing in both size and majesty. Even trapped here in this frozen hellscape, she was still the most beautiful thing he'd ever seen. Enormous, terrifying, and dignified, she gazed down at the cosmos with the kind of apathetic glamour only the rarest beauties could achieve. In the end, he couldn't blame her for trying to kill them. It was their fault for daring to approach her. She couldn't be ingratiated by the likes of them. She was as impervious as a god. It had been pure arrogance to think they could touch her and take anything away but pain.

So, of course, she got them in the end. That was to be expected. But gods dammit all if he hadn't managed to get some sliver of confirmation from her anyway. Somewhere down there, mixed into all her mountains of pomp and splendor, he'd left her an offering—a sweet and untouched youth. And she'd accepted. That's right. His gift had been good enough, deemed worthy, and she'd pulled it into her massive bosom to crown with glory. Glongkyle may not have been worthy, but his discovery was.

No. Screw that. Izo was better than worthy. Izo would be a magnificent, shining talent: a Marvel of the Mountain!

In his mind's eye, Glongkyle could see it all: the fame, fortune, and opulence. He'd gotten a tiny taste of that anointed life. Izo would be stamped with it forever. Who could ask for more?

I knew it, Glongkyle thought to himself as the cold began refreezing his limbs in place again. *I always knew he'd end up somewhere fancy.*

— ACKNOWLEDGMENTS —

To Alana, my editor—Thank you for seeing this story for what it could be and always knowing exactly what it needed. You really are the grooviest editor of all time.

To my husband—This story wouldn't have been half as funny or cool without you. Thank you for believing in it and me through our darkest moments. You are hilarious, handsome, genius, and generally amazing. You're my magic man.

To my og editor and best friend, Desire Jambiye—Thank you for teaching me how use quotes and sticking around through all those cringy first drafts.

To my mom—I love you. Thank you for pushing me. If I ever inexplicably end up at the Oscars, you're my date.

To my daughters—Never question how proud you make me every single day.* In some ways, you're both very different. Together, though, you're unstoppable.

To my amazing mother and father-in-law—Thank you for opening your home to us after Hurricane Michael. Without your support and warmth, I don't know how we would have survived that year.

To Jo Conklin, Sylvia Leong, Petty Crocker, and Taylor Rodgers—I don't know what I did to deserve running into you guys, but I'm damn lucky I did.

To all my wonderful, creative students—Thank you for your curiosity, bravery, and tenacity. It truly is an honor and inspiration.

To Elise and all the #AmQuerying writers—Thank you for your insight and support. Here's to all our book babies finding great homes!

To all the literary agents—Thank you for motivating me to get real and get off my butt. Because of you, I really will do everything to make this story a success!

Finally, to my father—You've always taught me to be confident, subversive, and unapologetically weird. So really, this is kind of your fault.

*As I type this your father is explaining how you've managed to lock yourselves out of both the doors to your shared bathroom. *sigh*

— ABOUT THE AUTHOR —

C.G. Volars is a 3rd generation Mexican-American author and wickedly sarcastic English teacher. A National Hispanic Scholar from the University of Alabama, she was born in Texas where her love for outlandish characters and subversive literature first took hold.

C.G. has lived in 3 countries, 4 states, survived a Category 5 hurricane, and is proudly banned for life from the Vatican. She currently resides in Northern California with her husband, daughters, and two grey cats—Skittles and Rosie. When not writing, she howls at high schoolers to read, gardens poorly, and collects hat pins.